Also by Brad Marlowe

Novels

Sleepwalker: The Last Sandman

Pop Shot: A Dex Wexler Production

Feature Films

Glass House

Second to Die

Wednesday's Child

Object of Obsession

At Home with the Webbers

House of Drums

Brad Marlowe

First Edition

Cover Design by SBM
Edited by Elisa Johnson

1. Horror—Fiction. 2. Suspense—Fiction. 3. Supernatural—Fiction.

4. Serial Killers—Fiction. 5. Contemporary—Fiction. 6. Literary—Fiction. I. Title.

For more information about Mr. Marlowe's books and films visit

www.bradmarlowe.com or email the author at brad@bradmarlowe.com

ISBN-10: 0615595812

ISBN-13: 9780615595818

For Taylor,
who loves to be scared.

He that eateth my flesh
And drinketh my blood, dwelleth in me,
And I in him

JOHN 6:56

Beware the teeth of a smiling goddess

SHANTU PROVERB

Part I

Dreams

1

Wind chimes, distant sirens, and the laughter of children floating up from the street below. Stillness. Peace. Then falling. Screams, rushing air, rustling leaves—and a brittle thud as flesh and bone meet pavement …

Allan Steele made a small sound like a trapped animal as his eyes twitched beneath their lids and the dream did something it had never done before: it began again. He screamed, "NO!" and awoke wide-eyed and gasping. Allan grabbed the phone and used a preprogrammed button to dial a long-distance number. He fought to control his racing heartbeat and turned to the special chart mounted on the wall opposite the bed to begin his eye exercises. Allan covered his left eye and worked the right, then alternated. He tried to make out the letters as he had every morning for as long as he could remember. The charts and exercises had changed over the years, but the results had remained the same: disappointing.

As the phone began its tenth ring, Allan donned the bulky eyeglasses he'd grown to hate. The magnifying elements made his eyes look like lifeless pellets. The heavy plastic frames, necessary to secure lenses this thick, had tagged him as a geek from the first grade. When Allan was a child, his mother had tried those awful frames in every possible color, hoping to assuage her son's shame, but the brightly-colored rims only served to transform Allan from a run of the mill freak into an outright clown.

To this day, no contact lens could approach the correction strength that Allan required. And laser surgery, though a promising possibility, was still years away from addressing his particular set of problems. Besides, even if the physical deficiencies could be dealt with, there was still the dyslexia—which had so severely limited his reading skills that Allan had been forced to spend the bulk of his twenty-two years in the cold company of private tutors and recorded books. As he grew older, the ever-present wall of glass and plastic had become a barrier between Allan and the rest of the world. A barrier no outsider had ever dared, or cared, to challenge; until Jenny. Allan tried to read the chart again as the phone began its fifteenth ring. Finally, he muttered, "Shit," and hung up the phone.

Allan stepped into a pair of lime green running shorts that he had tossed onto the floor the day before. He slipped the loop of twine that held his spare apartment key around his neck and hurried out into the sunlight. Allan fastened an elastic strap around the back of his head to secure his glasses and began to run.

The early morning air was clear and crisp, though Allan knew that by midday Santa Fe would reach eighty-five degrees. Allan started to pick up speed as he cleared his apartment complex, which had been built on the edge of a sea of sand and cactus. In a few years there might be apartments and condos as far as the eye could see, but for now it was just Allan and the desert; flat, serene and endless.

When Allan returned to his apartment, he exercised, showered and shaved, then began his hour of meditation, just as he did every morning. He had *always* been a creature of habit. During his Senior year of high school, Allan's obsession with behavioral rituals had gotten so out of hand that he couldn't leave the house if any single element of his morning routine was disrupted. One day Allan worked himself into a screaming frenzy because someone had purchased the wrong brand of toothpaste. His father had forced him to go to school anyway, despite his mother's impassioned pleas.

Allan's dusky complexion and quiet demeanor had always made him an easy target among the sea of white faces at his school, but that day was a stand-out among the long series of bad days in his young life. He spent most of the morning in a cold sweat, vomited twice—once on the shoes of a pretty Latin girl he had hoped to ask to the prom—and was finally sent to the school nurse when he broke into hysterical laughter in the showers after gym class. Allan didn't stop laughing for five long hours, not until he got home and brushed his teeth again, with the *right* toothpaste.

The psychiatrists concluded that this obsessive need for order was an attempt to exert control over his life. The rare form of neurological dyslexia, from which he'd suffered since birth, combined with profound vision problems, had forever robbed Allan of the ability to read or write with any level of proficiency. And, as fate would have it, dyslexia had also robbed Allan of his solitary childhood dream. Because, as other kids were playing cops and robbers; pretending to be doctors, nurses and fighter pilots—Allan imagined that he was a scholar. He would sit in a worn leather wing chair in the darkest corner of his father's den and pretend to read, the biggest books in the house balanced on his fragile legs. He would sit alone for hours at a time, staring at the pages, making up stories that the books might tell if only he could break their code.

Over the years Allan's mother had taken him to every known specialist, searching for the silver bullet that would kill the monster in her son's nervous system. A long list of ointments, exercises and odd-looking contraptions followed, with little result. Until finally, at nineteen, Allan had a devastating moment of clarity. He had just ingested a heaping spoonful of a foul tasting paste intended to realign the synapses in his brain. Perhaps it worked, to some small degree, because the thought that leapt into Allan's mind was clear and certain.

There will be no cure.

Not now. Not ever.

Allan wept in his mother's arms just like he had as a child after wandering off from a school field trip to the city and becoming hopelessly lost. He couldn't read the street signs and was afraid to ask strangers for help, so Allan had walked five miles in the wrong direction—ending up on the seedy side of town. Surrounded by violence, strange sounds and cold stares, he finally found a payphone that worked and plunked in his milk money. Allan closed his eyes and dialed by memorized touch, unwilling to trust himself to read the numbers on the dial. His dyslexia always made letters and numbers swirl and shift, but under stress the effect was downright nauseating.

Allan's mother answered on the first ring and assured him that everything would be all right, but there was an edge to her voice beyond mere concern. It wasn't anger; it was never anger, but a desperate sadness for this lonely child who had suffered so much so soon.

Of course Allan's mother couldn't drive, not anymore, so his father would have to be called away from the office. This meant that Allan would have to ride home with him? Alone. The thought of it made the fuzz on the back of his neck bristle. Being alone with his father was far more frightening than the things these strangers might do to him; almost more frightening than *anything.* Even the dreams.

The ride home was cold and silent. Allan's father had been called out of yet another important meeting to rescue his idiot son, and he was not pleased. Allan and his father had an unspoken agreement of sorts. Around Diti they worked hard to pretend a normal father/son relationship; her condition was too frail to shoulder the burden of truth. But away from her, all pretenses of warmth and affection were abandoned.

Allan avoided his father's eyes whenever possible, because in them he saw the nightmares: terrible things done in dark places, hatred and torment in swirling shapes of crimson and black, and phantom screams that caused him to sleep with the lights on until his sixteenth birthday. To little Allan, his father was a tortured demon. The fact that Argus had never once raised his hand or voice to Allan should have contradicted the nightly visions, but instead only served to confuse an already troubled boy. Allan fought back the urge to warn his mother on a daily basis, afraid that if he unmasked the demon, she might be its next victim.

In time the world taught Allan to doubt dreams and dismiss visions. And, in time, he learned to laugh at his childhood fears. But still, a vague, yet persistent dislike for his father had remained—

Focus.

And then there was his beloved mother—

FOCUS.

Blind and wheelchair-bound—

Goddamn it, FOCUS!

Why hadn't she answered the phone? And why had the dream repeated itself? Allan hadn't felt this distracted in ages. Not since he'd escaped New York and his father's house—and moved here to Santa Fe.

I escaped, but she was left alone to face the demon. I was just too weak ... too fucking spineless—
The mind must remain clear and unclouded by emotion.
The mind must remain clear and unclouded by emotion.
The mind must remain ... clear ... and unclouded by ...

Allan groaned and opened his eyes. Meditation would be impossible today. Normally the sweet smell of jasmine helped him focus, but today the incense only reminded him of his mother—and his weakness—and made him want to sneeze. He stood and stretched, working to release the kinks in his knees from the half-lotus, trying to shake the voice in his head that kept repeating "Something is wrong."

2

"Where've you been? The Weasel's crappin' his pants," chided Jenny as she helped Allan remove his backpack.

Allan hurried his bike into the bookstore's back room. "The good copier was down and the place was packed." He propped the bike against the wall and tried to tidy himself up.

"But you got it done, right? And you got your ticket?"

"Uh huh. Would you mind double-checking to see if the pages are all there," Allan pulled the newly bound thesis from his pack, "And, you know, in order?"

"Would I mind? After all the work we did on this little fucker? Try to stop me."

"I just thought with all the typing and proofing ... You've gotta be sick of it by now. I mean, even if I could read it straight through–" Allan stopped, knowing how much Jenny hated it when he belittled himself.

Jenny looked at her watch and proclaimed, "This time tomorrow you'll be at Yale. Yale! You must feel–"

"Sick. I feel sick." Allan took a deep breath, trying to fight a sudden attack of nerves. "I'd really rather not talk about it anymore. I still don't know why they're even considering me."

Jenny shook her head and sighed. "You're a real piece of work."

"Thanks—I think. And you're really ... You know–" Allan's cheeks reddened. He searched the walls for the words. "What

I mean is you're ... I just really ..." Allan clenched his teeth and nudged his glasses back up the bridge of his nose with his middle finger, disgusted by his social ineptitude. Finally, he found the courage to meet Jenny's deep brown eyes. He said, softly, "Thank you—that's what I mean. If it wasn't for you I'd still be hiding in my apartment, talking about all the things I'd do if only I was, you know, normal."

Jenny's quirky smile lit up the room. Something about this odd, lost young man had crept beneath the radar of her studied indifference and touched her beyond words. She said, "Just shut up and let me hold it." Jenny took the thesis in her hands, as if it was a baby, and read the title: "Classical Eastern Philosophies of the Soul and Transcendence and Their Relevance to Modern Society." Jenny beamed with pride. "Fuckin' A."

Allan laughed, "Pretty pretentious, even for Yale. What's that saying? If you can't dazzle 'em with brilliance–"

Jenny's mood darkened. She warned, "I'm not gonna listen to any more of your self-deprecating crap, Allan. Not today," and handed him the thesis. "The guests have all gone home, so pack up the goddamned pity party–"

"All I meant was—the ideas—they're not even mine. It's all stuff I got from my mother. She used to tell me these great stories about being a kid back in India—the things my grandfather and great-grandfather taught her–"

"Exactly! Your grandfather the fucking *Rajah*. Your mother the Indian Princess, for Christ's sake! How many people come from that? How many people are lucky enough to be exposed to that much culture and history, that much wisdom, in their whole miserable lifetimes? You're an honest-to-God descendant of royalty—and an amazing person on top of it." She cracked a smile and swiped a lock of hair out of Allan's eyes. "Plus you've got that swarthy, exotic look happening that drives us girls wild. What right have you got to whine about anything?"

Allan looked down at the floor and adjusted his eyeglasses again. "You still don't get it."

"You're blind as a bat, wear fucked up glasses, can't drive a car for shit and don't really read. What don't I get?" Allan glared at her, but Jenny refused to let it go. "Tell me."

Jason Blackhawk, the store's manager, burst into the room. "Where the hell have you been, Steele?" Blackhawk's beady eyes peered out from an oddly angular face atop his gangly frame. "I've got a truckload of paperbacks that have been awaiting an audience with your royal highness for over an hour—and my shelves look like crap."

"I'm sorry. I–"

"What, you can't even read a watch now? I swear to God, Steele, talk about poor career choices—a dyslexic in a book store. It sounds like the first line of a bad joke." Jenny whispered something snide, so that only Allan could hear, and it made him smile. Allan avoided his manager's impatient stare as he put on the warehouse-issued back support belt and headed out to the truck, cursing the pissy Navaho yuppie under his breath. Blackhawk smiled and said, "What was that, Steele?"

Allan choked back his anger, lowered his eyes and stuffed the thesis back into his pack. "Forget it." Allan left, ashamed of his weakness.

Blackhawk turned to leave, addressing Jenny on his way out; "You've got customers."

Jenny muttered, "Asshole," and fought the urge to club Blackhawk over the head with a nearby hardbound copy of the unabridged Heritage House Dictionary.

Blackhawk moved through the swinging doors that led back into the store. "I'll pretend I didn't hear that."

Jenny followed him into the store, speaking louder. "I said *asshole.*"

3

After Allan had finished unloading the truck, he returned to the storeroom—winded, soiled and brooding. He removed his glasses and stripped off his dirty t-shirt. After a moment of hesitation, Allan took a plastic-wrapped polo shirt from the shelf and tore open the cellophane wrapper. He pulled the fresh shirt over his head, thinking with pleasure that Blackhawk would be pissed.

The shirts had been emblazoned with the Golden Feather's logo and were intended for sale to tourists. They were Blackhawk's idea, but they never really sold. The Golden Feather was more of a local hangout than a tourist attraction. The eclectic mix of philosophical, religious, mythological and anthropological texts was too cerebral for most of the visiting yokels. Blackhawk had added a bestsellers' section, a complimentary cappuccino and pastry bar, and even some oversized souvenir volumes of traditional Indian artwork to the display window, in the hopes of attracting more tourist trade. But, to Blackhawk's dismay and Allan's delight, all attempts at commercialism had failed. The store had remained a haven for serious thinkers, and Allan's temple.

For Allan, the simple act of straightening the shelves could be a transcendent experience. Although he couldn't read the books— he could still hold them in his hands and imagine their secrets. Sometimes Allan could swear he heard them whispering to him, trying to reveal their contents, just as they had when he was a child. He especially enjoyed straightening the Classic Literature section where the books were mainly hardbound with embossed lettering on the spines. Allan would close his eyes and run his fingers across the titles like a blind man. He had, in fact, tried to learn Braille, but found his attention span too limited and his hands too clumsy for the mind-bending task of deciphering three or four hundred pages of raised text with his fingertips alone.

But that day the books had offered little comfort. He kept thinking about the recurring nightmare and his mother's failure to answer the phone. The regular customers noticed that Allan, who was normally friendly and upbeat, seemed distant.

"You okay?"

Allan emerged from his thoughts to find Jenny studying him with concern. "Yeah. Why, was I acting weird?"

"Only if you consider standing in one place for twenty minutes while staring at an unopened copy of Being and Nothingness weird." Allan put Sartre back on the shelf. Jenny asked, "What is it? Yale?"

"Just distracted, I guess. I keep thinking–" Allan stopped and listened intently.

"What?"

A moment later the store's phone began to ring. Blackhawk completed a sale and picked up the receiver and said, "Golden Feather."

Allan started toward the phone and Jenny called after him, "We just got the Joseph Campbell Omnibus Collection on CD. I slipped it in your backpack."

Allan reached for the phone before Blackhawk could indicate that the call was for him.

"Some guy named Argus? Claims to be your father." Blackhawk's tone was spiked with sarcasm. "You never said you had a father, Steele. I thought you were immaculately conceived by Her Holiness, the Princess." Blackhawk had just noticed the polo shirt and was about to start bitching when Allan took the receiver and turned away.

"Allan?" The voice on the other end of the line lacked its usual bite. Allan couldn't answer. He tried to catch his breath—tried to stop the room from spinning. "Are you there?"

Allan's response was barely a whisper. "Yes."

Jenny watched from the back of the store. As Allan listened, his face fell slack and his eyes fixed on a point far away.

To Allan, his father's voice was a jumbled, alien sound reaching his brain after light years of travel across the solar system; just so many coded blips that would take another set of untold years to decipher.

The blips continued: "I don't know if I'll ever be able to forgive myself for not checking that damned railing. She'd told me a month ago that it felt loose." Then there was a long pause. "Come home, Allan. I need you here. Son, it's time to set things right."

Allan barely made it to a chair before his legs buckled.

By the time Jenny reached him, the phone had slipped down from his ear. She asked, "Allan?"

"He said …" Allan swallowed hard, and when he spoke again his voice was small and frail. "He said it was an accident."

"Who said? What was an accident?"

"The railing was loose …"

Jenny knelt down and took his hand. "Allan, you're scaring me."

"He said to come home, but my home is gone. He said we need each other." Allan's breath hitched in his throat. "He said …" Jenny waited, but Allan couldn't seem to form the words. Finally, Allan found his pain mirrored in Jenny's eyes and the tears began to fall. "My mother is dead."

4

Jenny drove Allan home, his bike tossed in the back seat of her VW convertible. He stared up at the sky, clutching the thesis in his arms as if it might fly away. "All these years of nothing and she was here. And now just when things were about to happen ..."

Jenny searched in vain for words of wisdom, but settled for small talk. "Do you need anything else for the trip?" Allan continued to stare up at the sky. "Allan?"

"Huh?"

"Do we need to stop anywhere on the way?"

"No. I packed my bags a week ago." Allan's tone was flat. "The timing's perfect—I don't even have to change my ticket. The funeral will be in New York. The day after tomorrow. That gives me tomorrow for the interview." He tried to smile. "Maybe I can bring her some good news. My getting into Yale was her dream, too."

They drove in silence for a while, until Jenny said, "We've still got a few hours before the plane leaves. It's the red-eye, right? You wanna grab a latté or something?"

"No. I need to get home."

"But you just said ..."

Allan was suddenly agitated. "I said I need to get home."

"All right. But why?"

"I don't know why. I just have to—okay?"

———

Jenny waited in the kitchen while Allan dragged his battered suitcase to the door. He had been acting strangely, circling the apartment as if searching for something lost. Jenny spoke softly. "Can I help?"

Allan searched through a pile of books on tape and CD, and stuffed a few into his carry-on bag. He had a dozen more books in the MP3 format loaded onto his digital music player. Allan opened a cupboard and stared blankly into it. He said, "I don't know what I'm looking for, but it's gotta be here somewhere." Jenny carried Allan's suitcase to the car and met him back at the front door.

He stepped out of the apartment and locked the deadbolt, brow furrowed, muttering, "What is it? What is it ...?"

Jenny pulled several envelopes from the mailbox. "Want me to come by for your mail?"

Allan looked at the envelopes and suddenly knew. He snatched the mail from Jenny's hands and rifled through the stack.

"Should I take that as a no?"

Allan tossed aside the bills and junk mail. When he found the letter addressed in his mother's handwriting, a tortured sound arose from his throat.

Jenny saw the envelope and a chill ran through her body. It was mailed less than a week ago. For as long as she'd known Allan he'd had these subtle psychic episodes—and they always gave her the creeps. Allan called them his hunches, but Jenny knew better. Now Allan was staring at the unopened letter as if he could read it right through the envelope.

"Why would she mail you a letter? She knows you can't read it."

"I don't know." Allan was numb. "This is the first one she's ever sent."

"Did she have hunches—like yours?"

Allan caressed the parchment envelope, as if it was his mother's hand, and whispered, "All the time."

After a long moment, Jenny gave words to their shared thought. "You don't think ... she *knew*?"

5

Jenny hugged Allan goodbye at the boarding gate. There was no trace of her usual tough facade. She whispered, "Bye. I'll be thinkin' about you."

Allan generally disliked being hugged or touched by anyone other than his mother, but today the warmth of Jenny's body was comforting. He said, "Thanks, Jen. I'll call you when I know."

Jenny remembered the letter and retrieved it from her coat pocket. "Don't forget this." Allan accepted the opened envelope, and then looked to Jenny's eyes for reassurance. She offered an encouraging smile. "You're gonna be okay."

"Promise?"

"You call if you need me." The final boarding announcement for Allan's flight sounded over the airport's PA system.

Allan gathered his things and said, "I guess that's me." He forced a smile and began to move toward the door.

"Allan ..." He looked back over his shoulder, and Jenny said, "Blow those Yale snobs away. For you—*and* for her." Allan waved in agreement and hurried toward the plane. Jenny watched her friend cross the tarmac to board the DC-10, and was suddenly struck by a cloying emptiness in the pit of her stomach.

———

Allan stowed his carry-on and took his seat as the ground crew sealed the plane. The blonde occupying the window seat next to his was drop-dead gorgeous. Allan removed his glasses and cleaned them with the tail of his shirt to get a better look. He supposed her name was something like Morgan, or Krista with a K. She had a perfect face, a perfect body, and probably a perfect life.

Krista with a K skipped through the tracks on her metallic pink iPod while keeping her perfect nose buried in the new Vanity Fair, hoping to avoid conversation with the gawking geek seated beside her. Allan wrestled with his safety belt, wondering what it would be like to be Krista with a K. To be perfect and carefree, envied and admired. To live your life knowing that people are staring at you. Not because you're a hopeless dork, but because you're perfect.

Allan's train of thought was derailed when he noticed something missing from the seat pocket in front of him. He stretched the elastic pouch and rifled through its contents. Allan found the plane's escape route diagram, the airline's schlocky magazine, and a listing of all the available audio channels. He even found a half-eaten peanut butter and banana sandwich left by the former occupant of his seat. But what he didn't find was, for him, the most important element of flying; the air sickness bag.

Allan started to sweat, knowing that he would have to ask Krista for her bag. He thought, given the choice, she'd probably prefer *that* to vomit all over her perfect pink Armani suit, but the whole ordeal was bound to be unpleasant.

Yes, I'm a geek. I get airsick, carsick, seasick and homesick. I'm just about as pathetic as a human being can get without being on a daytime talk show, and I realize that you're probably thinking I might be better off dead. But if you'd just lend me your barf bag I'd be happy to shut up and let you get back to your perfect life.

The plane's engines roared to life and Allan decided that now was not the time for procrastination. He leaned over and said, "Excuse me–"

Krista pretended not to hear.

Allan felt the plane lurch forward, taking his anxiety level along with it. So he very gently pulled one headphone away from her perfect shell-shaped ear and whispered, "Excuse me."

Krista recoiled as if groped by a leper. "What are you doing?"

"Do you have a flight-sickness bag in there?"

"Excuse me?"

Allan leaned forward and pulled open her pouch, getting a heady whiff of her perfume in the process. "See there—you do have one. I hate to bother you, but I get air sick ..." Krista hid her revulsion behind a polite smile. "And the thing is, see, the thing is that I don't have one. An airsickness bag, that is. So, unless you need it, I thought we both might feel a little safer if I had it over here next to me."

Krista slipped the wax-lined paper bag from the pouch and handed it to Allan without a word, then moved as far away from him as her seat's armrest would allow.

Allan breathed a sigh of relief and accepted the bag. "Thanks a lot." He closed his eyes and settled in for takeoff as his perfect neighbor quietly pressed the stewardess call button, hoping to relocate. The plane accelerated and Allan tried to occupy his mind, but what immediately filled his thoughts was precisely the thing he had hoped to avoid: the letter. He heard it again in his mind, as if his mother was speaking softly in his ear.

Little One,

I must leave you now, but there is no room for sadness in my heart. I am filled with thoughts of you and memories of our times together. You have taught me so much about courage and strength, my son—so much about hope and determination. But it is your capacity to love that has been the light in my life, and may prove to be the key to your salvation.

Today you are a man and, as a man, it is your duty to seek out your destiny. It will do no good to avoid it, because if you do not find it—it will surely find you. Remember, all roads lead to the center, like the spokes of a wheel.

Your great-grandfather had the soul of a missionary. He was a great man who accomplished great things, traveling the world to relieve the pain of ignorance in others. That was his destiny and he sacrificed his life to it willingly. That was his road, just as this is mine. And now it is time for you to go out and find your own path, little one.

You will want to blame your father for what has happened, but don't. You must forgive him his destiny, just as God will forgive you yours.

I will wait for you, my love. At the center of the wheel.

6

By the time the plane touched down in Connecticut, Allan was physically and mentally exhausted. Flying had always taken a toll on him, but this flight and the troubling thoughts that had accompanied it had proven particularly brutal. The only bright spot had been during the landing when Allan had exaggerated his genuine nausea for the benefit of his perfect neighbor. He'd put on quite a show, feeling it was the least he could do. Krista had given him so much attitude during the flight that he felt obliged to give her a little something in return.

As he stepped off the plane Allan felt a strange sense of displacement. The time difference was only two hours, yet he felt as if he'd stepped through a hole in the universe. It was as if he'd left his real life behind and was now living out another, parallel existence. Perhaps his mother had been the anchor that had grounded him to the world and now, without her, he was left floating in some sort of psychic limbo. Whatever the reason, the feeling was quite unreal.

Allan emerged from the tunnel-like walkway that led from the plane to the terminal and looked for Professor Sumner. A sudden spike of sadness dug into his gut. The professor didn't know about Allan's mother, yet. Professor Sumner was an old friend of the family and was, in many ways, the father Allan had so often wished for: brilliant, kind, and filled with life.

How would he take the news? Not well, Allan supposed. There had always been something in the way that the professor looked at Diti. Allan never managed to put his finger on the emotion but often, when he was young, he pretended it was love. Allan would fantasize that the professor and his mother were married and that the professor was his father. They would be the archetypical happy family. But it was there that the fantasy stalled, because Allan never knew what a happy family was—couldn't even imagine one with any level of clarity. So his fantasies were vague, usually consisting of the three of them sitting together—reading and talking for hours on end in some far away place that had clouds for furniture. In these happy imaginings Allan's vision was perfect, and his mother was neither blind nor wheelchair-bound.

Allan scanned the sea of faces around him, but saw no sign of the professor. He saw families reuniting and old friends clasping hands; even Krista was met by a perfect man that could have only been her boyfriend. They embraced with such sincerity that Allan regretted his animosity toward her. He watched the perfect man slide his hands down the curve of Krista's lower back as they kissed, hesitating at the swell of her perky derriere. She wrapped her arms around him and slipped her hands into the back pockets of his designer jeans. Not only was she perfect, Allan mused with more than a twinge of jealousy, she was loved.

"Allan?" He turned toward the unfamiliar voice and found a rotund young college student, out of breath and sweating profusely. "Excuse me, are you Allan?"

"Yes."

The relieved young man extended a sweaty hand. "Thank God. I was afraid I missed you. I thought, 'the professor's gonna kill me', but I lucked out—here you are." Allan accepted the other man's hand, still a little confused. The young man grabbed Allan's carry-on and started walking. "The professor's down for the count, so he sent me. Name's Melniker. Chuck."

Allan trailed behind. "You said the professor's *down?*"

"You know, he's got his good days and his bad. Today was big-time bad. Couldn't even turn on the lights to call me. Said he dialed the wrong number three times before he got it right. I keep tellin' him to put me on the speed-dialer but—"

"He's sick?"

Chuck looked surprised. He said, "*Sick?* Man, he's ..." The blank look on Allan's face stopped the other young man in his tracks. Chuck's jovial expression changed to one of genuine sadness and compassion. He spoke quietly: "You don't know?"

"Know what?"

Chuck silently cursed his big mouth and walked on. "Lemme just get you there and you can talk to him yourself."

————

The drive to New Haven was brief and picturesque. The turning leaves were a welcome change from the sparse desert tapestry of New Mexico. Allan rolled down the window of Chuck's beat-up Ford to feel the bracing wind on his face. The rushing air was cool and damp. It made Allan's cheeks burn and his nose run. Chuck huddled into his faded parka and tried to make small talk, but Allan was unresponsive. With all that was on his mind chitchat seemed pointless; better to let the buffeting wind numb his face, allow his hair to beat loudly around his ears, and to dream that he could fly away.

Chuck pulled into the driveway of the professor's house. The structure itself was unimpressive, and the overgrown lawn was in desperate need of tending. Chuck hauled Allan's suitcase out of the trunk and lugged it to the door. He retrieved the key that the professor kept beneath a withered plant on the stoop and let himself in.

"You're not gonna ring the bell?"

Chuck spoke in a subdued tone. "Not if he's as bad off as he was this morning." Chuck entered the darkened living room. Allan followed.

"No need to skulk about, boys." Professor Sumner switched on a large overhead bank of fluorescent lights. He wore a ratty flannel bathrobe and was seated in the main portion of the living room, which he had transformed into his office. The professor looked disheveled, as if he'd just arisen from a long and troubled sleep. He rose to meet Allan, arms outstretched and smiling broadly. "My boy! It's *so good* to see you."

They hugged and Allan asked, "Are you all right, Professor?"

Professor Sumner patted Allan on the cheek. "I am *now.*"

Chuck watched from the door, glad to see the professor so happy. He said, "Professor, I should get back. I've got a paper to finish for Professor March's class."

"Not to worry Charles, the old windbag doesn't even read them. And you can tell him I said that."

Chuck hurried to the door, smiling. "I will. Allan, it was nice meeting you."

"You too, Chuck. Good luck on the paper."

"Thanks. I'll need it."

Professor Sumner pulled over a second chair and said, "Sit, sit." Under the harsh fluorescent lights, Allan could see dark circles etched beneath his friend's eyes. He noted that the professor had lost a lot of weight. "Stop staring, my boy. Didn't your mother ever tell you it's not polite?" The professor winked playfully in an attempt to dismiss Allan's concerns.

The comment was a stinging reminder. Allan decided to get the worst over with. He said, "We need to talk."

The professor checked his watch. "Indeed we do, my boy, but now is not the time. You should get ready for your interview with Dean Adashek. I'm looking forward to reading your paper. Your mother made me promise to call her with a full report."

Allan tried to smile. He checked his watch and said, "I don't have to be there for another four hours."

The professor patted his young friend on the shoulder as he passed. "Two hours, my boy. You've forgotten to reset your timepiece." The professor trundled off down the hall, favoring his left leg, as he had for as long as Allan had known him. He said, "I'll put out a fresh towel. Make yourself at home in the guest room. We'll catch up after your meeting." Allan sighed. His sad news would have to wait, as would his questions. The professor was right; he had to focus on this interview. It was his last, best chance at his dream.

7

Two hours and fifteen minutes later, Allan emerged from Dean Adashek's office feeling hollow and small. It took every ounce of Allan's strength to pull the office door closed—shutting the door on the world to which he had aspired for as long as he could remember.

The Dean's assistant offered a weak smile, in sympathy, but Allan didn't see it. He had removed his glasses before entering the Dean's office as a symbol of confidence. Maybe if Allan had left them on he could have seen it coming. The meeting had been little more than a courtesy—to Allan's father. As a generous alumnus, Argus had garnered the heartfelt thanks of the school, and of the Dean himself. They never had any intention of admitting Allan into Yale, though the Dean had called Argus personally to break the news.

He knew.

He knew and he didn't tell me.

And he didn't tell mother either because she was as excited about this meeting as I was.

Allan began to tremble. His growing rage turned his hands into fists and made his eyes well up. Dean Adashek had almost seemed embarrassed when he said, "I told your father that we had special programs for the handicapped for which you might qualify, but he insisted that you should be given no special treatment—apart from this meeting. Generally, this sort of thing is all done through the mail, by our admissions panel, but he thought that a few words of encouragement from me might help soften the blow."

Allan remembered saying, "I am *not* handicapped." But he must have spoken more loudly than he had intended, because Dean Adashek had winced, and then he'd adopted the calming tone of voice that one might use when addressing a mental patient.

"Mr. Steele, I *am* sorry. And this little paper that you've brought along ... I'm sure it's very good. Try to look at the time you've spent on it as an exercise. I'm sure you've learned a great deal in the process of writing it. And that's what's really important, after all, isn't it? Learning."

———————

Allan wandered the halls of Yale in a daze, trying to compare the numbers on the classroom doors to those scrawled onto the slip of paper in his hand. Allan stopped a passing student and said, "Excuse me, do you know where Professor Sumner's class meets?"

The girl gave him an odd look and moved through the very door that Allan had been studying. She called back over her shoulder, "You're here."

Allan followed her in and to the back of the lecture hall, where they took the last empty seats. The professor spotted Allan and gave him a broad smile and paternal wink as he paused for a sip of coffee. In this room he showed no signs of the pain that was so evident earlier in the day. Here, he was an enthusiastic performer who kept his students on the edges of their seats.

Professor Sumner addressed the students: "Aristotle said that before you can fully understand the nature of something—you must first identify its function and then work backwards. But what is the function of the soul? Is it a universal pool of knowledge—a Jungian divining rod designed to steer us away from evil and hopefully toward good? Or is it fused to our physical body—as doomed to mortality as we are? Maybe it's detachable. Plato thought so. You see philosophy and psychology ultimately mean little when dealing with questions of such intense personal significance. So, what is the soul?" He went to a coffee maker and refilled his Styrofoam cup, giving the students a moment to consider the question.

The helpful student whispered to Allan, "Isn't he great?"

Professor Sumner took a sip of his coffee, and continued: "Religion is each individual culture's attempt to find an answer to this question. The assumption being that whatever god or gods we worship will both define and determine the fate of our souls. As students of anthropology it will be your job to study how this quest for knowledge, in the form of religious and other belief systems, affects the lives and development of other cultures. Our challenge is to study without passing judgment—to remember that a culture that cremates a stillborn infant and requires the mother to ingest the ashes, hoping to recycle its soul into the body of the next child that the woman bears, is no more primitive or violent than one that pretends to drink the blood and eat the flesh of its savior." He took another sip of hot coffee and smiled through the steam. "If anything, the former might be seen as more committed to their beliefs."

Laughter skipped through the audience.

"All I ask is that, when the time comes, you approach these people with an open mind and a gentle heart. Despite some rather jarring first impressions, there is often method to what some might readily dismiss as madness." The professor closed his notes and embraced the crowd with a melancholy smile. "Good luck everyone—and have a wonderful summer."

The students gathered their things and began to disperse, discussing the professor's ideas as they left the room. A few grateful stragglers hovered around the professor, but he happily extricated himself when Allan approached. Professor Sumner said, "Well?" Allan didn't answer, but the look of utter devastation on his face spoke volumes. The professor threw his arm around Allan's shoulder and guided him toward the door. "No matter. I read your paper—and it convinced me."

"Of what?"

"You're meant for bigger things, my boy." His smile held a secret. "Much bigger things."

8

"In Elizabethan times they referred to death as the Pale Horse and jealousy as–"

Allan chimed in, "The Green-Eyed Monster," while buckling his seat belt.

"Exactly." The professor divided his attention between the road ahead and his conversation with Allan, which was unfortunate because the professor wasn't a very good driver to begin with. Irate motorists constantly honked and screamed obscenities, though the professor seemed oblivious. "You see, we've always used physical metaphors for elements of life beyond our control. And, like the Pale Horse and Green Eyed Monster, they're usually images of wild, uncontrollable creatures. That way we don't have to assume personal responsibility for giving in to them. And it's in that same vein that people have always clung to any idea—philosophical, religious, whatever—that perpetuates the idea of the soul as a tangible permanent essence. Christianity wouldn't stand a chance in Hell, pardon the pun, without the threat of eternal damnation. Catholics, Mormons, mystics all claim that they can save your soul. We laugh, but what if it's possible? What if we really could choose where our soul goes when we die?" The professor stopped to catch his breath. "I'm sorry, my boy. I'm still lecturing."

"The mothers who eat the ashes of their babies—was that really true?"

"Absolutely. In some parts of the world cannibalism is still an accepted practice. Fascinating stuff, really." The professor laughed at Allan's revulsion and he swerved to avoid a crossing pedestrian. "Admittedly, for a vegetarian like yourself, indeed, for most of us in the so-called civilized world, it would be quite a stretch. But for tribes who still eat their meat raw and steaming, fresh from the kill, it's not so strange."

The professor's tires screeched as he careened into a driveway and skidded to a stop. He stepped out of the battered Volvo and moved toward his house. Allan took a moment to allow his stomach to settle.

"Shut up, freak!"

Allan spotted a group of kids in the yard next door. They were tormenting a smaller kid who wore spectacles much like Allan's. Allan watched as the "normal" kids began to chant, "Zeke the freak! Zeke the freak!" The scrawny, bespectacled kid chewed his lower lip, trying to fight off tears, as the other boys prodded and poked him.

Professor Sumner wrestled with his house keys, hurrying to catch his ringing phone. "Could you grab those books in the back seat on your way in, my boy?"

"Sure," said Allan as he continued to watch the activities next door. The smaller kid, so like Allan as a child, had finally begun to cry and his tears fueled the fires of cruelty in the others. For a moment Allan stood, petrified, reliving that familiar pain and humiliation. But then anger replaced shame. He yelled, "HEY! KNOCK IT OFF OVER THERE! LEAVE HIM ALONE!" Allan ran toward the children and the pint-sized bullies backed away, insulted by the intrusion. "Get outta here you little assholes!" He stooped to make eye contact with the crying kid. "You all right?"

The little boy pressed his lips together and stared at the grass as he nodded. Allan retrieved the glasses from the muddy flowerbed, where they'd been thrown by one of the other kids. The bullies laughed and ran away. The tormented child accepted the dirty glasses from Allan and replaced them on his tear-stained face. He whispered, "Thanks, mister."

"You sure you're all right?" Allan was filled with empathy and painful memories. The boy nodded again, snuffling back tears. Allan stood and ruffled his hair. "Yeah, you'll be all right."

Allan overheard the professor's side of a heated phone conversation as he entered the little house. He wandered around the cluttered bungalow that looked like a library after an earthquake. Books were piled everywhere, along with hundreds of magazines and countless volumes of poetry. The only organized place was the office area, which took up half of the living room and stood in stark contrast to the rest of the house. It was an island of chrome amidst a sea of paper, stocked with state-of-the-art computer, audio/visual and graphics equipment.

Allan moved toward the living room's well worn leather couch, stumbling over a pile of old magazines along the way. As he gathered them, Allan came across a few of the more prestigious periodicals that carried the professor's photograph on their covers. There were also several awards that had been bestowed upon the professor, tucked away between back issues of The Anthropological Journal and Time. Allan smiled at the uncharacteristically formal photographs of his mentor. He put the last of the magazines back and stood, surrounded by some if the world's greatest literature. Allan was suddenly overwhelmed by all there was to know—and all that he would never know.

The professor slammed down the phone. "Can we sex it up a bit? *Sex it up!* I'm not writing a bleeding romance novel, for Christ's sake! When you write your book, Allan—" Allan laughed bitterly. "When you write your book, be forewarned—editors can be as neurotic as Hollywood starlets. This one I've got is a real piece of work." The professor flopped into his chair, massaging his temples. "Oh, to hell with it. Take a seat, my boy."

Allan was fascinated by all of the equipment. He picked up a pair of eyeglasses which appeared to be perfectly normal except for the thick temple pieces from which wires and a small junction box dangled. Allan asked, "What's this thing?"

Professor Sumner replied, "It's an early attempt at a personal video viewer that projects images on the inside of the transparent lenses rather than requiring isolating closed eyepieces, like the other ones currently on the market. As I get older I find it increasingly difficult to memorize my lectures, so I thought this might function as a teleprompter of sorts. It has real potential, though the software that runs it is still a little buggie."

Allan returned the gadget to the desk and directed his attention to the other hardware that littered the desktop. "And all that stuff?"

"Souped-up scanners and voice-to-text translators. I'm always fascinated with anything that might make life—and work—easier. But, more often than not, the time it takes to figure out and troubleshoot the damned things doesn't justify the reward. One of the Computer Science professors at the college reviews the stuff in his spare time for some computer magazine and sends the rejects my way. There's so much out there to learn, my boy. It's truly a brave new world." He arched his eyebrows and said, "And speaking of brave new worlds—I have a proposition for you."

Allan sat on the edge of the desk. "What kind of proposition?"

"I'm going to Zaire, and I'd like you to come with me."

"Zaire? Why me?"

"A colleague of mine is working on a project: physiological and psychological variances among tribal societies. Anyway, he's been hearing rumors about a river tribe called the Shantu." The impish gleam in Professor Sumner's eyes made him look twenty years younger. "The neighboring tribes consider them witches."

"Why?"

"Local legends claim that the Shantu have a way of preserving a man's soul—and tapping into the memories and knowledge that he's collected over the course of his lifetime." The professor limped into the kitchen, giving Allan's natural curiosity a chance to kick in.

Allan followed, the hook planted firmly in place. "But that's not possible. Right?"

"But what if it is? Can you imagine? If we could save the souls of our greatest scientists and leaders before they died. Maybe store them in some kind of computer. My God!" The professor paced back into the office, unable to stand still. "Come with me, Allan. Your metaphysical and spiritual insights could prove invaluable."

"Why?"

"I'm told they've been influenced by Eastern philosophies. An Indian yogi came to call on them about a hundred years ago. He intended to civilize them, help set them on the road to Nirvana I suppose, but ended up meeting a mysterious death while in the company of the tribe."

"I'm not qualified for this, professor. Not by a long shot. I don't know enough."

"Neither do I—nor does anyone else, for that matter!" Professor Sumner picked up the file folder that contained his research on the Shantu. "This is something brand new, Allan. We'd be the first to study these people." The professor put the folder aside and locked eyes with his young friend. "Look, this isn't a gamble that any 'reputable' scientist would be willing to take with me. The entire community is just so damned mentally constipated ... It takes too much work to think a new thought, or worse yet consider the fantastic. So we just rework the same tired old ideas and bat them back and forth like some blasted intellectual ping pong tournament. Frankly, I'm sick to death of the whole damned thing." The professor stood to pace. "Do you realize that every revolutionary invention and discovery in history was thought to be impossible by the intellectuals of the time ... until one person dared to defy their peers, their common-sense—and sometimes even their god? Until that first person dared make the impossible possible."

Allan wanted to say yes, wanted to believe, but he didn't think that he could handle another disappointment. Finally, he sighed and said, "I'm sorry professor–"

"No. Wait." Professor Sumner raised his hand, as if to ward off the unwelcome words, and turned to hobble off down the hallway—toward the bathroom. "Just think about it for a moment. Think carefully. I'll be right back."

Allan suddenly remembered his promise to Jenny and called out, "Professor, may I use your phone?"

Professor Sumner answered as he closed the bathroom door. "Of course, my boy. Do anything you like—just as long as you have good news waiting for me when I return."

Allan dialed Jenny's number several times before getting it right. Finally, her answering machine picked up and Allan said, "Hi, Jen. It's me. I ... uh ... I said I would call, but I don't want to tell you over the phone. Scratch that—that sounds like I got in ..." He hesitated for a moment, feeling the full impact of his disappointment again. "And, uh ... I didn't. I didn't get in. So ... I guess that's that. Anyway, I'll try you again later. Bye." He hung up the phone, took a deep breath and said aloud, "That's that."

Allan noticed the file folder on the desktop and flipped it open. He tried to read the professor's notes, but handwriting was even harder for him to decipher than typewritten text. Allan stared at the words and the letters began to shift. He tried to relax the muscles which controlled his eyes, as he had been taught, but the words continued to erode. He muttered, "C'mon ... don't force it. It's no big deal. Just relax." but the letters reversed into mirror-images and then ran off of the edges of the page as if they were water.

Frustrated and nauseous, Allan closed the folder too fast and the contents spilled onto the floor. And when he stooped to gather the papers—that was when Allan saw it: a familiar black and white image peering out from the scattered documents. Allan retrieved the newspaper clipping and brought it over to the light—just to make sure. The clipping was old and the newsprint had yellowed, but Allan knew this photo of an old Hindu royal on horseback.

"Aha! I knew your curiosity would get the better of you." The professor flopped into his chair and began to massage his temples with his fingertips. "That's the rajah who came to call on the Shantu. I believe that picture was taken on the first day of his crusade." Allan said something too softly to be heard and Professor Sumner answered, "What was that, my boy?"

Allan was still staring at the clipping in awe. He cleared his throat and repeated, softly, "I think this is my great-grandfather."

The professor stopped massaging his aching head. His eyes were open wide and his mouth was agape. "It *couldn't* be."

"I think it could." Allan looked up at his friend. "Professor, I think it is."

The professor thought it over for a moment and then said, "Well I'll be damned. I guess I owe your mother an apology. I always thought that all of that Destiny stuff was just a bunch of bunk, but ..."

Now it was Allan's turn to pace. He carried the clipping with him, checking it every few seconds—just to make sure that his defective eyes hadn't deceived him.

"It would just be you and me, my boy. There's no grant. No sponsors. Just an informal fact finding expedition." An edge of urgency crept into the professor's voice. "I need your youth. I need your hunger. And whether or not you're willing to admit it, you have insights that I simply do not." The professor looked Allan square in the eye and said, "Allan ... destiny aside, this may be the one adventure for which you are uniquely qualified. It may also be my last."

"What's that supposed to mean?"

"I suspect you already know." The professor searched Allan's face for a reaction. Allan *did* know. He knew from the moment he stepped into the house. "Do you still have your hunches, my boy?"

Allan sulked away, unable to face the desperation in his mentor's eyes. "No."

"Then you've stopped picking up the phone before it rings? And you no longer take your umbrella out with you on sunny days—only to have it rain by mid-afternoon?" Allan remained silent. "And the dreams ... You don't have them anymore, either?"

Allan lied: "No."

The professor sighed and turned his attention to his computer. "Well, good then. That must be a relief."

Allan returned to the chair, knowing that the professor saw right through him. "All right, yes ... That stuff still happens—usually when I meditate, but I try to ignore it."

The professor put his hand on Allan's shoulder and said, "Then you know what's growing inside my head."

Exhausted, Allan sank back into his chair and closed his eyes. "No. Only that whatever's wrong is–" Allan edited himself: "Serious."

Neither one knew what to say next and a long silence settled in and hung between them like smoke, obscuring everything but their love for each other.

Finally, the professor looked at his watch and said, "Well, you have a plane to catch." Professor Sumner stood and began to hunt for his car keys.

Allan spoke with painful deliberation: "She's dead, professor. My mother is dead."

Professor Sumner crumpled as if punched in the stomach. When his eyes met Allan's, they were those of a tired old man. Professor Sumner said, "Then there's nothing to keep *either* of us here."

9

Argus stood beside Allan while Professor Sumner grieved among the other mourners on the bank of Diti's favorite river; two hours outside of the city. Diti Steele had many friends and all were in attendance. Plans had been canceled and vacations delayed; a collection of treasured memories awaited each face in the crowd, beneath the sadness of a last goodbye to the kindest person they would ever know.

The Hindu priest chanted and prayed in words no one knew, but all understood. The sounds of sadness and the wind mingled on the grassy knoll beneath a weeping willow, overlooking a stream. Allan was struck by the irony of this tree that took its name from human sorrow. Perhaps the Buddhists were right: all living things had a soul and were conscious of their surroundings. As the leaves rustled overhead, Allan wondered if the limbs of this particular willow might not hang a little lower from this day forward.

Argus stood quietly, hands clasped behind his back, fingernails digging into the soft flesh of his palms in sync with the Vedic chant. Blood seeped from the wound and stained the cuff of his starched white shirt, yet he continued to dig. The priest stepped forward, extending the funereal urn, and no one noticed the blood that smeared the polished silver as Argus accepted the container, moved to the bank of the stream and committed Diti's ashes to the churning water. As he watched his wife's remains begin their long journey to the sea, Argus wept.

10

Saigon, January 23, 1968.

Argus finished his watered-down scotch and followed a young Vietnamese girl up the rickety stairs that led to the bedrooms. He noticed the girl's tacky, flowered dress was three sizes too big and that she hadn't quite mastered the art of walking in heels. These were good signs. She was probably new to the trade and less inclined to robbery and disease.

The girl clomped down the hallway, stealing a glance back at Argus to make sure that he hadn't changed his mind. She stopped at the fifth door on the left and turned to him with a desperate smile that was intended to be seductive. The bar girl cooed, "You no go, okie dokie? I super horny for you, baby." She took Argus' hand as she'd seen the other girls do and slipped it inside her dress to let him feel that her nipples were hard. It was a simple, but effective illusion accomplished with a dab of Preparation H. She smiled and promised, "We have good time, you bet."

Argus nodded in agreement, and she disappeared into her room. He could hear an animated discussion going on inside between the girl and two other voices.

In the fourteen months he had been in-country as an advisor, Argus had acquired a passion for purchased sex—to the extent that many of the enlisted men, and even some of the other officers, referred to him as Big John behind his back. It was one of two addictions Argus would bring home at war's end.

He had also picked up smatterings of Cantonese and Vietnamese, but the bastardization of both, mixed with French, eluded him. A moment later the girl emerged and gestured for him to enter. The room was cramped and smelled of fish and stale urine. A dirty sheet had been used to divide the tiny space. Argus could hear a whispered conversation taking place on the other side of the rustling partition. The girl scolded the voices in her bastardized tongue and they quieted. She turned on an old radio that played American rock and roll.

Argus looked toward the sheet and asked, "Who are they?"

"Only mother and sister." The girl turned up the radio.

Argus' lust had cooled a bit. He said, "I don't know–"

The girl raised a graceful forefinger to her lips and swayed seductively to The Doors, determined to pay her rent. She moved closer, slipping the straps of the dress over her shoulders, then closed her eyes and began to dance in her clunky heels. After what seemed like a long time, the pretty young girl allowed the hand-me-down garment to fall to the floor.

Argus' eyes drifted across her naked body. It was tight and lithe and the color of honey. She untucked his shirt and slipped her hands inside, wrapping her slender arms around his waist. She stood only chest-high to him. Her hands slid down, inside his trousers, and he took a quick breath in. Her hair smelled of cheap perfume and sweet adolescent sweat.

The girl unzipped Argus' pants and reached inside. He covered her mouth with his own. Her tiny hands found what they were looking for and she smiled a gap-toothed smile as they kissed. Any hesitation Argus may have had was no longer evident.

He made a guttural sound and tugged at his belt as the girl led him to the sagging cot in the corner. He peeled away his trousers and shucked off his skivvies as the soldier in the next room called out for God. The girl pushed Argus back onto the cot and straddled him. Her little sister was watching now from the edge of the hanging sheet. Argus heard movement and made eye contact with the curious child at the exact moment that he and the girl became one.

Footsteps hurried down the hall outside the room as the girl ground her hips and moaned in an approximation of pleasure. Just as urgency began to overtake Argus, the door burst inward and a soldier entered. "Lieutenant Steele?"

Argus convulsed. "WHAT THE FUCK ..."

The red-faced private averted his eyes and suppressed a smile. "Oh, shit. Sorry Sir."

Argus shoved the bewildered girl off and leapt to his feet, fumbling for his pants. "GODDAMN IT, PRIVATE! What the hell do you think you're doing?"

"General Cross needs you, Sir—A.S.A.P."

Argus yanked up his zipper, already feeling the painful ache of aborted satisfaction. He barked, "It couldn't have waited another thirty fucking seconds?!"

"Sorry, Sir." The Private handed Argus his shoes, smiled politely at the naked girl and nodded to the audience peering out from behind the dirty sheet. He couldn't wait to tell the guys back at the base about Big John's latest exploit.

The girl slipped back into her dress, allowing the Private's eyes to linger on her breasts a moment longer before she covered them. In her short career she'd already learned that it paid to advertise.

———

By the time Argus arrived at the base, all hell had broken loose. The General's secretary held ten people at bay, each insisting that they had to see General Cross immediately. An uninvited TV crew hovered outside the building, trying to get the scoop for their viewers back home. For them, the war had become a real live soap opera, complete with commercials.

General Cross spotted Argus and waved him into the office. Argus stood at ease in front of the General's desk. Cross slammed down the phone. "If he thinks I'm taking the fall for this mess he's sadly mistaken!"

Argus was clueless. "Sir?"

"What have you heard, Steele?"

"Heard, Sir? Nothing, Sir."

"Where the hell have you been the last three hours, Lieutenant?"

Argus searched for a decent response. He said, "We ... That is—myself and some of the other men—are on leave, Sir."

General Cross removed his glasses and pinched the bridge of his nose. "How many?"

"Men, Sir? Ten. Twelve including Lieutenant Krandle and myself."

"All from Yellow Fever?"

"All from Operation Yellow Fever, yes Sir."

General Cross studied Argus carefully, trying to decide whether he was an asset or a liability. "Then it looks like you're all I've got."

"Sir?"

"The Koreans captured the Pueblo. Three hours ago."

Stunned, Argus said, "There were over a hundred men on that ship."

"I'm painfully aware of that fact Lieutenant. One hundred and five. Plus another forty in the Yellow Fever unit."

"Then our mission, Sir ... Has it been—"

"No it has *not*, Lieutenant." The General tore open a roll of Tums and ate them like candy. "Your mission stands."

"But, Sir ... With all due respect, Sir, with only ten men left and only one officer—Lieutenant Krandle—to lead them–"

"*Two officers*, Lieutenant."

Argus got the message and was terrified. "Sir, I was with Yellow Fever solely as an advisor. I've never even seen combat, much less—"

"I'm aware of the situation, Lieutenant Steele. But the powers that be have decided that Operation Yellow Fever will proceed as planned. Word is that the North Koreans got wind of the mission, and that is why they took the Pueblo. They now believe that Yellow Fever has been crushed and, as a result, will have dropped their guard—creating a window of opportunity for you, Lieutenant Krandle and the remaining men."

Argus was numb with fear. "But, Sir—"

"Your men are waiting, Lieutenant. Good luck—and God's speed. That is all." The General turned his attention to the paperwork on his desk and Argus left—certain that death awaited him in Laos.

———

Argus studied the faces of the other troops as the transport truck bounced down a dirt road that led into the Laotian jungle. He was at least ten years older than the other men. At thirty, he should have been pushing papers, but had been convinced by a General friend that if he wanted to land a post in D.C. after the war he'd have to get his hands dirty, during. With a law degree from Yale it seemed only natural that Argus would be used solely as an advisor. But the taking of the Pueblo had changed everything.

The objective of Operation Yellow Fever was to locate the rumored safe house of Ho Chi Minh, the seventy-eight year old leader of the North. Word was that Minh was on his deathbed and had been moved to a secret location, deep in the jungle. Once located, Minh was to be neutralized, with all evidence pointing to the rival faction within the leader's own regime. It was a suicide mission and Argus had never intended to leave the command post. Krandle had checked him out on the M-16 and the other equipment, but he was still light years away from being ready for actual combat.

"You okay?"

Argus turned to Krandle and answered, "No. Are you?"

Krandle laughed, and said, "Hell no."

———

Two days later Krandle and Argus led the troops in on foot. They had abandoned the truck twenty miles back, when the overgrown foliage became too dense. By the time the troops of Operation Yellow Fever had arrived at the Ho Chi Minh trail, a squall had saturated the soldiers' clothes and gear, adding thirty pounds to each man's load. The lush terrain had been transformed into endless miles of muddy flypaper that slowed the unit's progress to a labored crawl. Argus had never experienced, or even imagined, such misery. Exhausted, dehydrated and unable to feel any part of his body, other than his badly blistered feet, he wasn't even thinking about the enemy when the first shot rang out from the trees.

Someone yelled, "SNIPER!"

The men dove for cover.

Argus and Thomas, the radio operator, scoured the treetops from their position behind a rotting log. Argus' voice cracked as he whispered, "See anything, Thomas?"

"Not yet, Lieutenant."

The stillness of the moment was unbearable. Seconds seemed like months as the men watched and waited. Rain spattered the leaves and drizzled down the rim of Argus' combat helmet. Then three shots sounded from above and a man on the ground screamed. The troops returned fire, but couldn't pinpoint the sniper's position.

A voice called out, "Lieutenant! O'Connell's hit! We need a medic over here—NOW!"

Harkness, the medic, emerged from the bush and ran toward the injured man, trailed by sniper fire. The men of Yellow Fever fired back. Another soldier on the ground was hit and someone yelled, "Where is he?"

"Is there more than one?"

"Fuck if I know!"

"This is bad, man! *Really* bad, man!"

Thomas spotted the sniper in the trees and aimed his M-16. "There you are, you little fucker." Argus watched Thomas pull the trigger. *Nothing.* "Sir—my rifle's jammed!" Thomas worked to free the frozen firing mechanism, pointing out the sniper to Argus. "He's right up there, Sir. See him?"

Argus saw him, a hundred feet above them, and a tiny figure barely visible among the bright green leaves. For the first time since his arrival in Vietnam Argus raised his rifle and took aim. He could feel the sweat running down his back. Argus willed his body to pull the trigger, but something kept him from firing. Fear? Or humanity?

"What the hell are you waiting for, Sir?" Argus held his breath to steady his aim. He found the enemy soldier in his sights. "Take him out, man!" urged Thomas, sensing Argus' hesitation. Argus watched as the sniper took aim at another of the ground troops— then suddenly turned his head toward Argus as if he sensed something. The sniper's eyes met Argus' and registered fear. Argus' finger jerked the trigger, more a result of surprise than intent.

BLAT.

The bullet took a chunk of the tree, right above the sniper's head. The enemy soldier swung his rifle around toward Argus.

Argus fumbled for the lever that switched the M-16 from single-shot to full automatic and squeezed the trigger harder than he had intended.

BLAT-TAT-TAT-TAT-TAT. BLAT. BLAT-TAT-TAT.

Argus' bullets hit home—shredding the sniper's face and trailing down his body, causing impact convulsions. Argus released the trigger and gasped for breath. He watched the sniper's lifeless body fall from the trees to meet the ground with a heavy, wet sound.

"Fuck yeah!" called Thomas, clapping Argus on the shoulder.

Argus tried to catch his breath, but his adrenaline was running too high.

A voice from the other side of the clearing warned, "We got company!"

That's when Argus heard them; clipped, singsong voices rushing toward the clearing from the North. And then more voices— from the South.

Krandle called out, "THIS IS IT, MEN!" and ran toward the Northern voices. The troops sprung from the trees and followed, as did Thomas and Argus, a moment later.

Argus moved through the trees, bringing up the rear, puffing like a runaway train. He heard the first shots up ahead—then another round of fire from behind. Argus and Thomas turned and fired on the advancing Viet Cong soldiers—taking out two. A bullet whizzed past, nicking Argus' cheek, but he didn't feel it. His eyes were suddenly alight with hatred, born of fear. He shot down three more Vietnamese as they entered the clearing, then hurried forward.

As he ran, rifle at the ready, Argus passed Harkness writhing on the ground in agony. He'd been gut shot. Argus continued to run, blood speeding through his veins and trickling down his cheek as the enemy closed in from the rear. Where was Thomas? Argus looked back and saw a Vietnamese soldier lifting the young radio operator from the ground by his uniform and pressing the muzzle of his rifle to his forehead.

Argus turned away and heard a single 'POP' a second later.

More bodies; ours and theirs. Argus leaped over Lieutenant Krandle. who was lying on his back staring blindly up at the sky. The dying man's voice had been replaced by an incoherent gurgling.

Finally, Argus caught up with the rest of his troops. They had pushed the enemy back to what appeared to be an abandoned coal mine. The ground between the trees and the mine was littered with Vietnamese bodies.

Argus called out, "We've got more behind!"

Three of the remaining six troops turned and joined Argus against the enemy at the rear. Argus fired into the advancing Viet Cong on full auto, watching them fall, one after the other, suddenly certain that his aim was guided by the hand of God. He felt invincible, immortal and more alive than ever before.

When Argus emerged from his reverie, there were no more targets and his ammunition was spent. The advancing enemy all lay dead or dying. Argus pried the weapon from the hands of a nearby Vietnamese corpse, turned back toward the mine, and began to fire.

The half-dozen remaining Vietnamese soldiers had entrenched themselves behind the massive vertical beams that supported the mine.

"You think that's where they got him, Lieutenant?" asked Jones. "Ho Chi Minh?"

"We'll find out soon enough."

"Not unless we can draw those little motherfuckers out into the open, Sir. We got no shot." Argus realized the truth in this and was suddenly clear on what must be done. He stepped over his men and moved toward the mine. Jones called out, "You outta your mind, Lieutenant?"

Argus ran toward the mine, firing. He felt superhuman. Enemy gunfire exploded all around him, but Argus continued. His men supplied cover as the Vietnamese moved out in the open to get a bead on him. A bullet tore through the soft flesh of his thigh, but it didn't faze him. Argus shot one enemy soldier in the chest as he reloaded and another as he emerged from cover to get a clear shot. Two more were taken out by Argus' men and the third abandoned the mine—running out into the jungle with unlikely dreams of escape.

And then there was one.

The last Vietnamese soldier's weapon had jammed and he was cornered in an alcove of the mine. Argus moved closer, rifle at the ready. His footsteps echoed in the mine shaft, along with the heavy breathing of the trapped Vietnamese, who was little more than a child. The prepubescent soldier's eyes were wide with terror and the cotton trousers of his uniform were soaked with urine. He dropped his weapon and raised his trembling hands in surrender.

Argus moved closer, pressing the barrel of his borrowed weapon to the boy's throat. The boy dropped to his knees, closed his eyes and began to whisper a Buddhist prayer. Argus followed the boy down, flipped the rifle into semi-auto mode and squeezed the trigger once. Blood sprayed across Argus' face, bright red and warm. The soldier clawed at his throat, trying to keep the blood in his body. Argus watched the kid buck and heave on the mine shaft's dirt floor. He switched back to full auto and used his foot to flip the kid over onto his back. Argus wanted to see the look in his eyes as he died.

He wanted *the secret.*

The remaining troops of Yellow Fever were just approaching the entrance of the mine shaft when the sounds began.

BLAT-TAT-TAT-TAT-TAT-TAT-TAT-TAT-TAT-TAT-TAT-TAT-TAT-TAT

Weapons up, the troops hurried forward—ready to assist in the battle. But they were unprepared for what they found. The kid's mutilated corpse was nearly unrecognizable as human …

BLAT-TAT-TAT-TAT-TAT-TAT-TAT-TAT-TAT-TAT-TAT-TAT-TAT-TAT

… just a twitching mass of pulp.

BLAT-TAT-TAT-TAT-TAT-TAT-TAT-TAT-TAT-TAT-TAT-TAT-TAT-TAT

Argus emptied his weapon into the long-dead boy, and continued to squeeze the trigger, even after his ammunition was spent.

Click. Click.

Jones stepped forward cautiously. "Sir?"

Click. Click. Click.

"Lieutenant?"

Click. Click.

Jones put his hand on Argus' rifle. "He's dead, Sir."

Argus looked up—and Jones would tell his wife, years later, it was an image he never managed to purge from his dreams. Blood and gore dripped from Argus' face and his eyes were open wide, pupils fixed and dilated. And on his lips: a smile.

11

Two months and four days later Argus revisited his favorite Saigon bordello. It was his first stop after his release from the hospital. Poking and prodding and endless questions had arisen from Private Jones' reported observations of Argus' actions that day in the cave; so much so that Argus had been forced to submit to a full psychiatric evaluation. After six weeks of inkblots and pointless psychobabble, the psychiatrist had finally asked the question that had been on his mind from day one: "Did you enjoy the kill, Lieutenant?"

Of course I enjoyed it! I'm not supposed to take satisfaction in defeating the enemy? Is it inappropriate to feel pleasure when you realize that you're not going to die today? You think I'm crazy—just because I felt a certain degree of satisfaction at having faced down the dragon in his lair? Who cares if we didn't find Minh? I found myself in that cave.

The pasty-faced shrink had released Argus, knowing full well that he had freed a monster with a taste for blood. But that was okay, because *here* monsters could be hailed as heroes, while the truly heroic were shipped home in plain pine boxes.

"Mmm ..."

Argus watched a pretty, cross-eyed prostitute work his flaccid penis in her hands like a party balloon being primed for inflation.

She sucked loudly, pretending to enjoy herself, and Argus wondered how long it had been since she'd washed her hair. The girl slipped him from her mouth with a soft, wet 'pop' and caught her breath while repeating the balloon routine.

She cooed, "You big man. Me need big man," and returned her attention to his unresponsive organ. Argus sensed her frustration. There seemed little hope of an erection tonight. In fact, the only recent arousal he could remember had accompanied memories of that day in the cave. He had never felt as much a man as he had in those few precious moments standing over the dead body of the young enemy soldier. Thinking about it now made him stiffen slightly. The girl whispered, "Oh yeah, Baby. I get it hard for you," and began to work faster, hoping for a quick orgasm and a big tip. She said, "You like Jesse, yes?"

Argus' thoughts turned away from the cave and he looked down into her hopeful eyes, but his passion was already fading. He muttered obscenities as he watched his erection die. The girl lowered her face into her hands, shamed by her failure, and Argus barked, "Stop that."

The young prostitute hadn't yet learned that patient sympathy in situations like these usually yielded bigger tips than tears. The girl wiped her face and said, "I do what you want. You tell me."

Annoyed, Argus pulled up his pants and moved toward the door. "Forget it."

The girl clung to him desperately. "No, mister—you no go." She slid her hands down his pants. "I make him work, mister, please—you no go." Argus tried to push her away, but she kept on coming. "You no go, you no go—"

"Get your fucking hands off me!" He shoved her hard and she stumbled back toward the bed, tripping over her own feet. The girl smashed her head on the edge of a cast iron table on her way down to the dirty wooden floor, and then lay motionless. Argus stopped in the doorway.

He took a step closer and saw the nasty gash on her forehead. Argus wondered if she might be dead. The possibility excited him. It would be another hour, maybe two, before she'd be missed. He would have all the privacy he could want.

Argus closed the door and moved to investigate. The cut was bleeding badly, but the girl was still breathing; alive but unconscious. His first reaction was disappointment, but then an unexpected thought aroused him: *I can still pretend.*

12

Douglas Geffner's fingers were beginning to ache again. It was always worse at night, and a full day of typing and filing hadn't helped. Four Aléve used to last five or six hours, but lately he was lucky to get three before the damned arthritic throb returned. Golden years? They felt more like tin.

Two years ago Elizabeth had finally convinced him to see a doctor, but there was no "cure," and the prescription pain killers dulled his brain as much as they did the pain. Sweet Elizabeth; another ache without a cure. He would have gladly sacrificed all eight fingers and both thumbs just to hear the sound of her voice again. He would have thrown in his toes for a kiss.

"Pop-Pop?"

"In here." Douglas closed the double-wide file drawer.

Bill Geffner, Douglas' thirty-four year old grandson leaned in the doorway, shirt untucked and tie askew, yawning and rubbing his eyes with balled up fists just like he had as a kid. Elizabeth would have said he was too thin, but Douglas knew it was just the stress of starting a new business. A few good months and he'd have his spare tire back, like it or not. Bill unbuckled his belt and unfastened his slacks, in order to tuck in his shirt properly, and said, "I've got the computer up and running, but this new router is driving me nuts. How can they sell a person brand new hardware that isn't compatible with the current operating systems and fail to mention it on the ever-lovin' box? Apparently there's a work-around—I found it on the user forums—but it's requires technical know-how far beyond my pay grade. Be nice if these tech companies would let us low-tech suckers in on the fine print *before* we buy the useless crap. Greedy bastards." He shook his head in disgust. "You ready to go?"

"Almost. I've got two policies that you had flagged—and one other."

"The flagged ones?"

"Avila and Fox."

Bill zipped up and said, "Toss them. They decided to go with another agent."

There was an impatient edge to Bill's voice. Douglas said, "But most of the others decided to stay with you, right?"

"About half."

"All in all, a good beginning."

Bill forced a smile. "The old bastard swore they would all stay. I hope the Florida sun gives him a nice case of skin cancer. He also told me that the heat in this dump worked—and he *also promised* ..." Bill stopped himself, shooing away the rest of his complaints as if they were flies. "Whatcha gonna do? Right, Pop-Pop? I was buying—he was selling. The old guy took me for a ride. Break out the violins."

Douglas retrieved the three files in question and handed the flagged ones to his grandson. "Well Billy, insurance salesmen have never been known as pillars of integrity." He saw the wry smile on Bill's face and added, hurriedly, "Present company excepted of course."

"Of course. And it's *insurance broker*, not salesman—if you don't mind." He looked at the folders in his hand. "What's the other one you've got there?"

Douglas handed the final folder to his grandson. "This one's got me stymied."

Billy opened the file and read the label aloud. "Steele. Argus and Diti. Goes after the Rs and before the Ts, right?"

Douglas waggled his forefinger. "Watch it with the smart talk, mister Insurance Broker. It's that name—Steele. It sounds very familiar."

"Sounds like a spy from the movies." He yawned again. "My name is Steele, Argus Steele."

"Exactly! That's what I thought." Douglas looked pained. "I know I've seen this name before—and recently. It's driving me crazy. I won't be able to sleep until I remember."

Bill glanced through the Steele file. "Our spy and his wife have matching his-and-hers life policies. Nice. Three million per. "Let's hope Argus and Diti Steele both live long and healthy lives." He closed the file and handed it back to Douglas. "For their sake *and* mine."

Douglas brightened. "That's it! The *wife*. It's *her* name that I've seen." He seemed on the verge of a breakthrough. Then his shoulders sagged. "But where?"

Bill dropped the two flagged files into the wastebasket and switched off the light. "C'mon, Pop-Pop. Janie's gonna be all over me for coming home late again, and not in a good way." Douglas opened his battered and unfashionably oversized leather briefcase and inserted the Steele file. Bill said, "What, you're taking one of my few remaining clients?"

"I'll bring it back. Maybe reading it over will jar my memory. I know I've seen that name. Diti Steele. *Diti Steele ...*"

Bill gestured toward the ugly briefcase. "You still shlepping that old thing?"

"This briefcase is older than you are, so show a little respect. What can I say? Old habits and old librarians die hard."

Bill smiled and said, "From your lips to God's ear." They walked out of the supply room, which contained the filing cabinet, and through the main office to the outer door. Bill put his arm around his granddad and said, "Thanks for helping me get settled, Pop-Pop. It's been nice having you around."

"Like my social calendar is so full these days."

They stepped out into the hallway and Bill locked the office door. "I hear retirement takes some getting used to, although it sounds pretty good to me right about now."

"You can have it." Douglas trundled off toward the elevator. "I feel like I'm sitting around waiting to die."

13

The new home care nurse was waiting by the door when Douglas arrived. She did not look pleased. Douglas set aside his briefcase and said, "I *know*, I'm late. My apologies."

She was already half way out the door. "Many nurses wouldn't have stayed 15 minutes past the end of their shift—much less an hour, you know."

"I know, and I appreciate it. Really."

The sincerity in his voice cut the chill, but only slightly. The nurse gave a half-hearted smile and turned toward the elevator. "All right then, goodnight. I'll be covering for Juana tomorrow, so I suppose I'll see you in the morning."

"Fine. How was she today?"

"Stable. You might want to prop her up on her side in a few hours—those bedsores are flaring up again."

"Thank you." Douglas closed the door and leaned back against it for a moment. He suddenly felt so alone. The apartment, which was once homey and well-kept, was now cluttered with medical paraphernalia, half-read books and magazines. Once the silence began to eat at him, Douglas called out, "Sweetheart, I'm home," and picked up a small stack of mail, mostly bills, from the coffee table on his way into the bedroom.

Elizabeth Geffner lay motionless, hooked to a ventilator, as she had been for the last thirteen months and seven days. Her eyes were wide open and glassy. That vacant, unfocused gaze was hard for Douglas to bear. Besides, she no longer blinked, and her eyes dried out quickly. So he closed them after giving her a kiss on the forehead and whispering, "Hello, beautiful. Miss me?"

Elizabeth was once beautiful, brilliant and vital; a scientist, an aspiring pastry chef, and one hell of a storyteller. She and Douglas and their uncommon love for each other were once the envy of all of their friends. But that was then and *now* there was only her alone in the bed that was once theirs, dwarfed by machinery, and him in the roll-away beside it. Golden years indeed.

Douglas recounted the minutiae of the day's events to his wife and then opened and read the mail aloud, hoping that the sound of his voice would comfort her. It could have been his imagination, but she seemed less agitated when he spoke. So he spoke at length, often until his voice was hoarse and he had nothing left to read except the boxes which held his frozen dinners: New and Improved! 99% Fat Free!

Douglas had finished the mail, and was just about to move on to the first of three newspapers to which he subscribed, when he suddenly blurted out, "Diti Steele! It was in the newspaper—that's where I saw that name!" He began to pace. "But which one? Which section?" He made a frustrated sound.

Douglas hurried to the closet where he kept the newspapers for recycling and found it overflowing. Elizabeth would have clucked her tongue and smiled that weary smile of hers. And he would have liked that. Undaunted, he rolled up his sleeves, grabbed a random stack, and returned to the bedroom.

14

Allan studied the stars from the balcony outside his parents' Park Avenue Penthouse. The air had always smelled different up here—at least, to him. To some it smelled like success. To others it smelled like money, power, and boundless possibility, blended into a heady perfume guaranteed to arouse ambition in even the most dedicated slacker. But to Allan, it had an oily, still quality—like the inside of a tool shed.

Allan peered over the edge of the railing and down to the sidewalk below; twenty stories. He wondered what was going through her head as she fell to her death. Allan's dream had just been a jumbled montage of images and sounds, with no real sense of what was going on inside his mother's mind. She couldn't see the ground rushing up to meet her so perhaps, to her, it felt like flying. God, he hoped so.

Allan placed his hand on the railing and then withdrew it suddenly, as if it had been on fire. His mother's ceramic wind chimes chattered behind him and Allan turned with a start.

"Don't worry. I had it fixed." Argus continued to strum the wind chimes with his hand. "Too little, too late, I know." He stepped into the moonlight and looked out over the city. Argus was a handsome and powerful man with strong, chiseled features. He inhaled deeply and held the scent in for a long time before exhaling. "I don't know, maybe I'll sell the place. I can't imagine living here without her."

Allan returned his attention to the sidewalk below where his mother had met her destiny. He couldn't see the chalk outline from here at night, but knew it was there. He said, quietly, "She told me not to blame you."

The look on Argus' face was the closest thing to surprise that Allan had ever seen. "She told you ..."

Allan enjoyed his father's obvious discomfort so much that he decided to change the subject. "I had my interview at Yale." Argus didn't respond. "Why didn't you tell me? I could have saved the trip."

"Allan ... Anything I say right now is only going to make you angrier. Why don't we just let it lie for a few days?"

"No. I want to hear it. You knew how important Yale was to me—and to her. Why didn't you tell us?"

Argus joined Allan at the railing and tried to sound sincere. "The specialists, the tests—the *torture* this thing has put us all through ... We have to stop fooling ourselves. You are and will *always* be ... limited."

Allan turned to face his father and said, "I'm going to Africa with Professor Sumner. We leave next week."

"Allan, don't be ridiculous. You don't have to prove anything."

"Yes—I do."

Argus sighed and turned to re enter the house. "I was going to ask a favor." Allan turned away, but Argus continued: "Your mother's things ... Would you sort through them for me? Whenever I ... It just makes it harder for me."

Allan answered, "Okay. I'll do it," and returned his attention to the stars.

15

Douglas Geffner stopped at the top of the steps in front of the New York Public Library after ten minutes of climbing up and down them. He pressed two fingers to his carotid, looked at his watch and started counting as the second hand breezed past twelve. He still had traces of newsprint embedded beneath his fingernails from last night's fruitless search for the elusive Diti Steele. Funny how something as trivial as a stranger's name could tug at a person's brain. Too much spare time on his hands, he supposed.

His heart rate was one-hundred and thirty beats per minute. Not bad, considering how little exercise he had done since his wife's illness and his resulting retirement. Every weekday for forty-plus years he had taken the 5:45 train to arrive at work a half an hour early, just so that he could climb these steps before opening. Over the years his eyesight had weakened and his arthritis had intensified, but his legs remained second only to Michelangelo's David, at least according to *Elizabeth.*

At first, when he was just an intern, the stair climbing had been to help him stay in shape for the NYU track team. Later, when he was a Reference Assistant, he continued out of habit. And finally, once he became the head Reference Librarian, habit became tradition. He had even named the lions some years back: Moe and Curly. As an intern he thought them pompous, but in time had become surprisingly attached to them. Moe and Curly—the ever-faithful guardians of knowledge.

"Doug, is that you?" Douglas turned his attention from Moe and Curly to find Arthur Walsh at the bottom of the steps, waving. "Long time no see."

Douglas met Arthur halfway down the steps and relieved him of an armful of books. Arthur, a short, stout man in his mid-forties, was already out of breath. Douglas said, "How have you been, Arthur?"

"Oh, you know me. I'm like that second frog in the vat of cream—you know, the one who *doesn't* drown—just paddling 'til the cream turns into butter. Hey, how's Liz?"

Douglas answered, "Not good," and nodded to Ernie, the morning guard, as Douglas and Arthur entered the building.

———

Arthur dumped his things on the oversized desk that was once Douglas' and said, "So, you wanna take a look at our fresh fiche."

"Ranging from two to six weeks ago. Local papers only."

Arthur headed for the office. "Why don't you grab a station and I'll check back here. I've been a little slow filing the new stuff, lately. They may still be in the pouches."

Douglas held his tongue and reminded himself that he wasn't the boss anymore. But he had thought—he had hoped—that he'd trained Arthur better. Douglas went to the bank of microfiche viewers and switched on number three. Unless Arthur had convinced the board to invest in some secondary repairs, which seemed unlikely, good old number three offered the sharpest images. In fact, in another hour all the quick-witted college students would be lined up for her.

Arthur said, "Here's what I've found so far." Douglas accepted several canisters of microfiche and loaded the first roll. "Have you got another mystery on your hands, Doug?"

"Huh?" Douglas was trying to concentrate on the tiny type as he scrolled through the roll. He said, "It's probably nothing."

"I remember you used to get a bug up your butt about something and you'd gnaw at it like a bulldog until you figured it out. That's what made you the best. No question was too arcane for you—you'd just dive into the stacks until you came up with the answer."

Douglas removed the roll and loaded another, thinking, "C'mon, where was it? The Society page?"

Arthur continued to prattle on; "I'd be happy to help, if you need anything. Especially if you've got a good mystery going. Gets pretty tedious answering the same old questions: what are the seven deadly sins, name the four horsemen of the apocalypse, when did the dinosaurs become extinct ... You know the drill."

"Extinct—that's it!" Arthur had jarred Douglas' memory. "It was an obituary." Douglas was excited now. He removed the current roll of microfiche and studied the dates on the remaining canisters.

"Look, I know you never really thought much of me as a reference librarian, let alone the head of the department, but I would like to help. I mean, I owe you so much—"

Douglas looked up and asked, "What did you say?"

Arthur tried to act casual, but his hurt feelings were showing. He said, "Nothing. I'd just like to help, if you want me to. That's all."

Douglas felt like a heel. Arthur was right about Douglas' opinion of his skills, though he had always tried to keep his feelings to himself. Apparently, he hadn't done a very good job of it. He suddenly saw Arthur in a whole new light. Perhaps he wasn't as lazy and unaware as Douglas had thought. Maybe he was just a guy with limited abilities doing the best he could. If Douglas was honest—he himself hadn't been good enough to be the head of the department when the job first fell into his lap. Maybe Arthur would grow into it, just as Douglas had.

Douglas selected four more canisters and handed two of them to Arthur. He said, "We're looking for an obituary. Diti Steele is the name."

16

Allan stood in the doorway of his mother's bedroom for a long time before crossing the threshold. The faint scent of Diti's herbal shampoo reached his nose, and Allan breathed it in slowly. He wanted to believe it was his mother's spirit still present in the room, but Allan guessed that it was coming from one of the pillows which, along with the other bedclothes, had probably not been changed since his mother's death. Allan stepped forward and looked around the room that held so many memories—wondering where to begin. Then he noticed something peculiar, at least in a *blind* woman's bedroom: a DVD. It stuck out like a rude silver tongue from the mouth of a DVD player atop a small TV in the far corner of the room.

Allan switched on the T.V. and DVD player, and nudged the disc back into the machine. When the television flickered to life, the colors were all wrong and the picture was skewed to the extreme left of the television's screen. Allan tweaked the brightness levels, color, and other settings on the old T.V., and he suddenly realized that this DVD contained video transfers of home movies featuring him as a child.

At first there was no sound—just the hand-held image of Allan at eight years old; sitting on his mother's lap as a tutor read to him. Diti looked deliriously happy, despite the wheelchair and dark glasses, as she smoothed Allan's hair and whispered happy secrets in his ear. The camera's image began to shift then, panning off of Allan and his mother and onto the sexy young tutor. The camera roamed over the tutor's voluptuous curves—then moved closer. The girl looked up from the book and into the lens—waving Argus away with a playful smile. Then the sound kicked in. "Hey, you—go point that thing somewhere else." The tutor stood and took the camera away from Argus. "Go on—sit over there next to your wife."

Allan sat on the edge of his mother's bed and watched the tutor nudge Argus into the frame with little Allan and his mother. It was an awkward family portrait at best. Argus was uncomfortable, Diti was focused exclusively on her son—and Allan was terrified.

"There we go. That's great."

Argus was growing more uncomfortable by the moment. He said, "Okay, *enough.*"

"No, that's nice. That's where you belong; with your *wife* and your son." The tutor pushed him back toward Allan, who was watching his father with a mixture of fear and suspicion." Allan, why don't you give your daddy a great big hug."

Allan backed away, taking shelter in his mother's arms, and Argus began to lose his sense of humor. Being this close to Allan made him visibly nervous. Argus said, "All right, Laurie. That's enough." Argus stood and left the frame, calling back, "I've got work to do."

"Touchy, touchy." Laurie turned the camera back to Allan and his mother, amused by Argus' discomfort. "Allan, sing that new song we learned for your mommy."

As Allan began to sing his song in his quavering little voice it became evident why Diti had cherished this piece of childhood memorabilia. Allan would sing, then forget the words, and have to start all over again; time after time, to the obvious delight of his mother and the tutor. It was a priceless moment of intimacy between mother and child in which they laughed and giggled together as if they hadn't a care in the world. Diti had probably played this part of the DVD a hundred times, just to hear the happiness in her son's voice. It was a sound that had been sorely lacking for many, many years. In fact, Allan himself barely recognized it.

Allan let the DVD play on as he turned his attention to the dresser drawers. He sifted through a collection of his own audio-taped letters; the older communications recorded on micro-cassettes and the newer ones on the little plastic memory cards that his and Diti's matching micro-recorders used. Allan gathered all of the audio correspondence and placed them into a fancy silk drawstring bag that looked like something intended to hold jewelry. Next, Allan began to pack his mother's photo albums into cardboard boxes. Allan transferred the last of the stack from drawer to box, and several photos and a scrap of paper fell to the floor. Allan stooped to retrieve it.

On the scrap of paper was a child's drawing depicting Allan and his mother in front of their old house upstate. Argus waved from a black airplane above. There were no flowers and there was no sun. Allan stood on a stack of books, waving to his father. Allan put the drawing aside and picked up the old black and white photos. The first was the one of his great-grandfather that he had seen at the professor's house.

His destiny.

The other photos were of Diti and the royal family. One was a formal portrait of Diti in which she was neither blind nor wheelchair bound. She was perfect. The last picture in the stack was a portrait of Argus in his Army dress uniform, young and handsome, with a spark of mischief in his eyes. Allan flipped through the photos once, then sat and turned back to the front of the album.

17

Argus paced the floor of the cheap hotel room like a caged animal, replaying the conversation with Allan in his mind. He caught a glimpse of himself in the dresser mirror: his hair was still wet and he had a towel wrapped around his waist. Argus tore the towel away to get a better look at his body; lean and hard. He turned to get a rear view, tensed his muscles, and was pleased with the fact that he was in great physical condition—not only for a man of his age, but for a man of *any* age.

Shauna, a voluptuous olive-skinned southern girl, wiped her hand across the steamy bathroom mirror and blotted the blood from the corner of her mouth. She asked, "What's the matter with you today, Sugar?" There was no answer from Argus. Shauna tried to sound casual as she covered the swelling around her eye with make up. "You have a bad day or somethin'?"

Still no answer, apart from the creaking floorboards. Shauna stepped into the bedroom and reached for her clothes, keeping an eye on Argus. He moved to the window to dress and she saw the vicious scratches up and down his back; one of his many odd requests. Finally, Argus spoke to no one in particular in a tone of quiet frustration: "It's not enough." He took a long drag from his cigarette. "It's never enough."

"Damned right it ain't enough." Shauna was annoyed, but tried to keep it light. "A girl's gotta work you know. I got rules about bruises." She grimaced and reached down into her panties to scratch herself. "Besides, I'm all itchy now. How am I supposed to explain this to the next guy?"

Argus said, "Tell them you're a princess," and moved to the night stand to collect the small mound of pubic hair he had shaved from Shauna with a straight razor. He went to the jacket, draped over a vinyl chair, and carefully tucked the hair into the inside pocket. Argus pulled out a handful of cash and tossed it onto the bed. He said, "I'm sorry—for everything," and avoided Shauna's eyes as he stepped into his pants. "Can you forgive me?"

The money was more than the prostitute had expected. Just looking at it made her wetter than any man ever had. She said, "Only God and Oral Roberts can forgive you baby, but we can sure try to put the whole thing behind us. And you know how much I like *that.*"

Argus' expression turned cold. This wasn't the response he had been looking for. He said, "Don't come again."

His tone made Shauna nervous. She said, "Look Sugar, the rough stuff—that's just not my thing, but I got a whole bag of tricks ain't even been opened yet." She pressed her body against his. "Just tell momma what turns you on." Argus finished dressing and moved to the door. Shauna tried again: "All you gotta do is tell me, Sugar."

He took a step closer—too close—and looked deep into her eyes before whispering, "Do you really want to know?"

Shauna took an involuntary step backward, wondering how she could have missed it. It was as if she was seeing him for the first time: raw and dangerous, with only a paper-thin veneer of civility to mask the darkness in his soul. She had always taken pride in being a good judge of people—especially johns. So how could she have missed it? After what seemed a very long time, Argus turned and walked out the door without another word.

Shauna would never know just how close she came to death that afternoon. But she did know that this had been her last trick. Beauty school, the spare bedroom in her sister's shabby apartment, and a life of honest struggle all seemed infinitely bearable in the shadow of those cold, dead eyes.

18

Allan leaned against the balcony's railing, watching the sunrise. He didn't see the creeping shadow move up from behind, until it had already consumed him. Without warning the railing gave way and Allan toppled over the side. His screams were muted by the traffic sounds as he plummeted toward the dirty pavement below. At the moment of impact—

Allan woke with a start. He had a painful crick in his neck after falling asleep in his seat. Professor Sumner looked up from his paperwork. "Bad dream?"

"Always." Allan tried to shake the cobwebs from his head and work the kink from his neck. "How much longer?"

The professor checked his watch. "Three and a half hours—and two more plane changes." The airliner hit some turbulence and Allan's nausea returned with a vengeance. When the plane lurched a second time, he bolted from his seat.

———

Allan flushed the 727's toilet, splashed cold water on his face, then turned on the air vent and leaned against the sink. The plane began to bounce again and he returned to his knees. There was a knock at the door. Allan responded between heaves: "Go—away."

"It's me."

Allan groaned and unlocked the door. The professor squeezed into the tiny room while Allan reclaimed his position at the stainless steel commode. The professor dampened a paper towel and handed it to his young friend. "I'll see if they have something to settle your stomach."

"No, I'll be okay. I just need a minute." Allan tried to pull himself together, but his problem wasn't purely physical. He said, "It's my mother—and him. I can't shake the feeling that he–" Another round of turbulence silenced Allan's accusation.

The professor dug an amber vial from his pocket and popped the top. He shook out two Tylenol with codeine and swallowed them, along with a handful of water from the tap. "My boy, he loved her. I *know* that." More turbulence. Allan covered his mouth and groaned in misery. The professor tried to get Allan's mind off his stomach. "I first met your mother at an alumni party, just a few months after she and your father returned to the states. Anyone could see that they were crazy about each other." The professor dampened another paper towel. "Did you know he saved her life?"

Allan wiped his mouth. "That was her favorite story. It was after Vietnam. He was sent by the Army to help grandfather negotiate with the rebels. Bengal was about to get into a civil war." Allan leaned his forehead against the stainless steel and closed his eyes as he continued. "My great-grandfather was away on a crusade when an assassin got into the palace and gutted grandfather's wife and all of mother's step-brothers. But they took grandfather alive, so they could execute him publicly. Argus got her out of the palace alive, brought her back and married her." Allan wanted to laugh, but couldn't. "And they lived happily ever after." Allan stood and splashed cold water on his face. "It always sounded like a fairy tale. I asked her once how things could've changed so much between them."

"And what did she tell you?"

"Nothing really." Allan smiled, remembering his mother. "You know her—she always talked in riddles and proverbs, like a walking fortune cookie. I used to tease her about it."

"She never gave you an answer?"

"All she'd say was that she and Argus were caught by destiny."

"Your mother was a very loyal woman." The professor smiled sadly, opened the lavatory door and reentered the main cabin.

Allan followed, his curiosity piqued. "What? There's more?" He returned to his seat and buckled up. The professor pretended to be engrossed in a book on tribal religions. Allan said, "Are you gonna tell me or not?"

The professor turned a page and avoided Allan's eyes. "I shouldn't have brought it up. I'm sorry, my boy. It really isn't my place."

"Then whose place is it?"

The professor considered the question for a moment before setting aside his book. "Did your mother ever tell you about her pregnancy?"

"Just that I was a miracle. Whatever *that* meant."

"About three years after your mother and father married, she became very ill. We thought she was going to die. She'd been sick for almost a year, but had never told anyone. Not even your father."

"Why?"

The Professor lied, "I don't know." He stopped a passing stewardess. "Vodka tonic, please." He turned back o Allan, looking miserable. "Because the illness had gone untreated for so long, she lapsed into a coma. I remember thinking that if she died Argus would undoubtedly kill himself. He was *that* guilt ridden. Well, she didn't die. But she came out of the whole ordeal blind, paralyzed and sterile—"

"Sterile?"

"That was what the doctors said. I don't think Argus ever forgave himself, though she did. In fact, afterwards, she seemed more loving and devoted to him than ever. Diti wanted a child desperately. It was all she talked about. Your father knew it was hopeless, but couldn't stand to take away her last dream. So they tried. It was a purely a symbolic gesture—once or twice a year."

"Jesus." Allan was stunned. "It sounds like a fucking soap opera." The professor finished his drink and flagged the stewardess down for a refill. Allan said, "So, I really *was* a miracle."

"Ah, but a dyslexic miracle, thanks to the neurological damage passed on to you from your mother. I'm surprised your father's fared as well as he has. The guilt would've driven me mad."

Allan tried to process the information, but a piece of the puzzle was still missing. He asked, "Why would he feel so guilty. It wasn't his fault that she got sick."

The professor averted his eyes, already feeling the guilt of deception. "I suppose because he didn't pay enough attention to her. If he had, maybe they could have caught the illness sooner. I don't know, my boy, he just felt responsible. Let's just leave it at that, shall we?"

"Why did she stay with him?"

"Once upon a time, he truly *was* her knight in shining armor." The professor placed his withered hand on Allan's knee and added, "And, I believe she thought that she could save him."

At a loss for words, Allan directed his attention out the window and considered the past as the professor gratefully accepted a fresh drink from the stewardess.

19

Washington, D.C., December 1972.
Argus paced the honeymoon suite in silk pajamas, awaiting his young bride's emergence from the dressing room. His thoughts were all of love and the new life he would share with Diti. Argus hadn't sought the company of a prostitute since his return to the states and, although the war still visited his dreams, he had every reason to believe that Diti would be the only woman to share his bed from this day forward.

"My love?"

Argus turned to find Diti standing in the balcony's breezy doorway. She wore the flowing white negligee that her American girlfriends had given her. Diti's smile was nervous, yet she radiated a magnetic inner peace. Diti somehow managed to simultaneously embody the sexuality of a goddess—and the innocence of a schoolgirl. Argus was speechless.

She hugged her arms across her breasts. "Aren't you cold?"

"Yes." Argus couldn't stop staring. "Freezing." He moved toward her.

Diti opened her arms to embrace him and whispered, "Then let me warm you."

————————

Argus moved slowly, touching his bride's inexperienced body with deliberate tenderness. She was tense at first, but eager to please. When he asked her to remove the nightgown, she stood from the bed without hesitation and let it fall to the floor, revealing her hairless body. She stood before him, eyes lowered, hoping that he would like what he saw. "I have removed the hair from my body, as is the custom of my family. I wish to hide nothing from you, my husband, as I hope you will hide nothing from me. For truth is the foundation of all great love." Argus was struck silent by Diti's beauty and vulnerability. After what seemed like forever, Diti looked up to find his face in the moonlight. He had tears in his eyes. Diti's voice was soft and low. "Do I not please you, my love?"

Argus sat on the side of the bed and rested his cheek against her golden skin. He wrapped his arms around her waist and spoke into her soft, warm flesh: "More than you know."

They stayed like that for a long time—Diti stroking his hair as he clung to her in the dark and wept. When they finally returned to the bed, Argus and Diti cuddled, kissed and laughed for hours before he positioned himself between her legs. He hesitated, knowing this would be her first time and that it held a place of spiritual significance, as well as emotional, in eastern culture. He whispered, "Are you ready?"

Diti was suddenly frightened. She answered, "Yes, my love."

They shared one last gentle kiss before Argus pushed slowly forward. Then, without warning, his erection failed. He tried to recover, but his frustration quickly turned to anger. Argus said, "Shit!"

Diti was confused. She asked, "Is something wrong, my love?" Argus remained silent as he tried to manually stimulate himself, but it was no good. He closed his eyes, trying to conjure an arousing fantasy. Still no good. Diti whispered, on the verge of tears, "Did I do something wrong?"

Argus snapped, "NO," then whispered apologetically, "No ..."
His mind was searching for something—*anything*—that that might
avert the disaster at hand. Finally, an image popped into his mind
that hardened him instantly. Argus closed his eyes again, allowing
himself to remember the dying boy in the cave, and then entered
Diti in one hard thrust.

Diti cried out and tried to pull Argus closer, but he was lost
in his violent fantasy; able to make love to her only by entertain-
ing images of death in his head. Argus clenched his teeth and
drove into Diti as the Vietnamese boy bucked with the impact of
his bullets.

Diti pleaded with Argus to open his eyes, but every time he
tried—he began to soften. So Argus kept his eyes closed as he took
his new bride's virginity with the same fierce passion which with
he had taken the young soldier's life. Near the end, Diti begged
for Argus to look at her, and when he opened his eyes and saw the
spots of blood that stained the bed sheets—Argus climaxed.

———————

After Diti had drifted off into a troubled sleep, Argus returned
to the balcony and stood naked in the freezing wind. But he didn't
feel the cold. He was numb.

Did you actually think that she could purify you, just by loving you?
What gives you the right to dirty her? A piece of paper? A few vows? You're
nothing! You don't deserve her, or her love. You don't deserve anything but
the pain you'll feel every time you look at her and know that you can't make
love to her. Did you really think she'd play the game—like the little whores
in-country? Or did you think you wouldn't need the game with her?

Argus looked down to find Diti's blood caking on his withered
flesh.

You made her bleed, that's how you got through it. This time. But what
about next time?

Argus' expression hardened and he confided to the wind: "I'll
find the blood somewhere else."

Part II

ಐ ◈ ಚ

The House of Drums

20

The battered Cessna bounced to a graceless stop on the rocky patch of dirt local pilots affectionately referred to as the Mbandaka International Airport. A group of villagers on the ground had watched the approach with great interest. From the Cessna's port window, and from the depths of his own gastrointestinal misery, Allan had assumed that they were the welcoming committee. But as he gingerly departed the plane Allan noticed that the bystanders had already started to disperse and that they seemed disappointed.

Allan helped the professor down from the plane and then sat in the dirt with an unexpected thud, suddenly too weak to stand. Allan cradled his head in his hands and groaned, "Why did they leave? I'm gonna need someone to carry me out of here."

François Tubere, a shaggy, sunburned behemoth in his mid-forties, loped across the makeshift runway with his arms extended. He and the professor embraced while Allan watched from the ground. François raised his voice to be heard over the little plane's ill-tuned engines. "Good to see you, John! Welcome to the Republic of Zaire!"

The professor shouted, "Allan, this is François—an old friend."

François reached down to grab Allan's trembling hand with the strength of a bear. "Call me Frank. Good to meet you, Allan."

"Hello." Allan winced, as Frank continued to squeeze his hand, wondering if this friendly giant might be willing to carry him the rest of the way.

"My Jeep's over here. We'd better get a move on. It gets dark early these days and you've got a long road ahead." Frank helped Allan to his feet, and the group headed for the Jeep. Allan still looked as if he might launch his lunch at any moment. As Frank squeezed behind the wheel, he said, "Looks like you did pretty well, Allan. Jokko had to hose out the inside of the plane after my first trip in." Frank waved to Jokko and the Cessna coasted down the makeshift runway, leaving the trio in the middle of nowhere.

Frank started the Jeep's engine and Professor Sumner said, "We had an audience when we arrived, but they left as soon as the plane landed."

"This is their Monte Carlo. They come to wager on the planes." Frank pulled the Jeep off the runway and started down a narrow back road. "Some wager that the pilot will overshoot the runway and end up in that ditch at the end. Others bet on the pilot. And if the plane does end up in the ditch—the pilots pay the men to help drag it out." He swerved to avoid a coconut vendor on his way to market. "But you landed safely, so it was a total loss. No one ever bets on Jokko."

The professor said, "Beautiful place, this. Don't you think, Allan?"

Allan lowered his head between his knees and moaned, "Oh yeah—it's great."

The older men shared a smile, and then Frank dug a grimy bottle of the jungle equivalent of Pepto Bismal out of the glove compartment. He tossed it back to Allan. "Go on, son—drink up. It'll help."

Allan unscrewed the crusted, rusty cap and was immediately hit by the smell. He held his breath, raised the bottle to his lips and gagged on the chunky green sludge, but somehow managed to keep it down. He asked, "How do we get back? When we're done."

"You can talk. That's a good sign." Frank shot the professor a good-natured wink. "I helped Jokko out of a messy case of the clap. As long as his number one wife's alive and well we've got unlimited passage. John knows how to reach me." Frank called out, "Hold on!" and veered off of the narrow road—and onto an even narrower footpath.

Allan yelped as low-hanging branches slapped him in the face. "Are all of the roads like this?"

"This is a shortcut. If we don't make up some time, I'm afraid you'll miss your ride." Frank controlled the Jeep much like a rodeo cowboy rides an unbroken colt. "John—reach into the glove box and grab the masks.

Professor Sumner did as instructed, retrieving three bacterial filtration masks—the type that surgeon's wear. He asked, "Has there been another outbreak?" and grabbed the roll-bar just in time to avoid ejection from the vehicle by a nasty set of ruts.

"Unfortunately. Hollywood and the Red Cross have come and gone, but Ebola and company appear to be in no rush to leave. The masks won't offer much protection, but if we keep moving— we'll probably be okay."

Allan put on his mask and whined, "Probably?"

Frank laughed, "What—are they offering *guarantees* back in the city these days?"

———

Frank downshifted as they approached the village proper. He said, "This is Mbandaka," and waved to a barefooted man pushing a cart piled high with sugarcane and tea leaves.

Although the town itself was only four square miles, the bustling trade activity and crowded streets made Mbandaka seem enormous. The ramshackle storefronts were little more than clapboard shacks held together with baling wire and good intentions. The rest of the town's edifices took the form of traditional tulkas: small dwellings made of mud and rubble, topped with thatched straw or sheet-metal roofs.

Allan spotted a group of somber youngsters watching the Jeep and waving slowly with both hands. He asked, "Why do they look so serious?"

Frank answered, "It's the masks. They think we've come to quarantine another house." He directed Allan's attention to a passing shack that had been boarded up. A huge red "X" had been painted across the doorway. "That one's new—since the last time I was here."

The professor said, "There are a lot of children."

"Almost half of the population of Zaire is under fifteen." There was a traffic jam ahead—of goats. Frank slowed to a stop.

Allan felt something touch his hand and turned to find an emaciated young woman stroking him. She had run out into the street and was talking so fast that Allan wouldn't have been able to understand her; even if he had spoken the language. He recoiled, instinctively, but she continued to walk alongside the Jeep as it began to move, pleading with Allan and occasionally pulling aside her pagne to reveal a flash of thigh. Allan said, "Frank?"

Frank looked back and said something in Bantu that made the woman stop and return to her doorway. "That's the worst of it, really. Housewives forced to sell themselves to put bread on the table. And forty percent of them are already infected with the AIDS virus. Their husbands have all gone off to Kinshasa to try and find work. I'm afraid it won't be a very pleasant homecoming. Poor devils."

As the Jeep cleared the goats and sped away, Allan couldn't help looking back at the desperate woman in the doorway. Her eyes had been so weary—and so incredibly sad. Allan hoped that her husband would return home soon.

———————

Ten miles later Allan wished he was dead. He whimpered and moaned in the bucking back seat like a colicky child: "Please tell me we're almost there." The Jeep burst through a wall of brush, accelerated up an embankment and then slid to a stop. In the sudden calm, Allan heard a cheetah calling to its mate. He whispered, "Oh shit—what was that?"

Frank set the parking brake and climbed out. He was in a hurry. "Okay—gather your things. You'll be set to go in just a few minutes." Frank hurried away.

"Go? I thought we were *here*." Allan turned to his friend. "Professor?"

Even Professor Sumner had been shaken by the roller coaster ride through the untamed jungle. He took his time getting out of the Jeep. "Sorry, my boy—I'm just along for the ride, just like you." The professor reached into his pocket to retrieve a few more codeine-laced Tylenol.

Allan relinquished his vice-like grip on the Jeep's roll bar, but left imprints of his fingers in the weathered foam padding. He climbed out of the vehicle and wrestled the oversized backpacks out of the Jeep. "Allan?" The professor cocked his head. "Do you hear them?"

Allan stopped and listened. He said, nervously, "Drums." He followed the professor up the embankment and found himself at the edge of the Ubangi river: a narrow waterway less than two hundred feet across.

"Allan, John–" Frank was beckoning them from down-river. He was standing among a group of Mbinga men, bickering over the price of passage. Frank called out, "Bring your gear. I think we've struck a bargain."

Allan and the professor grabbed their packs and started down the shoreline toward Frank. The Mbinga, small men under five feet tall, studied the two oversized tourists and their oversized bags with open curiosity. The leader of the nomadic tribe wore an animal skin loincloth and a tattered K.C. and the Sunshine Band concert t-shirt. He accepted some money from Frank and shook his hand. The leader called to another Mbinga and the second man pushed his canoe into the shallow water. To Allan, it looked like a homemade version of the sculling boats he had seen in Ivy League college competitions on ESPN.

Frank clapped the other tribesmen on the back and hurried over to Professor Sumner. "Okay. You're all set. He's not thrilled about heading into Shantu territory. But the hunting's been bad, so they can use the cash."

The professor handed his pack over to the boatman, who positioned it onto the long, narrow craft in a way that would best counterbalance his passengers' weight. Professor Sumner shook Frank's hand and said, "My friend, how can I thank you?"

"Just come back safely." Frank helped the professor into the boat and then turned to Allan, who was staring at the water with a look of terror. Frank handed Allan's pack into the skiff and then reached out to steady it. "Okay, Allan."

"I ... uh ... I can't."

Frank suppressed a smile and said, "Don't tell me you can't swim?"

"Okay." Allan swallowed hard. "I won't tell you."

Frank laughed loud and hard, then the professor and the boatman joined in, and finally Allan began to laugh. Then, without warning, Frank picked Allan up and plunked him down into the canoe before he had a chance to protest.

Allan closed his eyes tightly, grabbed the sides of the rocking skiff and cried, "Ahh!"

Still laughing, Frank waded into the cool water and launched the boat onto the Ubangi. He called out after the skiff as it drifted away: "If they decide to have you for dinner—just make a run for the river. Someone's bound to pick you up."

Allan's hands were already cramping from their death grip on the sides of the boat, and he was tired of being afraid. So Allan finally let go, and he opened his eyes. Frank had disappeared from view, as had the other Mbingas. The man at the oars was watching Allan as he rowed, wondering what the cowardly tourist would do next. Allan forced a smile, hoping to convey a sense of confidence that he did not possess. The oarsman wasn't fooled.

"Admit it my boy, *this* is truly spectacular."

Allan looked into his friend's face and couldn't help but be calmed by his euphoria. The oars broke the surface of the water with a soothing, rhythmic regularity and the sounds of the jungle, which Allan had perceived as random and threatening before, now seemed orchestrated. The wind through the trees created the melody, while the birds formed choruses, the larger animals supplied soloists—and through it all the steady oars kept the beat. It was as if everything was in perfect harmony.

Allan and the professor lost track of time, immersing themselves in Zaire's music, until the Mbinga clucked his tongue and directed their attention to the shore. A group of okapi, dwarfed relatives of the giraffe with striped zebra legs and auburn-colored upper bodies like a horse, were grazing on the grassy banks of the river. The oarsman said, "Bwa bwa," and pointed to the okapi as if he was imparting a crucial piece of information. "Bwa bwa."

The professor repeated, "Bwa bwa."

The Mbinga smiled and nodded "yes," then looked at Allan.

Allan repeated, "Bwa bwa," proudly and noticed for the first time that their guide wore a necklace adorned with a variety of animal teeth and a small wooden cross. The boatman smiled again and nodded sharply in the affirmative, pleased with his students. Allan whispered, "Professor, he's wearing a cross."

"Don't tell me that you assumed they all practiced voodoo." Professor Sumner laughed. "That's Haiti dear boy, and the numbers are vastly overstated. Most Zaireans are Roman Catholic. Now, the Shantu–" The professor stopped and turned. The Mbinga had muttered something in Bantu and was now rowing faster.

Allan looked around and spotted a giant hippo that had left his place in the sun to pursue the skiff. Now only his eyes, ears and nostrils were visible above the surface of the water as he approached. Allan tried to suppress his fear. He said, "Professor? Should we be worried?"

The Mbinga began to grunt as he labored at the oars.

"That depends on whether or not he catches us." There was no humor in the professor's voice. "Hippopotami are responsible for more deaths than crocodiles."

"Crocodiles?" Allan had forgotten all about crocodiles. In fact, he had been so terrified by the water itself that he had never even considered the hungry creatures that made their homes there. "He looks pretty fat. Maybe he isn't hungry."

The hippo was gaining on them slowly, but surely.

"Hippos don't eat people. They're vegetarians. We must have breached his territory."

The hippo opened its mouth wide, displaying an impressive set of incisors.

Allan stammered, "Look ... He's getting tired."

"I'm afraid that's not a yawn. It's a show of aggression."

But then the hippo, as if picking up on Allan's suggestion, suddenly abandoned its pursuit. The little boat began to pull away and the animal bared its teeth one more time, just for show, and then turned to rejoin his pack on the riverbank.

Allan scanned the water for other threatening creatures and found none. He asked, "Are we okay?"

"I think so." The professor was relieved. "You see—I've always said that vegetarians' barks were worse than their bite."

After a moment, the oarsman slowed to a normal pace as he caught his breath. He gave his passengers a look of relief and said something in Bantu that could have meant, "That was a close one."

The Mbinga took a moment to survey the area. He appeared concerned again, even though there was no apparent danger. Caught up in eluding the angry hippo, he hadn't realized that they had already entered Shantu territory. He rowed much slower now, as if fearful that the sounds of the oars in the water might awaken an evil spirit. And then the boatman began to repeat something, very quietly, that Allan guessed might be the rosary.

A half mile farther, a rock the size of a baseball plunked into the water about twenty feet from the boat. The native skipper immediately back-paddled to a stop, and crossed himself. Allan watched as the Mbinga searched the shore for the pitcher. Finally, he raised his arm and pointed to a cluster of wild banana trees. He looked as though he had seen a ghost.

Allan spotted the Shantu escort, barely visible among the foliage, and pointed him out to the professor. "Do you see him? There—about thirty feet up the mountain."

"He doesn't look especially friendly, does he?"

Allan said, "Oh thanks—thanks a lot. That was just what I needed to hear."

The professor was excited now. He gestured toward the shore and addressed their guide impatiently: "Well, get us over there, man! Please—before he gives up on us." The Mbinga shook his head "no" and pointed to the water. Professor Sumner answered, "What? You'd like us to swim?" He gestured to the backpacks. "With *these*? No. NO! You take us there. *Now.*" The boatman considered the request for a moment and then, reluctantly, paddled toward the shore, but stopped ten feet short. Professor Sumner said, "No, no—*all the way*. Now really, I must *insist*." The Mbinga's response was to shove the professor's backpack overboard—followed by Allan's.

Allan yelled, "Hey, what the hell–" but the boat's equilibrium was so unstable from the shift in weight that he found himself in the water, along with the professor, before he had a chance to finish his thought. Allan thrashed in the river like a drowning man, until the professor said:

"Allan! ALLAN! We're in *shallow* water."

"What?" Allan stopped flailing and stood up. The water was only chest-high.

"Go on. Get the other one before we lose it." Professor Sumner grabbed one of the sinking backpacks and started for the shore.

Allan cursed the Mbinga, who was already paddling fast in the opposite direction, as he retrieved the second pack and waded to shore.

"I guess that will teach me to be insistent, eh?" The professor looked like an overgrown terrier that had been caught in the rain. "You all right?"

Allan spat a bit of algae back into the water. "You can catch malaria from the water, can't you?"

"No, you catch it from mosquitoes." Professor Sumner tried to don his backpack, but the weight of the water had doubled the load. "Give me a hand up with this, would you?"

Allan helped his friend with his pack and then mounted his own. He moaned, "Jesus Christ! This thing weighs a ton now." The Shantu escort clapped his hands twice to get their attention, and then started up the mountain. Allan whined, "I can't believe I let you talk me into this."

————

It was a few hours before sunset and both Allan and the professor were having a hard time keeping up with their guide. The swift-footed Shantu scurried up the densely-wooded mountainside with maddening ease, keeping fifty yards ahead at all times. When the professor and Allan stopped—so did the guide, but only for a moment. Then he was off again, and the exhausted foreigners were forced to continue on or risk being left behind.

The professor stopped and tried to catch his breath. "The mountain ... didn't look nearly this steep ... from the bottom." He wiped the perspiration from his brow with the sweat-stained sleeve of his shirt. "It can't be much farther now."

Allan dumped his pack and slumped against a tree. "Why not?"

The professor thought about it for a moment and answered, "I don't know. It just ... seemed like the thing to say. I suppose it could be a great deal farther." He began to laugh, exhausted. "I suppose it could take days to get there. I certainly hope not."

Allan gave the professor a look and re-shouldered his load. "Now I know why I've always lived in the city. I hate trees."

"At least the weather looks good."

The guide signaled with a high-pitched click/whistle and took off again, gazelle like, through the trees. Allan whined, "There he goes again."

"C'mon my boy—keep your pecker up." The professor started off after the guide.

"Excuse me?"

"Keep your pecker up. You know—'hang in there,' as the kids say." The professor picked up the pace. "We'd better hurry. The little bastard's getting away from us." Allan and the professor hacked their way through the jungle, punctuating their conversation with machete cuts. "How is it that he skips through the blasted jungle without a trace, yet we have to chop our way through as if we were in some damned safari film?"

Allan didn't answer. He seemed to be venting some unspoken anger on the greenery.

The professor used a tree root as a handhold, inching his way up the steep incline. "The little bugger's probably watching us from a tree, laughing."

Allan still didn't answer. He just continued to chop, his scowl apparently permanent.

"Is it something I said?"

Allan executed a young banana tree that blocked his passage. *Swak.*

"Just thinking about my father."

Swak. Swak.

"Guess it's time to grow up and face facts. He hates me, and I hate him."

Swak.

The professor stopped to drink. "He doesn't hate you, Allan. He's afraid of you." Professor Sumner offered the canteen.

Allan took a swig and choked on the water. "Yeah, right. I'm pretty scary."

"You're like a mirror to him. In you he sees both the greatest good and the most unforgivable sins of his life. Every day your struggle must remind him of the irreparable harm he's done your mother—and you."

Allan got back to work.

Swak.

"Yeah, well ..."

Swak.

"My heart bleeds for him." Allan struck a tree trunk with his blade, making it stick. Milky sap bled down the edge of the machete's rusted blade.

"Don't hate him, my boy. Pity him. Your mother was probably the only person who ever truly loved him." The professor capped the canteen and continued on. "And now there's no one left to save him from himself."

After a moment's thought Allan sighed, retrieved his machete, and continued to cut a path—with a little less venom than before.

21

The rain blanketed the jungle in liquid crystal, refracting the golden light of sunset through a billion tiny prisms. The terrifying face, carved from wood, was the first thing Allan saw as he entered the clearing near the top of the mountain. Professor Sumner followed, stunned by the intricacy of the totem that stood twenty feet high and ten feet wide.

"Oh my God," whispered Allan, "It's Kali."

The wooden idol was an amazingly intricate piece of work. A wild eyed goddess wielded a large knife and wore a necklace of human skulls. Her expression was fierce, her hair matted and disheveled. Kali's tongue hung from her mouth, as if to lick, and she had one foot resting triumphantly on a corpse.

"She's amazing." The professor was elated. "Quite beautiful—in a morbid sort of way. Not exactly the type you'd bring home to mother, though."

Allan asked, "How could they know about Kali?"

"I suppose your great-grandfather must have taught them. He must have really hit it off with the tribe. They say he never left."

"But why Kali?" Allan seemed disturbed. "She's the most blood-thirsty goddess in Hindu mythology. I mean, really ruthless."

The professor gave Allan an affectionate pat on the back, shucked off his pack and circled the massive carving. "I knew there was a reason I brought you along."

Allan couldn't take his eyes off of the angry goddess. "This place must have been where he met his destiny." Allan's mind reeled as his mother's words came rushing back.

Your great-grandfather had the soul of a missionary. He was a great man who accomplished great things, traveling the world to relieve the pain of ignorance in others. This was his destiny and he sacrificed his life to it willingly.

The professor was speaking, but Allan heard only his mother's voice.

Spokes of a wheel ...
Your destiny ...
All roads lead to the center ...
Your destiny ...
If you do not find it, it will find you ...

"Allan?"

Allan's legs were suddenly very weak. He said, "Huh? What did you say?"

"I said—can you imagine a trip like this at his age?"

Allan moved to the foot of the totem, transfixed by the hideous beauty of the goddess and, with trembling hands, reached out to touch his destiny.

22

It was dusk and the rain had slowed to a drizzle by the time the guide led Allan and the professor into the Shantu colony. The travelers were soiled and stained beyond recognition. In fact, to the villagers who watched them pass, *Allan and the professor* appeared to be the primitives.

The professor was fascinated by the Shantu dwellings. He said, "Very unusual."

"What?"

"The huts. They're round."

"Looks like they'd be hard to build."

"Exactly my point. Quite advanced. They've even topped them with teardrop-shaped roofs, reminiscent of the Taj Mahal. I haven't a clue how they managed that. And the women—do their robes look familiar to you?"

"They look like the saris my mother wore, but these are made of animal skins."

"Indeed. A truly amazing fusion of Indian and African traditions." The professor put his hand on Allan's shoulder. "I'd say your great-grandfather made quite an impression."

Allan noticed warriors guarding each entrance to the camp, while children played by the fire and adults conducted their lives—relatively unmoved by the gawking visitors. Allan noted that many of the Shantu showed some form of physical deformity. He nudged the professor and whispered, "I don't see any old people."

"That's odd. Normally, they would head the welcoming committee."

The guide motioned for the professor and Allan to follow, and then led them to a hut where they were greeted by two young girls. The prettier of the two girls had been born with only one ear. Allan looked to the guide for some indication of what was to come, but he just gestured for Allan to follow the girls.

Once inside the hut, Allan and the professor were taken to opposite sides of a wooden partition, where a tub of water awaited each man. Allan said, "Professor ... I don't know about this."

Professor Sumner called across the divider, "Just relax and enjoy it, my boy. And make sure to smile a lot. We wouldn't want to start our visit by insulting our hosts."

So Allan plastered a smile onto his face and kept it there, which proved challenging when one of the girls insisted upon undressing him. The timid young man tried to convey, through a desperate grin, that he preferred to do it himself—but the pretty Shantu kept tugging at Allan's clothes as if removing them was her sworn duty. At one point they got into a tug-of-war over Allan's jockey shorts; the girl kept trying to slide them down—while Allan fought to hold them up. And even after Allan conceded the shorts, to his great embarrassment, the girl became fascinated with the elastic waistband of his underwear while he stood before her, buck-naked, hands positioned awkwardly over his genitals. But Allan managed to maintain his smile throughout, even when the girl stared openly at his body while he stepped into the tub. And she smiled back, seemingly amused by Allan's modesty, as her hands disappeared beneath the soapy water.

———————

An hour later the visitors were cleaned and dressed in hand-woven corn silk tunics which had been adorned with wooden beads and fringed with fur. Allan felt like a virgin being prepared for sacrifice. All he needed now was an active volcano and a little push. They were left waiting outside the chief's hut, so Professor Sumner dug into his backpack, unsealing the various plastic bags that had protected his belongings from the river. After some poking around, he extracted a battery-operated camcorder and a small tripod.

A group of young boys were playing a soccer-like game near the fire. The ball was kicked out of bounds and it came bouncing over to Allan. A clubfooted twelve-year-old, wearing an ornate golden necklace unlike any of the other boys, hobbled over to retrieve the ball. Allan picked it up, made eye contact with the boy, and smiled as he extended the ball. The boy smiled back and nodded his thanks, then returned to his watchful friends.

The professor said, "They're curious, but not afraid."

"Is that unusual?"

"Tribal cultures are notoriously suspicious of strangers. But then again, this tribe has never met a white man, so–"

"They don't know what assholes we can be?"

The professor smiled. "Precisely. And I hope to keep it that way."

Allan saw a little girl watching him from the porch of her hut. Her eyes were filled with questions. Allan asked the professor, "How are we supposed to communicate?"

"The chief speaks English." The professor dry-swallowed another pair of pills to fight his perpetual headache.

Allan asked, "How?"

"I would assume that he learned that from your great-grandfather, as well. He spoke English, didn't he?"

"And French, and Spanish. I think mother said he studied at Oxford. How old is the chief?"

"I'm not sure. But this tribe, with its current belief systems—its entire culture really—is in its infancy. They began incorporating the Hindu's teachings less than a hundred years ago." One of the chief's attendants motioned for them to enter. Professor Sumner took a deep breath and said, "Here we go."

Allan and the professor entered the chief's quarters and the door was immediately closed behind them, leaving them in total darkness. Allan could hear the breathing of others in the room, but he couldn't see them. He whispered, "Professor?"

"I'm right here." He spoke quietly. "Let's just give our eyes a moment to adjust before we assume the worst."

Allan smelled food, sweat—and something else. Incense? He spoke quickly: "But what if it's a trap. What if–"

The sharp sound of stone striking stone stopped Allan cold. A second later the sound came again, and this time Allan thought he saw a spark a few feet away. The sound repeated in regular intervals, as did the spark, and in the brief bursts of light—Allan thought he saw faces.

The woman trying to start the fire–

Two odd-looking children seated together in the corner–

A warrior with his spear trained on the professor–

And then a spark caught, and the small mound of twigs and leaves for which it was intended began to burn. The woman at the center of the room cupped her hands around the tentative flame. Her slender fingers appeared to glow in the dark as she leaned close to coax the fire with her breath. Allan was captivated by this primitive ritual, despite his fear. It felt as if they were witnessing the birth of man's first flame in this tiny hut, half a world away from home.

Once the flame had stabilized, the woman used it to ignite a long reed, which was in turn used to light an oil lamp. The smell that Allan had been unable to place earlier was the animal fat that fueled the lamp. The other fires were extinguished and the oil lamp was then dimmed until the single flame was barely a flicker.

An open-ended box, made of a simple wooden frame with tightly-stretched leather panels, was then placed around the lamp to subdue the feeble light even further.

As the tiny, muted flame danced behind its screen, Allan thought of a single firefly—captured in a paper bag. And it was in this flickering glow that Allan saw the room and its occupants. The flame-tender and the guard with the spear were much as he has guessed, though he hadn't noticed the large, raised scar that spread across the light-skinned African's chest. It was in the shape of a human eye.

Allan whispered to the professor, "Did you see his scar?"

"Probably had the design carved into the flesh. Possibly to assign social status—like the Eastern caste system. Or maybe as a symbol of protection."

"But why an eye?"

The children in the corner made a sound—as if to silence the strangers. In the momentary flashes of light, Allan hadn't been able to place what was so odd about them. But now he realized that they were not two young boys seated back-to-back, they were in fact Siamese twins joined at the spine. They were watching Allan closely now. With strange eyes. Old eyes.

From what Allan could discern, the room itself was perfectly ordinary, except for the fact that the window openings had been boarded up from the inside. Large pillows had been placed on the floor around the cloistered flame. They reminded Allan of the cushions that he used for meditation. The only difference was that these were covered in the skins of leopards and zebras.

In addition to the pillows on the floor there was a throne of sorts: a massive, carved monstrosity, positioned several feet from the lamp. A huge platter of fruit and meats waited beside the throne, reminding Allan that he hadn't eaten since his vegetarian meal on the plane—and even that had been purged during the hellish trek through the jungle.

There was movement from the other side of the room. Through the darkness, Allan saw a beaded curtain parting—and then the man who he assumed was the chief being led into the room by a young girl. The chief's eyes were closed tightly against the light—and he was so shriveled and frail that Allan was unable to determine his age. He was also sweating profusely. The chief was taken to his chair and the long, braided hair, which hung to his knees, was gathered and then pulled aside so that he could sit.

Without opening his eyes, the old man gestured to the unoccupied cushions on the floor and said, "You sit."

With his eyes still closed, the chief reached for a bone that bore roasted meat and began to eat as if he hadn't seen food in days. Allan noticed that his fingernails were at least four inches long and that they were as gnarled and brown as the man himself.

Allan and the professor sat, as instructed, and then waited in silence. Finally, the chief opened his eyes, slowly, and said, "I am Nala Manu Tonga," then reached for more food, as if there were nothing more to say. As he chewed, the chief studied the professor's eyes and appeared to make a mental note. But when he turned his attention to Allan's eyes—the chief winced, as if he'd looked directly into the sun.

Allan's trepidation suddenly increased and he whispered, "Professor—" but he was silenced by a sharp elbow to the ribs. Allan said, "But—"

"Boy—" Tonga spoke in a crackling hiss: "Be still." The chief returned his attention to Allan's eyes, this time squinting against some unseen luminance.

Allan wished he could dismiss this feeble old man as a savage, an eccentric—or even a lunatic, but his intuition told him otherwise. Tonga was far more dangerous. Allan began to squirm beneath the chief's hungry gaze. Tonga's eyes were the color of pale jade, with broken capillaries zigzagging out from the irises. The cool green of his eyes stood in eerie contrast to his weathered skin, which was so black that is was almost purple. But it was the intention lurking behind those eyes that really frightened Allan.

"I am Professor John Sumner." Professor Sumner used expansive hand gestures as he spoke. "And this is my associate, Allan Steele."

The chief smiled at Allan, revealing a mouthful of rotting teeth. He said, "Good. I been wait for you, Allan Steele," and bit into a luscious mango. "You come far. You want sleep—yes?"

The professor tried to tear his attention away from the young lady at the chief's side that was cutting Tonga's overgrown fingernails short with a small bone-handled blade. But she had neglected to address the nails of his thumb and forefinger on his right hand. Professor Sumner said, "Sorry? Oh, yes. It was a long trip."

"Maybe my speak—like you speak—not so good. Been many years since I speak it out."

The professor continued to gesture with his hands. "No. You speak very well. We are both very happy to be here. And we are very grateful to you for allowing us to visit."

The chief looked to Allan for confirmation of this professed gratitude, but found only fear. Allan tried to smile while pushing back the voice in his head that told him to run from this room, this country, and the irresistible pull of the chief's haunting eyes.

Tonga continued to smile at Allan like an ancient crocodile as he ate. It was as if he had heard Allan's thoughts—and he enjoyed scaring him. He said, "Good. We all very much happy."

The professor said, "I'm sorry. We must be staring. It's just that—" the professor lied,"—you look very ... very well, for your age."

Tonga began to laugh and nearly choked on his food. This stranger did not know how to hide his thoughts. The chief responded, "Today—not so much." He then gave the girl at his side a command and she mopped the sweat from his withered torso with a sea sponge. She then retrieved a larger blade and began to sever Tonga's serpentine braids by the handful, cutting them as close to the scalp as possible.

The professor said, "May I ask, Sir—how old are you?"

Tonga answered, "One-one-two, I think." He addressed Allan: "Do you think Tonga look good, boy?"

"Uh ... yes." Allan had seen healthier looking relics in museums.

The chief laughed again, and then lapsed into a coughing fit which concerned his attendants. The back-to-back twins rose in an amazing move that appeared as if a single child was backing his way up a mirror. They then waddled across the room like a mutant crab to bring Tonga a gold cup filled with water. The Chief took a sip and waved them away, then returned to eating. Allan tried not to stare as the twins waddled back across the room and did their mirror movement again—in reverse.

Professor Sumner filled the silence as the chief attempted to catch his breath. "So ... you have been chief for a long time?"

The chief furrowed his sweaty brow and gestured into the distance with his newly-manicured hands—indicating a great expanse of time. He then said something unintelligible to his other female attendant, who then turned away to prepare a special drink for the occasion. The chief turned back to his visitors and flexed his muscles, proclaiming, "One-one-two! Chief is strong!" He watched with acute interest as the beverage was served to Allan.

Allan accepted the silver chalice and said, "Oh, uh ... thank you." He brought the cup closer and smelled it, but couldn't bring himself to drink.

The professor whispered, "Drink it."

Allan took a deep breath and raised the cup to his lips again—but he still could not bring himself to drink. Something just didn't feel right.

The chief's withered tongue slid across cracked lips as he watched Allan grapple with the decision. Tonga almost seemed amused. "Drink—and maybe you be old like chief."

Allan tried again, but he lacked the strength to override his instincts. He lowered the cup and said, "I'm sorry, but I—"

"My friend is just tired." Professor Sumner took the cup from Allan's hands. "As you said—it's been a long journey. And I, for one, am very thirsty." The professor shot Allan an admonishing glance and took a big swallow.

Allan cried, "Professor—NO," and knocked the chalice from his mentor's hand. The cup clattered to the wooden floor and the remaining liquid splashed everywhere.

The professor was mortified. He blotted the stray droplets from his lips and spoke in a somber tone. "Chief ... I am very sorry. Please forgive our rudeness. My friend is young and–"

Suddenly, an agitated Shantu warrior rushed in. His chest bore the mark of the eye, just like the guard in the room. The chief motioned for the warrior to approach and they whispered in an archaic form of Lingala. The chief then conferred with his twin advisors and gave the warrior instructions. After another word with his advisors, the chief waved the warrior away and returned his attention to his guests. The news seemed to have tired him. He said, "We have fight with Binjee people. Soon, big fight."

The professor had gone pale and clammy.

Allan asked, "Professor? Are you okay?"

The professor's eyelids drooped and he said, "The day must have caught up with me." Allan helped him lie down. The professor continued to mumble as consciousness ebbed: "I'm sorry to be such a bother." Professor Sumner saw concern on Allan's face, and the chief standing over him with an odd look of interest.

And then everything went black.

23

The world was a shadowed blur to Professor Sumner as he fought to regain consciousness. He had been moved to a hut at the far end of the village. The windows of this room had been boarded up, just as those in the chief's quarters had been. The firefly in a paper bag served as sole illumination.

"I'm here, professor. What can I get you?"

"Allan?" The professor found Allan's hand. "Water ... please."

The chief stood nearby, eating and sweating. He motioned to an attendant who brought the professor another cup of the ominous black liquid.

The professor gulped it down and asked, "How long?"

"Three days." Allan handed the cup back to the attendant after his friend had finished. "You had me worried."

"Three ..." The professor tried to sit up, but he was too weak. "What have I missed?"

Even Allan's profound concern for the professor couldn't quell his excitement. He said, "The Hindu influence is everywhere. The way they cook, their sanitation system—even their customs. Remember that carving at the entrance? I was right. They worship Kali, but I haven't figured out why, yet. Kali is the most terrifying and destructive goddess in Hindu mythology. But the passive Hindu traits seem to be dominant over the violent rituals of Kali's devotees. They still draw on some of the more primitive tribal

traditions, though. I guess they had to, in order to survive here."
Allan began to pace. "You were right. This is absolutely incredible!
You have to get well, so we can start."

"Sounds like you're doing pretty well on your own." The professor managed a smile as he parroted Allan's own words. "For a
kid with *nothing* to contribute."

"The chief's been helping me communicate, but I could sure
stand a little sunlight." He whispered, "Everywhere he goes—they
board up the windows and take along this rancid oil lamp."

"And the preservation of the souls?"

"That, you won't believe. They claim they can transfer the souls
of the dying into the bodies of the living. Supposedly all the knowledge of the donor goes with the soul—into the new body."

"My God. Then it's true?"

"I'm still having a little trouble wrapping the Western part of
my mind around the concept, but I spent two hours talking to a
ten-year-old who knew a hell of a lot more about life than I do. I
mean, even his eyes looked ... I don't know ... wise."

"But why choose a child?"

"According to Tonga—when they die, the souls of the oldest
members of the household are transferred into the body of the
youngest member—figuring that the children are gonna be the
leaders someday, so they're gonna need all the wisdom they can
get."

"How do the older members of the tribe feel about it?"

"There aren't very many around to ask, but the few I found
seemed to like the idea. They say this way they get to hang around
the family forever. Tonga hasn't told me how they do it, yet. I think
he's waiting for you. So we have to get you well, okay? I can't do
this on my own."

Professor Sumner seemed to have exhausted what little strength
he had. His speech was slurred. "It's all quite amazing. I wonder
how many souls can be contained in one body." The professor's
eyes slipped shut. "Wake me in a few hours. We must ... find out
how they do it."

Allan stayed by his friend's side until he had lapsed into unconsciousness, and then stepped back to allow access to the young
lady who had been attending the professor.

24

That night Allan paced while trying keep all of his observations clear in his mind. One of his better tutors had taught him a technique by which he could organize his thoughts, just as a student might use acronyms to cram for an exam. But there were just too many disparate elements to this tribe—and he was too excited about the possibilities ... if the Shantu could really do what they claimed.

Allan suddenly remembered the micro-cassette recorder he'd thrown in with his clothes at the last minute, and he hurried over to his unopened backpack. Every morning one of the Shantu women had shown up at his doorstep with a new tunic that they'd made for him, along with anything else that he had requested, as offerings—of sorts. And Allan had the professor's mini DVD camcorder along with the watertight container that held six spare NiCad batteries, a nifty little solar charger, and two dozen blank DVD-Rs. So he hadn't needed anything else that he and Professor Sumner had dragged through the jungle; until now.

Allan smelled the mildew, and remembered the river, as soon as he opened his pack. His white t-shirts had patches of green mold growing on them. And the micro-cassette recorder, which had also been left unprotected from the muddy waters of the Ubangi, was useless. He yelled, "Goddamn it!" and tossed the water-logged recorder aside, then returned to the grass-filled mattress where his friend slept. The professor's shallow breathing troubled Allan, as did his persistent high fever. Powerless to help, frustrated and restless, Allan went to the professor's pack and dug out a pad and pencil.

The moment that Allan sat down to write, his palms began to sweat.

Just relax! It's only a piece of paper, for Christ's sake!

He touched the pencil to the paper and willed his body to write, but the resulting scribbles were illegible. Allan tore away the page and tried again. The results were no better. Enraged, he threw the pad across the room, followed by his glasses, and snapped the pencil in two.

Allan started to pace, but stumbled over an unseen object after only a few steps and fell headlong onto the earthen floor. He wiped the dirt from his eyes and mouth and tried to get his bearings. To Allan, the room was a poorly rendered impressionistic painting in dire need of interpretation. He couldn't remember the last time he felt this helpless—or this *alone.*

Allan crawled across the room in search of his glasses, hands sliding in semicircles on the ground. Eventually he found the hated spectacles and put them back on. His tantrum had cracked the right lens. Allan mumbled, "Great," and extinguished the oil lamp, then flopped down onto his mattress—eager to put this night behind him.

25

It wasn't the eerie sounds of the jungle that woke Allan from his nightmare. Nor was it the spotted owl holding court in the tree outside his window. It was the footsteps. Allan shook the confusion from his brain and donned his damaged glasses before creeping to the window. Outside, groups of Shantu filed past, carrying wooden bowls filled with fruit and handmade dolls. Brightly colored beads of bone and wood chattered as the Shantu hurried through the darkness and into the trees.

After a quick check on the professor, Allan grabbed the camcorder and his shoes. He waited until the last Shantu had passed, then ventured out into the night that was blacker than any he had ever known.

———————

He did his best to keep up with the agile Shantu, but even the stragglers seemed to leave Allan in the weeds. After running for what seemed like an eternity, Allan finally arrived at a crossroads. Unable to discern which way the others went, he chose the wrong route. The otherworldly sounds of the jungle surrounded and terrified Allan as he moved through the overgrown foliage, his head filled with fearful banter.

If I get lost out here—I could die. Actually die. There must be animals all around me. Watching from the trees, crouched behind the rocks—just waiting for me to stumble, or stop to catch my breath so they can pounce. Fucking WILD animals that don't eat Alpo and peanuts through the bars of their cages. You're definitely *not in Kansas anymore, Dorothy.*

Lions ...

and tigers ...

and bears ...

"Oh, shit." Adrenaline flooded Allan's bloodstream, transforming every shadow into a monster, every sound into a final warning. He would have happily returned to the relative comfort of his hut, had he a clue how to find it.

Finally, Allan saw firelight up ahead, peeking through the trees like an evil eye. He made it to an opening in the dense underbrush and peered through, praying that his thundering heartbeat wouldn't give him away.

To his right, along the river bank, sat the majority of the tribe. Waiting. Allan ducked back, fearful of discovery, but then realized that the Shantus' attention was focused in the opposite direction, toward the water. Allan crept out from the trees and craned his neck to see what the others saw.

A large, round, floating platform had been anchored at the center of the river. Around the edge sat twelve priests, wearing leather thongs and ceremonial paint. Allan wondered why they were just sitting there, silent and immobile. But a rustling in the trees behind him put an end to his musing. He scanned the area, desperate for a place to hide, and spotted small raft-like structure with a tent built on top of it.

Allan hurried to the raft and ducked inside the tent, but realized his mistake too late. A small candle illuminated the interior and a large, ornate cushion awaited the guest of honor. Allan turned back to the opening of the tent, and then the raft shifted. Someone else had stepped aboard. He dove for cover in the darkest corner, using an animal skin blanket to hide himself and the palm-sized digital camcorder. A moment later the tent's flap was opened and someone entered.

Allan heard the flap close and then felt the raft launch. Although there were others on the raft, Allan sensed that only he and the late arrival occupied the tent itself. It took him several minutes to summon the courage to move the blanket, just enough to glean the identity of his traveling companion. It was the boy who had been playing ball by the fire the day Allan and the professor first arrived.

Allan adjusted his position and the boy must have sensed the movement because he turned without warning and yanked away the blanket. Just as the boy started to call out to the others, he recognized Allan. This was the stranger who had returned his ball. Allan was about to speak when the boy raised a forefinger to his lips and re-covered him. A moment later, one of the priests on board pulled back the flap.

Speaking in his native tongue, the boy reassured the priest that everything was all right and the flap was once again lowered. The boy pulled away the blanket again and smiled, then made a throwing gesture with one hand. Allan returned the smile and sat beside him, then inched the flap back to see what was going on outside.

The raft was approaching the floating platform. It was then that Allan noticed that all of the priests circling the stage had shaved heads and bindees on their foreheads. An empty wooden bowl waited on the platform in front of each man in the circle.

The chief sat at the opposite side of the circle. He wore a robe made of human hair in a patchwork of scalps. And although his face was covered by a mask that had been fashioned from the skull of some great horned animal, the eyes were unmistakable, eerie and unflinching. Chief Tonga gestured, and one of the priests began to beat an odd-looking drum. The sound was slow and rhythmic, almost hypnotic. The other priests began to hum.

Allan reached for the camera and flipped a switch to put it into infra-red night vision mode as ashes were scattered from an urn onto the center of the platform. The humming intensified while the single drumbeat thumped in the background. The sound was very peaceful. Allan found himself comforted and drawn to it in some mysterious way. Without even noticing, he had begun to rock back and forth to the beat of the drums as he surveyed the eerily green-tinted night through the monochromatic eye of the viewfinder.

A body, wrapped in animal skins, was tossed into the center of the stage from a canoe that had been moored to the platform. For a moment—all sound stopped. When the drumming resumed, the priests rocked back and forth while the cocoon center-stage writhed among the ashes.

Allan's mind drifted off for a moment and he saw the stage from overhead, as if he had left his body. The shape of the floating platform, with the priests at its edges and the writhing cocoon in the center of the circular scattering of ash, created the appearance of a huge human eye.

Something touched Allan's hand and the sensation brought him back into his body. It was the boy; he had reached out to touch the camcorder. The child stared at Allan and the camera with curiosity. Allan whispered, "Here. Look," and held out the camera.

The boy looked into the finder, saw the sacred ceremony through the unflinching eye of the camera, and panicked. He jumped away, as if bitten, and whispered something in Lingala which Allan surmised was a prayer for forgiveness.

Allan took the camera back, but the boy continued to study it, and Allan, with suspicion. Allan turned the camera back toward the ceremony, panning the platform to find the chief—and then met those eyes. The chief was looking directly into the camera.

Allan pulled the camcorder away from his eye, just to make sure that he had seen what he thought he had seen, and the chief was still there—staring directly at him. Allan whispered, "Oh, shit," and his blood ran cold. "Shit, shit, shit ..."

But instead of exposing Allan, the chief just smiled his rot toothed smile and returned his attention to the action on the stage. He stood and moved to the center, carrying a small sickle in one hand. The chief's body gleamed with sweat as he forced the squirming bag to the ground with his foot and raised the sickle high above his head. Then all sound and movement stopped and, for a moment, the crescent shape of the sickle mirrored that of the moon.

Finally, the chief swung the blade down, slashing the fleshy fabric of the man-made cocoon. The movement within stopped. Then the oldest priest in the circle rose and began to chant in a blend of East Indian and African tones.

The chief slashed the bag a second time and the crowd on shore went wild.

The chief slashed the bag a third time and all hell broke loose; Kali exploded from the cocoon—whirling into a dance of total abandon. She leapt into the air, writhing and twirling, fueled by the fires of the damned. The goddess was naked, except for a necklace of shrunken human skulls and a mask which had a grotesquely large mouth. An animal tongue protruded from the opening and hung to one side. Her eyes were wild and unseeing as she began to whirl a serrated machete around her body in a gleaming blur. The music and chanting intensified as Kali flew around the circle, her energy growing with each step. The priests continued to hum and rock, hum and rock ... And then without warning, Kali jumped to one side of the stage, raised her blade, and howled as the standing priest's chant was cut off in midstream. She had decapitated him with one clean blow.

The boy helped Allan poke his head out of the back of the tent so that he could empty the contents of his stomach into the river. Afterward, still horrified and nauseous, Allan returned his attention to the stage.

Kali had dragged the headless body to the center of the floating platform and now stood triumphant with one foot resting on top of the corpse. In her right hand she brandished the bloody knife. In her left—the head. She then sat upon the lifeless body, as if it was a throne, and waited.

Two priests approached the tent.

The boy hurried Allan back into his hiding place before the flap was raised and he was escorted onto the stage. The child was brought to Kali and he showed no fear. The goddess extended her bloodstained hand to him and he accepted. She took him to her bare breast, like a mother, stroking his hair tenderly in a moment of decision. It was time. He would either die, or be judged worthy and fill the vacant seat among the circle of priests.

"Don't do it, you bitch. Don't do it ... don't do it ..." Allan held his breath, watching from the tent, terrified for the child's life. Then the boy bowed his head to Ma Kali—and she kissed it. He had been accepted as one of her own. The boy rose to accept the bloody sickle from Kali, the Dark Mother, and then turned to the shore. The crowd leapt to its feet in celebration as the boy made his way around the platform, bowing to each of the surviving priests and listening intently while they offered him a private pearl of wisdom. About halfway around the platform, the boy bowed and listened for a long time to the oldest surviving priest. It took a while, because the priest had much to say. Once the pearl had been dispensed, the boy stood, bowed deeply, and then slashed the old man's throat with a mercifully quick swing of the sickle.

Allan blanched, caught completely off-guard by this final assault. He felt dizzy and weak.

The boy battled his club foot as he dragged the body of the dying man to the center of the stage and then returned to take his place among the other priests. The chief rose and approached the old man. The priest twitched and gurgled as blood gushed from his severed jugular, but he made no effort to stem the flow. Chief Tonga raised his hands to the heavens, his long, brown fingernails like ancient daggers—then tore out the old man's eyes.

Allan retched as the crowd cheered and Tonga consumed the eyes of the dying priest. The chief's body shuddered as he enjoyed a moment of ecstasy, then Kali rose to approach the two lifeless bodies at the center of the stage, her knife at the ready.

The last thing Allan saw before losing consciousness was the remaining priests in the circle, bowing their heads and lifting their bowls, awaiting the sacramental meal.

26

The chief had put his mask aside. He ate and sweated and watched from the corner as Allan awakened. Tonga found it hard to believe that this pathetic boy might actually be The One.

Allan groaned, "What happened?" and his hands went instinctively to his face to adjust his glasses. "Where am I?" He tried to get his bearings while the girl who had played the Dark Goddess mopped his brow. Allan spotted the Kali mask nearby and suddenly the memories of last night's events came flooding back with unwelcomed clarity. He removed his glasses, covered his eyes with his forearm and muttered, "Oh my God ... It wasn't a nightmare." Tonga continued to study Allan from the shadows.

Allan squinted against the sunlight streaming through a window opening. He saw the professor's digital camcorder on the ground. It had been smashed and discarded. He said, "Thanks for taking care of the camera," and the woman whispered something to the chief in a language that sounded vaguely familiar to Allan. He asked, "Was that Hindu?"

The chief stepped closer and spoke with his mouth full: "It is the holy language. She say you must be slow." Chief Tonga smiled. "She say we make you afraid."

Allan said, "Afraid? AFRAID? Who *are* you? Where is—" and then stopped to put on his glasses. He had assumed that the man in the corner was a guard—he was young and muscular, though he didn't bear the scar on his chest as the other warriors had. But now, as the man approached, Allan recognized those eyes–and his mind reeled. He stammered, "But ... it's not *possible.*"

Tonga stepped into the sunshine, looking proud and vital, and answered, "All things are possible, boy." The chief made eye contact with Allan, with no need to squint or look away, and added, "For a price." The woman spoke again and the chief laughed.

Allan was still in shock. He knew that this couldn't be happening. It simply couldn't. He asked, "What did she say?"

"She say you have fear of me. She say you like Tonga old and weak better."

"Yeah, well—she's right." Allan sat up with the help of his beautiful nurse. "I don't understand. The little boy–"

"Boy, now man. Man, now holy man. Ma Kali has smiled on him." Tonga went to the door and said, "All will be told. But your friend—he die now."

―――――――

Allan burst into the professor's hut, frantic and out of breath. Professor Sumner's complexion was deathly pale and his lips were blue. Allan hurried to his friend, whispering to himself, "Jesus Christ." He turned to the chief and said, "I thought you were taking care of him."

The professor wheezed, fighting the paralysis in his lungs. "He did just that, my boy."

Allan turned on the chief, screaming, "What did you do to him?"

The chief offered a wicked smile, but no explanation.

The professor supplied the answer; there was no time to waste. He swallowed hard and said, "I finally placed the flavor of the tea, yesterday. Belladonna. He was testing your psychic abilities by putting the poison in the cup. I drank …"

"When I *didn't*." Allan remembered: "I didn't know why. I just couldn't." Allan watched the professor's suffering and felt wholly responsible. "Professor, if I'd known why–"

"No, my boy—don't. He was testing your psychic abilities. He said he sensed them the moment he saw you, but he had to be sure you were the one that he had been waiting for. A little drastic, if you ask me, but ..." The professor managed a feeble smile. "The good news is that my headache is gone."

"We've gotta get you to a doctor."

"Judging by the paralysis in my legs and arms I would guess it's too late for that, although toxicology really isn't my field."

"I can't just let you die."

"I'm glad to hear that."

Allan took the professor's hand and asked, "What should I do?"

"I think that's a discussion that you and the chief will have to have. Under normal circumstances I'd love to know the details, but ..." He patted Allan's hand, suddenly frightened. "I'm sure you understand."

Allan turned to the chief and asked, "What can I do?"

"Togu Ma."

"What's Togu Ma?"

There was a quaver in the professor's voice. "It's the soul transference process."

"The soul trans–" Allan stopped, stunned, and turned to the Chief. "What do you have to gain by killing him?"

The chief said, "Not Tonga. *You*."

Allan moved closer, enraged. "You son of a bitch!"

The chief smiled again but there was evil in his eyes. He said, "When he die—smoke will pass through here." The chief pointed to the professor's eyes. Allan noticed that his fingernails had already grown an inch in less than a week.

"What smoke?" Allan asked the professor, "What the hell is he talking about?"

"The smoke is the soul. He's talking about my soul."

The chief said, "You wait for smoke. Then you take—and you keep."

"Take what? Where? And how?" Allan walked away, frustrated. "You're outta your fucking mind!"

"Allan. Listen to what he has to say. Please. I don't think we have much time."

Allan shook his head in disbelief and took a seat. He said, "This isn't happening," and chewed on his thumbnail nervously. "You want me to take what?" The chief pointed to the professor's eyes. "His eyes? You want me to take his fucking eyes?! And then what am I supposed to do with them?"

The chief tore into a drumstick of roasted meat with his gruesome teeth, and smiled.

Allan's laugh was one part disbelief, two parts hysteria. "Eat them?! I don't even eat meat—and you want me to eat his ..." Allan searched the faces in the room for a punch line, but soon realized that there was no joke. The blood drained from his face as he recalled the climax of the ceremony on the floating stage. "Jesus ..." Allan slumped back into his chair. "You're serious."

The chief adopted the patient tone of a father with a difficult child. He said, "When the Great Man came–"

"The Great Man?"

The professor said, "Your great grandfather, Allan."

Chief Tonga continued: "The old chief—he had much strength. Then the Great Man come and he want change Shantu. He no want hunt. He want pray. Old chief no want pray—he want hunt. They make big noise for many days." He confided, "I hide near sleep place of chief and listen. Old chief say we must hunt. We must kill the spotted cat and drink blood for speed. Kill the big ape and eat heart for strength. That our way to take smoke and keep."

"That's ridiculous."

The chief smiled again. "That what Great Man say. He say smoke not tree, smoke not rock ... how could it be heart—or blood?" The chief gestured with his hands as he spoke. "He say smoke fly away when die—from here." He pointed to his eyes. "But normal man no can see it."

Allan said, "Their beliefs were totally opposite. How could they ever agree?"

"They never do. But *both* were right."

"Both ... What do you mean?"

"When night come I sneak into sleeping place and I make old chief and Great Man dead." Tonga was excited, now. "Great man right, smoke came here." He directed a filthy fingernail toward Allan's eye.

Allan felt sick again. "And you ..."

Tonga took another bite of food. "I take smoke."

"Jesus." Allan's voice was flat and hollow. His mind was numb.

"And I eat hearts—to be sure. Now both live in me and I know what they know." The chief was amused by the look of repulsion on Allan's face. "Sometimes they still make big noise ..." He tapped his forehead and said, "In here."

Allan was still trying to process what he had just heard when the professor mumbled something and slipped into unconsciousness. Allan asked the chief, "What makes you think I could do this? Even if I wanted to?"

The chief looked Allan in the eye and said, "I know you, boy. You stronger than you think. You from Great Man." He smiled. "Now you from *me*. I wait long time. I know you come to me. Your road—it begin *here*. With Tonga."

"Like the spokes of a wheel—" Allan paced, scrubbing his face with his hands, muttering his mother's words: "—all roads lead to the center."

27

Washington, D.C., October 1973.

She looked so peaceful lying there, long blonde hair arranged on the pillow to frame her ashen face. Her expression was serene, with just a hint of a smile bowing her crimson lips. Her hands had been crossed on her chest.

Argus paced naked across the room as he admired his hand-iwork. It had taken a long time to get the smile just right. His erection bobbed as he circled the hotel bed, and then he stooped to take the serrated survival knife from his attaché case. Argus trembled with excitement as he moved to the clothes on the chair and used the sleeve of his uniform to polish the steel blade. Argus stared at the motionless girl on the bed as he polished and paced—polished and paced—until finally he could stand no more.

He knelt on the bed and removed the girl's shoes. Her toenails had been manicured for the occasion. He slid the knife, edge up, under the cuff of her slacks until the tip of the blade pierced the fabric just below the knee. Argus closed his eyes and savored the soft tearing sound as he pushed the blade through the cloth to its hilt and pulled it back toward him. When he'd cut a long slit from knee to cuff on the right leg—he moved to the left. When that was done, he straddled her and carefully cut upward from each knee, until he sawed through the waistband of the slacks. At one point Argus heard voices in the hallway and stopped, dead still, until they had passed.

His breath came hot and fast. He pulled away the dissected slacks, making every effort not to disturb the body, and then Argus slid the shiny blade across her skin to the waistband of her panties. The serrated edge cut through the silky fabric in one gentle tug. He removed the girl's underwear, like a child unwrapping a gift, and found that she was a true blonde—just as she had promised. He would have to shave her before they began. Argus gently parted her legs and knelt between them, before reaching for the straight razor.

Her nostrils flared slightly. Then her nose twitched and she sneezed. Argus climbed off of the sniffling call girl, his erection flagging. "Goddamn it!"

The girl sneezed again. "Shit. I'm sorry."

Argus stalked away. "You're sorry? What did I tell you about moving?"

She sat up to blow her nose. "You told me not to, but–"

"That's fucking right! I TOLD YOU NOT TO!"

The girl was annoyed by Argus' tone. "Well, *I told you* I have a cold. Christ, I said I was sorry." She studied her shredded slacks with casual disdain, glad that these were not among her favorites. "You wanna try again?"

Argus headed for his uniform, face flushed, sulking. "Forget it. You ruined it."

The call girl suddenly remembered the diamond tennis brace-let she had seen at Tiffany's and moved to take Argus' limp penis in her hand. "Come on, lover. We can get him going again."

Argus pushed her away, enraged. "Get your hands off me! I told you what to do, but you were too fucking stupid to follow instructions! I told Monica to send someone with a brain, but I guess that was too much to ask." He stepped into his skivvies and then into his pants. "So now I'm not getting fucked, and you *are*."

The girl stormed off to gather her things, wiping away the powder that had given her that ashen look. "Monica didn't tell me about the knife! You think I would've taken this job if I knew you were gonna cut my clothes off with a fucking knife? And what about my pants? You're gonna at least pay for those!"

Argus tucked in his shirt, zipped up his fly and moved toward the door. "I'm not paying for anything, you stupid cunt."

She put on her overcoat, buttoning it to disguise her lack of pants as she mumbled, "Freaks."

Argus stopped in the open doorway, seething. He narrowed his eyes and asked, "What was that?"

She stomped toward the door. "I said I'm done with *freaks*. I get five hundred for a straight fuck. I don't need this bullshit. No more leather, no more pissing on people, and no more acting like a Goddamned corpse so limp-dicked FREAKS like you can get it up!"

Argus punched her square in the face without warning—send-ing her sprawling back onto the bed. Just then a maid passed by, but Argus didn't notice. He was busy inside, attempting to silence the screaming prostitute with a brutal series of blows.

———————

Argus was kept waiting for two hours and twelve minutes before Colonel Bryant finally waved him into the office. Maggie, the Colonel's secretary, had been staring openly at the scabby scratch marks across Argus' face. The Colonel limped to the chair behind his desk and sat with a heavy sigh. "At ease, Major."

"Yes, Sir." Argus sat, noticing the little crucifix on the Colonel's wall for the first time.

Colonel Bryant looked Argus over as if he was also seeing something for the first time. "The girl's got friends in high places, Steele. But we've convinced her not to press charges."

Argus wished he'd killed her but he said, "That's good, Sir."

"Good, Steele? There's nothing good about this whole damned—" He took a deep breath, trying to contain his rage and disgust. "I realize that many other commanding officers turn a blind eye to this kind of behavior—", He grimaced, "—prostitutes and all, but I thought you knew where I stood on this issue."

"Yes, Sir. You've made yourself very clear on—"

The Colonel raised his hand and Argus stopped talking. "Just shut up and listen, Steele. I'll let you know when to talk." Argus dammed his anger behind clenched teeth. Colonel Bryant continued. "You've had a problem ever since Nam. Haven't you, Steele?"

Argus flushed. "No Sir. Not a *problem.*"

"Are you forgetting who walked your lovely bride down the aisle, Major?"

"No, Sir."

"Have you forgotten how beautiful that girl of yours is, Major—foreigner or not?"

Argus felt a bead of sweat trickle down his back. "No, Sir."

"But you *have* forgotten that you took some vows that day. And you have forgotten that paying whores to do—whatever it is you have them do—is not only against the laws of this great country of ours, but a violation of God's laws."

"No, Sir." Argus' shame and rage echoed in his voice. "I haven't forgotten any of that, Sir."

Colonel Bryant was repulsed by Argus. He opened a file folder and slid it across the desk without looking at it. "You proud of that, Steele?"

"No, Sir." Argus' attention was drawn to the MP's photograph of the beaten call girl. He was aroused, despite his shame. The gleam in his eyes as he studied the photo confirmed the Colonel's suspicions. Bryant slid a typed document across the desk. Argus read the heading and was stunned. "What is this?"

"Sign it, Steele. Then get the hell out of my office."

"This is a letter of resignation."

The Colonel checked his watch. "I know what it is, Steele." He met Argus' eyes with a long, cold stare. "And now I know what *you* are."

28

Allan wandered aimlessly through the jungle surrounding the Shantu camp, allowing the rain to wash away his tears. Could this horrible place and this horrible act truly be his destiny? After countless hours of walking and thinking, he found himself back where he began—outside the window of his dying friend. He watched the girl who had played Kali try to still Professor Sumner after an extended convulsion. Allan's last words with the chief still echoed through his tortured brain.

"How did you know when to do it?"

"When smoke in eyes you take."

"What if you're wrong? What if I can't see the smoke?"

"You will. You have magic. Hotter fire make lighter smoke. Your friend very wise. Very strong. Fire will be bright."

"If everything you've said is true how do the other Shantu keep the souls? Do they all have magic?"

"My people had magic. Like yours."

"But the others ... The children–"

"All children come from me."

"That's why so many of them are deformed ... You killed everyone from the old chief's tribe?"

"Tonga no kill women—until after."

"But all the others ..."

"Others not dead. They live inside Tonga."

"But if they all have the power why are you Chief?"

"Tonga strong, like you. When you take smoke, stronger other is, stronger you must be to hold flame. Strongest flame will be chief."

Allan turned away from his friend's pain and wandered for a while longer. After a time, he had reached one of the huts near the entrance to the camp. His eyes met those of a Down syndrome child, watching from a doorway. Her expression was weary beyond her years. Her young eyes had already seen too much.

"My boy, I'm truly sorry I won't be there to see this. Though I suppose, in a way, I will be."

"Professor, I'm scared."

"Good. Then I'm not the only one." Professor Sumner patted Allan's hand. *"My time was nearly over, anyway. The old bastard just gave me a bit of a nudge."*

"I don't want to lose you."

"You won't—if this works. In fact, we'll be spending a lot of time together."

Allan's mood lightened as he remembered his friend's unexpected laughter in that dark moment. But Allan's smile soon faded as he made his decision and set out to find the chief. The professor's final words offered little solace.

"If it has to be—I'm glad it's you, Allan. I can think of no one I'd rather spend eternity with."

"I still don't know. I can't decide what to do."

"Pray, my boy. For both our souls."

29

He knelt at the center of the floating stage, surrounded by the night. The angels wept as Kali danced and Allan did his best to shield the unconscious body of his dying friend from the pelt of falling tears, both the angels'—and his own. There was no audience on the shore for this rite of passage. Nor was there cheering or celebration. There was only misery.

Chief Tonga warned Allan from behind his ceremonial mask, "Once your foot is on road, boy—is no going back."

Allan cradled the professor's head in his lap and raised his voice to be heard above the rain. "Just tell me what to do."

"Do you take the Dark Mother as your own?"

The professor convulsed and his eyes fluttered open. Allan panicked. "Whatever! Let's just get this over with! He's suffering—can't you see that?"

Kali stood before Allan, awaiting his response. The rain had transformed her body into a glistening silhouette in the moonlight. The heat of her efforts returned ghostly trails of steam to the night.

The chief's tone was urgent. He said, "You must answer."

Professor Sumner made a small, desperate sound. His body began to twitch and his eyes rolled back in his head. Allan screamed, "YES! JUST TELL ME WHAT TO DO!" Kali drew his head to her bare breast and stroked his rain-soaked hair. Allan felt her warm heartbeat against his cheek and began to sob, "Please, just tell me what to do—before it's too late."

The professor jerked and screamed as death's final spasms took hold of him. Kali moved away and the chief held Professor Sumner's eyes open. "Now, boy! Look!"

Allan saw nothing but the glazed stare of a dying man. His heart sank. "There's nothing."

The chief insisted, "Look!"

Allan swiped the tears and rain out of his eyes and leaned in closer, determined to see the smoke. He said, "There's nothing! There's ..." Allan's heart stopped. He blinked and focused on the speck of silver buried deep within the black void of his friend's eyes. *Oh my God. Is that it? Maybe it's just the moon's reflection. But it's* ... "Growing." Allan blinked, and looked again, unwilling to trust his senses. He repeated, "It's *growing*."

"You see smoke, boy?"

"Yes." Allan's voice was low and reverent, his eyes locked with the professor's. It was as if he'd seen the face of God himself. He whispered, "I see it." The professor drew in a final breath, tensed for a moment, then exhaled as the silver smoke glittered like a newly-minted coin spinning up from the darkness beneath a golden spotlight. Allan whispered, "It's ... beautiful."

The chief traced his razor-sharp fingernails across the professor's cheek. "It is time."

Allan pulled the professor closer and screamed, "GET AWAY FROM HIM!" The chief smiled beneath his mask and backed away. He recognized the hunger. Allan leaned forward to say goodbye to his friend and saw himself reflected in the silver mirrors of the professor's eyes. He whispered a pledge: "You will always have a home with me." Allan raised his hands to his friend's face, averted his eyes and pushed his fingers into the soft flesh and fibrous ligaments that surrounded the professor's eyeballs. But when his fingers met behind them, and tore them from their sockets, they were no longer flesh and blood. They were the ripened fruits of the gods; fruits of wisdom that would have rotted on the vine if Allan hadn't plucked them at that precise moment.

Now, the rest of the professor's body was nothing but a lifeless husk that's only purpose had been to protect the seeds through their years of maturation. And when he raised the fruit to his lips and tasted, Allan was amazed at the sweetness of the juice. He closed his eyes and swallowed, reveling in the wave of hedonistic pleasure that washed over him. His body shuddered as the professor's blood ran down his face and their souls met.

Then the pain struck without warning and Allan screamed— his body jolted by an unseen cardiac probe. He looked to the chief for guidance, but it was too late. Allan's eyes glazed over and his perceptions turned inward.

Falling through space and time. Icy winds rushing past. Frost on eyebrows ... Consuming numbness ... Fear closing his heart in its huge black hand. Something below, rushing up. A light ... No—a fire. Silent screams engulfed in flames as he continues to plummet down. Sucking fire into his lungs.

No air.

NO AIR.

Passing through the fire, his skin begins to bubble black and his eyes sear shut. Until ... SPLASH. Engulfed in water. Sinking fast. Eyelids burned away and bathed in salt water, lungs aching—clawing at nothing. Still sinking.

And then ...

... finally ...

... reaching bottom.

Kali continued her dance on the floating stage, moving to the ghastly music of Allan's screams, her image reflected in the blood-spattered lenses of his glasses. Allan's pain intensified as his bones softened, and then began to shift. He stared blindly up at the stars as he sucked air and rainwater into his lungs. Suddenly, the structure of his face and body melted, becoming indistinct, and then tried to coalesce again. And then, gradually, Allan began to resemble the professor. He wailed and thrashed as his soul fought his friend's for dominance of the body until, finally, the professor was absorbed back into Allan and the body stabilized.

Beneath the murky water, Allan's fear disappears and he begins to float upward. In time, he reaches the surface and the horizon of the water shifts sideways until it stands vertically—beside Allan—who is now on dry land.

He moves toward the wall of water and sees Kali on the other side. She dances and gestures, calling him home. Unafraid, he walks through the water wall which envelops him like a sheet of plastic wrap. It molds itself to his body, thickens, then hardens; becoming solid ice. Allan struggles to escape until the ice finally explodes outward and he is free.

On the floating stage, Allan lay dead still. His eyes were open wide and staring, a look of euphoria on his face. He took a deep breath, held it, and then tensed in an orgasmic moment.

In a sunlit room within Allan's mind, a voluptuous young woman lays her head on his chest. She's out of breath and smells of sex. The room is by the sea, but the details of the location, and the girl, are unknown to Allan. This memory is not his own, but somehow feels right. The girl kisses him and says, "I'll love you forever."

Allan whispers back, "And I'll love you," in the professor's voice.

The girl stands away from the rumpled bed sheets and goes to the open French windows. She is more beautiful than any master's painting. The sea breeze carries her salty scent back to Allan as she wraps a towel around her head to absorb the sea water, leaving her body nude and glistening in the sunlight. Allan's eyes caress her body and then drift to the swimsuits draped haphazardly over the balcony, drying in the sunshine. The girl smiles at him and he stands to join her, catching a glimpse of himself in the dressing table mirror. He sees the face and body of the professor as a young man.

But when Allan looks back, in search of the girl, he finds instead an audience full of applauding scientists. Dressed and polished, he steps forward to accept the professor's award. The photographers' flashes fire and Allan remembers this pose—this moment—from the cover of one of the professor's magazines. After shaking the moderator's hand, he turns to exit.

Allan stared up blindly from the floating stage, his expression registering a bittersweet memory.

He sees Diti through a crowded Yale Alumni party. She sits quietly by Argus' side. Allan is confused by his own feelings mingled with those of the

*professor. He makes eye contact and she smiles at him. It is a soft, bright
smile that is proper on its surface, but hides a hint of something else. But
just as Allan thinks he might discover what is hidden—she catches herself
and averts her eyes. When Diti looks back, any potential attraction has been
set aside and replaced by cordiality. Allan feels the professor's sense of loss,
but then brightens as infatuation turns inward, into admiration ... and
something deeper.*

30

When Allan awoke, sixteen hours later, he was delirious. The
young woman who had played Kali sponged the sweat from his
body as she hummed to herself. Allan's mouth was dry and his
stomach churning.

Chief Tonga waited nearby, eating and smiling, knowing exactly
what Allan had just experienced. Allan tried to speak, but he was
too parched. The girl helped Allan drink. Finally, he found his
voice and said, "That was incredible. I was the professor. I felt what
he felt, I thought what he thought. I knew everything that he had
ever learned."

The chief said, "You still do. He lives inside you now."

Allan brushed a lock of matted hair from his eyes and quickly
realized that something was missing. He said, "My glasses ..." He
scanned the room, and when he found his glasses without having
them on—he leapt to his feet. "I can see! I mean—I can see *everything.*" He ran out the door.

Allan bounded into the professor's hut and hurried to the
knapsack. He tore through Professor Sumner's pack until he
found what he was looking for: a book. After a hurried, silent
prayer, Allan turned to page one and began to read easily for the
first time in his life. The act was effortless and his comprehension
was unmarred by swimming letters. As his eyes skipped across the
page, devouring the thoughts contained within as a starving man
might devour a loaf of bread, Allan began to weep. A few moments
later the chief appeared in the doorway. Allan looked up with the
bright eyes of a child and said, "I can read this."

The chief answered, "Now, you can do many things."

31

Allan put his shovel aside and pounded the simple wooden cross into the earthen mound that marked Professor Sumner's grave. He had locked himself away with the professor's books and thoughts for a week and had emerged into the sunlight both older and wiser.

Several Shantu watched from the bushes, fascinated by this odd ritual of putting the dead into the ground, as Allan touched the carved wood where he had inscribed the professor's name, along with a passage from Yeats which read;

> Cast a cold eye
> On life, on Death,
> Horseman, pass by!

Allan removed the battered eyeglasses from his pocket and placed them on the professor's grave like a vestigial limb onto a sacrificial altar.

———

After Allan had buried the professor's body, he locked himself up with his friend's books, and thoughts, for ten solid days. He read until his eyes and head ached, and his body screamed for sleep. Allan read the anthropological reference texts, which he found among Professor Sumner's clothes, from cover to cover twice. And he reread Professor Sumner's favorite volume of poetry so often that the pages began to come loose from the binding.

The professor already knew much of the information contained in the books, so Allan had inherited that legacy along with renewed sight and a greater sense of confidence. But it was just the simple act of reading—after all these years—that Allan cherished. In fact, Allan became so caught up in his reading frenzy that he read every single thing on the professor's knapsack—even down to the instructions on the dehydrated vegetarian lasagna and the labels on the clothes.

32

In the following weeks Allan devoted himself to the study of the Shantu. He scribbled notes as he watched them work together to build a new hut, as they shared stories around the fire, and congregated on the banks of the murky river that had witnessed his rebirth. He also observed sessions in which the soldiers were counseled by the children with wise eyes. Allan was even included in tribal council meetings where chosen children, and the few remaining elders, discussed the future of the tribe and the imminent war with the Binjee. He even tried to help Tonga with his English. It was the happiest and most intellectually rewarding time of Allan's life.

———————————

Then one evening Allan was summoned to Tonga's quarters. As he waited in the main room, Allan helped himself to the food that was always kept in abundant supply around the chief. Ever since the ceremony, Allan had developed a voracious appetite. He heard a woman whimper as he chewed.

Allan looked toward the bedroom and noticed a gap between the beaded curtains. Another whimper followed, this time of a higher pitch, and Allan saw shifting shapes in the dark. A rhythmic thumping and the sounds of skin against skin began to fill the room and raise Allan's temperature. He cleared his throat in an attempt to make his presence known but the only responses were a giggle and a moan. Allan looked away and tried to occupy his mind, but the sounds of sex kept calling him back. He was having a hard time deciding whether to leave, or take a closer look.

Opting for the latter, he moved quietly toward the gap in the curtains. Was this what the chief had intended? Allan peered through the opening, into the bedroom, and his mouth went dry. Tonga knelt on the bed behind a buxom girl, pumping away while an older woman devoured the sweat that ran down his back and buttocks as if he was the Fountain of Youth. A third woman lay on her back with the first girl's face buried between her legs, whimpering. The girl on all fours began to make a high-pitched whining sound that grew louder as the chief moved faster. Then the girl shuddered and screamed into the other woman's crotch. The chief grunted like a rooting pig and continued to drive into her. Gradually, the screams turned to shrieks, and then evolved into a prolonged, breathless wheeze. The girl's body went limp and she collapsed face down onto the bed. But the chief wasn't satisfied. He moved between the legs of the girl on her back.

Allan watched in amazement as the chief revisited each of the three women twice more, climaxing three times in two hours of non-stop intercourse. When Tonga finally emerged from the bed chamber, his naked body was drenched with sweat and he was still erect. The chief took a seat opposite Allan and began to eat. Allan averted his eyes. He was spent after merely *watching* the coital acrobatics. He said, "That was some show."

"With each smoke come strength." The chief tapped his head with a long, brown fingernail. "In here ..." He thumped his chest. "... here ..." He grasped his still-raging hard-on proudly. "And *here*." Allan reached for an animal skin blanket and tossed it across the chief's lap. Tonga laughed at his modesty as the women began to file out of the bedroom. Allan noticed that their eyes were lowered and their expressions contented. But the contentment appeared to be more spiritual than physical. It was if they'd just returned from church after accepting communion.

The chief stopped the most attractive of the three girls. He cupped her chin in his hand, turned her face toward Allan, and asked, "You like?"

The blood rushed to Allan's cheeks. He addressed the girl directly. "You're very pretty."

"See. Good." The chief pulled the girl's robe aside, revealing her breasts. He said, "You take—yes?"

Allan pulled his eyes away from the girl's body. "No. Thank you."

"She like you. Look."

Allan looked into the girl's face and saw a hospitable smile. He said, "Let her go home to her family." The chief waved the girls away and returned to his food. Allan was suddenly angry. He asked,

"What was this all about?" The chief looked perplexed. Allan over enunciated, "Why did you bring me here?"

The chief answered with his mouth full, "I teach you."

"Teach me. Teach me what?"

"To be a man. And the ways of the goddess."

Just as Allan was about to respond, a group of Shantu soldiers burst into the room. The news wasn't good. Tonga grabbed his robe on the way out the door.

———

When the chief and Allan arrived at the hut of the little Down syndrome child, a crowd had already begun to gather. The entire family had been murdered. The chief scolded the soldiers and stormed into the hut. He rolled the corpse of the household's patriarch onto its stomach. Allan watched as chief Tonga placed his foot in the small of the dead man's back and dislodged a long hunting arrow. He examined the chiseled obsidian tip. "Binjee," he sighed, suddenly very tired.

33

Manhattan, June 1975.

As Argus emerged from the subway station to join the Times Square foot traffic, he concluded that prostitutes and sorority girls had a lot in common.

They tended to hang out in groups.

They dressed alike.

And they were always eager to share the latest gossip.

Argus had discovered the latter similarity the hard way when he'd first moved to New York from D.C. and tried to hire a call girl from an exclusive escort agency. The owner of the agency had been enthusiastic over the phone as Argus explained his interest in regular visits from two or three of the agency's top girls. But when the madam pressed for specifics relating to the tasks her girls would be asked to perform, and Argus told her—the phone interview was abruptly ended. Argus called back, but the madam dodged him. When he called the other top flight agencies in town, the response was the same. The hooker in D.C. had apparently put the word out, and now Argus was a sexual pariah.

At first he considered giving up working girls completely and limiting himself to the awkward couplings with Diti that required his violent fantasies as aphrodisiacs. But after a few lackluster performances and the sadness they brought his eager young wife, Argus grudgingly accepted his sexual fate.

He could use the escort girls for standard kink as long as he gave a phony name, but if he wanted to get rough—or play his favorite game—Argus had to come here, to the streets, where the night was well-stocked with fresh faces and short memories.

The primary sacrifices of slumming for sex were education and hygiene. Argus often had to force the streetwalkers to bathe before he could touch them. And their fingernails usually had so much grime and God-knows-what caked beneath them that the only quick solution was a fresh coat of nail polish. Argus always brought a bottle along for just such occasions. But the street walkers all had breasts and legs and asses, just like the high-priced whores, though they weren't as tanned or toned as their cultured counterparts. And the occasional bruises and fat lips didn't seem to faze the street hookers, as long as Argus paid for his violent pleasures.

Over the years Argus had achieved an odd version of contentment. He worked toward partnership during the day at the law firm that had taken him on after his early retirement from the military—capitalizing on his knack for hostile corporate takeovers. Then, two or three nights a week he would cruise the square for a new girl to play his game. And finally—he would come home to the woman he loved, to play the good husband, even managing a perfunctory round of marital sex every few weeks. It wasn't idyllic, but it paid the bills, supplied his sexual habit, and kept the dark dreams to a minimum.

But Diti was having dreams of her own: disturbing visions of her husband's future that she dismissed as imagination, rather than prophecy. She had become withdrawn since the move to New York, though Argus barely noticed. What he chose to perceive as quiet contentment was actually Diti's heroic efforts to mask the pain. At first it was the pain of loneliness and disappointment, but later—after Argus had unknowingly brought home a severe case of syphilis—the pain was physical.

Argus had a brief bout of VD in Vietnam, so when he felt the familiar burning—he visited a doctor immediately. He never even considered that he might have infected Diti. After all, they had sex so infrequently. An injection, two rounds of antibiotics, and the whole thing was forgotten, though Argus did become a little more selective in his choice of sexual playmates.

But Diti had no idea what was happening to her body, and wasn't about to burden Argus with her worsening condition over the months that followed. In her father's palace she had been sheltered from any knowledge of sex or its consequences. So she interpreted and embraced this pain as a penance for her failures as a wife. On a subconscious level, Diti believed the unnamed illness to be a purifying fire that would devour her fears and weaknesses, strengthening her for the battle to save her troubled husband's soul.

Argus had absolutely no idea, trolling Times Square that night, that Professor Sumner had joined Diti for tea. And he didn't know that she had finally revealed her pain to her friend at the very moment that Argus had approached a young girl in shredded jeans and whispered his own dark secrets. He had no way of knowing that Diti had collapsed in the kitchen while pouring the tea. Or that she had been rushed to the hospital and into intensive care around the time he was bathing and powdering his young prostitute in preparation for the game. And he had no clue that his own wife lay motionless on starched white linens while he arranged his "corpse for hire" on a sagging cot, rented by the hour, and readied his erection.

———

Four hours later, Argus listened to the doctors' news in silence. Even if Diti regained consciousness, she would never walk again, there would be no children, and she would probably be blind. Argus knew the surgeon was judging him, just as Colonel Bryant had, even though nothing in the doctor's tone revealed his contempt. But the surgeon's stare was hard and merciless as he described in agonizing detail all that Argus' infidelity had put Diti through. And when Argus' eyes welled up with guilty tears—there was a faint look of satisfaction on the doctor's face.

34

After avoiding the chief for days, Allan had finally made his decision. He had learned all he could from the Shantu. But Allan wasn't sure how Tonga would react. He had taken a liking to Allan. Or was it something else?

Allan asked for the chief and was directed to an overgrown path which led out of the Shantu village and up the mountainside. An hour later he reached the secluded cave that lay halfway to the top. Allan was fascinated by the grotto, which was filled with drums of all shapes and sizes. Intricate, handmade carvings and orna-ments made of animals' bones adorned each unique instrument. The drums' skins were very delicate, almost translucent. Most were dry and cracked like ancient parchment.

Allan had spotted several dozen sleeping bats hanging from the ceiling in the darkest corner of the cave when he entered. He had also sensed something else: a very subtle sound, like a whisper. Allan heard a noise behind him and turned—startled.

The chief said, "This is House of Drums. Where the old ones sleep—from the time before the Great Man." The chief picked up one of the drums, taking care not to damage the fragile bone frame. "When someone die his people make drum from bones and use skin—for here, and here." The chief indicated the tightly stretched skins at the top and bottom of the instru-ment. Tonga blotted the moisture from his forehead with the sleeve of his robe and pointed out a funereal urn. "Other parts go there—after fire. When afraid, or not knowing, we came to this place to ask our old ones what to do." He thumped the head of the drum gently and listened. "They answered with the sounds—to help us know what is right." The chief walked deeper into the cave. "But that was before ..." The chief's voice trailed off, and when he turned back to Allan he looked neither fierce, nor powerful. Just tired. He gently returned the drum to its rightful place.

Allan had noticed that in the month since his arrival, the Chief's hair had almost grown back down to his knees. And his nails had grown back, too. Allan wanted to ask Tonga about it, but was afraid to hear the response—because Allan thought he had detected a slight acceleration in his own nail and hair growth since that night on the floating stage. But then again, maybe it was just his imagination.

Today Tonga looked haggard. The youth that he had acquired after the ritual had begun to fade. That day he had looked powerful and fierce, but now he carried himself like a middle-aged man with the weight of the world on his shoulders.

Tonga said, "I been wait a long time, boy. But I knew you would come."

"How?"

"How did you know not to drink from the cup?"

Allan spoke gently: "Then you also knew that there would come a time that I would leave."

The chief would have been surprised—would have been angry, but he was just too tired. He said, "*That* I did not know."

"Then you don't know everything."

The chief walked even farther into the cave, waving off Allan's comment. "With all the voices—it is hard. You will see."

Allan followed Tonga. "That first day—you looked into my friend's eyes and you saw something."

"I saw his smoke. It wanted to leave."

"And what did you see in my eyes?"

The chief stopped and turned to face Allan. He almost looked proud. "I saw a great flame. You are strong, boy. You are from me."

"And what do you see now—in my eyes?"

The chief looked into Allan's eyes for a moment, and then shrugged. "I see smoke, but is not the same without The Sight." He sat on a rocky ledge to rest. "Your people had magic—like mine. We see what others do not." He sighed, "And now we serve Kali together." The chief retrieved a stray tibia from a nearby drum that had crumbled and drew a dot in the dirt. He then scratched a circle around the dot and marked an "X" on the upper edge of the drawing, at the twelve o'clock position.

Allan said, "We serve her—how?"

Tonga tapped the "X" with the bone. "She will give you the hunger." Tonga drew another mark at the three o'clock position. "And she will give you the sight." He marked a third "X" at the six o'clock position.

"And what's that supposed to be?"

"The sacrifice that you will give her."

Allan stood back. "Look, you don't understand. I'm not going to make any sacrifices—"

"You *have.*" He brought the jagged tip if the leg bone down on the dot at the center of his circle. "*Your friend.* When you took the goddess as your mother."

"I did not—" Allan began to pace. "Look, I could never do that again. I still can't believe I did it *once.*"

Chief Tonga smiled sadly and marked the final "X" at the nine o'clock position on the circle.

Allan was very nervous now. He said, "Okay—tell me."

The chief tapped the final mark and said, "You are reborn."

Allan laughed. "You mean—like a baby? Like reincarnation?" But then he remembered the chief's transformation and moaned, "Oh, my God." He thought about it for a moment and finally concluded, in a small voice, "I'm really fucked—aren't I?"

Tonga didn't know the word, but he certainly knew the feeling. He drew lines outward from the dot in the center of the circle which connected with each of the four marks. The chief spoke slowly and carefully, as if to a child: "You will hunger. You will have the sight. You will sacrifice to Ma Kali. You will be reborn."

"And then what?" Allan felt trapped and desperate as he watched Tonga retrace the circle with the bone of his ancestor over and over again. Allan looked down at the drawing and whispered, "Like the spokes of a wheel ..." Tonga watched as the boy turned what he had been told over in his mind. Finally, Alan shook his head sharply and barked out a hollow laugh. "Uh-uh. No way." He erased the circle in the dirt with his foot. "I'm sorry, but I don't accept this." Allan sulked away and leaned against the cold stone wall of the cave.

After a moment, Tonga approached Allan and said, "There is no hiding, boy. You are The One."

"The one? The one for what?"

"To lead my people."

Suddenly it all made sense to Allan. His inclusion in tribal meetings, the gifts and attention—even the revelation of the ritual itself. Tonga had been grooming him to be his successor. Allan asked, "You want me to replace *you?*"

"I gave you the magic. Now you must give to me." Allan was speechless. The chief's mood turned dark and his tone became threatening. "Boy, if you will not give—I can *take.* I will put my smoke into your body and it will be mine."

Allan said, "You'd have a new body, but you'd also have another voice to fight." Allan wanted to back away, but he held his ground. He met the chief's eyes. "And I'd *never* stop fighting."

Tonga sighed and said, "Yes, you are strong. Stronger than you know." He changed his tack to seduction, speaking softly: "With the things I know and the things the Great Man and Old Chief know—with all this—and with what you and your friend know ... We would know much. We would be *very strong,* boy."

Allan wondered what it would be like to command such wisdom. The thought was exhilarating and terrifying. But finally he answered, as if to a question he had asked himself, "No. I couldn't kill like you do."

"You did. You *will.* Kali is your mother now, and her hunger grows in you." The chief's tone turned melancholy. "And she never let you go, boy." Allan touched the delicate skin of a large, slender drum as he considered his future. The chief said, "The lost souls need a place." The hiss of the chief's voice was like the devil whispering in Allan's ear: "*We* are the place, boy. You and Tonga are the same now. We are the House of Drums."

"I'm sorry." Allan backed away slowly, wondering if he could outrun the chief—if it came to that. "I don't belong here."

The chief chose to ignore Allan, instead focusing on another drum. He said, "This is my grandfather. His people came to this mountain–"

Allan moved to leave and the chief turned on him, eyes burning, but then seemed to soften as another, gentler personality claimed dominance over his body. For a brief moment Allan thought he caught a glimpse of his great-grandfather in the chief's pained expression. Then Tonga resurfaced, and turned away, defeated. He said, "We don't belong anywhere, boy. Not now."

Allan hurried from the cave without a backward glance. Tonga stopped to consider his situation and found himself at a loss for the first time in his long life. Finally, he approached the drum of his grandfather, thumped it softly, and listened ...

35

Darkness had blanketed the Shantu village by the time Allan found his way back. He had never thought to question the sense of urgency that had overtaken him on the return trek from the caves, when he suddenly felt the need to *run*—not walk. Allan's heart was racing and sweat ran in rivulets down his face and back as he ducked inside his hut like a man pursued by demons. Allan took off the Shantu tunic and snatched a shirt and a pair of shorts from Professor Sumner's bag. He had to cinch the belt to its minimum circumference to keep the shorts from falling around his knees. Allan picked up the smashed DVD camcorder and pressed the eject button. Nothing happened. He mashed the button again—then forced open the plastic panel that protected the recordable media. Allan plucked the mini DVD from the ruined camera and stuffed the undamaged silver disc, the other DVD-Rs that he had used to document the Shantu, his journal and notes—into one of the plastic insulation bags. A final glance around the hut—and Allan was out the door. In light of the new desperation that had gripped Allan, hitching a ride on the river suddenly didn't sound so bad.

Allan stopped at the professor's grave and knelt at the make-shift marker. His glasses had been partially buried by wind blown dust and weeds. Allan dug them up and placed them in their right-ful place atop the mound. He heard a noise from the trees but before he could turn, the girl in the Kali mask was upon him. She slashed Allan's shirt—her knife a silver flash in the moonlight—and she tore at him with her hands while biting his flesh with her teeth.

The crazed Shantu knocked Allan onto his back. He caught her wrist as she swung the dagger down, and they wrestled until she finally regained the advantage and straddled Allan. The girl grimaced beneath her mask as she used every bit of strength to force the blade down toward Allan's chest. But then there was a sound—like a breath exhaled too quickly—and the girl dropped her knife and began to writhe atop Allan, clawing at the sky and screaming like a banshee, before collapsing bonelessly atop her intended victim. Allan pushed the dead girl away and saw the arrow in her back. He grabbed his bag, leapt to his feet, and hurried into the jungle: running with speed and grace that was new to him.

A moment later three Binjee warriors moved into the clearing. One started off after Allan, but the group leader stopped him, motioning in the opposite direction, toward the Shantu village.

———

Two days later a very rough and ragged Allan shook François Tubere's hand and happily boarded the Cessna from hell. As Frank slammed the hatch shut, Allan thought he saw a distant trail of smoke rising from general location of the Shantu camp.

36

The Binjee had done everything in their power to erase the memory of the Shantu from the world. The village had been burned to the ground, every last man, woman and child had been slaughtered, and the house of drums had been sealed forever with large stones and mud. No one would be allowed to live or hunt in the territory that had once belonged to the Shantu, and the Binjee chief would proclaim that his people were never again to speak their name aloud for fear of conjuring evil spirits. But the Binjee children would still dream about the Shantu, and when they grew, their children's children would tell tales of "the witches" around secret campfires.

The place where the Shantu encampment once stood was littered with bodies, which had been left out in the open for the animals. Other than the occasional crackle of a dying ember, the only sound was that of the wind rustling the clothes of the dead. Chief Tonga had been crucified on a post at the center of the village so that he could watch his people die. He hadn't uttered a sound during the death and destruction—and his stoic silence had only served to bolster the enemy tribe's belief that he was not human. In fact, the Binjee warriors had thrown stones at Tonga and had jabbed him with their spears—just to see if he would cry out. But they never looked into his eyes.

The Binjee had left those eyes for the vultures. And now Tonga stared blindly off into the distance, his head cocked at an unnatural angle, still awaiting an answer from the drums.

Part III

Karma

37

Washington, D.C., July 4, 1976.

As the nation celebrated its second century of independence, Diti readied herself for a different type of ritual. She had begged Argus to return to D.C. for the bicentennial, hoping to recapture the happiness they had once shared there—even if it was only for a weekend.

They had checked into a suite in their favorite hotel and dined at a chic new restaurant. To Diti's surprise and delight, laughter seemed to come easily that night. Usually Argus' guilt cast a long shadow over their time together, but that night he seemed able to see past the tragedy of this beautiful and vibrant twenty-three-year-old woman who had been crippled by his infidelity.

In the restaurant they held hands and talked about the future, just like any other young couple. After dinner, they ventured out into the night to take in the festivities. Argus even managed a playful wisecrack when he had to push Diti's wheelchair up a steep incline to get a better view of the spectacular fireworks display. And there were no unexpected ambushes of painful memories or unwelcome reunions with people from the past to mar their good time. In short, it was a perfect evening.

But the good time came to an abrupt halt when Diti asked Argus if they might make love that night. Since the doctors had pronounced Diti barren, and her paralysis prevented any sensation below the waist, sexual intimacy between the Steeles had pretty much been forgotten. Not because the doctors forbade it, or because Diti requested it. It had been Argus' choice. His excuse was fear of worsening her condition, but in truth he was relieved. It had always been difficult for him to make love to Diti. Now, he no longer had to try.

In fact, despite her feelings of loss and disappointment, Diti had given Argus permission to find sexual satisfaction elsewhere. She said that she realized that men had needs and that she could no longer perform her marital "duties," so Argus was free to take a lover, though Diti didn't want to know the details. At first, Argus accepted her permission as a windfall. He thought now he could pursue his dark desires with impunity. But the reality was that Diti's saintly understanding and forgiveness had only served to strip the eroticism from Argus' infidelities, while simultaneously increasing his torturous feelings of guilt. Diti had asked only one thing in return for Argus' sexual freedom."What did you say? I couldn't hear you?"

Diti spoke louder to be heard over the fireworks. "I SAID—I WANT YOU TO MAKE LOVE TO ME!"

Argus heard that time, as did a few other people in the vicinity. He was the only one that wasn't amused. He said, "Honey ..." Diti saw the look on his face and knew what he was about to say. Frustrated, she turned her wheelchair around and moved away through the crowd. Argus followed, calling, "Where are you going?"

Diti fought back tears as she wheeled her way through the bustling crowd. "I want a baby."

"You know that's not going to happen." He took control of the chair, but she continued to struggle. "Why do you do this to yourself?"

"You promised we could still try, but we never do. They could all be wrong."

Argus started to say something cruel, but stopped himself. Instead he said, "Okay."

She reached back to touch his hand. "Okay ... what?"

"We can try."

Diti pulled Argus down and hugged him fiercely. She said, "I'm sorry. I just have to try. It's all I have left to hope for."

———

Three months later Argus had rushed Diti to the hospital, despite her reassurances. After five long hours of tests and scans, the doctor emerged with the worst news imaginable. At least for *Argus*. He asked, "Is it a tumor?"

The doctor paced and smoothed his thinning hair. "No, it's not a tumor."

Diti closed her eyes. Tears were streaming down her face. Argus gripped her hand tighter and said, "Then ... What is it?"

The doctor sat and looked Argus square in the eye. He said, "It's a baby."

"A ..." Argus looked to Diti, who had been smiling through her tears ever since the doctor entered the room. "A baby? That's not possible." Argus' head was spinning. "But they told us ... They told us ..."

The doctor shook his head in disbelief. "I know what they told you, what *I* told you, and by all accounts we should've been right. Her ovaries are severely damaged, her fallopian tubes are almost completely blocked by scar tissue, and her body has stopped producing estrogen. But the fact remains—Diti is pregnant. And, with a few precautions and an increase in her hormone injections, I see no reason she can't bring the baby to term. If that's what you both want."

Diti was laughing and crying and squeezing Argus' hand so tightly that his fingertips were turning white. She cried, "Of course we want the baby!"

"I must warn you—there is a very real risk of birth defect."

"I don't care." She brought Argus' hand to her heart and held it close. "We don't care about anything but having this baby—in whatever condition God sees fit to give him to us."

The doctor and Diti discussed her miraculous condition, and the horrifying list of the possible birth defects that could result from the damage to her nervous system, for over an hour as Argus stared at the wall, stunned. Diti pronounced this child a gift from God, the answer to her nightly prayers. And the doctor, though not a religious man himself, seemed to offer no better explanation.

But Argus knew what this child was. A gift from God? No, far from it. This child, this *thing*, was a curse: a punishment for Argus' sins—an avenging angel that was in fact sent by God to torment, and ultimately destroy him.

38

"Sir?"

Argus didn't respond.

"Excuse me—Sir?" Argus emerged from the memory of that moment in the doctor's office and found himself standing at the counter of the Waldorf Astoria's coat check room. The perky attendant was smiling at him. She said, "May I take your coat?"

Argus slipped out of his topcoat and handed it to the girl. He asked, "What time is it?"

The girl hung Argus' coat and handed him a ticket as she checked the clock. "Nine o'clock, Sir."

Argus surveyed the crowd in the Waldorf's cocktail lounge and spotted a striking, light-skinned black woman sitting alone at a table in the far corner. He crossed the room as piano music and idle chatter mixed, creating a pleasantly frenetic atmosphere. Argus sat at the stranger's table, uninvited, and said, "Kendra?" The leggy young lady ignored Argus. She just sat there smoking her thin cigarette, looking incredible. Argus studied her for a moment longer and actually began to feel a little intimidated. He fingered the glass ash tray at the center of the table and said, "I'm sorry. I was supposed to meet a friend here."

The stranger took a deep drag of her cigarette as her sea green eyes assessed Argus with cool disinterest. Then she exhaled the smoke into Argus' face, ground the burning butt of her cigarette out into the back of his hand, and said, "I'm Kendra. Let's go." Argus winced and watched, stunned, as Kendra stood, smoothed her skirt and walked toward the registration desk without a backward glance. After Argus got over the initial shock and pain—he smiled.

39

Kendra watched Argus untie her limbs from the bedposts. Once free, she got up and extracted a pale pink silk robe from her crocodile bag. As she slipped into it, the clingy fabric outlined the curves of her well-toned body.

Argus reclined on the bed, enjoying the view. He smiled to himself, thinking that this whore's skin was the color of café latté, and said, "Sorry if I got a little too rough. Can you forgive me?"

Kendra smiled and said, "No," then walked away, adding: "Next time it's *my* turn."

Argus laughed, exhausted. Kendra stepped into the bathroom and closed the door. Argus couldn't remember the last time he'd found so much pleasure in a woman's walk—or in the relatively "straight" sex he had just purchased. Kendra hadn't even allowed him to shave her, which was usually a condition of employment for which Argus often paid dearly. But that was all right—this time— because she'd been good. Very good.

Kendra washed her face and hands with soap and very hot water for a long time before burying her face in the plush towel that bore the hotel's monogram. Then she lit up a cigarette and inhaled deeply. Her hands were trembling. She let the silk robe fall to the cool tile floor and avoided her own reflection in the mirror. After taking a moment to pull herself together, Kendra stepped into the shower, turned on the water and began to scrub her body viciously.

Argus listened to the soothing sounds of running water. He stretched and sat on the edge of the bed, then noticed that Kendra had forgotten her purse. Unusual for a working girl, he thought. But then again, this one was anything but usual. Argus picked up the purse and began to rummage through, smiling to himself. Perhaps she might be willing to play the game.

40

Jon, Ellen Chonce's perfectly-coifed assistant, checked Allan out as he stepped from the elevator and set the professor's suitcase aside. Allan's wavy black hair had grown shaggy and wild during his trip—and his skin had tanned to a golden brown. The assistant let his eyes wander down Allan's body as he wrapped up a phone call and Allan approached the desk. Jon said, "Jane, I *promise* you, I will get Ellen to look over the changes as soon as she gets back from lunch. Don't worry. I'm sure they're fine." He smiled at Allan and rolled his eyes as the writer on the phone droned on. "Okay ... okay ... No, Jane—honestly, we're all very excited about it. Gotta go Sweetie. Okay. Ciao." The assistant punched a button, removed his headset, and groaned, "God save me from virgins."

"I guess that would include me."

"Now, *you* don't look like you'd be any trouble at all." Allan smiled awkwardly and looked away, not quite sure how to respond to the off-color double entendre. The assistant cooed, "Oh look—he's blushing. How *adorable.*"

"I had an appointment with Ms. Chonce. My name is Allan Steele."

"Sorry, Sweetie—Ellen won't be back for another hour. Her lunch ran long. But you're welcome to wait—right over there, where I can keep my eye on you."

"Oh. I guess I could just leave this with you." Allan placed his manuscript on the desk. "I just got in from Connecticut. I've been typing for a week straight. I hope everything is okay."

Jon hefted the eight-hundred page manuscript in his hands, but his flirtatious gaze was trained on Allan when he cocked an expertly-shaped eyebrow and cooed: "Oooh ... It's so *big!* You must be very proud."

Allan laughed uncomfortably and said, "The credit really belongs to Professor Sumner. I couldn't have done it without him."

Jon suddenly dropped the licentious come-on and did an almost comic double take, as if seeing Allan for the fist time. "Oh, *you're* the one who went to Africa with the professor. He was a real kick. Ellen was so upset after you called. To die alone like that—in the middle of some God-forsaken jungle. How *horrible.*"

Allan bristled, insisting, "He wasn't *alone.* I was there."

"And thank God you made it back to us safe and sound. It's great that you were able to finish his work. I'm sure he would be pleased."

"He is." Allan reconsidered his wording. "I mean—yes, he would be." Allan headed for the elevator.

"Allan—you didn't put a contact number on here."

"I'm not sure where I'm staying. I'll call as soon as I know."

Jon began to flip through the pages of the manuscript. "I still can't believe you made a trip like this all by yourselves. How did you manage?"

Allan collected his bag and pushed the call button for the elevator. "Oh, well—you know how it is. We just kept our peckers up." Jon smiled and said, "I like the sound of that."

41

Argus walked Detectives McCrae and Lucci, out of his office and into the reception area where Allan had been waiting for the last twenty minutes. McCrae was a lanky African-American with a quick wit, a sharp gaze and a handsome, easy smile. Lucci was his opposite: short and gruff with a disinterested demeanor that masked an acute eye for detail. McCrae offered his hand and to Argus and said, "Sorry we had to bother you again, Mr. Steele. We just needed verification on those gray areas so we could close the file."

Argus said, "Did you reach James?"

"Yes we did. Mr. Wilmington confirmed your meeting on the day of the accident. Thanks again for your cooperation. We know this must be a hard time for you."

Argus shook McCrae's hand and adopted a sober tone. "It's just so painful—going through the whole thing again. You understand."

"I do, and we're truly sorry for your loss."

Lucci added, "We have to check out all fatal accidents, especially falls, as if they were potential homicides. Just procedure. Nothing personal."

Allan, who had been watching from a distance, approached, and Argus was taken aback by his son's new look. Allan said, "Do you need to talk to me?" McCrae turned toward Allan. "I'm her son."

McCrae and his partner exchanged a look and Lucci referred to her notes. She said, "You were out of state—New Mexico—at the time of the accident, right? Then out of the country for a while after that?"

"Yes. I just returned last week. I've been at a friend's house in Massachusetts since then. I came into the city today to meet with his editor."

The elevator doors on the other side of the reception area opened and Douglas Geffner emerged. He approached the group, but kept a respectful distance.

Lucci closed her notepad, looked at McCrae and shrugged. "I don't have any questions for him. Do you?"

"No." McCrae addressed Allan: "Not unless you've got anything that you think is pertinent."

Allan thought, *Pertinent? I've got dreams, hunches and a real bad feeling, but I doubt a cop would consider any of that pertinent.* Then he looked at Argus, who was staring into his eyes as if he knew what he was thinking. It was almost as if he was daring him to say something, but surely that was Allan's imagination. Finally, Allan said, "No, I guess not," and then noticed that now everyone was staring at him. He said, "I'm sorry—I'm still a little scattered. It's been a hard couple of months."

McCrae handed Allan a business card and said, "No problem. Give us a call if you think of anything." He addressed Argus: "Again, sorry for the intrusion." Lucci and McCrae nodded goodbye and passed Douglas on the way to the elevator.

Argus said, "Come on in," and led Allan into his office.

As Argus and Allan passed, Miss Pearl, Argus' secretary, looked up from her paperwork and said to Douglas, "Mr. Geffner, I've told you *several times* now that Mr. Steele's calendar is full—"

Douglas ignored her and followed Argus and Allan toward the office. "I just wanted to ask Mr. Steele a few quick questions. It'll only take a second."

Miss Pearl stood to block his path and said, "Mr. Steele is not interested in additional life insurance."

Argus moved to close his door and Douglas answered loudly, "It's not about additional life insurance—it's about the *existing policy* on his wife. I've been trying to get an appointment for six weeks now. Is there some reason that Mr. Steele is dodging my calls?"

Argus didn't turn, but he knew that Allan had heard the old man. He said, "Fine, come in. But this will have to be brief. My son and I have a lot of catching up to do."

Miss Pearl stepped aside and Douglas entered the office. He approached Allan and extended his hand. "My name is Douglas Geffner. I'm sorry about your mother."

Allan accepted Douglas' hand and said, "Allan Steele. Thank you."

Douglas sensed something odd about the young man's handshake, but it wasn't until later that he figured it out: his palm was very hot, as if he was running a fever.

Argus took his place behind his massive stone desk and said, "What's your question, Mr. Geffner?"

"Like I said, it's about your wife's policy. The accident was well over a month ago, but you haven't filed a claim yet."

Argus was having a hard time disguising his irritation. He said, "They sent you out here to encourage me to file a claim?"

"Oh, no. In fact my grandson, he owns the brokerage that purchased your account, doesn't even know I'm here." Douglas sat and placed his briefcase on his knees to open it. "You see, I was helping him get his files organized, and I ran across yours. I had seen your wife's obituary in the newspaper, so it rang a bell. To be honest, I couldn't place the name for a while and it was driving me crazy–"

"Do you have a question or not, Mr. Geffner?"

Douglas extracted the file from his briefcase. "Yes. I did a little research—an amazing story by the way, how you and your wife met—and something just doesn't make sense."

"Get to the point, Mr. Geffner."

"I checked your building's maintenance records. Boy, they really do things right over there, don't they? You see, that railing was repaired just two months ago."

Allan was suddenly very interested in what Douglas Geffner had to say.

Argus said, "So?"

"So, it was *already* loose again? Loose enough to fall away at the touch of a hand?"

"Apparently."

Geffner seemed troubled. "I don't know. It just doesn't sound right to me."

Allan asked, "What are you saying, Mr. Geffner?"

"Was your mother unusually depressed lately? I mean, with her health problems it must have been really hard on her."

Argus said to Allan, "He's asking if you think it was suicide, so that his grandson doesn't have to pay. Right, Mr. Geffner."

Douglas didn't answer.

Allan said, "My mother was the most positive person I have ever known. If you're asking if she could have killed herself, the answer is no. Absolutely not."

Argus added, "Frankly, Mr. Geffner, I think you've got a lot of nerve coming here and suggesting—"

Allan added, "But she did send me a letter."

Argus was caught off guard. "She sent a letter?"

Geffner asked, "And the subject of this letter was?"

Allan considered his answer as he studied his father's face, sensing something urgent behind the puzzled expression. Finally, Allan said, "It was about her death."

Argus asked, "Why didn't I know about this?"

Allan faced his father with his new confidence and said, "She sent it to *me*, not you."

Geffner watched the tension build between father and son, and he knew that he had stumbled onto something strange. He asked, "Did she say anything that might be helpful?"

"Just that I shouldn't blame my father." There was a long silence as Douglas considered his next move. When he closed his file and stood to leave, Allan turned away from his father to say, "I'm not sure what it meant, though. I guess the timing could have been a coincidence."

Douglas answered, "I'm not a big believer in coincidences, myself."

Allan answered, "Neither am I, Mr. Geffner. May I see that file?"

Geffner handed it to him and said, "Of course. You *are* the beneficiary."

It was obvious by the look on Allan's face that this was news to him. Allan accepted the file and looked through it as another uncomfortable silence settled over the room. Argus shuffled papers on his desk and checked his watch twice while Geffner surveyed the office: oversized furnishings, morbid art, framed medals of valor beside a black and white photo of Argus and his troops in Vietnam—and a tension between father and son that could be cut with a knife. Perhaps Arthur was right; there *was* a mystery here after all.

Allan said, "Thank you," and closed the file, then returned it to Geffner.

Geffner said, "Again, I'm very sorry about your mother." To Argus: "And I'm sorry to have upset you, Mr. Steele."

Argus did not to respond to the subtle accusation. He said, "Goodbye Mr. Geffner," and followed Douglas to the door. When Douglas had gone, Argus returned his attention to Allan. Argus said, "You look different. And you're not wearing your glasses."

"I don't need them anymore."

"Don't need them? Since when?"

"I got contacts."

"They don't make contacts that can correct–"

"Look, I don't know how they did it." Allan paced. "They just did."

"*They?*" Allan had never been a good liar, but Argus decided to let it slide. He studied Allan for a moment longer, as if seeing his son for the first time. Argus said, "I can't get over it. You look so different."

"I think I'll be in town for a while. Until the book's ready to go to print." Allan was thinking aloud now: "I have a line on an apartment I can afford, but the old renters aren't out yet. I dumped my bags in a hotel this morning on my way in from the airport, but I can't afford to stay there long."

Argus said, "You'll stay at the apartment. Problem solved."

The thought of seeing Argus every day without Diti as a buffer made Allan nauseous. He said, "Thanks, but I'd just be in the way. I'll find a cheaper hotel. "It'll only be for–"

"Allan, stop this foolishness." Something was definitely going on with Allan, and Argus was determined to get to the bottom of it. He said, "I'm out of town so much these days, you'd practically have the place to yourself. Besides, affordable apartments in the city are impossible to find. If you've found one ..."

Allan was trapped and he didn't like the feeling. He tried for a smile and mumbled, "Okay. Thanks. It won't be for long."

Another uncomfortable silence settled in. Argus watched his son fidget and stare out the window. He said, "How did it go with John's editor?"

"She wasn't there, but I left the manuscript."

"John would be pleased that you were able to piece all of his work together." Argus joined Allan at the window. "Your mother would be proud, Allan. And I'm proud, too." The last words stuck in Argus' throat like a rancid chunk of meat. "I didn't think you had it in you."

Allan looked at his father without fear for the first time in his life and said, "You'd be amazed by what's in me." He started for the door. "I guess I'll see you later."

"Okay. See you later." Argus' smile faltered as the door closed. Allan was up to something. Perhaps God's little messenger had toyed with him long enough and was finally ready to finish the job. Diti's miracle had always been Argus' thorn in the side, and he was sick and tired of it—and him. Argus grabbed the phone and dialed. After a moment, he said, "It's Argus Steele. Send Kendra." He didn't like the response and barked, "All right then, tomorrow." Another bit of information irritated him even more. "When will she be back?" The person on the other end of the line had barely begun to speak when Argus slammed down the phone. He pushed away from his desk and moved to the window, fists and jaw clenched as he paced.

———

Miss Pearl caught Allan as he entered the elevator. She said, "Mr. Geffner left cards for you and Mr. Steele, in case you had any more questions about your mother's policy. He said he wrote his home number and address on the back—he doesn't spend much time at his grandson's office." Allan took the card from Miss Pearl. She said, "Allan, I'm really sorry about your mom."

Allan said, "Thanks," as the doors slid shut.

42

Allan wandered into the cafeteria of Saint Luke's Hospital. Chet waved and called out, "Hey, Allan!" and the two men hugged in the middle of the food line. "The great white hunter returns!" Chet was a second-year surgery resident who always looked like he was on the last leg of a forty-eight hour shift. He took a step back to get a better look at his old friend and said, "What'd you do to yourself, man?"

"Contacts." Allan smiled, and relaxed for the first time since his return. He said, "You look like crap."

Chet handed Allan a tray and continued through the line. He said, "I'm whipped." Chet took another look at Allan. "And you don't look so hot, yourself."

"Got a lot on my mind. Haven't been sleeping much." Allan piled food onto his tray. "I've been working on that idea I mentioned on the phone."

Chet watched Allan reach for a second entrée. "Hungry?"

"I don't know what's with my appetite lately. I eat and eat and never gain a pound. It's like I just can't get enough."

"Maybe something's up with your metabolism. You should get it checked out."

"You think?" Allan craned his neck, eager to see what food lay ahead. "Everything looks great."

Chet laughed as Allan tried to decide between another pot roast dinner or the meatloaf. He said, "They've got vegetarian stuff down at the end."

"I think I'll try a burger." Allan added a greasy, paper-wrapped cheeseburger to his overloaded tray.

Chet was shocked. He said, "You've gotta be careful, man. Your body's not used to meat. This stuff could cause some serious digestive problems." Allan wasn't listening. He had moved on to the desserts. Chet said to himself, "What am I—your mother?" and slid a diet plate onto his own tray. He said, "Hey, tell me more about this gizmo of yours?" and followed Allan to a table. He watched for a reaction as Allan picked up a hamburger and took his first bite of meat.

Allan chewed for a while and then said, "Tastes like salty rubber," and took another bite. "I like it."

Chet shook his head in amazement and started on his own lunch. "So, this thing of yours—it's for blind kids?"

"More for dyslexics, although I think it could be adapted for the blind, later." Allan pushed the food aside, dug four neatly folded cocktail napkins out of his back pocket, and opened them up. He smoothed out the wrinkles and pieced the napkins together like a puzzle on the Formica tabletop. Each meticulous drawing had tiny notations surrounding it, with arrows pointing out the relevant aspects of the sketch to which the notes referred. Allan said, "Here's a rough schematic I did on the plane."

"A screen and a pair of glasses?"

Allan was excited now. He said, "See the eight and a half by eleven inch panel on *this* napkin?"

"Uh huh."

"You've heard of those new flexible electronic readers with the smart screens, right?"

"Yeah. Julius Verner over in Oncology has nearly every textbook, journal, and paper on the subject on his. Full color touch screen, wireless internet connection, and the battery lasts for a month. Those things are *amazing*. He was showing it to me in the lunchroom last week."

"This would use one of those panels—with a few important tweaks. You know how the different colors on one of those electronic ink screens have different positive and negative charges, right?"

Chet looked confused. "No, but I'll take your word on it."

"Okay. Well, they *do*. So, this panel gets placed on top of a page of text, or the check at a restaurant, or *whatever*. The positively-charged particles in the scanner are affected by the text lying beneath it and they, in effect, "push up" the text, so it appears on the panel just as it was typed or handwritten."

"Okay, you lost me. The two-dimensional text *pushes up* through the panel?"

Allan let out an exasperated sigh and shook his head abruptly. "No. The lighter, *negatively charged*, particles in the panel are unaffected by the blank 'negative' space on the page beneath it. The text on the page is dark, right? So it occupies *positive space*, in a purely visual sense." Allan looked expectantly at Chet, smiling broadly.

"Okay ... I'm *still* lost."

"But instead of displaying the text contained in a digital text file, as these panels do on an e-reader, they would now reproduce the negative and positive visual space on the paper beneath them."

"So, it's like that kids' toy with all of the little hanging metal pins mounted on a frame that you push your hand or the side of your face up into and it makes a pin replica of the object beneath it. The text acts like and electronic version of that physical pressure on the pins?"

"Exactly!"

Chet asked, "I don't mean to crap on your birthday cake, but how is this better than just reading the text through a sheet of plastic? And what does it have to do with the glasses?"

"This panel, *which already exists in the world*—super lightweight, durable, flexible, requiring no light, and whose battery will last a month on a charge—wouldn't be simply duplicating the text, it would be *scanning* it into memory."

"Scanning it. For what purpose?"

"Once the text is scanned it goes through a very basic OCR program …" Allan caught the question in Chet's eyes and added: "… *optical character recognition* … and then the dyslexic user trains the device for his or her specific needs."

"Trains it?"

"Have you ever used a text-to-speech program? Or a speech-to-text program for dictating notes onto a computer?"

"Sure. I used one of those to proof my papers in med school."

"And I used them a lot before there were very many books available on audio CD and MP3. The problem was that the program would mispronounce a lot of words."

"And record words incorrectly when you're dictating—if you had an accent or a speech impediment. My dorm mate was from Egypt, and he used to complain about that."

"Right! So just like you would train one of those programs with your pronunciation preferences—if you're talking about *it* reading to *you*—or your particular speech anomalies—if you're using a speech-to-text program, we could *train* this panel to *translate* the text beneath it to suit a specific dyslexic's needs."

Chet seemed more perplexed than ever. He scratched his head and asked, "What do you mean *translate?*"

Every dyslexic perceives words on a page in their own unique way. Some of us see 'b's and 'd's reversed, others see all the letters backwards, and there are dozens of other perceptual variations. It's as individual as a thumbprint. And, as you know, it's not a learning disorder—so no amount of 'training' can *fix* us."

"Of course. It's a brain abnormality, like colorblindness."

Allan shot Chet a hard look. "Hey, are you saying I've got an abnormal brain?"

Chet smiled and replied, "Spectacularly so, my friend. And I wouldn't have it any other way."

"So, we *can't* train our brains to see the words as they are written but we *can* train this device to show us the text in a way that makes sense to our spectacularly abnormal brains. You need everything reversed, like a mirror image, you got it. I need all of the 'b's and 'd's switched—I just tell the genie in the panel and my wish is its command."

Chet asked, "I don't recall the latest estimates, but I know there are a hell of a lot of dyslexics out there."

Allan spoke through a mouthful of French fries: "Upwards of fifteen percent of the world's population."

Chet sat back in his chair and stared at his friend in open amazement. "Jesus Allan, this could help *a lot* of people. This could be *huge.*" Chet studied the napkins on the table. "Could this really work?"

"Unless I'm missing something—the core hardware and software already exist, even though they've been designed for other applications. It would just be a matter of funding, tweaking, and testing."

"And the glasses?"

Allan took a big bite of his now-cold burger. He spoke as he chewed: "Wirelessly connected to the panel. The adapted text is projected onto the inside of the transparent lenses. There's a semi-reflective layer embedded in the glass so the wearer sees the projection but no one else does—so he doesn't have to feel so much like a freak." Allan tapped the napkin that showed the sketch of the panel and said, "I think we might even be able to make it so that we could type on the panel and it would show the words as they were intended to be—after running our input through the personalized translation protocol that the user has created. These panels are touch screens with the ability to display virtual keyboards, that could be adapted to the dyslexic's perceptual idiosyncrasies, so I don't see why not. But *that* would come later—after I get a working prototype."

"This could *completely* transform the lives of millions of people."

Allan smiled, pleased with himself, and arched his eyebrows. "Best thing since sliced bread." Chet was dumbfounded. He stared at Allan and shook his head in amazement. Allan asked, "What?"

"I just can't get over the change in you, man. Blows me away."

"I know. Pretty incredible."

"Miraculous is more like it. We should run some tests. Maybe we can find something about the change in your system that'll help other dyslexics."

"Yeah." Allan returned his focus to his food. "Maybe I'll do that." Allan caught Chet staring at him again. "What?"

"I'm sorry. It's just too much, man. Honestly, Allan, I'm so happy for you. Of all the people I've ever known, *you* deserved a miracle. *And you got it.*" Chet suddenly realized something. He said, "Hey, *that's* what's been bugging me: those contacts! They make your eyes look lighter."

Allan averted his eyes. "I don't know. Maybe."

Chet tapped Allan's napkin schematic and said, "When you're ready—I'll introduce you to Dr. Minlow in the Learning Disorders Treatment Center. He'd be a fool not to jump on this."

"Yeah? That'd be great." Allan popped the last bite of his burger into his mouth and then looked over the remaining food on his tray, trying to decide what to eat first.

Chet insisted, "You're fucking *brilliant*, man. What the hell happened to you over there?"

Allan shoveled a forkful of pot roast into his mouth and smiled as he chewed.

43

Douglas gave Janie a kiss and stepped into the house. "Hello, beautiful. Is Billy around?"

"He's helping me with dinner—if you call making messes and giving orders helping." She called into the kitchen, "Bill. Pop-Pop's here."

Douglas asked, "Is he any better?"

Janie tried to shrug off her concern, but she looked tired. She confided: "He worries all the time, doesn't sleep and snaps at the kids over the silliest things. I don't know. Maybe this buyout was a mistake."

Bill Geffner emerged from the kitchen wearing the frilly apron that he had purchased for Janie as a joke. He looked exhausted, but managed a smile for his grandfather. "You're just in time for dinner. I've almost got these amateurs whipped into shape." Janie gave Douglas a look and returned to the kitchen. Bill slumped into a chair.

Douglas said, "I can't tonight, Billy. I've got to relieve the nurse."

"So what's the occasion?"

"It's that Steele claim."

"They haven't made a claim, yet. Thank God."

"I finally spoke to the husband today."

"What?" Billy stood up, ready for a fight. "You went to his office again?" I told you—the *last thing* I need is for that guy to make his claim. I mean, I know he will eventually, but don't hammer the nails into my casket for them. With this kind of shock loss I lose my gold card and go from PUA to LUA just like that." He snapped his fingers.

Douglas said, "PUA?"

"Preferred Underwriting Authority. It lets me bind customers on the spot, and offer special discounts. Limited Underwriting Authority means I have to go through the company for everything. Less autonomy and no special discounting ability. Combine *that* with the increased Loss Ratio, and it could cost me a hundred thousand dollars a year in bonuses for the next *three years*." He began to pace. "Do you have three hundred thousand dollars Pop-Pop? 'Cause I sure don't."

Douglas allowed his grandson to cool down a moment before he spoke. "I'm not sure you'll have to pay on that policy."

Billy sat again, dropped his head into his hands. "The police ruled it an accident, right?"

"Yes, but I think there's more to the story."

Billy's eyes lit up. "Suicide? You think it was suicide?"

Douglas said, "I don't know, yet. But I do know that something is wrong. Do you want me to keep poking around?"

"Hell yes. I don't have time to do it, and if you think there's *any chance at all* ... I'll just try to stall the claim—if they file one—until we know for sure."

Douglas went to Billy and ruffled his hair before starting for the door. "It's only money, Billy. It comes and it goes. But your family is with you forever."

Billy sighed, and nodded in agreement. "I'm sorry, Pop-Pop."

Douglas looked toward the kitchen and said, "Don't tell me. Tell *them*."

44

The black Jag stalked the trash-strewn streets on the seedy side of town. It was dusk and Argus knew exactly what he needed. He cut through an alley and emerged on a block inhabited by factories and abandoned warehouses.

Argus spotted a hooker up ahead wearing a short skirt and long boots. The Latin girl kicked old newspapers aside and dragged her gloved hand across dirty bricked walls, making the handcuffs that she wore as a bracelet jingle. She heard the Jag's engine purring behind her, but didn't look back. Argus followed for a long block. Then the hooker stopped.

Argus rolled down the window and flashed a hundred-dollar bill. The hooker checked out the car, arched an eyebrow, and started to walk again. Argus pulled ahead and onto the sidewalk, blocking her path at a secluded spot.

She stopped and copped an attitude.

He stepped out of the car and took three hundred-dollar bills from his wallet. Her gaze traveled from his dark eyes to the bills. He folded them neatly and tucked them down the front of his pants. She wetted her lips and took a step forward, removing the glove on her right hand. Her smile was crooked. Long fingers with lethal, red tipped nails slid down the front of Argus' shirt and disappeared into his trousers.

Their eyes connected again as she moved her hand in search of the treasure. She teased for a moment and then her teeth showed as she tightened her grip, just a little. He pulled her close and attacked her neck, biting a little harder than she would have liked. She pushed him away.

His tone was low and cautious. "I'm sorry. Can you forgive me?"

The hooker's voice was weathered gravel: "For three hundred bucks I can forgive a lot. For five hundred I could be your own personal Mother Theresa."

His voice trembled. "Say the words. Say, 'I forgive you'."

She moved close and whispered in his ear and Argus sighed, relieved. She stepped up onto the bumper of his Jag and walked across the hood, the heels of her boots bowing the enameled metal. Then she sat on the roof of the car in a way that was clearly an invitation.

Argus moved quickly then, grabbing her ankle and pulling so that she slid down the windshield and onto the hood. He tore at her clothes like an animal. She laughed and thrashed around, as if it was a game, enjoying his frenzy.

He exposed her breasts and bit them with his teeth.

She unfastened his trousers and pushed them down.

He hiked up her skirt and ripped away her panties, then saw that she had already shaved herself bare and smiled, thinking of destiny.

She clawed at his ass, pulling him into her, and their sounds echoed in the empty space as frenzy built toward explosion.

Hot breath, sporadic and incomplete ...

Rustling clothes, grinding flesh ...

And shifting metal, as the Jag settled beneath their weight.

She sensed that it would be over soon. She'd be home in time to catch the news and she would pay next month's rent in advance. Then he put his hands on each side of her face and began to squeeze. Her smile faltered as his rhythm intensified and he hooked his thumbs into the corners of her mouth, drawing them upward to simulate a smile. His huge hands slid down to her throat and her eyes showed fear for the first time. Her mouth opened wide, working for air, as Argus tightened his grip. She reminded him of a fish that had been plucked from the water.

The hooker tried to buck him off of her, but his full weight slammed her back onto the Jaguar's hood with every vicious thrust. She tried to claw at his face, but was too weak—and suddenly it didn't seem as important as it had a second ago. Her vision was blurring now and his hateful stare seemed to soften and transform into something gentle. Something *kind*. Then the world went black.

45

Allan was too hot and restless to sleep. He pushed the scattered books from the bed and moved to the guest room's desk in search of a notepad. He switched on the halogen desk lamp and immediately regretted the action. He winced and cried out, "Ow, *shit!*" and knocked the lamp to the floor. He muttered, "Too fucking bright." Annoyed and irritable, Allan stripped off his T-shirt, picked up his journal, and began scribbling notes in the dark.

———————

It was late afternoon when he padded across the marbled floors of his parents' penthouse. His night had been restless and his thoughts troubled. Allan stopped, suddenly struck by the silence. His mother had a habit of leaving the radio or TV on constantly, just for the noise. He couldn't remember when it started, but he'd noticed that she'd done it more frequently over the years. The noise must have kept her company in the cold vacuum of her life with Argus. Allan had always understood the underlying motivation, but it had driven him crazy nonetheless. He would tease her about becoming one of those Pavlovian housewives who lived for the next installment of their favorite soap.

And she would smile a gentle, radiant smile that always had a healing effect on Allan. For him, it was a magic elixir that cured melancholia and sugar-coated pain. Allan suddenly missed the noise, and her, with an intensity that left him feeling heavy and dull. He said, "Mom," aloud and was startled by the hollow sound of his own voice as it bounced off the cold, stone floors, skipped across chrome and glass, and hovered in the stagnant air like a secret thought. When Allan spoke again it was with the breathy, solemn reverence of a heartfelt prayer. "I miss you."

After a lingering silence, Allan switched on the stereo, turned up the volume and moved into the kitchen. He made himself a cup of coffee, catching a glimpse of his own reflection in one of the high-tech room's chromed surfaces. He touched his face, concerned by its haggard appearance.

46

The subway station was a little over a mile away from Ellen's Brooklyn Heights home, and the walk left Allan drenched in perspiration, despite the cool night air. He stopped at the door to Ellen's house and gave himself a quick once-over. His hair felt too long. It kept getting in his eyes. Allan took a deep breath, pushed his nervousness aside, and knocked. The door opened immediately and a very chic young woman emerged. Allan smiled a little too broadly and said, "Hi. I'm Allan Steele."

"Well, *there* you are!" The elegant woman whisked Allan in, kissed him on the cheek and peeled his coat away from his sweaty body in a single, effortless movement that would have put Baryshnikov to shame. "Ellen's been telling us tales from your new *masterpiece* all night."

"She has?"

The woman led Allan into the living room. "I'm Bibi." She looked around the room, which was crowded with guests. "Now where is she? I know Ellen was *dying* to meet you." Bibi confided, "But you know how she is."

"Actually I don't." Allan was already extremely uncomfortable. He hated large gatherings, and he felt as though everyone in the room was staring at him.

Bibi cocked her head and said, "Well, *of course* you don't! What's *wrong* with me?"

"Allan!" Jon pushed his way through the crowd. "So glad you could make it." He turned to Bibi and asked, "Where's Ellen?"

Bibi whispered, "M.I.A.. *Again.*"

Jon muttered, "Fan-fucking-tastic," and turned his attention back to Allan as Bibi disappeared into the crowd. "Allan, have I told you how much I love your hair?"

The lights were beginning to give Allan a headache. He said, "Huh? My hair?"

"You look like that pianist. What's his name?"

"I ... I don't know."

"Oh come on—*you know who I mean*. The one who was photographed in flagrante delicto in Spain with that TV actress with the bad hair." Allan shook his head in bewilderment. Jon insisted, "You look *just like him*, but without the mustache and the piano." Jon gently guided Allan through the minglers, scanning the crowd for Ellen. "Can I get you anything?" Jon summoned a waiter with a gesture. "Drink?"

"No thanks."

Jon said, "Are you sure?" The waiter hovered nearby.

"Um ... all right. A vodka tonic, I guess." The waiter nodded in acknowledgment and returned to the bar.

"Ellen's got to be around here somewhere." Jon spoke through a frozen smile. "There's Raul, her no-good-two-timing-piece-of-shit-husband." Jon put his hand on Allan's shoulder and lowered his voice. "But if you tell her I said that I will deny it." Someone waved from across the room. Jon smiled and waved back as he whispered to Allan, "Oh, Gawd. I'd hoped *they* wouldn't come. Or had died or something. Excuse me, Allan. I have to greet some of Ellen's wretched friends."

Allan started to say something, but Jon had disappeared into the crowd. Allan spotted the food table and began to work his way toward it. En route, several strangers stopped him to say hello and introduce themselves. Allan nibbled pâté while loading his plate with food. As he ate, an elegant couple joined him at the table.

The man said, "William Hapner. Call me Dr. Bill," then the man turned to the sleepy-looking woman at his side and said, "This is Pandora."

Allan shielded his mouth, which was full of pâté, and answered, "Nice to meet you. I'm Allan Steele." He extended his hand, but when the doctor shook it, he winced and pulled back his hand.

One of Allan's fingernails, which had grown to nearly an inch long, had broken the skin of Dr. Bill's palm.

The doctor looked at Allan's nails and quipped, "Good thing I've had my shots."

Allan withdrew his hand and mumbled, "I'm sorry," then stuffed his hand into his pocket.

Doctor Bill wiped the speck of blood from his hand with a cocktail napkin and said, "You're Ellen's wunderkind, right?"

Allan's nervousness intensified. "I don't know. I guess so."

Dr. Bill locked onto someone else across the room just as Bibi breezed by. She winked and slipped Allan's drink into his hand as she passed. Allan turned to say thanks, but she was already out of range. Dr. Bill whispered something to Pandora and then turned to Allan. "Sorry Al. A patient of mine. I'd better make a quick house call." He slipped Allan a business card. "Let me know if there's ever anything I can do for you."

"Okay. Thanks."

"Allan—you just disappeared. I want you to meet someone."

Allan turned as he pocketed the doctor's card and saw Jon and Laughton Hince approaching. Allan seemed agitated. He said, "I'm sorry, Jon. I'm really not feeling well. I should probably—"

"No, no, no—you can't go, yet. You just got here. I know Ellen is here somewhere. I mean, it is *her* fucking party."

Allan downed half of his drink and tried to get a grip.

Jon said, "Besides, Ellen wanted you to meet Laughton." He turned to Laughton, who had been quietly studying Allan. "Allan Steele—Laughton Hince."

Allan said, "Hello," and Laughton offered his hand, but Allan kept his own in his pockets.

Laughton withdrew, feeling a little foolish, and said, "Great name, Allan. Is it real?"

"Huh? Is it ...? Oh. Yes."

Jon put his arm around Allan. "Laughton is the best literary agent in New York and a good friend of Ellen's. You two should get to know each other."

Allan said, "Nice to meet you, Mr. Hince," and continued to hide in his drink.

Laughton said, "Allan, if you're interested I think I can get you on Nighttime New York."

Jon added, "And how about the college lecture circuit?"

"Good idea. His youth would be a big plus."

Allan fidgeted. "Uh ... I appreciate everything you're both trying to do for me, but–" Allan closed his eyes and held onto the edge of the food table, feeling dizzy.

"But?"

"I just need to ... Think about everything ... Figure out what I'm gonna do."

Laughton and Jon exchanged a look of concern. Clearly, there was something wrong with this kid. The big question was whether that "something" would prove to be a major P.R. nightmare, or a just minor pain in the ass. Laughton turned to Allan and spoke as if to a child. "Sure, Al. You think about it?" To Jon: "Have Ellen call me."

Laughton moved away and Jon spoke quietly. "Have we got a problem, Allan?"

"I don't feel well."

"Look, when your book hits the stands, it's gonna be–"

"Where's your bathroom?"

"What?" Jon sighed. "Upstairs. To your right."

Allan headed for the stairs, weaving through the crowd. "Excuse me. I'm sorry."

Jon called after Allan, "We also need to set up a shoot for the book jacket. There's a photographer here that I want you to meet ..."

Allan had made it to the top of the stairs. He turned back to respond to Jon, but a drunken guy with a ponytail and granny glasses got in his face. The guy said, "You're *him*, huh?"

Allan said, "What?"

"Him. *The guy.* Ellen's new discovery." He leaned in closer, studying Allan as if he was inanimate. "You don't look like a genius."

"I'm not. Excuse me."

The drunk grabbed the back of Allan's sweater as he moved away, pulling him back like a toy on an elastic leash. He said, "I'm Ellen's old discovery. My first book was Chemical Nirvana. Perhaps you've heard of it?"

Allan's nausea increased a notch. He gripped the banister tighter squinted against the light. "No. I'm sorry."

The man dismissed Allan's ignorance with a courtly gesture and said, quite loudly, "Four weeks on the New York Times' Bestseller list. Thrice reprinted, translated into seven languages, promos on radio and TV, thank you very much."

Allan said, "I'm sorry, you'll have to excuse me."

"No, wait." He raised his voice to catch the attention of those below. "Prithee regale us with a tale of your mystical journey into the deepest heart of Botswana, brilliant boy."

"It was Zaire," He addressed the partiers below, who had begun to stare. "Not Botswana. And it wasn't mystical—just tiring. So please excuse me."

The troublemaker grabbed Allan's arm again and taunted, "Come now, brilliant boy—surely Ellen's new golden child has something to say for himself. How about a scary story?" He turned to the crowd and said, "Something about monsters and demons and horrible, horrible deaths."

Allan was feeling odd and the guests were all staring at him ... awaiting a response. He braced himself against the wall and muttered, "I've seen all of those things—you'll have to be more specific."

"Then tell us about death, brilliant boy."

Allan tried to think of something—anything that would get this guy off of his back. Finally, he remembered something one of the children with the wise eyes had told him. He said, "There was *one story*. About a monster that lived in the jungle." The guests below crowded closer in order to hear.

Laughton asked Jon, "What's he doing up there?"

"He's either going to vomit on that prick—or tell a story. I can't tell which."

Laughton said, "I was beginning to wonder if he could speak at all."

The fog in Allan's brain suddenly cleared and he felt completely in control. He stepped to the banister and said, "The Shantu say that back when the world was new a young boy's village had run out of food. He was sent into the forest to search for something to eat, and it was there that he stumbled across a sleeping giant, covered in long, silken hair that stretched as far as the eye could see."

A chic-looking man with shoulder-length hair called out, "Who was his stylist? Mine isn't worth shit," and the group laughed.

Allan continued: "The boy tried to sneak away, but the giant was awake and he demanded to know why he had been disturbed. The boy explained that he was hungry and the giant offered to supply all the food the child could eat—*if he would be his servant.* The boy agreed and the giant said that his name was Death."

The drunk turned to the crowd and said, "Aha! Death is a chickenhawk!"

Someone chided, "Shhh, let him finish," and the drunk returned to his drink.

Allan said, "Anyway, the boy stayed for a long time and grew fat on the giant's exotic food. Then one day the boy became homesick and asked if he might return to his village and Death said, 'Fine, as long as you send another boy to serve in your place.' So, the boy brought his brother to the giant and returned to the village, but food was still in scarce supply, so eventually he returned to Death and asked to be fed. The giant agreed, on the condition that the boy would work for him again. The boy worked and ate with the giant for a long time after that, but was surprised that he never saw his brother. When asked, the giant explained that the other boy had been sent away on business. The boy eventually gets homesick again and this time the giant says that if he brings him a bride he will let him return to his village. So, the boy convinces his sister to marry Death. Time passes and the boy is hungry again for the giant's exotic meats, so he returns to the jungle"

Someone said, "Uh oh, here it comes," and his wife elbowed him in the ribs.

"This time the giant is impatient with the boy, but tells him to go into the inner room of his house and help himself. But when the boy goes into the meat locker, he finds—"

Someone called out, "His sister."

Someone else insisted, "His *brother.*"

Allan smiled and said, "Right. The boy runs back to his village and returns with the bravest tribesmen and they light the giant's long hair on fire and watch him scream and burn, and ultimately die, from a safe distance. Once he was dead, the group moved closer to examine Death's head and noticed a small packet of mysterious crystals in roots of the giant's hair. So, hoping they might contain some sort of magic, the boy took the crystals to the giant's house and sprinkled some of them on the bones of his brother and sister—and they were instantly brought back to life.

The wisest man in the group suggested that they hurry back to the village to store the magic crystals in a safe place, so the boy hurried back with them, but tripped over the giant's head, spilling the remaining crystals onto one of the giant's eyes. The eye opened once and everyone ran away in fear." Allan took a breath. "And that is how Death came to mankind. Now, whenever the giant opens and shuts his eye—someone dies."

The group burst into spontaneous applause.

Laughton turned to Jon and raised his voice to be heard above the clapping. "Not bad. You may have something there after all."

Allan slipped off down the hallway.

47

A middle-aged woman sat at the antique desk in the den, smoking a joint and gorging herself on hors d' oeuvres. She was gluttony personified, and if she hadn't been bulimic she would have probably weighed three hundred pounds. Currently, she was no more than voluptuous, and still quite attractive. Allan wandered into the room, drink in hand, and interrupted the unhappy woman in mid toke. He mumbled, "Oh, sorry," and turned to leave.

She tried to focus. "Hey, great story. I was coming back from the john when you gave 'em the punch line." She scrunched one eye closed and began to blink the other one slowly, singing a bad rendition of the Queen song *Another One Bites The Dust*. After the first chorus she stopped, brow furrowed, and said, "Goddamn it. I hate it when I forget the words. Oh well, fuck it. Hey, you know any good death jokes?"

Allan closed his eyes and massaged his temples. The headache was getting worse. He covered his eyes with his hand and approached a floor lamp that was causing him considerable pain. "Do you mind if I turn this off?"

The woman behind the desk tried to focus. She asked, "Are we setting a mood, here?"

Allan switched off the light. Now the little desk lamp was the sole light source in the room. Still, Allan was miserable.

"H-e-l-l-o? Anyone there? These are the *jokes?*"

Allan shaded his eyes from the lamp in order to look at the woman. He said, "Hmmm? Jokes?"

"Did you know that, pound for pound, fat people have the best senses of humor? I bet you didn't know that. You're looking at two fucking tons of fun here, mister." Allan recognized the anguish and loneliness in the woman's eyes, and pushed his own pain aside. He moved to a nearby chair and sat, thinking that perhaps she just needed someone to listen. The woman said, "Know what I like about death? It's so cyclic. When somebody dies—even a rotten shithead kind of person—when that shithead somebody dies, another person is born to take their place in the world. So it really doesn't matter so much if you, personally, are alive or not—as long as the space is filled." She popped another canapé into her mouth and asked, "Right?"

"No. I think it matters."

She thought about it for a moment and then held up her wrists for Allan to see. They were badly scarred by botched suicide attempts. "I feel bad keeping that other person waiting to fill my spot. You see, I'm really just trying to be efficient."

"But what about the child?"

The woman's face blanched and she asked, "What child?"

Alan said, "The child that would take your place. Would you want it to come into the world carrying the weight of your suicide on its soul? You would've just replaced one miserable life with another."

The unhappy woman harrumphed and muttered, "Goddamned *Catholics*," then lowered her head to the edge of the desk as she thought it over, mumbling, "What to do, what to do ..." Allan heard Jon walking down the hall, calling his name, but Allan didn't respond. Finally, he started for the door, unable to take the light any longer.

The woman said, "God! I have fat thighs. I mean really, *really* fat thighs."

Allan stopped in the doorway and said, "Stand up."

She mumbled, "Huh?"

"Let me see." The woman pushed away from the desk and stood. She hiked up her dress, displaying her thighs. Allan was more concerned with her needs than her thighs. He said, "I think you're *beautiful.*"

"Oh yeah, sure, *I am.* But it's my thighs we're talking about."

"Incredible."

She found refuge in Allan's eyes. "Yeah?"

"Yeah." Allan noticed something odd about the woman's eyes, but he couldn't pinpoint it.

The woman walked over to a mirror and studied her thighs, a little happier. Allan smiled as he watched her posing in front of the mirror—until the sickness consumed him once again, and he left the room.

48

Allan hurried from the house and ran for the subway station, looking lost and confused. Every street lamp caused him to cower, and the headlights of passing cars made his head feel as if it was about to explode. The party seemed to have taken ten years off of his life. He looked like an aging junkie in desperate need of a fix. After a few blocks, Allan doubled over and began to cough until he vomited into someone's meticulously manicured shrubs.

His footsteps echoed as he stumbled down the stairs that led into the subterranean station. He clung to the railing for support and then, when he reached the bottom, staggered to the edge of the platform. Allan peered into the darkness of the tunnel, hoping for the sounds of a train, but heard none. Two of the three fluorescent light fixtures on this side of the tracks were out. Allan was thankful, but he still huddled into the darkest corner that he could find.

Two young couples on the other side of the tracks laughed as they climbed the stairs to ground-level, while Allan paced in the shadows like a sick, caged cat. His skin suddenly felt three sizes too small and his eyes burned like red-hot coals. Allan could feel the sweat running down his legs, as if he'd wet himself.

The wind whispered through the tunnel, along with another sound: an undercurrent. Something subtle; throbbing like beating drums. Allan studied the ceiling of the cave's enclosure, attributing the distant thumping to cars passing overhead. He gathered his coat around his frail body and returned to the edge of the platform.

Voices …

Two drunken men, loud and aggressive, descended the stairs on the other side of the tracks. Their bickering seemed well-worn, familiar, as if this scene had been played out a hundred times before. Both men were in their late forties. The Italian man jabbed his finger at his red-cheeked, Irish friend and said, "You're wrong, so fuck you!"

"And I say fuck you! You know damned well I'm right."

"Because you're always right, huh?"

The muscular Irishman got up in the little Italian's face. "That's right, boyo! So why don't ya' just go off and fuck yourself in the arse!"

"Yeah?"

"YEAH!"

Allan was miserable. He was trembling and sweating, and all sound seemed to be amplified tenfold. He watched the men from the other side of the tracks, while backing away and covering his ears with his hands. The argument continued to escalate, voices bouncing off the cavernous walls and assaulting Allan from all sides. He jammed himself into the corner again, trying to hide from the sounds, but the thumping continued to build—punctuating the drunken banter. And then came a new sound: the train. Allan rocked back and forth, pale and sweating, trying to find comfort in the approaching rumble of the subway train. Soon he would be home.

Then the men squared off.

"C'mon ya' little guinea fucker."

"That's it, Shawnesy! That's it! You push me too far this time!" The two men circled each other, fists up, looking for an opening. The Italian took a swing and missed.

"Oh, C'mon son? Is that all ya' got?"

The Italian thumbed his nose and said, "All right—that's really it!", and the men continued to circle, seeming to genuinely enjoy this sport. They taunted each other, but there was no malice. They probably never made contact, just did this "dance" as a sort of ritual.

As the train drew closer, the drums in Allan's head grew louder. He jammed his fists into his ears and mumbled, "No,no,no,no,no,no,no."

The Irishman, who looked as though he might have been a boxer in his younger days, jabbed with his left, but the punch fell short. The Italian laughed, a little out of breath, and said, "I feel sad for your mama."

"I was sparin' you is all."

Allan opened his eyes for a moment and saw the men dancing around each other, inching closer to the yellow safety line at the edge of the platform. And then he saw it again—in their eyes. The same odd glow that he had see in the unhappy woman's eyes, but different somehow. The little man's seemed dimmer, but the Irishman's eyes were burning brightly. Allan hoped he was imagining things, but he knew he wasn't.

The train was coming fast, only a few blocks away now. The Irishman took another half hearted poke at the Italian. This one connected, surprising them both. The Italian stumbled backward, tripping over his own feet and fell to the dirty concrete just as the ground began to tremble. Allan saw the look on the Italian's face and moved forward, wanting to stop them.

The shocked Irishman lowered his fists and leaned down to help the other man up. He said, "Jesus, Mary and Joseph, Tony I didn't mean to ..."

The Italian looked up, suddenly enraged, as the train rounded the last corner before entering the station. Allan took another step forward as the Italian lunged without warning and landed a solid blow to the jaw of the larger man. The Irishman stumbled backward, toward the tracks, trying to right himself. The Italian saw the approaching train too late and tried to grab his friend's hand. For a moment the Irishman teetered on the edge of the platform like an awkward ballerina, and then he fell against the side of the speeding train. His screams filled the station as he slid down the side of the moving train and tumbled down to the tracks below.

Allan waited on the other side of the station, his view blocked by the passing train. Gradually the sounds of the train began to fade away and those of the drums took their place. Allan shuddered as the hunger overtook him. He knew what lay ahead. After the train had finally passed, Allan saw the little Italian man with the bloody lip. He was just standing there at the edge of the platform, staring down at the tracks. Staring at what was left of his friend.

Allan moved closer, his head filled with the drums of the Shantu ceremony, and saw the mess that was once a man. But the Irishman's eyes ... his eyes were beautiful—like stars.

The Italian's lips moved for a long time before he finally managed to form the words; "Oh my God ... He's still alive."

"Go get help." Allan's voice was devoid of emotion. "I'll stay with him." The Italian looked up at Allan without an ounce of comprehension. Allan said, "Hurry, before it's too late." The Italian backed away slowly and then, suddenly, snapped out of his daze. He turned and ran up the stairs, taking two at a time, calling for help at the top of his lungs.

Now Allan was alone with the dying man. Drawn by the drums and his inescapable hunger, Allan lowered himself to the tracks. The Irishman gurgled and sputtered as Allan knelt beside him. The ex fighter's lower body had been caught beneath the train and was crushed beyond recognition. He stared up at Allan, gushing blood as he slipped into shock. In another minute, he would be dead.

There was a distant rumble. Another train was approaching. Allan moved closer, casting a cold shadow over the mangled Irishman. He looked around for something sharp to make the job ahead easier, and then remembered the incident with Doctor Bill. He would have to remember to cut his fingernails—afterwards.

49

Allan wandered the streets of Manhattan in a daze with the Irishman's blood smeared across his face. He had walked across the Brooklyn Bridge, still high from the fusion process. Passers-by barely noticed Allan as he tore off his shirt and discarded it. His eyes were bright and his cheeks were ruddy from the heady infusion of new life.

He walked through Central Park in the dead of night, footsteps crunching in the dirty snow, oblivious to the danger that surrounded him. His promise to the goddess fulfilled, and his hunger satisfied, Allan's eyes had already begun to lose their hypersensitivity. And in this moment of exhilaration—Allan had also lost all sense of remorse.

He felt electric. *Invincible.* The resident hoods and outcasts huddled around their refuse fires studied Allan carefully, but decided that he was not the victim they had hoped for. It might have been the fact that he was walking shirtless through the park in October that discouraged them. Or it might have been the blood.

Allan knelt at the edge of Central Park Lake to try to wash the blood from his face. And when he saw his reflection on the surface of the water, Allan thought he could almost make out the fragile young man that used to greet him in the mirror each morning. But then the ripples swept the young man away, and when the murky water quieted Allan saw exactly what he had become.

———

When Allan returned to the empty penthouse, he grabbed the nail clippers from the medicine cabinet and the cordless phone from its charger before stepping out onto the balcony that overlooked the city. It was still dark, though the sun was threatening to show itself on the horizon, and Allan was still on fire. He pulled off his remaining clothing and turned to meet the howling wind as he dialed a long distance number. Allan closed his eyes and waited, still sweating in the icy breeze. A groggy female voice answered, and Allan hesitated. The voice on the other end of the line grew impatient, but Allan still seemed unable to find his own.

Jenny slammed down the phone in the dark, sending her alarm clock clattering to the floor. "Goddamn it." As she fumbled for it, the phone began to ring again. She read the luminescent hands of the clock and mumbled, "Motherfucking son of a ..." and Jenny snatched the phone from its cradle. She challenged: "You gonna *talk* this time, asshole?"

"Jen ... it's me."

It only took an instant for the familiar voice to cut through the cobwebs. Jenny sat up in bed. "Allan?"

"Yeah. Did I wake you?"

"Are you okay?"

"No. I don't think so. What time is it there?"

"Three a.m. What's up? Why didn't you call me? I'd be pissed if I wasn't so tired."

"So much has happened ..."

"Where have you been?"

"I'm in New York. At my parent's place."

"Well, fuck Yale. Come on home. We'll be miserable together."

"I can't come home, Jen. That's why I called. I want you to ship my stuff."

"What? Allan, what's going on? You sound weird."

"Please Jenny ... just ship my stuff for me. Maybe I'll tell you the whole story some day, but I can't now. Okay?" There was a long silence. "Jen?"

Jenny sighed and reached for a pad and pen. She was hurt, but knew Allan well enough not to push when he got into one of his dark moods. "You gonna give me an address? Or is that a secret, too?"

They talked for a while longer about nothing in particular, just to hear the sound of each other's voices, and then Allan gave Jenny the address. The sun was beginning to rise in Manhattan, so Allan said goodbye and retreated into the apartment.

50

Allan was shown into a portrait studio by the photographer's assistant and seated in a straight backed chair in front of a mottled backdrop. The assistant said, "Okay, Allan, she'll be with you in a few. Can I get you anything? Cappuccino? Herbal tea?"

Allan's stomach growled. "Got anything to eat?"

The assistant said, "I'll check," and hurried out of the room, passing Ellen in the hallway. "Go on in. Allan's waiting for Sandra."

Ellen Chonce entered the studio looking like she'd had a rough night. She smiled at Allan and said, "Bet you hoped you'd never see me again."

Allan turned and recognized Ellen immediately; she was the unhappy woman from the party. He said, "You're the photographer?"

She stepped forward timidly and extended her hand. "Not quite. I'm Ellen Chonce." Alan was as dumbfounded as Ellen was mortified. Finally Ellen said, "It's nice to finally meet you, Allan." She added quickly, "Properly, I mean. I'm so sorry about the other night. My husband and I had just had a huge fight and I was ... Well, I was ..." She trailed off, unable to finds words that were sufficient to express her pain.

Allan tried to lighten the moment: "Your husband—he's the 'no-good-two-timing-piece-of-shit'?"

Ellen laughed. "Oh, so you've met him?"

"No, but I heard about him." Allan gave Ellen a tender, compassionate smile, and asked, "How are your thighs?"

"Fabulous ... or so I've been told." Ellen took a deep breath. "Well, anyway, it was totally unprofessional, and I hope that we can pretend it never happened. I love your book, and I'd really like to continue working with you."

Allan considered her words for a moment, and then said, "All right. I'd like that."

Sandra entered the room, bringing with her a gust of frantic energy. "Morning all ..." She began to check the settings on her Hasselblad. "Do we feel beautiful?"

Allan replied, "A little nervous."

Ellen took a seat in the back, and Sandra turned her attention to her camera's viewfinder. "Okay, enough of this happy crap. Off with your clothes and on with the big fan! Lick your lips, babe. Give it to me!" Allan laughed and began to relax. Sandra clicked off the first shot, triggering a *pop* as the strobes positioned around Allan fired. She said, "Give me your eyes, Allan. Right here. That's it."

Pop.

Sandra said to Ellen, "He's got incredible eyes. There's so much going on in there. Talk about intense."

Ellen said, "But he's also got that boyish charm."

Still nervous, Allan said, "Hey, no whispering."

Ellen said, "We were just saying how fuckable you are, Allan. We can't decide whether to market you as an author or as a teen idol."

Allan smiled.

Pop.

"Great!" Sandra said, "Try talking. It'll loosen you up. Just let yourself ramble. The more personal the better."

Allan laughed.

Pop.

Allan searched his mind for a topic. "Okay. Did you know that most primitive cultures won't allow their pictures to be taken?"

Pop.

Ellen asked, "Why not?"

"They believe that when a camera records a person's image it also steals their souls."

Pop-Pop.

The photographer looked up for a second, but kept her finger on the shutter's trigger. Allan relaxed as Sandra considered what he had said. "I never thought about it that way. But I guess in a way it does. It captures an emotion. A thought."

Allan looked off to the side a little, thinking about it.

Pop.

Allan had been caught off-guard and Sandra smiled. "Gotcha."

51

Allan allowed his eyes to recuperate in the deep red light of Sandra's darkroom as she slipped an exposed sheet of photographic paper into a large rectangular tray of developing chemicals. Allan and Ellen watched over Sandra's shoulder as a monochromatic image began to blossom from a field of white that had been tinted blood red by the dim light. Allan said, "I didn't know anyone still took pictures on film anymore, much less developed paper prints in actual darkrooms."

Sandra harrumphed and insisted, "I won't even shoot my *dogs* on digital," while prodding the submerged print with rubber-tipped tongs.

Ellen said, "But digital cameras are so simple. I just take picture after picture and never worry about running out of film or developing it later."

Sandra said, "Who said "easy" is better? The discipline required for shooting on film helps focus my energy. Besides, digital shooters who give a shit about the end result spend all of their time after the fact trying to use computer effects to fix up their crappy pictures—and to mimic the character that comes with film grain naturally. It's like screwing every guy you meet in the hopes that one of them will clean up well enough to introduce to your parents." Sandra seemed troubled by the emerging print in the tray, and she raised the eyeglasses, which hung from a librarian's chain around her neck, into position. She muttered, "Been there, done that. No thanks."

Allan said, "Well, I appreciate your taking us back here. This is fascinating."

Sandra spoke distractedly as she inspected the strange image before her: "I figured if you could give us your soul, the least we could do is give you a tour." She scowled at the print. "What the hell?"

Allan and Ellen leaned forward to see what Sandra saw. The shot in the tray was the one of Allan looking off to the side, but there was a ghost image overlapping Allan's. As the picture continued to develop, the "ghost" evolved into the faces of the professor and the Irishman, superimposed over Allan's.

Sandra pulled the paper from the tray to take a closer look. She said, "Who the hell are these guys?" She removed the negatives from the enlarger and brought them over to the light table. Sandra flipped on the table's internal lamps and peered at the negatives through a loupe.

Allan's mind was reeling. How could this happen? Ellen reached for the print to get a better look, but Allan feared that she might recognize Professor Sumner, so he kept it close, pretending that he hadn't seen her efforts.

Sandra said, "It's in the fucking negatives. Every single shot." She called out the darkroom door, "Jamie! Goddamn it I've got a used roll of film in my fucking camera!"

Allan retrieved the 8x10 and stared at it. He was terrified.

"Allan, I don't know what to say. I'm really sorry." Sandra turned on the overhead lights and stormed out of the room, screaming obscenities at Jamie. Allan watched as the light overexposed the print in his hand and turned it black.

52

Argus smoked as he passed a midtown bookstore window. The clerk was putting the finishing touches on a huge display that featured Allan's book: *Pale Horsemen.* In the center of the display was a blowup of the back of the dust jacket, which carried a pencil sketch illustration of Allan. The clerk transferred another stack of Allan's books from the display to the counter and handed a copy to a waiting customer. Argus dropped his cigarette and ground it out with his shoe.

Argus watched from a corner booth as Kendra crossed the room, looking fantastic. When she reached the table he snapped, "You're late."

Kendra said, "I know," and lit up a cigarette, making deliberate eye contact—just as she had in their first meeting at the Waldorf.

"You can save the act. I want you to do a job for me."

"I don't do parties."

"I need your unique talents."

"Why me?"

"You're a good actress."

"How the hell would you know?"

Argus smiled and slipped his hand under her skirt. "You had me fooled."

Kendra stabbed Argus' other hand with a fork and said, "That was nothing." Argus laughed as he pulled his hand back and sucked the blood. She asked, "What's the job?"

Argus pulled out a thick stack of hundred-dollar bills and placed the pile in the center of the table. He said, "I want you to get to know my son."

"What's the catch?" Argus didn't answer. Kendra gathered her things. "Look, if you're not gonna be straight with me I'm out. I don't care how much money you've got."

"My son went to Africa a witless loser and he came back brilliant. Now he's on his way to becoming famous."

"Good for him." Kendra lit up another cigarette, trying hard not to stare at the money.

Argus bristled. "I think he's planning something. Against me."

"So call the cops."

Argus was trying hard to control his temper but was losing the battle. "Look, I don't like these sudden changes in him. I want to know what's going on. I want to know what he's planning. Now, you either want the job or you don't."

53

Journal Entry: Tuesday Morning, 3 a.m.: I haven't left the apartment since the incident at the photography studio except for brief excursions for parts. When I go out I wear the sunglasses so that people won't see my eyes. I still haven't decided what to call the gizmo. Maybe the professor will come up with something if I can manage to sleep again. He's already done that once—helped solve a problem on the panel modification. It was a little creepy to wake up to a note that I had no memory of writing, but the advice was good, and I think we've got the problem solved.

I don't think the boxer likes it here with us. He seems restless. Next time I'll choose more carefully. I think I still have some time, but I don't know how much.

I've moved my things into Mom's room. Maybe her spirit will protect me from Kali. Maybe it will protect me from myself. The hunger's building again and I'm afraid I'm not strong enough to fight it. I think the fear of giving in to the hunger keeps me awake as much as anything.

I've only seen Argus twice in the last few weeks. He says he's been traveling a lot and sleeping on the couch at the office when he works late. He keeps his distance as if he's afraid of me. Good. I walked up behind him once in the kitchen and said something, and he jumped. I wasn't wearing my glasses and he noticed my eyes, though he didn't say anything. But he was watching me too closely.

I've gotten used to the constant sweating. I just wear lightweight clothing when I go out and nothing when I'm here alone. My increasing appetite is a problem, though. I had twelve bags of groceries delivered, and ate everything in less than three days.

After two trips to get my hair cut in one month, I decided to just do it myself. I suppose I could just go to a different place each time or make a schedule so that I only return to each place in a "reasonable" period of time. But still—it's a risk.

Ellen's been hounding me to do TV and radio advertising for the book, but the thing at the photography studio has me worried. What if it happened again—on national TV? Ellen showed up at my door one day, unannounced. I guess she's right, I can't hide in here forever. If I don't find it ... my destiny will find me.

54

Laughton Hince watched Allan pace in the wings as Dean Adashek crossed the stage and thumped on the microphone. "Testing, testing ... Hello?" The dean cleared his throat and looked to the sound booth. "Is this thing working?" The Yale anthropology students gathered in the auditorium snickered amongst themselves.

Allan approached Laughton as the dean began his introduction. He said, "I just forgot everything I was going to say."

Laughton massaged Allan's shoulders as if he was loosening up a prize fighter. He said, "Just take a deep breath. Opening night jitters. Happens to everyone." He removed a handkerchief from his pocket and blotted the perspiration from Allan's forehead. "You'll be fine once you get out there." Allan looked toward the stage. Dean Adashek had finished his introduction, and the audience was clapping. Laughton nudged Allan through the curtains and said, "That's your cue, babe. Knock 'em dead."

Allan walked stiff-legged toward the podium. It seemed to be miles away, and everything was a blur and his heart was thumping so loudly that it drowned out the applause, along with any glib satisfaction that he might otherwise have felt. And then, halfway across the stage, Allan's mind began to drift. He suddenly felt disoriented, out of phase.

As Allan approached, Dean Gruff noticed that the boy was limping in a way that he hadn't during their first meeting. By the time Allan had reached the lectern, something had begun to shift in the deep recesses of his brain. On a conscious level it was like slipping beneath the surface of a vast black lake. Allan reached out to shake the dean's hand and held on tight—more to maintain his balance than as a gesture of affection or respect—and he took a slow breath inward as he sank deeper and consciousness ebbed.

Allan thought, *Professor Sumner is taking over my body.*

It was similar to the experience he'd had at Ellen's party, except that at the party Allan hadn't been as aware of the change. Now he actually *felt* himself slipping away as his personality was subjugated by the professor's. The applause died down and Allan's eyelids drooped closed, as if he'd fallen asleep, but then his grip on the dean's hand tightened once again as Professor Sumner took possession of the body. Dean Adashek said into the microphone, "Allan Steele, ladies and gentlemen—a young man with as much appreciation for education as anyone I've ever had the pleasure to meet."

Allan kept Dean Adashek at the microphone by refusing to break the handshake as he addressed the crowd: "Yes, Dean, but I also agree with Oscar Wilde when he said, 'Education is an admirable thing, but it is well to remember from time to time that nothing worth knowing can be taught'."

The students snickered and Dean Adashek's face reddened, then he quipped, "I don't know, Mr. Steele, I believe I would have to side with Claus Moser, who once said, 'Education costs money, but then so does ignorance'." With that, Dean Adashek headed off-stage.

As Allan watched the dean exit the stage, he spoke into the microphone. "Ah, but Krauss says, 'Education is a crutch with which the foolish attack the wise to prove they are not idiots'."

The crowd began to laugh openly, and Dean Adashek stopped to consider yet another retort. But nothing sprang to mind, so he just hurried off into the wings—to the delight of the student body. Allan turned his full attention to the audience and said, "Which brings us to the Shantu—a tribe who, though uneducated, devised an amazing technique by which knowledge could be passed from person to person." He lowered his voice conspiratorially, "And it's tuition-free."

Kendra watched from the audience as the students cheered the comment and the speaker. Allan didn't strike Kendra as a guy who had ever been a loser, witless or otherwise. He seemed bright, focused, and unquestionably in charge. And, although Allan's physique was a bit reedy for her taste, Kendra thought to herself that this might not be a such bad gig after all.

After the lecture, students filed past Allan on their way out— stopping to comment or just to have him sign their copy of his book. Kendra was the last in line. She had made a conscious effort to dress conservatively in a sweater, blazer, and blue jeans, but it was hard to downplay a body like hers.

Allan spotted Kendra, and she smiled coyly. She said, "Wow, you were great tonight."

Allan's pulse quickened as Kendra's playful gaze lingered. His cheeks reddened and he stammered, "Thanks." Kendra handed him her copy of *Pale Horsemen* and he signed it.

"You're welcome." Kendra smiled and touched his hand as she accepted the signed book. "The lecture was fascinating." Allan smiled back awkwardly. Kendra hesitated for a moment and then said, "Can I ask a personal question?"

"Sure."

"Are you biracial? You've really got a great look. It's so ..."

Allan remembered Jenny's words, and volunteered, "Exotic?"

Kendra's smile was bigger this time. She had grown so sick of hearing that word used to describe her own beauty over the years, especially by "clients", but as a descriptor for this awkward young man—it seemed funny. She said, "Yes, exotic. And very sexy."

Allan shifted his weight from one foot to the other nervously. He couldn't seem to keep the blood from his cheeks. He said, "Oh ... uh ... thanks. My mother is Indian. East Indian. Um, I mean she was." Allan grew sullen. "She died. Recently."

Kendra saw the pain in Allan's eyes, but chose not to open that door. Instead she asked, "And your father?"

"White." Allan's smile was a distant memory now. "German."

Kendra thought back to Argus' cold stare and touch, and was amazed by the difference between father and son. She said, "Well, it was great meeting you, Allan," and turned to leave.

Allan suddenly snapped out of his funk and sputtered, "Um ... would you like to get something? With me." Kendra turned back, waiting for the rest, and Allan cursed his social ineptitude. "I mean ..." He ran his hand nervously through his hair. "... I don't know what I mean. Dinner?"

The tip of Kendra's tongue emerged to touch her upper lip as she looked into Allan's eyes again. She said, "I'd love to, but I've gotta catch a train back to the city."

"You live in the city?"

"Uh huh. I just came in to meet you."

Allan was amazed. "Honest?"

Kendra laughed. "Is that so hard to believe?"

"Well ... yeah." Allan fidgeted. "I'm staying in the city, too." Kendra's gaze made his body itch. "Could we do something, I don't know—next week maybe?"

"I'd like that. Give me a call." Kendra wrote something in her book and handed it back to Allan, along with a playful smile filled with promises. "I'm in the book." Kendra checked her watch and cried, "Oh shit, I'm gonna miss my train! I've *really* gotta go. Bye."

Allan called after her as she hurried out the door, "Wait. I don't know your name."

"Kendra."

"What about your book?"

"I'll get it next time."

After she'd gone, Allan said, "Kendra ..." aloud. He liked the sound of her name in his mouth so much that he said it again. But a moment later his elation was dampened when he tried to remember Kendra's last name. Had she told it to him? Allan struggled to remember—then flopped down into a nearby chair and muttered, "Great."

55

Allan knocked on the apartment manager's door, catching the burly Persian on the way out to dump his garbage. The manager was a gentle, hairy giant who was usually very friendly. But today his smile seemed forced. He said, "Oh good. It's you. I was gonna call you."

"Hi, Mr. Mirshafi. I just came by to pick up the key. I'll be moving in on Monday."

The manager closed his door and started down the hall, toward the trash chute, avoiding Allan's eyes. "Yeah, like I said—I was gonna call you."

Allan asked, "What's wrong?"

The manager opened the chute and dumped his garbage. He said, "It's the apartment. The thing is—I rented it."

"I know. To me."

"Yeah, well ... I didn't call you 'cause I thought maybe one of the others would open up. See, the old man on four's been ready to kick for months now."

Allan fought to suppress a growing rage. "Are you telling me—"

"Look, it's not like I'm gonna stiff you for your deposit or nothin' like that. Let's go back to my place and I'll—"

"I don't want my deposit. I want my apartment."

"Look kid—I'm sorry. It's business, you know? This guy comes in—wants to pay a year in advance cash up front. What am I gonna do?"

Allan began to sweat. He closed his eyes and put the flat of his hand on the wall for support. He closed his eyes and spoke through clenched teeth: "You can't do that. It's my apartment. I had all my stuff shipped from New Mexico."

"Yeah, and we stored it for you—no charge. Some of the boxes busted on the way so me and the wife re-packed 'em for you—"

Allan felt himself beginning to slip beneath the surface of the black lake. He reached out to a dirty wall for support and fought to stay afloat. "You went through my things?"

"I wasn't sure you were comin' back."

"I told you I was coming today!"

"Look kid, I'm sorry." The manager watched as Allan held on to the wall for support—eyes fluttering—trying desperately to retain control. The manager added, "Besides, I hear you're movin' up the social ladder. What do you need this dump for anyway?"

"You heard—" Allan drew a sharp breath and sank like a stone into the cold, dark void of his own subconsciousness. When he spoke again, it was with the boxer's impatient Irish brogue. Allan stood away from the wall, his posture slightly hunched, his hands in ready fists at his sides. He growled, "I'll tell ya' what I need this dump for—ya' fuckin' greasy pig ..."

The manager was taken aback by the abrupt change in Allan. He said, "Hey—you wanna watch your mouth there, kid."

Allan grabbed the metal lid off of the manager's trash can and began to beat him with it, screaming, "I'll tell you what I want, pig! I'll tell ya' what I fuckin' want ..."

"Jesus, kid!" The manager wrestled the lid away from Allan and tried to use it to shield his body as Allan delivered a brutal beating with his fists. The manager cried, "What the fuck! Whattaya want from me?"

"I want my fuckin' place—that's what I want! Do you hear me, fucker? Do you?!"

The manager pleaded, "Y ... yes. YES! Please, kid! For Christ's sake!"

Allan delivered one last flurry of blows to the other man's midsection and then knocked him off of his feet with a savage left hook. A nosy tenant peered out from her apartment and screamed as Allan began to kick the battered and confused manager. Allan turned toward the terrified old lady, spittle hanging from his mouth, and he suddenly regained control of his body. His expression softened and he looked down at the bloodied manager in shock, as if someone else had done the damage. He said, "Mr. Mirshafi?" Allan reached out to help the beaten man, and the manager recoiled in fear. Allan backed away, disoriented, and then ran from the building.

56

Douglas had just taken the first bite of his sandwich. He was settling in to read the materials to Elizabeth that Arthur had dug up for him on Argus Steele when Allan knocked on his door. Douglas set his lunch aside, and padded through the living room in his stockinged feet, calling out, "Coming ..."

Allan was still disoriented from his encounter with the apartment manager. There were smears of blood on his stark white shirt. Allan looked down at the business card in his hand, to remind himself where he was. He said, "Mr. Geffner?"

"Mr. Steele?" Douglas was taken aback by the difference in Allan's appearance and demeanor. "Come in, please." He stepped aside and Allan entered. Once inside, Allan began to pace. Douglas asked, "Are you all right?"

"Huh?" Allan looked up from the floor, but continued to pace. "I ... I don't know."

Douglas waited for Allan to announce the purpose of his visit, but he seemed lost in thought. Douglas prodded, "Did you have a question about your mother's death benefit?"

This roused Allan from his daze and seemed to remind him why he had come. He said, "I was wondering how soon I could get it. I have to get out of my father's house." Allan's face twitched involuntarily and he began to scratch his forearm. "I mean—I don't have to, but I need to."

"Well, we're still trying to tie up a few loose ends." Douglas was fascinated by the change in Allan. He had seemed so sedate the other day. Douglas supposed he could be dangerous—on drugs or something—but his intuition told him *no*. He asked, "Would you like to sit down?"

Allan answered, "Thanks," and sat in a nearby chair—then popped back up like a jack-in-the-box and continued to pace. "So ... how soon did you say?"

"I'd have to check with Bill, my grandson, but my best guess would be a month—maybe two—after we close the case." Allan made a trapped sound and began to scratch faster. His knuckles were bloody. Douglas asked, "Are you sure you're okay?"

Allan said, "I'm not sure of much these days, Mr. Geffner," and sat, then stood up again. "Not much at all."

Douglas heard a sound coming from the bedroom. He said, "Excuse me," and hurried from the room.

Elizabeth had become agitated for no apparent reason. Douglas smoothed her hair and whispered reassurances in her ear, but he couldn't calm her. Douglas hesitated for a moment before going to the automated morphine induction device at his wife's bedside. He pressed the button that would infuse one dose into Elizabeth's IV drip, and then returned to hold her hand. It didn't take long for the drug to take effect. Douglas stroked his wife's fragile hand, which had been bruised by the invasion of the IV tube, and he whispered, "I'm here, baby. I'm right here." When Douglas looked up, he realized that Allan was watching from the bedroom doorway. He had stopped twitching and scratching and now seemed very calm.

Allan said, "I'm sorry."

Douglas looked at his wife's face, which had gone slack, and said, "So am I."

Allan stayed in the doorway, sensing that crossing its threshold would be a violation of the Geffners' sacred space and, in a voice far too wise and tired for his years, he said, "I don't know which is better—to lose someone suddenly without a chance to say goodbye ... or to watch them waste away with plenty of time to wrap things up, each day dying a little inside, yourself, while you put on a happy face for them." Douglas considered the question for a moment, but had no answer. Finally, Allan confided, "Death follows me wherever I go these days."

"Then leave, Mr. Steele." The tone of Douglas' voice was gentle but firm. "Please."

"I wrote down the phone number and address at my father's apartment. Please ask your grandson to send the check as soon as he can. And call me if you find out anything about him." Douglas' eyes inadvertently jumped to the files beneath his sandwich. Allan said, "Detective McCrae and his partner seemed satisfied, but I'm not. I think he did it," and walked away.

A moment later Douglas heard the front door close, but he was in no hurry to release his wife's hand. The files and the troubled young man could wait.

57

Later that night, Allan unpacked the last of the cartons containing the professor's books and added them to the shelf in his mother's room. He hated being forced to stay at his father's house, but seemed to be short on options, at least for the time being.

There had been another message from Jenny on the machine. Allan had erased it. Things were too weird right now—*he was too weird*—and he wasn't about to drag Jenny into his madness.

Allan retrieved a framed magazine cover that bore the professor's picture and dusted it off, wondering how long he'd be stuck in New York. The advance on his book had been small, but Laughton had predicted that his first royalty check would be impressive. Maybe that money could buy a new life for Allan—away from his father and the painful memories of his mother and the professor's deaths. But what about the drums? Was there anyplace he could hide from them?

Allan placed the framed magazine cover on the shelf, reading the caption as he recalled the moment. He looked around the room at all the books and began to run his fingertips along the leather spines, remembering what was contained in each precious volume. Allan moved to the desk, picked up the copy of his book that Kendra had given him, and flipped through the pages, muttering, "Kendra what? Jones? Smith? Abromowitz?" Allan finished fanning the pages and tossed the book onto the bed in frustration. But as he turned away, something registered. "She said ..." He grabbed the book and turned back to the title page—where Kendra had written her phone number. Allan smiled and shook his head as he spoke her parting words aloud: 'I'm in the book.'

Part IV

ॐ ◈ ॐ

Hunger

58

Orange blossom water was sprinkled from long silver shakers into Allan's and Kendra's open hands as the remains of a lavish nine-course meal were cleared from the ornate, low table near the edge of the stage. A belly dancer gyrated beneath the spotlight, sending Allan into a silly, drunken giggle. Kendra was still amazed by Allan's innocence. She said, "I can't believe you've never tried Moroccan food before."

Allan shrugged and rubbed the scented water into his hands. The wine had hit him hard and he struggled to speak clearly, "I've never been very adventurous."

Kendra laughed, drawing Allan's attention to her copy of his book. "What would you call this? Fiction?"

Allan pushed the book aside, wanting to forget that part of his life—at least for tonight. He just wanted to be a normal guy on a normal date. He said, "I meant apart from that."

The server freshened their drinks and Kendra brought Allan's hands to her face, inhaling deeply. "Mmm ... I love that smell."

Allan looked at her, dopey-eyed, and cooed, "This is great."

Kendra looked away, already a little uncomfortable with this job, and noticed a woman sitting alone at a corner table. Kendra asked, "Do you ever look at people and wonder what they're thinking? You know—what their lives are like?" Allan smiled, sensing a kindred spirit, while Kendra continued to study the solitary woman. "I do. All the time. That's one of the things that fascinated me about the Shantu. I think we all wonder what and how other people think, but they actually get to find out. What impressed me most about your book was the empathy you had for the people of the tribe and your friend, the professor. That's why I had to meet you. How did you get into their heads like that?"

"Sorry." Allan finished his drink. "That's between me and my journal."

"Aha! You keep a journal." Allan clammed up and refused another refill of his drink. Kendra studied the troubled look on his face and decided to drop the subject, for now. She said, "I just knew you'd be brilliant and sensitive ..." She touched Allan's hand. "... just like you are." Allan's sudden smile was broad and childlike. He looked away, deliriously happy, and Kendra asked, "Is it my imagination or do you not get out of the house too often?"

"Until the professor—I never got out of the house. I mainly sat around feeling sorry for myself."

"Then I feel honored."

"Yeah?" Allan was liberated by the alcohol. His eyes were filled with pure, trusting, puppy love. He said, "And I feel like I want to kiss you." Kendra was about to encourage him, but then she stopped herself. She found everything about Allan to be very curious, and a little sad. But whatever Allan was—he certainly wasn't what she had expected.

The belly dancer stepped down from the stage and began to move through the audience while Allan continued to search for his own reflection in Kendra's eyes. And just as Allan leaned forward to kiss Kendra, the dancer interjected her rolling abdomen between them. The audience laughed and clapped as the dancer teased Allan, dancing around him, flirting with her eyes, and generally embarrassing the hell out of him. Kendra sat back and enjoyed Allan's predicament. She sipped her drink and watched Allan squirm, genuinely affected by his unguarded, boyish charm.

59

Kendra unlocked the door to the penthouse, supporting Allan with her free hand. Allan whipped a forefinger to his lips, inadvertently poking himself in the eye in the process, and said, "Shh ... Listen ..." He rubbed his watering eye and peered into the shadowy apartment. "Is he here?"

"He who?"

"The big bad wolf."

Kendra's smile faltered. She said, "I don't know. I don't hear anyone."

Allan whispered into the darkened room like a frightened kid into an ancient cave. "Hello ... are you here?" There was no answer, which relaxed both Allan and Kendra. Allan gave an exaggerated shrug and said, "I dunno where the heck he goes. He's never here." Allan's knees buckled and he cried, "Whoops!" Kendra strained to keep him standing, and they ended up in an awkward embrace. Allan whispered, "Thanks for the ride home—and for my first date."

Kendra laughed. "First date?" The sincere look in Allan's eyes wiped away her cynical smile. "Ever?"

Allan shushed her by raising his finger to his lips again, more carefully this time. He did his best island accent: "You know, if I'd taken the train home by myself I might have ended up in Jamaica and I'm definitely not dressed for it, man."

Kendra said, "By the looks of this place you could afford a car."

Allan stifled a volcanic belch and fought to keep the contents of his stomach down. He said, "I don't drive. I guess I could now, but I've never been able to before. So I never have, and I probably won't—simply because I haven't." Allan replayed what he'd just said in his head. "Does that make any sense?" Kendra smiled and kissed him. It was a soft, sweet, genuine kiss that caught Allan completely off-guard. A huge, dopey grin spread across Allan's face and he said, "Wow."

"Is that all you have to say? 'Wow'?" Allan shook his head and spoke in a tone so low that it was virtually inaudible. Kendra moved closer, brushing the tip of Allan's nose with her own, and asked, "What was that?"

Allan blushed as he repeated himself: "Another, please." Kendra kissed him again, but just as things were beginning to heat up, she broke away. Allan said, "Wh ... What? Did I do something wrong? Was it the tongue thing?"

"Was this really your first date?"

"First date, first drink ... first kiss." He searched his memory. "Well, at least, you know, like that." Kendra stared at him, wondering. Then Allan kissed her, and when the phone began to ring they ignored it.

The answering machine finally picked up and Argus' voice said, "It's me, Allan. You there? I'm not going to be home again tonight. See you tomorrow." The message ended and the machine clicked off.

Kendra pulled away, affected by Argus' intrusion. Allan looked at her, breathless and confused by the sudden chill. He asked, "Wh ... what?" After a long moment, Kendra embraced him again, but this time it was all business. She unbuttoned his shirt with one hand as she undid her own blouse with the other. Allan pawed Kendra clumsily as they moved to the couch. Jackets, shirts, pants and socks rained down across the furniture as Allan tore the clothes from their bodies. Kendra knelt and slid Allan's briefs down around his ankles, then led him to the couch before standing back to remove her stockings.

Allan watched, slack-jawed, hypnotized by the way she moved, his heartbeat pounding in his ears, drowning out the voices of insecurity and fear. His eyes devoured Kendra's flesh with laser-like attention as she offered it to him, bit by bit:

The tendon of her graceful neck ...

Her smooth, brown shoulders ...

The sway of her breasts, freed from the lacy bra ...

The oblong ridge of her navel, rimmed by moonlight ...

And the white cotton panties that ruffled glistening hairs—then inched their way down miles of legs before coming to rest on the floor.

Allan made a low, guttural sound, and Kendra returned to the couch to lie lengthwise in front of him. He laid down behind her, so that the back of her body was pressed to the front of his. Allan noticed that the shades of their skin, where the curve of his hips traced the swell of her behind, were almost identical. Kendra took Allan's arm and wrapped it around her, and the heat between them intensified. He kissed her neck and she guided his hand up her thighs ...

... to the top, and let it linger there

... then moved his hand slowly across her stomach

... up to her breasts

... to her neck

... and finally to her lips, where she kissed and teased his fingertips. Kendra was surprised and a little excited by the length of Allan's fingernails. Everything about this boy was odd. But why hadn't she noticed the long nails before?

Allan moaned, "I'm sure glad one of us is good at this," and Kendra laughed. Allan's breath became sporadic, and she continued to tongue his fingertips, allowing each one to slide into the wet heat of her mouth. He moved his hands back to Kendra's breasts and caressed them with a little too much vigor. She smiled patiently and showed him, then pressed her body back against his. Allan said, "I ... I don't know what to do. I mean I know what to do, it's just ... You know what I mean."

Kendra reached down to her purse, which she'd left on the floor near the couch, and pulled out a foil-wrapped square. She extracted the condom from its wrapper, reached back without looking, and expertly unrolled the prophylactic onto Allan's burning flesh in a series of fluid movements that would have impressed the hell out of Allan—if he'd had any blood supplying his brain. As it was, Allan just moaned at her touch, and then watched dumbly as Kendra's hand moved between their bodies to guide him as she continued to kiss and lick Allan's fingertips. Kendra arched her back and pushed against him. He drew a quick breath inward—and she whispered, "Slowly. Slowly ..." Allan closed his eyes and tried to concentrate, wanting this feeling to last forever. Kendra moved her body away from Allan's and paused, pressing the tip of his forefinger to her lips. She said, "I'll show you. Just do what I do," and allowed Allan's finger to slide between her lips—just a little. Allan pressed his hips forward—just a little. She said, "Mmm ..." and took the finger deeper and Allan followed suit.

Perspiration beaded on Allan's forehead and beneath the sparse hair on his chest. He groaned, "This is *incredible. You* are incredible," as Kendra continued her tutelage. Allan following her lead, synchronizing his hips to her lips, for a long time. And when his movements finally became urgent, Kendra reached back and stroked Allan's thigh in a gesture that was more maternal than passionate.

60

Later, in the kitchen, Allan and Kendra laughed and played as they made hot fudge sundaes in the nude—still sweaty and rumpled from sex. Kendra scooped out the ice cream while Allan chopped nuts, sending an occasional wayward walnut flying to the floor. Kendra said, "You're getting nuts everywhere."

"You're making a pretty good mess, yourself."

"That's *different*." Kendra smiled and licked melted ice cream from her fingers.

The microwave beeped and Allan checked its contents. He said, "The hot fudge is ready to go ..." then crept up behind Kendra and wrapped his arms around her, moving his hands up to cup her breasts, "... and so am I."

"You're gonna make me drop this on the floor." Kendra squirmed as she scooped huge mounds of ice cream into dessert bowls. "Then what are we gonna do?"

"Gee, I don't know." Allan nibbled her neck.

"Mmm ..." Kendra pushed her body back to meet his and said, "You weren't kidding. You are ready." Allan turned Kendra around and kissed her hard, sliding his sweaty body against hers. She nibbled his lower lip and said, "You know, we don't have to do all of your catching up in one night." Allan pulled Kendra closer and kissed her again. She reached down between their bodies to touch him. "God, you're so hot."

Allan smiled and said, "Thanks."

She continued to stroke him as they kissed. "I meant your body's burning up." Allan groaned and slid his hands down the curve of her lower back. Kendra reached over and quietly grabbed a scoop of ice cream from one of the bowls with her bare hand. She brought it between their bodies, without notice, and applied it to Allan's—

"JESUS CHRIST!" Allan tried to pull away, but Kendra held him close, massaging him with the melting ice cream.

She nibbled Allan's earlobe and whispered, "Cooling down?"

"Yes and no." Allan panted as Kendra continued to move her hand. "Ah ... Wow!"

"I'm not hurting you, am I?"

"It's very, very cold" She kissed him and continued her movements, causing steam to rise from his fevered skin. Allan began to ramble, between kisses: "Your mouth ... It's so hot ... Must be the contrast. Heat differentials are greatly dependent upon levels of contrast. That is, *perceived contrasts* as opposed to bona fide, *proven* contrasts."

"Hmm ... What an *interesting* phenomenon. Perhaps we should investigate further." Allan tried to catch his breath as she kissed, licked and nibbled her way down his sweaty torso. Kendra said, "You're very salty," and let her tongue slip into his belly button before continuing south. She sank to her knees and Allan's jaw dropped. Kendra purred, "Mmm ... Sweet. Now this is my idea of dessert." Allan gripped the edge of the counter, feeling suddenly weak in the knees. And, after a prolonged moment of indulgence, Kendra said, "Allan?"

"Y ... Y ... Yes?"

"Pass the hot fudge."

61

That night Kendra suffered strange dreams in Allan's arms as he lay awake exhausted, but as always, too wired to sleep. Allan kissed Kendra's bare shoulder, slipped out of bed, and crept to the window to open it. He closed his eyes and let the icy winds cool his overheated body while the restless voices within murmured their troubled secrets and his heartbeat drummed wildly.

Kendra shivered and pulled the covers close. She opened her eyes and saw Allan staring off into the night, his boyish face so tired and haunted. Allan suddenly thought of Kendra and closed the window. He turned to see if he had disturbed her, and she closed her eyes again just in time. Allan slipped on a pair of jeans, sneakers, and a thin sweatshirt before taking his keys from the bedside table and creeping out of the room.

Kendra waited to hear the front door close. When the sound came—she jumped out of bed and looked around the room, adrenaline pumping, wondering where to start. Deciding on the bureau, Kendra rifled through the drawers as she listened carefully for the front door. Nothing but socks and underwear in the first two drawers. Sweaters in the third, and something else ... way in the back.

Kendra extracted the journal and one of the mini DVDs that had been tucked behind the sweaters. She switched on the bureau lamp. A black Sharpie had been used to label the silver side of the recordable DVD "Shantu Ritual 1: Kali," in Allan's awkward hand. Kendra felt lightheaded and sat back onto the bed. Surely this wasn't what Argus was after. This was too easy.

Kendra fitted the little DVD into the inner circular indentation of the loading tray of the bedroom's DVD player, hit PLAY, and switched on the TV before returning to the bed. She hugged her knees to her chest and chewed her nails as the TV's screen flickered to life and the Shantu ritual began.

62

As Kendra learned his secrets, Allan shuffled aimlessly through the city. After a while, he strayed from the uptown neighborhood of his father's penthouse into a darker, more densely populated place. Allan's eyes were fogged by exhaustion and his mind was a cyclone of foreign memories and emotions. As he walked through the windy streets, Allan's body seemed to move of its own accord to a predestined location.

He turned a series of corners and finally stopped in an alley. Allan studied the dilapidated brownstone that stood before him, and was overcome by an eerie sense of déja vú. He heard heavy, uneven footsteps approaching from behind, but couldn't tear his eyes away from a dark, broken window on the third floor. In his mind, Allan saw the crumbling brickwork around the window restore itself, while the warm yellow glow of a table lamp cast graceful shadows on lacy curtains that hadn't hung there for thirty years.

A woman's silhouette enters the window's frame and Allan smiles. But his nostalgic pleasure soon falters as the shadow of a man joins her in the golden lamplight. The silhouettes embrace, the woman steps back to unfasten her dressing gown, and then she lets it drop. Allan is devastated, though he doesn't know why. He hears a wolf-whistle echo through the alleyway behind him, but he still can't pull his eyes away from the window.

"Hey Shawn, yer old lady—she ain't bad. Looks like somebody's gonna get himself a nice little piece of ass tonight." The voice speaks with a lisp from a fat lip. "Hey, we could all take turns. Whattaya think? With a dame like dat you're probably used to sloppy seconds, huh?"

Allan turns to find an oafish, bush-league boxer laughing at him. He is a prematurely balding bulldog with cuts and bruises scattered across his face and fresh stitches over his swollen left eye. The boxer carries his shoddy boxing gloves draped over one shoulder, tied at the laces. Allan watches the stranger hawk up a mouthful of phlegm. Allan whispers, "Manny? Manny Vitelli?"

"Yeah right, like you don't know me—you crooked mick piece a shit."

"Fuck you, ya' spineless guinea bastard." Allan hears himself speaking in the clipped, gruff tone of the Irishman, but feels utterly disconnected from his body.

"How 'bout I fuck yer old lady instead?" The boxer looks up to the window and shakes his head in mock disappointment. "Nah ... Guess I'd have to get in line."

Allan feels his face flush. He clenches his fists and says, "What, one beatin' a day ain't enough for ya', Manny?"

"One woulda been plenty if I'da had a straight shot at it. But I don't see any bought refs back here, so I guess it'll do." Manny closes the space between himself and Allan, retrieving a splintered baseball bat and metal trash can lid from an overflowing cluster of garbage cans along the way.

Allan looked back up to the window, anger rising like bile in his throat, and then he returned his attention to Manny. But the other boxer was gone, and a young thug had taken his place. The thug said, "Hey, man. You deaf? I said what the fuck you doin' in my alley? I don't remember givin' you permission to be in my fuckin' alley."

Allan reemerged from the cold black lake of his subconscious, confused and disoriented. He said, "I ... I couldn't sleep."

"No one trespasses my alley, man."

"I didn't mean to. I just ... It was the voices."

"Voices, huh?" The punk softened, smelling a potential customer, and extracted a handful of plastic bags from his pocket that had been stocked with brightly-colored pills. He took a deep drag from his cigarette and said, "Why didn't you say so, brother? I hate those fuckin' voices." Allan studied the other man with suspicion. "Oh yeah, baby. I got voices up the ass." The thug spoke in a low, confidential tone. "But I got a way to shut 'em up. If you got the cash." He dangled a bag in front of Allan's tortured eyes, tempting him. He said, "I can help you out, man."

Allan started to step closer, but then changed his mind. The dealer reached into his other pocket and began to pull something out. Allan saw a flash of silver in the moonlight and his instincts took over. He shoved the dealer into the trash cans and ran from the alley. The dealer screamed, "Shit, man!" and picked himself and his pills up out of the garbage. He swiped withered lettuce leaves and rotting meat scraps from his clothing, calling out, "No need to get mental." The dealer reached back into his pocket and extracted a shiny silver flask. As Allan's footfalls sped away, the dealer shouted, "Fuck you, man. FUCK YOU!"

63

Kendra watched as Kali stood triumphant—her foot on the priest's headless corpse and her knife held high. Kendra averted her eyes from the gore, but it didn't take long for morbid curiosity to draw them back. As she studied the woman who played Kali, Kendra opened her robe and let it fall to the floor, and compared herself in the bureau mirror to the goddess on the DVD.

Their breasts were similar in shape and placement on their torsos, though Kendra's were slightly smaller. Both women appeared to be within inches of each other in height. But Kendra noted, with more than a little pride, that her ass was higher and firmer than Kali's. Nice to know that all those dance classes and countless hours on the stair-climber hadn't been wasted.

Illuminated only by the flickering blue light of the TV screen, Kendra raised one hand in triumph, posing like her video counterpart. She scowled and postured until she became so immersed in the charade that she didn't hear the front door open and close.

Allan moved through the penthouse, and heard the distant drums coming from the TV down the hall, but he assumed the all too familiar sounds were in his head. Allan neared the bed-room, mouth dry, breath coming in shallow, panicked gasps. Allan gathered his courage before rounding the corner to his mother's room, and he entered just as the DVD ended and static filled the large TV screen. Allan saw Kendra silhouetted against the erratic flashes of light behind her—posed as Kali—and he gasped. Kendra turned toward the sound and saw Allan frozen in the doorway, like a deer in the headlights of an oncoming truck. Kendra took a step toward Allan and he backed away, terrified, until he stumbled over a table. He fell to the floor screaming.

Kendra moved to help him, at a loss for what to do or say. "Allan ..."

"NO! Get away from me!" Allan cowered in the corner, wide-eyed and trembling, unable to speak.

"It's me ... *Kendra*... Are you okay?" She reached for him and he recoiled.

"Wha ... What do you want?"

Kendra switched off the TV and turned on a small bedside light. Being caught in the blatant invasion of Allan's privacy had sent her heart racing, but Kendra was baffled by the intensity of Allan's fear, nonetheless. She asked, "What is it? Talk to me."

Allan whimpered, "Kendra?"

"It's okay." Kendra was torn between genuine sympathy and curiosity at Allan's bizarre reaction. She said, "It's only me."

"Why were you standing there ... like *that*?" Allan leapt to his feet, suddenly furious. "What are you trying to do to me?"

Kendra retrieved her robe and slipped it on, her instincts telling her to play dumb. Kendra asked, "What are you talking about?"

Allan saw concern in Kendra's eyes, and tried to calm himself. Suddenly, nothing made sense. He said, "I don't know," and began to pace. "It's my mind. I can't focus. I'm confused."

Kendra tied her robe and sat on the edge of the bed. She asked, "Where did you go?" Allan remained silent and continued to pace, staring at the floor and rubbing his face with his hands. He was unable to answer because he didn't remember most of it. After a moment, Kendra moved closer and put her arms around him. "Did you sleep at all?"

He closed his eyes and held her a little too tightly. "I don't know. I don't think so."

"Allan, what's going on?" Allan remained silent. "I mean, if you need someone to talk to—"

Allan pulled away, suddenly angry and suspicious again. "Why do you care?"

Kendra was caught off guard. She turned away, face flushed, and answered, "What kind of question is that?"

"An honest one. How about an honest answer?"

"I don't know why." Kendra was frustrated and dealing with her own confusion. She finally met his eyes and said, "That's the truth, okay? I don't know why I care. But I do."

Allan's anger softened and then turned inward—into torment. He said, "You'd better go," and traced his finger along the curve of her cheek. Before Kendra could respond, Allan had turned away and was heading for the bathroom. He said, "I'm sorry," and closed the door.

Kendra removed the mini DVD from the player. She studied the little silver disc, wondering how the images contained upon it could have inspired such fear in Allan. Finally, at a loss, she returned the DVD to its rightful place and gathered her things.

Allan emerged soon after Kendra left and made a beeline for the desk. He tore through the drawers and rifled stacks of papers, exhausted and desperate. "C'mon ... Goddamn it! Where is it?" After an exhaustive search, Allan finally found what he'd been looking for: Dr. Bill's card.

64

"I'm looking for a goddess."

"Aren't we all?" The plump young man behind the reference desk hadn't even bothered to look up from his paperwork. "Greek, Egyptian, Vedic ...?"

Kendra thumbed through the pages of Allan's book. "Either African ... or Indian."

"American Indian or East Indian?"

"East."

The pimple-faced kid still hadn't looked up from his work. He said, "You've got about thirty to choose from. Can you be a little more specific? Where does she hang out?"

The brainy kid's impatient tone made Kendra feel like an idiot. She said, "Um ... I don't know. I'm sure he went into that in the book, but I don't really remember."

"Trees, churches ... caves ...? Most ancient deities were either location- or event-specific. Gods of the forest, goddesses of the hunt ..."

Kendra suddenly remembered the label on the DVD she found in Allan's drawer and blurted out, "Kali. That's it—*Kali.*" The kid looked up from his books, suddenly interested, and Kendra asked, "Have you heard of that one?"

Kendra studied photographs of ancient sculptures and carvings of Kali as Mr. Reference lectured from memory: "Kali, also known as Ma Kali—roughly translated as "Dark Mother." Hindu, but specifically Bengali. She and all of the other goddesses in Hindu mythology are aspects—or *elements*, you might say—of a goddess named Devi. Now, Devi's the big *Kahuna*, right? The sum total of all existence. But Kali didn't really show up until post-Vedic times. She's the patron goddess of thugs and lost souls—basically people on the fringes of society—and is renowned throughout Hindu literature as the most frightening and bloodthirsty of all of Devi's aspects. Her first big splash was at the site of the slaughter of the Pandava army by the Kaurava warriors." He quoted proudly from memory: "'She was black as the night, her mouth bloody, her hair disheveled and in her hand she held a noose in which she led away the souls of the dead.'"

Kendra said, "Nice," and turned to the next page, feeling queasy.

"Yeah, she was a real kick-ass bitch. You remember the last scene in Aliens—where Ripley comes out all bloody and sweaty in this freakin' awesome mech suit to fight the ginormous alien who has that little girl cornered? Well, Kali was like *that*, totally fierce. There are other stories that have her jumping into the heart of battle—beating the crap out of everyone with this skull-handled staff, or flinging herself at demons and crushing them in her mouth. And then there's the one where she grabs the enemies of her children by the hair and decapitates them with her sword."

"Her children?"

"Her devotees. Once they vow allegiance to her, Kali becomes their mother in an incestuous kind of way. But she's just as ruthless in her punishment of wayward children as she is in defeating their enemies." He leaned in close enough for Kendra to smell the chocolate on his breath. "They say that those who deny her the sacrifices she demands are driven to madness."

She gave him a dreamy 'You're s-o-o-o smart' look and cooed, "Wow! Anything else?"

He let his gaze drop to her breasts and said, "Kali is supposed to be as beautiful as she is terrifying. She hangs out in trees, caves, mountains, crossroads, cremation grounds ... And her dance is *central* to her iconography. She performs this Dance of Death on the plane of the human soul."

"Dance of Death?"

"Pretty wild, huh?"

Kendra took a moment to process what she'd heard and then said, "Tell me more about this dance."

65

Someone had been pounding on the door for what seemed like hours. At first the sound had no effect on Allan's murky, drug-induced sleep. Gradually, the persistent thumping found its way into his nightmare.

He was running along the subway tracks and something was chasing him. The thing had a headlight like a train, but it wasn't a train. Allan couldn't see the beast itself but he could feel it behind him—closing the gap—breathing down his neck like a dragon with a single scorching eye. The pounding kept growing louder, and then the sound warped and changed into the drums of Kali. Allan ran for his life without looking back—not wanting to know what was behind him. The subway dragon quickened, and now the light from its eye was so close that the heat of it was burning the back of Allan's neck. He could smell his own searing flesh ...

Allan opened his eyes, still drugged and gasping for breath, and tried to make sense of the distant pounding that had bridged the chasm between his dream and consciousness.

The door. It had to be the door.

Allan staggered from the bed, sweating and naked, willing his leaden feet toward the insistent rapping. He mumbled, "Coming," as he shuffled down the hall. The light seemed too bright, so Allan pulled the living room drapes closed.

When Allan finally reached the door, he struggled with the locks, and then opened it just wide enough to peek through the crack. He said, "Go away," and closed the door before the impatient face in the hallway had registered in his muddy brain.

The voice on the other side of the door said, "Allan! Open the fuckin' door."

"Jenny?" Allan turned back to the door and opened it. "Jen?"

Jenny pushed past him, her duffle bag slung over one shoulder. She said, "Would you get some clothes on, please? I'm pissed off, and I don't wanna be distracted."

Allan was still disoriented. He asked, "Pissed off? At me?"

"Who else, Allan?" Her eyes skated across his sweaty body and then returned to his dazed expression. "What's this bullshit about not being able to tell me what's going on? You didn't even bother returning my fucking phone calls! I *was* worried. Now—I'm pissed."

Allan was too tired to stand. He slumped into a nearby chair, but still lacked the presence of mind to cover his nakedness. He said, "Jesus, Jen. I'm sorry. I just—"

"You just what?" She pulled a copy of his book from her duffel and tossed it onto a chrome and glass table. The *thwack* that rang out as the book landed made Allan jump. Jenny asked, "Wrote a book? Got famous? Started doing fucking daytime talk shows and forgot to mention it?"

Allan said, "I don't do TV," and offered a timid smile.

"Cute. You know what I fucking mean, Allan." She was glaring at him now, though her eyes were still tempted to wander. She asked, "What the hell's going on?"

Allan pinched the bridge of his nose between his thumb and forefinger and said, "I'm sorry, Jen. I'm all fucked up."

She sat, feeling better after the release, and sighed, "No shit." Then she added, "But you've got a better body than I'd imagined."

Allan blushed, suddenly realizing that he was nude. He said, "Shit. I'm sorry Jen," and retrieved the book to cover himself on the way back to his bedroom. He called back, "I took some pills to help me sleep and they really knocked me out. I'm sorry."

She watched him go, smiling for the first time. "You're sorry and I'm fuckin' *horny*. You're the first naked guy I've seen up close in almost a year. How pathetic is that? Nice ass, by the way." She stood to check out the place, and snuck a glance back into Allan's room. He was blotting the perspiration from his body with a towel before stepping into a pair of jeans. Jenny said, "You got a girl back there?"

"What?"

"Did I interrupt something?"

Allan reentered the living room, slipping a lightweight shirt over his head. "A girl?"

"You're sweating like you just ran a marathon—or I interrupted something. I mean, it's thirty degrees outside."

Allan's thoughts turned to Kendra. He said, "No. No girl. Not anymore." There was a look on Jenny's face, but Allan couldn't tell if it was jealousy or concern. But either way, he liked it. Allan said, "I'm just hot."

Jenny arched her eyebrows and replied, "You certainly are. What's with the makeover?"

"Huh?"

"Your glasses, or lack thereof—and the hair extensions."

Allan played along. "Oh, yeah. Do you like the new look?"

"I haven't decided. You don't really look like you anymore, but I must admit that the whole package is pretty damned sexy."

She smiled and gave him a playful wink. "C'mon, take me out for breakfast before I start humping the furniture."

66

The waitress brought Allan's second stack of blueberry pancakes to a booth in the darkest corner of the deli. Jenny watched in amazement as Allan attacked the food. "You eat like this all the time?"

Allan answered with his mouth full. "I'm always hungry. Chet thinks it's all part of some kind of metabolism problem."

"What's he doing about it?"

"Nothing yet. We've been waiting to see if it goes away on its own." He noticed that Jenny had only eaten half of her omelette. Allan gestured with his fork. "You gonna finish that?"

Jenny pushed the plate toward him. "But I still don't understand how the metabolism thing fixed your dyslexia. And your eyes getting more sensitive to light—*that* can't be good." Allan shrugged and continued to eat. Jenny studied his face. "This girl—Sandra— did she break your heart?"

"*Kendra,* and I still don't wanna talk about it."

"She turned you gray."

"Huh?" Allan reached for the syrup.

"You're going gray around the temples. That's new, too. If I were you I'd get out of this city quick, before you self-destruct completely."

"I can't leave. Not yet."

Jenny was worried, but she decided to let it slide for now. She asked, "So, do I get a tour of the city or what? I told Geronimo I'd be gone for a week, so if you can fit me into your busy schedule ..."

Allan had mixed feelings about Jenny's visit, but he feigned unabashed enthusiasm. He said, "A week? That's *great,* Jen. I've gotta pick up a library book I've been waiting for. Why don't you go back to the apartment and unpack? I should be home in an hour or so."

67

Kendra had become a regular in the mythology section of the New York Public Library over the last two weeks. Howard, the brainy kid who had helped her on that first day, had developed quite a crush. He had already been admonished several times for abandoning his desk in order to devote his full attention to her needs. So, when he stopped at Kendra's aisle with an eager smile and a cart full of books to be reshelved, her tone was patient. She said, "Hi, Howard."

"Finding everything you need?"

"Yes, Howard. Thanks."

Howard's boss must have gestured to him then, because he gritted his teeth and waved back in acknowledgment, then headed away. Howard grumbled, "See ya'."

"Bye, Howard." Kendra smiled to herself and returned a book to its place on the shelf.

———

When Howard returned to the reference desk, Arthur was engrossed in a private conversation with Douglas Geffner. Arthur saw Howard attempting to eavesdrop and said, "Howie, there's a reference call on line two. Would you pick it up, please?"

Howard muttered, "Yeah," and headed for the phone.

Douglas turned to Arthur and lowered his voice. "How did you get all of this?" He flipped pages. "Medical files, military records ..."

Arthur puffed up like a peacock and said, "Some pretty juicy stuff in there, huh?"

Douglas mused, "This guy is bizarre. He blows a fuse and goes on a killing spree in `Nam, gets awarded the Silver Star and Purple Heart—then gets asked to resign for beating up a call girl."

"So I did good, huh?"

"You did great." Douglas seemed troubled. "But none of this actually proves anything. Steele appears to have been totally devoted to his wife."

"Guilt and love share many of the same symptoms. Hey, who said that?"

Douglas answered, "I don't know."

Arthur said proudly, "I guess I did."

Douglas clapped Arthur on the back. "Thank you, Arthur. I guess it's up to me now."

"Hey, have you read his son's book yet?"

"I just finished it the other night."

Arthur said, "Pretty wild stuff. That kid must be a trip."

"He is."

"But you know, he never really said how they did it—the soul transfer, or whatever they call it."

Douglas considered that for a moment. "No he didn't, did he? But the tribe's focus on Kali was interesting."

"Know who's become an expert on Kali lately? Howie. He's trying to impress this sexy young thing who's been in here boning up on goddesses. Last time I checked she was still over there." He added, "Definitely worth a look."

Douglas checked his watch and said, "I should get going. I'm supposed to have dinner with Bill and his family."

"Okay, see you later, Doug. Let me know what happens with your mystery."

"I will." Douglas waved as he headed for the exit—by way of the mythology section.

———

"Kendra?"

She turned from the shelves, expecting to find Howard back for another gawk, but found Allan instead. She said, "Allan? What are you doing here?"

Allan adjusted his sunglasses and held up a book of near-death testimonials. "I've been trying to get this for weeks. It just came in today. What are you doing here?"

Kendra tried to mask her guilty conscience with a veil of indignation. She straightened her back and said, "Excuse me? I think I should be offended by that." Kendra edged toward another section.

Allan laughed and stepped into the aisle. "I didn't mean it that way. It's just that ... I'm sorry. I didn't mean it that way."

Kendra decided that the best defense was a good offense. She said, "I don't even know if I'm *talking* to you. You blow up at me, two weeks go by, and you don't even call to apologize ..."

"Look, I don't blame you for being mad. I don't know what happened. My mind—it just *snapped*. I hadn't been sleeping and when I saw you there by the window it reminded me of ... a nightmare I'd been having."

"How can you have nightmares if you don't sleep?"

"Okay, a *daymare*." Allan wandered back to the section where he first saw Kendra. "What were you reading?"

Kendra almost lied, but decided to take another tack, and answered, "Hindu mythology."

Allan's smile faded, and he studied Kendra with suspicion.

Douglas rounded the corner and almost didn't recognize Allan beneath his dark glasses. He said, "Mr. Steele?"

"Mr. Geffner? What are you doing here?"

"I used to work here." Douglas took a moment to choose his words carefully. He asked, "Do you have a moment, Mr. Steele?" He held up the research on Argus. "I've discovered some things about your father that you might want to know." Allan looked at Kendra and then back to Douglas. Douglas took note. "Oh, I've caught you in the middle of something. This must be the young lady who's been researching goddesses. Is she helping you with your next book?" Allan gave Kendra an accusatory look, which Douglas took as his cue to leave. He said, "I'm sorry, I didn't mean to interrupt. Call me if you'd like, Allan."

Allan answered without breaking eye contact with Kendra. His tone was flat and lifeless. "Okay. Thank you." Douglas left, and Allan took a step toward Kendra. He tried to sound casual. "You've been researching goddesses? Which ones?"

Kendra's lips moved silently for a moment before the lie emerged: "Not just goddesses—Hindu mythology in general."

"Why?"

"I wanted us to have something in common ... that we could talk about." Allan was still watching her a little too closely. Kendra explained, "I guess I just wanted to know more about you. You know, where you come from—spiritually speaking."

"Really?"

Kendra moved closer and asked, "Why are you so surprised?"

It took Allan a moment to decide whether or not to believe Kendra. Once he decided, all doubt evaporated and in its place was shame at having ever doubted her in the first place. Allan said, "I guess I've never had anyone care enough about me to want to know more," and put his arms around her.

Kendra arched an eyebrow and said, "Shouldn't you be out inventing something, or writing another bestseller?"

"Oh, shit." Allan checked his watch, grimacing. "I told Jenny I'd be back to show her around town."

"Who's Jenny?" The twinge of jealousy in Kendra's voice was unintentional.

Allan smiled. "A *friend*. From Santa Fe."

"Is she a dumpy, ugly kind of friend—or the cute, horny type?"

Allan decided to milk it. "Definitely horny. And she *did* say I have a nice ass."

She put her arms around him and grabbed his butt. "Why was your *friend* checking out your ass, Allan?"

"It's a long story."

Kendra loosened her grip. "Well, she's right. And I've missed it."

Allan kissed her, then turned away to survey the books that surrounded them. He asked, "Have you ever noticed when you open a book—at least, a *great* book—and flip to a random page ..." He pulled a random book from a shelf and did just that as he continued, "... the words always seem to apply directly to your life? It's like the author wrote this personal note to you, stuck it in a bottle, and tossed it out to sea, somehow knowing that fifty or a hundred years later you'd find it."

Kendra watched Allan gently close the book. He caressed the cover, lost in his thoughts. His boyish innocence and sincerity continued to amaze her. Kendra asked, "You okay?"

"Yeah. It's just *this place*." He spoke in the quick, giddy tone of a zealot: "All of this *knowledge* ... It's addicting. I used to come here just to hold the books in my hands, imagining the secrets they could tell me. But my fantasies weren't even close. I get lost in their words. All their beautiful words ... It just makes me so—"

"High."

Allan laughed. "I don't know if I'd say *that*."

"Why not? You get high off books."

Allan considered Kendra's observation for a moment, and then admitted, "Yeah, I guess I do."

A recorded announcement came over the P.A. system stating that the library would be closing in five minutes. Kendra moved closer, turned on by Allan's oddities—despite her efforts to keep him at arm's length, emotionally. She moved close and whispered, "Hey, junkie. I've got an idea."

68

Allan groaned as he straightened his legs. At first, the idea of hiding in the restroom until the library closed had seemed daring, in a juvenile way. But an hour and a half crouched on a lidless plastic toilet seat with his knees folded beneath his chin had stripped the adventure bare of romance. As he unlatched the stall door and hobbled from his 3'x4' Formica cell, Allan suspected that his most vivid memories of this particular adventure might be the explicit prose etched into the stall walls and the pungent lemon bite of the janitor's industrial-strength disinfectant.

Although the lavatory's overhead lights had been switched off by the security guard before he left for the night, Allan had no problem seeing in the darkened room. He took a step forward and jumped when he caught a glimpse of a gaunt, gray man in the lavatory's warped steel mirror. Allan's fear of discovery was quickly replaced by clinical interest when he realized that the stranger was *him*—aged by the time-accelerating side effects of his super-charged metabolism.

Upon closer inspection Allan realized that Jenny had been right—he *was* graying around the temples. Allan had cut his hair to the nub the morning after the traumatic incident with Kendra, but it had already grown back down to his shoulders. Luckily, he had never had much of a beard, so the persistent stubble on his face just appeared unkempt, rather than alarming.

If the phenomenon hadn't been so fascinating Allan would have been terrified. His face was drawn and ashen, the soft flesh around his eyes was creased with lines of experience and wisdom beyond his years. As he splashed cold water onto his face, brushed his hair back from his forehead, and fought the nagging hunger, Allan wondered if Kendra would find his new look distinguished.

Allan crept from the men's room into the shadowed silence of the abandoned library. The stillness of the place struck him as intensely monasterial. Allan roamed the massive rooms filled with bloated bookshelves that towered over him like ancient mono-liths. He allowed his fingertips to caress the books' spines as he passed. The night watchman approached—Allan ducked into the Modern Philosophers section. When the guard had passed, Allan continued on to the place where he and Kendra had agreed to rendezvous.

Allan rounded the corner to find Kendra lying naked atop a bed of opened books she had piled in the center of the aisle. Kendra pretended to read casually, as if she were in her own bed-room. Allan moved closer and whispered, "You're kidding, right?"

Kendra smiled and stretched, catlike, across the books. She tossed the current book aside and chose another, flipping to a page at random and reading aloud: 'Put off that mask of burning gold with emerald eyes.'"

Allan moved closer, supplying the next line from his 'collec-tive' memory. "'Oh no, my dear, you make so bold to find if hearts be wild and wise and yet not cold.'"

Kendra read, "'I would but find what's there to find. Love or deceit?'"

When Allan spoke the next line, its irony did not escape him. "'It was the mask engaged your mind and after set your heart to beat. Not what's behind.'"

Kendra was also affected by the poem's relevance. She recited, "'But lest you are my enemy—I must enquire.'"

"'Oh no, my dear, let all that be. What matter, so there is but fire in you—in me?'" Allan lowered his lips to the back of Kendra's calf, moving upward as she chose another book, and another random page. She read, "'As virtuous men pass mildly away ...'"

Allan's mood darkened. The professor knew this piece all too well. "'... and whisper to their souls to go ...'"

"'Whilst some of their sad friends do say the breath goes now and some say no.'"

"'Such wilt thou be to me, who must like th' other foot obliquely run; Thy firmness makes my circle just ... and makes me end where I begun.'"

Kendra looked back over her shoulder and found Allan's lips. She rolled over and pulled him closer, then tore at his shirt. He stood to remove the rest of his clothes and pulled a book from the shelf at random. He read the title of the first poem his eyes fell upon: "My Love in Her Attire." Allan smiled, seeing Kendra as genuinely vulnerable for the very first time. He knelt beside her and discarded the book, reciting from memory: "'My love in her attire doth show her wit, it doth so well become her: For every season she hath dressings fit for winter, spring, and summer. No beauty she doth miss when all her robes are on; but Beauty's self she is ... when all her robes are gone.'"

Kendra was breathless when Allan joined her on her bed of books. She reached for him, speaking softly in his ear: "So you think you know everything, huh?"

"Not everything." Allan kissed her neck and whispered, "Not yet."

69

Jenny was asleep by the time Allan returned from the library. He found her curled up at the foot of the guest room bed. A TV evangelist was sobbing less than two feet from her head. She wore a ratty old tank top with a Greenpeace logo fading across its front and a pair of pinstriped men's boxer shorts. Alan had never noticed her body before. She had always been good old Jenny, like an older sister. But as he crept across the room to switch off the television, Allan found himself aroused by Jenny's bare, tanned legs and her easy beauty.

Allan gingerly pulled the blankets up to cover his friend's newly discovered legs and was tempted to kiss her—to touch her. But he didn't. It felt good to have Jenny there with him, and that was enough. Perhaps her mere presence could keep the drums and the voices at bay. And what about the hunger? Allan was doubtful that anything or anyone could suppress that, but still, it was a nice thought. At the very least he would be forced to keep up a front of normalcy for the coming week. If he could make it through one week without giving in to the hunger . . . maybe he could go two. Allan stood in the doorway, watching Jenny sleep, and longed for the days before the Shantu and his pledge to Kali—for the days before his transformation—when the worst that could be said of him was that he was a geek.

———

Allan slept like the dead that night. The last thing he remembered was returning from Jenny's room, lying down fully clothed, and … sinking. Allan hadn't even had a chance to take a Valium. He was just awake one moment and then:

Comforting, thick, black liquid enveloping him as if he was like slipping into a warm mud bath …

And then it was morning, and he was awake again. Allan's clothes were folded on the chair near the door.

Folded? I don't even remember taking them off. And I don't fold my …

Allan heard Jenny's door open and hurried footsteps moving down the hall, then a crash and Jenny swearing. Allan threw on a robe and stepped out of his room.

Jenny was crouched to investigate the shattered crystal sculpture that she had toppled with her duffel bag as she passed. When she saw Allan watching her, Jenny averted her eyes and continued on toward the front door, offering a hollow "Sorry."

"Jen? Where are you going?" Allan padded after her. "Jen!"

"Home."

Allan tried to skirt the crystal shards that had exploded across the marble floor, but still ended up with one in his foot. He yelled, "OW! Shit! Jenny?" and hopped after her. Allan called out, "Why are you leaving?"

Jenny paused at the front door with her hand on the knob. She said, "Gee Allan, I've got *no fucking clue*. Do you?"

"Would you talk to me?" Allan trailed bloody footprints across the foyer as he limped toward the door. "*Please!*"

"Talk?" She turned back to glare at him. A bruise was blossoming under her right eye and there were purple fingerprints around her wrists. "I thought you were through talking, Allan! I thought you'd had enough of my 'fuckin' cock-teasing'." Jenny was determined not to cry, but her heart was in worse shape than the toppled sculpture.

"Cock-teasing?" Allan was desperately confused and bleeding badly now. "What are you talking about, Jen?"

She saw the innocence in his eyes and was amazed. She spoke slowly and clearly: "*Last night*, Allan. That's what I'm fucking talking about."

"Last night ...? I don't understand."

Jenny was dumbfounded by Allan's denial. She swatted away a renegade tear and spoke each word as if it were a sentence: "It's called *rape*, Allan."

Allan took a step back, away from the accusation, and slipped in the blooming puddle of his own blood. He groped his way to a chair and felt the pain in his groin for the first time. It hadn't registered before, but now—the way he had slept, the folded clothes ... the black lake ... and the pain. Allan pulled open his robe and found scabbing scratches across his chest. He looked up at Jenny, his eyes brimming with horror and tears. When Allan finally found his voice again, it was little more than a faint, trembling whisper: "I raped you?"

Jenny tried to dismiss Allan's innocent act, but it seemed so damned real. She took a cautious step closer and said, "No. But you tried. I had to knee you in the nuts to get you off me."

"Oh, Jesus ..." Allan closed his eyes and sank back into the chair. "Oh, fuck ..." His head was pounding and his heart was threatening to burst through his chest. If he could do this to Jenny—that meant he was capable of *anything*. It also meant that he no longer had control over his own body.

"You were talking funny, too." Jenny was torn between outrage and pity. Allan was clearly devastated. This was no act. She added, "With an accent or something."

Allan blanched and whispered, "The Irishman," and then folded his arms in a self-comforting gesture. He began to rock back and forth, muttering, "Oh my God. What am I gonna do? What the fuck am I gonna do?"

"What are *you* gonna do?" She took another step closer, lowering her bag to the floor. "What's going on, Allan?" Allan searched in vain for a plausible explanation, rocking and mumbling, rocking and mumbling. Jenny moved closer. She said, "Allan? You're scaring me. Stop that. *Please.*"

Allan began to giggle hysterically. "What's going on? What's going on ... What's going on ..."

"Allan?" Jenny reached out to touch his hand.

Allan laughed through his tears as he held Jenny's hand and said, "Karma's going on, Jen. I am so fucked. You have no idea."

"Tell me."

"I can't." Allan felt like the last man on earth. He reached out to touch the bruise on Jenny's face. She stiffened, but allowed him to make contact. "I'm so sorry, Jen. I don't know what to do ..." He was suddenly a frightened little boy, begging for forgiveness: "Please don't hate me, Jen. *Please* ..."

Her own pain dismissed for the moment, Jenny cradled Allan in her arms. She said, "Don't be an asshole. I don't hate you. I just ..." She stopped to choose her words carefully. "... wanna know who the fuck this Irishman is."

"One of the ..." Allan censored himself. "... voices." Allan began to babble: "I have voices in my head, Jen. I can't tell you how they got there, but they're there. I thought I could hold them but—oh shit, Jen—what am I gonna do? If they can take over when I'm *asleep*—what am I gonna do?"

Jenny was at a loss. She'd seen her share of troubled people in her life, but not like this. This was a full-fledged meltdown. She rocked Allan, stroking his hair as she tried to sort out her own warring emotions. "We've gotta get you to a doctor."

"Doctors can't help me. No one can. Not now."

Jenny cradled his face in her hands. "I *can*—if you'll let me."

Allan wanted desperately to believe. "How?"

"I don't know yet." Jenny set her jaw. "But we're starting with a doctor."

Allan reached out to touch her bruise again, and he experienced a devastating moment of clarity. Allan said, "No, Jen. You have to leave."

"What?"

"*Right now*. If you don't it could happen again, or something even worse, and I couldn't stand that."

Jenny took Allan's hand away from her face, turning it up to kiss his palm in an uncharacteristically gentle gesture. She said, "It won't happen again. We're gonna find out what's wrong with you and we're gonna fix it. Okay?"

Allan was about to say something when the elevator outside the front door arrived and Kendra stepped out carrying a bag of hot bagels. "Allan? I brought breakfast—" She stopped in the doorway, taken aback by Allan and Jenny's intimate posture. Kendra said, "Oh … I'm sorry."

Jenny made eye contact and regained a bit of her hard veneer. She asked, "Is this the one who broke your heart?"

Kendra forced a smile and put the bag down. "You must be Jenny." She offered her hand. "My name is Kendra." Jenny reluctantly accepted the handshake.

The tension between the two women was crushing. Allan stood, dumbfounded, still trying to pull himself together. Finally he said, "I'm gonna … uh … take a shower and, um … try to pull the glass out of my foot. You two aren't gonna exchange blows or anything … are you?"

There was another long silence, and then Kendra commented, as Allan tottered away on shaky legs, trailing bloody footprints on the floor behind him: "Jenny looks like she's already done that today." Jenny wasn't amused, but she held her tongue. She watched Kendra take the bag into the kitchen and settle in as if she owned the place. Kendra called to Allan, "Don't forget about the hospital. You said you had an appointment this afternoon."

Allan said, "The hospital?" Allan stopped at the door to his mother's bedroom, suddenly recalling the appointment to see his invention in use. He asked, "Would you call Chet and see if we can reschedule?"

"Sure."

Jenny said, "Hospital? Is Chet a doctor?"

Allan knew what she was thinking. He replied, "Not *that* kind."

"Okay, but he must know someone."

Allan smiled weakly and sighed, "All right, Jen."

"So it's settled," said Jenny as she joined Kendra in the kitchen and took a bagel from the bag. "We'll all go."

70

Argus asked, "So what's this *Kali* got to do with the sudden changes in Allan?"

Kendra seemed uncomfortable. Things felt different now, and it wasn't just Jenny. She said, "I didn't have time to read the journal." She avoided Argus' cold stare. "Maybe the link, if there is one, is there."

Argus was pleased. He mused, "So he was terrified—thinking you were this Hindu goddess?" Kendra checked her watch again. She was supposed to meet Allan and Jenny at the hospital in less than an hour. Argus pressed: "Maybe you could shake him up a little more."

Kendra rose to leave. "I'm meeting Allan and his little friend."

Argus grabbed her by the wrist as she tried to pass. "Don't forget which side you're on. I don't care how good the sex is."

"You've been spying on me?" Kendra glared at him.

"Just keeping an eye on my investment."

"Look, he's just a kid. Why can't you leave him alone? Why can't you just, I don't know … let him be happy?"

Argus seemed genuinely surprised. "Just when you think you know someone … *Sincerity.* I would have never expected it from you." He pulled her close, digging his fingers into the soft flesh of her forearm, and warned, "Don't do it."

"Do what?" Kendra cursed the tremble in her voice.

"Fall in love with my son. Think you'll save him from me. Hope he'll save you from yourself—" He snickered into his drink, "—and your wicked, wicked ways."

Kendra said, "Go fuck yourself," and tried to pull away. "I hope Geffner nails you." She regretted the comment as soon as it passed her lips.

"Geffner? The old man from the insurance company?"

"Forget it. He's harmless." She was desperate to get out of this place, and to get away from Argus. Kendra said, "Just some old guy snooping around."

"And?"

She knew she was going nowhere until she told him, so she sighed and said, "He told Allan he had some information for him."

"About?"

"I don't know."

Argus squeezed harder. There would be a bruise there tomorrow. "You." She continued through clenched teeth, "He has information about you."

Argus filed the news under "potentially dangerous annoyances" and resolved to deal with the nosy old fuck later, then he looked Kendra directly in the eye and said, "Make no mistake. My son is damned."

"Why?" She ripped her arm away from Argus and rubbed the place where he had bruised the skin. "What could he have possibly done to deserve so much hatred?"

"He lived. And now he's gaining strength." Argus dismissed her bewildered expression with a wave and returned his attention to his drink. He spoke to Kendra's back as she walked away: "Even if he never learned the truth about your part in this—you'd still have the guilt." His words followed her toward the door. "You might as well get used to it, Kendra. It'll be with you long after he's gone." She kept walking. "And there's *Passaic* to think about."

Kendra stopped. All the blood had drained from her face. She returned to the table and tried to sound casual. "What are you talking about?"

"Do you actually think I would give a whore this much money without making sure that I had collateral? I know everything about you, Kendra. So just do your job and we'll all live happily ever after." Argus made his choice from the menu and flagged the waitress, adding pointedly, "Except Allan, that is."

71

"Hang on. I'll find Lois."

Allan, Kendra, and Jenny waited as Chet crossed the one-time cafeteria, now converted into St. Luke's new Learning Disorders Treatment Center. There were children everywhere; some were working with adults, some paired off with other children. Allan spotted a therapist working with a preteen girl in the corner, using the prototype of his invention, and he approached them.

The girl, who appeared to be eleven or twelve, held a notepad-sized plastic panel in her hands. She positioned the device over a flyer that looked as if it might have been taken from a break room bulletin board, and then laid the panel down on top of the paper. The girl handled the jury-rigged prototype, which had a tangle of multicolored wires sprouting from one end and several exposed electronic components hot-glued to the other, with a level of enthusiasm and confidence that implied she had used it before. An insulated cable the thickness and color of a number two pencil connected the junction box—which received data from the tablet assembly via the dozen wires that led from its plastic frame—to a modified pair of pink and white Hello Kitty sunglasses, with which the young lady kept fidgeting whenever the weight of the yellow cable threatened to unseat the glasses. Once the scanning element was in place, the girl pressed a grey button on the panel.

For some reason, even though he had designed the device himself, Allan expected some sort of sound when the prototype was engaged—the hum of electricity, the whine of a cooling fan, or the mechanical clack and whir of a scanning element as it moved across the text below—but Allan's invention didn't utilize a traditional scanner and it generated very little heat, so it was virtually silent. The only sound was the girl's delighted giggle as the flyer's text and a single clip art image rose to the surface of the frosted white plastic panel with perfect clarity, as if the markings on the page beneath the prototype had disengaged from the paper and floated to the surface of a milky pool, forming tiny black islands of text, as well as a larger continent in color. The paper beneath the panel had been askew so its digital doppelganger was also crooked. This caused an alignment grid to automatically appear over the recreated text, and then the entire page was shifted until the rows of letters ran true. Once this had been accomplished, the grid disappeared.

The girl wriggled in her chair as she watched the process, insisting, "I love this next part."

Allan saw a yellow LED on the panel's frame blink, and then the letters began to dance; one by one each letter 'b' reversed itself, as did the 'd's. The 'w's and 'm's did vertical flips, and then something in the alignment of some of the sentences themselves shifted, although this and a half-dozen other adaptations happened too quickly for Allan to identify. When the character reversals and other adjustments—already "trained" into the device to counter the little girl's particular perceptual anomalies—were complete, the custom-formatted flyer looked like a grade-schooler's word jumble, although the colorful illustration of a dancing man with a lampshade on his head remained unchanged.

The LED turned green and the therapist working with the girl asked, "Do you have it in your glasses, Elisa?"

Elisa's lips moved a little as she read: "'It's a party! Joey M. in radio …'" She furrowed her brow and tried again: "'… radio log …'"

The therapist slipped the flyer out from under the scanner and located the troublesome word. He said, "Sorry, Elisa. That's my fault. Guess I might want to actually read these things beforehand, huh? You've just been making such great strides that I assumed you can read just about anything now."

Elisa smiled broadly and boasted, "Well, I can. Almost."

The therapist smiled back and explained, "That word is *radiology*, Elisa. It's the place where people have x-rays taken."

The girl continued, "'Joey M. in radiology's last day is Friday, so help us send him off this Thursday night at 6:00 p.m. in the third floor break room. Contact Tess in billing if you'd like to bring something.'" The girl whipped off the Hello Kitty glasses as soon as she had finished reading the translated text. Elisa beamed with pride and excitement as she asked, "Was that it? Did I get it right?"

———

After the tour of the Learning Disorders Treatment Center, Allan wandered off on his own while Kendra listened to Jenny and Chet's excited discussion about the miraculous invention, which Allan had named the Sumner Adaptive Reader. Allan mopped the sweat from his forehead, looking haggard and troubled despite the success of the day. The voices and the drums were back with a vengeance.

Kendra saw Allan heading off down the hall, shielding his eyes from the lights with his hand, and she hurried to catch up with him. Kendra asked, "Allan? Are you okay?"

"I don't know." Allan blinked. "They're getting louder."

Jenny was glad when Kendra left. She'd been trying to get a moment alone with Chet all afternoon. Jenny interrupted Chet's rambling dissertation on the hundred-and-one uses of Allan's device. "I need to talk to you about Allan."

"What about him?"

Jenny spoke in a hurried whisper, keeping an eye on Allan and Kendra. "He's hearing voices. I think he needs to see someone—a shrink or something. You must know some, right?"

Chet looked concerned. "Yes, but—"

"Look, I'm not fucking around!" Chet took a step back and Jenny took a breath. "I'm sorry. I'm just worried about him." She showed Chet the bruises on her wrist that had started to yellow. "He did this last night ..." she removed her sunglasses "... and *this*. And he didn't remember a thing about it this morning. I mean he had no clue. He said it was one of these ... *voices*." Jenny withdrew her wrist and folded her arms. "So, do you know someone or not?"

Chet said, "I'll ask Schultz. He's a Psych intern."

"You don't know any real doctors?" Jenny saw the look on Chet's face and back-peddled. "You know what I mean. What if it's serious?"

"Don't worry, Schultz is good and he knows it. That's why everyone hates him."

"I just hope I can get Allan to go along with it. He's gotten so fucking weird." Chet asked, "Does Allan still have that metabolism problem?"

Jenny was distracted. She'd been watching Kendra kiss Allan. "Huh? Oh, yeah ... He eats like a family of four, if that's what you mean."

Chet said, "Okay, bring him in for tests on that. I'll figure out how to bring Schultz into it."

Kendra noticed that Jenny was watching her and Allan. She asked, "How long is your little friend going to be in town?"

"I don't know." Allan felt disoriented and dizzy. The headache was getting worse by the moment. "A week maybe."

Kendra checked her watch. "I've gotta go. We still on for tonight?"

Allan was trying desperately to ignore the voices and drums in his head. He didn't respond for a moment, and then said, "Huh?"

"Dinner? Tonight. I'm cooking. Remember?"

"Yeah, sure. Don't forget about Jenny."

"I wish." She kissed him and hurried off down the hallway.

Allan called out, "Can you give her a ride home?"

Kendra forced a smile. "Sure." She addressed Jenny curtly. "You ready?"

"Coming, Mom." Jenny exchanged a look with Chet before following Kendra to the exit.

Chet had been paged. He called out, "Allan, don't forget the meeting with Scheel." Allan looked back toward his friend with a blank expression on his face. Chet sighed. "Six o'clock? Empire State Building. Suite 808." Allan waved in vague acknowledgment and wandered off again, not really paying much attention to where he was going. Chet's page was repeated and he hurried off in the opposite direction.

72

Some time later, Allan found himself in St. Luke's Intensive Care Unit. He stopped in a shadowed corner near a break room to allow his eyes to recuperate from the pulsing fluorescent lights. At first, Allan thought the voices coming from inside the room were in his head:

"Oh, please. That's nothing. The old man in bed 224 claims he saw God when he was out."

"God?"

"God, or heaven. Or it coulda been hell. I'm not sure, but whatever it was sure scared the bejesus outta him."

"224? Isn't that the bypass that flat-lined for three minutes?"

"Almost three and a half. Dr. Wincott brought him back."

"Dr. Wincott's such a cutie. Three and a half, huh? No kidding? That's gotta be a new record."

Even in the midst of Allan's pain, he couldn't help wondering what the face of God might look like. Perhaps it was his destiny to find out. Allan mumbled to himself, "Bed 224," and continued off down the hall, trying to stay out of the lights as much as possible.

———

The panicked octogenarian in bed 224 was arguing with a nurse as he attempted to pull the tubes and wires from his body. The old man's bed was in a small, dark corner of the room. He wailed, "I can't stay here. I ... I can't ... breathe ..."

The nurse fought to keep the patient in his bed, asking, "What can I do to help you, Mr. Fisher?"

"The walls ... keeping the air away ..."

"Mr. Fisher, just tell me—"

"The window ... Move me ... Please ... "

The nurse checked the patient's chart and realized that he was listed as severely claustrophobic. She cursed the admitting nurse under her breath. "Okay, we're going to move you over to the window, Mr. Fisher, but you have to promise me that you'll lie quietly until I get back."

The patient nodded yes, but his eyes were still wild. He whimpered, "Please hurry. And ask them to find my glasses." He watched the nurse leave the room. A moment later Allan stepped into the doorway. The patient whispered, "Father?" and extended his bony hand. Allan checked the hallway for a priest, but found himself to be the only person in the vicinity. Then Allan remembered that he was wearing a black shirt with a white collar. The miserable patient said, "Father, *please* ..." and reached out to Allan again. The old man said, "I'm so frightened, Father. I can't die. Not now."

Allan asked, "What did you see?" and took a step closer.

The old man screamed, "I can't die now! Not *now!*"

Startled by the outburst, Allan looked around, but there was still no one else in sight. He said, "It's all right. Just tell me what you saw."

"I HAVE TO GET OUT OF HERE!" The old man tore the IV tube from his arm and ripped the heart-monitoring electrodes from his chest. Allan rushed to restrain him. The old man wailed, "You don't understand, Father. I've seen it! I've seen the other side!" and then he began to sob: "Please, Father ... You have to *warn* them."

Allan fought the hunger and the drums and the voices in his head that urged him on. He whispered, "I will. I'll warn them. But I can't warn them if you don't tell me what you saw."

The patient tried to verbalize what he had seen, but it had been too horrible. His eyes grew wide, his mouth moved, but still—he made no sound. Allan watched as the old man relived the moment. The patient's eyes fixed on a point far away and a tear slipped down his cheek. Then he began to whisper, "No ... sweet Jesus ... I can't die now ..." Allan heard laughter from the hallway moving closer, and the old man repeated, "Someone has to warn them!" Frustrated and disturbed, Allan broke away from the patient and hurried from the room.

73

Argus pulled back the plastic curtain and stepped out of the shower. He wrapped a towel around his waist, wiped the steam from the mirror and lit up a cigarette. Argus began to sharpen a gleaming straight razor on a worn leather strap as he spoke to someone in the next room: "I may have overestimated her. She's soft. Like everyone else." He dampened his face with cold water and raised the blade to his stubbly skin. "In the army they taught us the true meaning of discipline, and life teaches you about pain; both very valuable lessons—discipline and pain." The shiny blade glided up Argus' throat, completing his last stroke. "I've always seen the connection."

Argus took a long drag from his cigarette as he moved from the bathroom to the bed. He said to the girl lying there, "Pain *is* discipline, and discipline is *everything*. Can you understand that?" A lifeless hand with chipped nail polish was tied, palm up, to the bed's cheap headboard. Argus stubbed his burning cigarette out in the tender flesh, using the dead girl's hand as an ash tray, and then inhaled the sweet scent of burning tobacco and seared flesh. The young prostitute's eyes stared blankly ahead at some unknown horror. Argus nodded slowly and said, "I knew you could."

74

At ten after six Allan pushed through a throng of tourists who were waiting for the express elevator to the roof. His head felt like it might explode at any moment. Allan gave the guard at the main elevators his name and cupped his hands around the gaps between the sunglasses and his face where the light seeped in. One of Allan's overgrown fingernails scratched his forehead and drew blood, though he didn't notice.

But the guard did. In fact, he had pegged him as a freak from the moment Allan entered the building: dark sunglasses worn indoors, long hair and nails—this guy was either a drug addict, a homo, or from Los Angeles. The guard thought the freak looked too frail to be dangerous, but he called up anyway. When he hung up the phone, the guard still seemed unconvinced, but he said, "Okay, you can go on up. Mr. Scheel says he's expecting you. Invisible Inc. is on the eighth floor. Suite 808."

An elevator arrived and a weary businessman exited. Allan mumbled, "Thanks," to the guard and hurried in before the doors closed.

———————

Invisible Inc.'s reception area was a testament to success, but not to good taste. Grossly enlarged photographs of Kevin Scheel's most successful infomercial products and real estate ventures screamed for attention from the walls, which had been papered in garish green velvet with a gold-leaf design. Allan recognized a fitness device that was usually advertised on TV in the wee hours of the morning.

"Mr. Steele?" Allan turned to find one of the most beautiful women he had ever seen studying him through cool, green eyes. She smiled and said, "He'll see you now. This way, please."

Allan followed the shapely young lady down a long hallway that displayed another gallery of Scheel's successes. Allan heard the receptionist's stockinged thighs whispering beneath her short, tight skirt as she walked, and he became instantly and unexpectedly hard. Allan's eyes slid down to the young woman's perky derriere and the well-toned muscles there that clenched as she moved. The muscles clenched and unclenched … clenched and unclenched … as Allan stared, transfixed, inhaling the heady perfume the young woman left in her wake.

The receptionist reached the end of the hall, knocked twice, and opened the door to Scheel's office to announce: "Allan Steele." She stepped aside and saw her own reflection in Allan's sunglasses as he passed. She also noticed the erection that Allan tried to hide with his awkwardly positioned hands.

Kevin Scheel, swimming in a garish and ill-fitting designer suit, was leaning back with his feet propped on a massive rosewood desk. His right arm was extended toward a video game running on a fifty-inch flat screen TV. The thumb and forefinger of Scheel's hand were trained on the monitor, like a gun. The nebbishy little man behind the desk took aim and twitched his thumb twice, which resulted in the booming sounds of gunfire. Scheel leaned to the left and the photorealistic S.W.A.T. officer in the game took cover behind a Grecian pillar. The president and founder of Invisible Inc. glanced over at Allan and said, "Be right with you, man. This last level's a real bitch." Scheel used his "finger gun" to take out a sniper, who had appeared on a distant rooftop, and then mimed a grenade toss with his left hand. He said, "I see you met Irma."

"Irma?"

"My receptionist: the gorgeous girl with the horrible name. You look like you're going camping." Allan was mortified when he realized that Scheel was referring to the front of his khakis—which *did* look a little like a tent. Allan turned away and put his hands into his pockets to adjust himself.

"Oh, shit …" Scheel suddenly began to pump his arms in a parody of running and his on-screen counterpart sped away from the grenade that had been tossed back at him by an enemy combatant, but it was too late. An explosion boomed from the speakers and shook the office walls, then a wash of red covered the game screen and the dying groan of Scheel's character signaled the loss of his digital life. Scheel cried, "Motherfucker!" and then turned his attention to Allan, who was still attempting to manage his inopportune erection. Scheel smirked and said, "Don't feel bad. That's why I hired her. Inspiration." Scheel adjusted his tortoise-shell eyeglasses and smiled, revealing a mouthful of yellow teeth. There was something about this nerdy tycoon that Allan liked. Scheel gestured toward an oversized couch.

Allan sat, crossing his legs uncomfortably, and said, "Chet said you went to Yale."

"Timothy Dwight, Class of ninety-five. Summa cum laude. I was Silliman."

Allan's headache was now a constant dull throb at the base of his skull. He said, "It didn't take you long to reach the top."

"The Bible says the meek will inherit the earth, but I think there was a typo. It shoulda been *geek*. The freaks and outcasts with nothing to lose and lots of time on our hands to think, thanks to our unencumbered social calendars."

"You and Chet met in junior high?"

"Summer camp. He had really bad acne in those days, so he hung out with me and the other invisibles. In all these years he's never called to hit me up for anything, until now. And I'm glad he did." Kevin returned to his desk to retrieve a file. "I saw your invention in action the other day. Fucking *brilliant*, man. Very smart to adapt existing technology instead of trying to reinvent the wheel. Cuts way down on R&D."

"Thank you." Allan wandered over to the wall to take a closer look at Scheel's Yale diploma. He was starting to think that his erection would never wane.

Scheel chewed on his fingernails as he referred to his notes. "Allan, I think we could help a fuck of a lot of people with this thing of yours *and* make a lot of money doing it. Any reason we couldn't work together on this?"

Allan turned. "None that I can think of."

Scheel grinned and offered his hand. "That's great. I'll have the legal department get started on an agreement in the morning."

Allan shook Kevin's hand. "Okay. But this was almost too easy."

"The hard part comes later—when you find out what a greedy bastard I am." Scheel laughed and looked down at Allan's fingernails. "Can I ask you something, Allan?"

"Sure."

"The fingernails and the sunglasses ... Do the ladies go for that stuff?"

Allan thought about it for a moment and replied, "Actually, they *do*."

Kevin looked down at his own gnarled fingernails, thinking it over. Then he had an idea. "Hey, I've got an extra ticket to an Off-Broadway show tonight. I heard it's a little too long, but the lead actress gets naked in the third act and she's supposedly got a pretty nice rack. Wanna come with?"

"Thanks, but I have a date."

Kevin took the extra ticket from his desktop and handed it to Allan. "I've got more money than God and I still get stood up every now and then. So take it anyway, just in case."

75

Kendra knew this might be her last chance. After a full day of watching her every move, Jenny had finally left to take a shower. Kendra had ten minutes, fifteen tops. She hurried into Allan's room, opened his dresser drawer, and hesitated a moment before taking the journal from its hiding place. Did she really want to know? If he had done something *really* awful might it help curb these unfamiliar feelings that had begun to cloud her mind? Kendra reached for the journal and opened it.

I had no choice. It was either let the professor die or do this ... thing. He had nothing to lose and I had everything to gain—but at what price? My soul? My sanity? I'm lost, frightened and more alone than ever, though his voice has joined my dreams at night. In the blink of an eye everything I have known to be true has been proven false and I have turned my back on God—

"Find anything juicy?" Kendra jumped and the book slipped from her hands. Jenny was watching from the doorway with a bottle of conditioner in her hands and a towel wrapped around her waist.

Kendra stammered, "It's mine. This is my diary."

"And you keep it in Allan's underwear drawer. How trusting. You two must have a great relationship."

Kendra retrieved the journal from the floor and offered it to Jenny, putting on her best poker face. "Here, take a look. There are a lot of intimate details about our sex life. You want juicy? It's all here."

Jenny accepted the book, but didn't open it. She considered Kendra's challenge for a moment, then set the journal aside. "Look, we got off to a bad start." Kendra eyed the journal, but didn't allow herself to reach for it. "I'm sorry. I've been a real bitch."

Kendra answered, "Yeah, you have. But I haven't been much better."

"Okay, so I'm jealous." Jenny's smile was genuinely sad. "For the last five years I've been like ... *everything* to him; his best friend, his sister—even his parent sometimes."

A blanket of guilt had enveloped Kendra, and Jenny's openness was only making the smothering sensation worse. She said, "He loves you, Jenny. It's obvious."

"I know. But now he loves *you*, too." The two women made eye contact and a look of understanding passed between them. The sound of a key in the front door's lock made Kendra jump again. Jenny turned away, holding her towel in place, and headed back toward the shower. "I'm gonna hang out in my room tonight. Tell Allan I'm not mad. Just tired."

Kendra waited until Jenny had turned away, and then jammed the journal into her purse and closed Allan's drawer.

Allan called from the living room, "Kendra? Jenny?"

"Be right out." Kendra's voice was tense.

Allan pulled back the living room blinds, revealing the huge picture window that spanned most of the wall. The view of the city at night was spectacular. He stripped off his shirt and mopped his torso with it as he stared out into the night. Allan turned off all of the lights in the room, and then discarded his sunglasses. He couldn't get the incident at the hospital out of his mind—or the old man's words: "Someone has to warn them."

Kendra emerged from the bedroom smiling. She said, "Why are all the lights off?"

"My eyes are bothering me."

"I'm making dinner, but it won't be ready for a while. I didn't think you'd be back so early. Did the meeting go okay?" Allan studied the night sky in silence, wondering how much longer he could keep Kali at bay. Kendra approached Allan from behind and hugged him. "You okay?"

"She used to say the stars were the flickering souls of the dead. They watched over us. Protected us. Whenever I was afraid or confused she would tell me to turn to the stars. She said they would guide me in my search for truth."

"So which one are you—afraid or confused?"

Allan turned in Kendra's arms to face her. "I feel like I'm losing myself." He pulled her close, in need of contact. "Have you ever done something and it seemed like the only choice you had but then, afterwards, you weren't sure anymore? Maybe you did the wrong thing for the right reason, or maybe it was just the wrong thing. But you're just not sure." He searched her eyes for understanding.

Kendra felt transparent. She said, "Yes."

"This ... *thing* ... has a hold on me. And I don't know how—or if—I can get free." The self-pity in Allan's voice was replaced by frustration. "I just wanted to be able to help people, you know? I just wanted—"

Kendra interrupted him with a tender kiss. She said, "What about meditation? Isn't that supposed to help, I don't know, *center* you or something?"

Allan smiled, appreciating her efforts at comfort. He kissed her nose, then her forehead, and said, "I think it's gone beyond meditation."

Kendra had a devilish gleam in her eye. She said, "Well, the books say that the ancient Hindus believed that sex was almost as purifying as meditation."

Allan arched an eyebrow and said, "Oh yeah? What about Jenny?"

"She's in her room for the night." Kendra traced the sparse line of hair that led down from Allan's belly button. "I think she's trying to make up." Kendra played with the top button of Allan's jeans. "You know, according to Hindu mythology, male and female life forces are only complete when they're joined together. The legends say that those yogis who lived on mountain tops would make love to their partners for a thousand years at a time. They believed it purified the soul."

Allan kissed her. "Well, my soul could certainly use a good scrubbing." He slipped the straps of Kendra's dress down over her shoulders and they made love among the meditation pillows and rumpled clothes, watched by the stars and city lights. And the burden of guilt that weighed on each one's soul was transformed into tenderness.

They had no way of knowing that another, uninvited, spectator lay hidden behind a full city block and a telescope positioned in the window of a rented room.

Waiting.

76

Later that night Allan tossed and turned in a troubled, chemical-induced sleep as the sounds of distant drums grew louder. Finally, he opened his eyes and was horrified to see Kali dancing in the moonlight. Allan looked to Kendra, just a shape beneath the covers, and wanted desperately to save her from the goddess' fury. Kali howled, demanding his attention, thrashing around the room—knife in one hand and staff in the other. Her movements beckoned him, demanding blood.

Allan dragged himself from the bed, his body and bedclothes soaked with sweat, and moved closer. But Kali danced away, taunting him, her necklace of bones and shrunken skulls chattering as she moved. Allan followed, groggy and off-balance, and when he finally cornered the elusive goddess, Allan bowed down at her feet. Kali howled again and raised her hands to the heavens—then clubbed him with the skull-headed handle of her staff. Allan's vision blurred as he looked up at Kali through a trickle of blood … then collapsed to the floor, unconsciousness.

Kendra tore away the carved tribal mask and positioned Allan's body so that he could have reasonably tripped and fallen, hitting his head in the process. She slid the mask, staff and her iPod—which had been fitted with a small speaker that plugged into the head-phone port—under the bed and removed the pillows she'd put under the bedclothes as her proxy. Kendra climbed beneath the covers, curled up into herself, and tried to catch her breath as she waited for Allan to regain consciousness. The sense of shame and guilt that she felt now was deeper than any she could remember.

After what seemed like days, Allan began to stir. Kendra closed her eyes and tried to regulate her breathing. Allan struggled to his feet and looked around the room, confused. He stood by the window for a long time as he tried to get his bearings. Suddenly, Kendra felt something digging into her neck and a voice in her head screamed, "The necklace! You're still wearing the fucking necklace!" Kendra must have made an involuntary sound then—because Allan looked toward the bed. Kendra had to think fast; another step closer and Allan would see. She moaned and turned, as if caught in the throes of a nightmare, and managed to pull the covers up high around her neck in the process.

Allan moved to Kendra's side of the bed and stooped down, his bare foot only millimeters from the mask beneath the bed. Allan reached out to Kendra and smoothed her hair. She was wet with sweat and her breathing was shallow and quick. He thought, Now, my insanity has even given her nightmares, and kissed Kendra gently on the cheek before standing away from the bed.

Kendra watched from the corner of her eye as Allan grabbed his clothes and left the room. As soon as the front door closed she sat up, tore the necklace from around her neck, and threw it against the wall.

77

Allan emerged from the 42nd Street subway station at 8th Avenue wearing only a pair of slacks and a thin shirt. The theater ticket that Kevin Scheel had given him was clutched in one hand. Allan knew what he had to do to quiet the drums and Kali, and he was determined to make a better selection this time. Allan was in agony beneath the glaring neon lights, despite the dark glasses.

He compared the address on the ticket to the street signs, mumbling to himself as he shuffled barefoot along 42nd—just another lost soul in an endless parade.

To the passers-by, Allan looked like a raging monk down from the mountaintop on a mission from God. To Allan, the passers-by looked like demons with glowing eyes that covered the entire color spectrum. He wondered why the night-dwellers' souls seemed so dim tonight. Some eyes offered only a flicker of light, and even the strongest among them barely managed a soft glow.

A shabby street corner evangelist with dark eyes stabbed his finger at Allan and cried out, "He that eateth my flesh and drinketh my blood dwelleth in me, and I in him. Do you know who said that, son? J-e-s-u-s said it!"

Allan continued on, and eventually found the street name that had been printed on the ticket, and lowered his eyes as he rounded the corner, shaking his head in silent conversation. A few blocks later Allan saw a group of theater-goers breaking up and heading off in different directions. He wetted his lips and watched from the shadows like a junkie in need of a fix. Kevin Scheel emerged from the theater, and even from a distance Allan could see that his eyes burned with a brilliant blue light.

Kevin waved to a group of friends and headed off alone down an alleyway that was a shortcut to his subway station. Allan followed at a distance, not feeling or thinking, pulled by the call of the drums. Kevin soon sensed someone behind him, and quickened his pace without looking back. Allan continued after him, mumbling in response to the voices in his head. Kevin turned a corner and broke into a panicked run, thinking, *Where the fuck is the station?*

Allan climbed a fire escape ladder with a sudden burst of energy.

Kevin looked back over his shoulder as he continued to run. There was no sign of the crazy stranger behind him, but Kevin kept running and panting: "C'mon, c'mon, c'mon ..."

Allan was careful not to let Kevin see his face as he followed across the rooftops of souvenir shops and fast-food joints, sensing every turn his prey made. He leapt from building to building with increasing grace and speed. His eyes burned bright and his senses felt keener than ever before.

Kevin stopped to catch his breath. There was still no sign of the crazy guy behind him. He laughed at his own fear and said to himself, "Fucking pussy." Then there was a clattering from above. Kevin saw a figure sliding down the fire escape ladder on a nearby building like a crazed pirate shimmying down his ship's mast. Kevin ran, screaming, "Help! Someone help me!"

Allan reached the ground and sped after Kevin. His breathing was steady, his strides long and powerful. Kevin pushed his glasses back up to the bridge of his nose as his arms pumped. He threw off his cashmere overcoat, screeching at nearby pedestrians as his feet slapped the pavement, "Somebody Fucking help me!" The pedestrians just stepped aside and watched as Kevin and Allan disappeared around another corner. Allan was closing the gap, his feet making contact with the ground in sync to the beat of the drums in his head.

Twenty feet ...

Fifteen ...

Ten ...

Kevin heard the relentless footfalls behind him and made the mistake of trying to look back for a glimpse of the pursuing psycho's face while speeding around the corner. He slammed into the side of an abandoned theater and crumpled to the dirty pavement, losing his glasses in the process.

Allan stopped, his breath quick and visible in the cool night air. Kevin was trapped and bleary-eyed. His nose was broken and bleeding and he had a gash on his forehead that mirrored Allan's. Kevin tore the wallet from his pocket and stammered, "Here—take it! There's five hundred in cash and credit cards. Lots of credit cards." He scrambled across the filthy concrete, clambering for his shattered glasses, pleading blindly, "Just tell me what you want and I'll give it to you."

Allan stood silently over his prey, wild and wind blown—steam rising from his overheated body in the cold night air.

"Please ..." Kevin squinted, trying desperately to bring his attacker into focus. "Don't kill me! Please don't kill me."

Allan looked into Kevin Scheel's helpless face, and it was like looking in a mirror. The fire in Allan's eyes began to cool as his murderous resolve crumbled and horror took its place. Horror at what he'd become and terror at the thought of where he was headed.

Allan turned away and vomited onto the street as Kevin listened, petrified. Allan turned away, ashamed, and wiped his mouth on his sleeve. When he turned back to Kevin, Allan's eyes were filled with compassion. He said, "I'm sorry," and extended a helping hand.

Kevin recoiled, screaming, "No! Please!"

Allan saw himself reflected in the burning glow of Kevin's eyes and backed away, muttering, "I'm sorry." Then Allan ran from Kevin, from the alley, from the memory of cold, ruthless hunger that he had felt. He ran without direction, as if every mile he put between himself and Scheel would distance him from his own destiny. Finally, he collapsed to the ground, exhausted beyond reason. He saw his own shadow cast on the dirty pavement and looked up, squinting against the light.

High in the sky a huge cross glowed from the fluorescent tubes within. It was St. Luke's Hospital. Devastated, Allan stood to face his destiny, convinced that there was truly no escape.

78

The night nurse had seen her share of horrors in fifteen years of service: from drug babies barely two days old dying of heroin withdrawal to jumpers bleeding from every orifice of their bodies. She had even assisted one Thanksgiving when an impeccably-dressed gentleman was brought in with a meat cleaver embedded in his skull after a particularly nasty domestic dispute. He was awake and lucid the whole time, despite the cleaver lodged firmly in his frontal lobe. Apart from a world-class headache and an impressive battle scar, the patient sustained no long term damage, though he did complain of a lingering odor of spoiled potatoes.

Horrible? Yes. But shocking? Shock implied disbelief, and the nurse had come to believe that people were pretty much capable of anything. But when she pulled back the fluttering privacy curtain to check on the patient in bed 224 that night, the nurse was well and truly stunned.

She said, "Mr. Matteo, I've told you about leaving that window open ..." She slipped on the blood that covered everything, including the floor, but managed to regain her balance. "Mr. Matteo?" At first she thought the patient had ripped out his IV tube, tearing a vein in the process. But then she saw his eyes—or, more accurately, the gaping sockets where they had been. That was when she began to scream.

79

The F train hissed to a stop. Allan stepped in, bloody and dazed. The scattered passengers barely spared a second glance for the grizzly specter who collapsed into a seat near the doors that divided the trains. Allan saw his ghastly reflection in the graffiti-engraved window, and smashed the glass with his fist, but it was safety glass—and the only damage was to Allan's hand. The other passengers watched with distant curiosity as he began to cough and retch.

Anticipating what lay ahead, Allan hurried through the connecting doors and out onto the small platform between the train's compartments. He raised his arms to grab the edge of the next car and pulled himself up, then sat atop the speeding subway train, fascinated by the canopy of concrete and steel flying past. Suddenly, Allan broke into hysterical, drunken laughter. He laughed until he was out of breath, and then Allan's eyes dropped to the tracks, which seemed to be calling him. He pleaded, "No more ..." but his words were lost in the whoosh and clatter of the speeding train. Allan closed his eyes and began to sway back and forth, leaning a little farther over the tracks with each repetition, as he whispered his mantra, "No more ... No more ... No more ..."

But just as gravity threatened to take Allan over the edge—his body convulsed. He jerked back onto the roof of the train, screaming as pain coursed through his veins and overloaded his senses. Allan barely managed to make it back down to the platform before his trembling legs gave way. He crumpled to the shifting steel floor as the bony structures of his face began to shift and change beneath the surface of the skin. Allan's eyes rolled back in their sockets and he heaved and twitched. Then he began to take on the physical characteristics of the old man. And as the old man's soul battled Allan's for dominance of the body, Allan saw what the old man had seen:

He stands on a narrow dirt road in the middle of nowhere. A hill rises before him, so he begins to climb. Toward the crest Allan begins to notice a sound. But it's not a sound—it's an absence *of sound:*

No birds.

No crickets.

No wind.

Allan picks up the pace, hoping to find a light or a golden tunnel on the other side of the hill; anything that might resemble one of the happy versions of the afterlife that the believers of the world have promised. But when he finally reaches the top of the hill he sees a vast black emptiness as deep and cold as the ocean.

Allan stands at the edge of the precipice, and knows true fear for the first time. He turns back to the road, but the road is gone. He looks around, desperate for another path, but realizes that the small patch of earth on which he now stands is the only island in this dark and lonely sea.

The un-sound intensifies, becoming an inhuman howl that sucks the bits of earth from around Allan's feet. He feels an odd sensation in his fingertips, and lifts his hand to investigate. Allan's body is beginning to degenerate into a kind of congealed smoke. He watches helplessly as the howling void sucks little wisps of his body away, bit by agonizing bit. He tries to scream, but the swirling black abyss takes that, too. Just as the last square foot of dirt crumbles beneath his feet, Allan is snatched from the void.

Glistening chrome and glaring white light assault his eyes. It takes Allan a moment to pinpoint his whereabouts. He's in an operating room, and he is the patient. Allan tries to scream, but the tube running down his throat muffles the sound.

"Clear!"

Allan watches helplessly as the emergency team steps back in unison, as if performing a minuet. He feels something cold on his bare chest.

Zap.

Allan's body convulses. He bites into the plastic tube.

Zap.

Another convulsion, and then a small sound like a radar blip. A moment later a huge face fills Allan's field of view.

"All right. Looks like he's back."

Allan's eyes fluttered as he fought his way back into his own thoughts, and his own reality. Still panicked, he squirmed in the small space in which he found himself, feeling as though the shimmying compartments on either side were closing in on him. Allan began to gasp for air, suddenly feeling the full weight of the old man's claustrophobia. He clawed at the door latch that would allow passage back into the subway car.

Allan hurried through the compartment door, stumbled over to a window and slammed it down into the open position. He collapsed into the seat and hung his head out of the window, trying to hold onto what was left of his sanity as he gulped the rushing, fetid air.

80

Kendra checked her watch, pacing past the bedroom window. Why did Kali terrify Allan so? And how did the bizarre ritual figure into it? Kendra had watched the DVD again and again, but couldn't bring herself to read more of the journal. It felt like a betrayal. One of many, perhaps, but one *too* many. Still, there was Argus. And Passaic.

Kendra stuffed the journal into her bag along with her costume, and headed for the front door. She reached for the knob and heard someone fumbling with a key on the other side. Kendra tossed her bag behind a chair and tried to sound calm. "Allan?"

A craggy voice answered, "No, but I got him. It's Johnny. The doorman."

Kendra asked, "What's going on?" as she untucked her shirt, rumpled her hair and unlocked the door.

"Hell if I know." Johnny supported Allan's weight as he struggled to get him to a chair. Allan's youth had been restored again. "Johhny said, "He came into the lobby all covered with blood and just fuckin' collapsed."

Kendra remembered her blow to Allan's head and panicked. She asked, "Is all this *his* blood?"

"Can't tell. Looks like he's been in either an accident or a helluva bar fight."

Jenny emerged from her room and followed the voices down the hall. She yawned, "What's goin' on?" and then saw Allan. Jenny hurried to him, adrenalin slapping her wide awake, and cried, "Allan!" Jenny began to look in vain for the wound that had covered him in blood. "Is he breathing?"

Johnny said, "Yeah, he was mumblin' all the way up."

Jenny said, "I'm calling Chet," and went to the phone to dial information. "It's Saint Luke's, right?"

"Yes." Kendra studied the cut on Allan's forehead that she had inflicted. He wasn't supposed to get *that* close.

Jenny spoke in a rush into the phone: "I need to find one of your interns. His name is Chet something. I don't know what department, but it's an emergency."

81

Allan was wheeled into a curtained exam area on a gurney, mumbling incoherently as Jenny and Kendra trailed behind. His eyes were closed. His head lolled from side to side.

Chet appeared in the doorway, looking haggard. He said, "Here you are," and referred to the chart in his hand. "They had him down as an overdosed junkie." Chet checked Allan's vital signs. "Jesus, his BP's through the roof." He retracted one of Allan's eyelids with his thumb and shone his penlight into the pupil. A few hours ago Allan would have screamed in pain, but now he only seemed mildly annoyed by the light. Chet turned to the women and asked, "Where are his contacts?"

Kendra answered, "I don't think he wears contacts. But his eyes are *really* sensitive to light."

"Since when?" Chet unbuttoned Allan's shirt and began to check for broken bones.

Kendra said, "As long as I've known him." She sensed Jenny's eyes on her and added, "But that hasn't been very long. It *has* seemed to bother him more in the last few days, though."

Chet continued to examine Allan, speaking more to himself than to the women as he did so: "No broken bones that I can see … No major wounds. So where did all this blood come from?" Chet took Allan's face in his hands and said, "C'mon, buddy. Talk to me."

Allan's response was a drunken, giddy babble: "I have to warn them …"

Chet said, "Let's get these clothes off so I can get a better look at him." Jenny helped Chet pull Allan up to his feet while Kendra began to undress him. "Jesus, he's *burning up.*"

Kendra felt Allan's skin. "He's always like this."

"That's not good. He must be running around 101 or 102."

Kendra said, "He's *always* hot."

Jenny nodded in agreement. "It's true. He sweats all the time."

Chet asked, "What else should I know about? *Anything* out of the ordinary."

Jenny said, "He's hungry all the time."

Kendra began to say, "And he's—" but then she stopped herself.

Chet saw her hesitation and pressed: "He's *what?*"

"It's just that he's …" Kendra felt the blood rushing to her cheeks, and was caught off-guard by her own uncharacteristic modestly. She finally said, "He's very … sexual."

"How sexual is 'very'?" Chet opened Allan's mouth and shined the light down his throat.

Kendra didn't look at Jenny when she answered, "He, uh, wants sex all the time."

Jenny would have laughed if she hadn't been so worried. She said, "What guy his age doesn't?"

"No, I mean *all the time.* Two, three, even four times a night."

Chet leaned in close to peer down Allan's throat and recoiled. He said, "Jesus, his breath is foul. Maybe it's gastrointestinal." He stepped back, thought for a moment, and turned to Kendra. "He *wants* sex four times a night or he can actually *perform* four times a night?"

"He wants sex constantly, but we've done it four times in a night and he still wasn't satisfied." Jenny held her sarcastic tongue while Chet wrote a note to himself. Kendra asked, "Does that mean something."

"Has he been using Viagra or any other drugs?"

Kendra shook her head. "Valium. He can't sleep."

Jenny said, "The voices," and addressed Chet: "He says *the voices* keep him up at night." Kendra removed the last of Allan's clothing, and they eased him back onto the exam table.

Chet continued to search Allan's body for clues, growing increasingly bemused. He said, "He's got a cut on his hand and this one on his head, but nothing to explain all this blood. I want to get him cleaned up." Chet sighed and turned to Jenny. "Then we'll run those tests we talked about. Fever, sleeplessness, dramatically increased appetite and sex drive. Maybe they're all related to this metabolism thing. I'll be right back." Chet stepped out of the room, leaving Kendra and Jenny alone with Allan.

After an uncomfortable silence, Kendra's eyes drifted to her purse. The corner of Allan's journal was poking out. Kendra pretended to check her watch. "Oh shit—I've gotta go."

"It's fucking five a.m." Jenny pulled a chair over beside the bed. "You gotta date or something?"

Kendra ignored the barb and headed for the door. "I won't be long."

82

An hour later the rising sun revived Manhattan's ancient brownstones, kissing them sweetly on the forehead and whispering loving affirmations in their weathered ears. Gentle breezes skipped off the Hudson, transforming tattered theater posters into rustling puppet shows of shadow while skyscrapers rose from the heart of the city, tinted windows refracting the dawn like the facets of a dusty diamond. On a morning as perfect as this one it was only the void where two gleaming towers once stood that reminded otherwise self-involved city-dwellers that evil did, in fact, exist in the world.

Kendra emerged from the postal center after depositing Allan's journal into the designated box, just as Argus had instructed. Then she walked the streets through the lazy sunshine, trying to justify her actions. How odd it was that this awkward, troubled boy could have such a profound impact on her life and thoughts.

When she returned to Saint Luke's, Kendra found Jenny dozing in the chair beside Allan's bed like a long-suffering wife. Kendra stood in the doorway for a moment, watching Allan and his friend sleep. She thought, I bet there are no secrets between them. *It must be nice to have one person who knows everything about you and still wants to hang around. Maybe that's what love is.*

Jenny stirred, as if she had felt the heat of Kendra's envy. She looked to Allan, who was still asleep, and stretched. Jenny asked saw Kendra standing in the doorway and asked, "What time is it?"

"Almost seven."

Jenny yawned, "Short date."

Kendra let it slide and moved to Allan's bedside. He looked so normal now, all cleaned up and sleeping peacefully. There was even a hint of a smile on his face. In this light he looked so young. She asked, "Did they do the tests?"

"Yeah." Jenny studied the look on Kendra's face as she watched Allan sleep. There was tenderness there, and real concern. Jenny asked, "You actually care about him, don't you?"

Kendra was caught off guard by the directness of Jenny's question. She thought it over for a moment and then answered carefully, "Not as much as you do."

Jenny continued to stare, assessing the sadness in Kendra's eyes. After a moment she said, "You're lying. But why?"

Kendra averted her eyes. "You need some coffee or something? I'll stay with him."

"Okay. Thanks." Jenny started for the door, still trying to figure Kendra out. "I'll see if I can find Chet."

Kendra waited until Jenny had left the room, then brushed back a lock of hair that had fallen into Allan's eyes. When she touched his face, Allan stirred and mumbled, "That tickles." His speech was slurred and sticky, but his eyes were bright. He squinted against the light and asked, "Could you turn that off?"

Kendra went to the light switch on the wall and switched it off. From across the room she could barely make out Allan's silhouette in the dim light of the fluorescent cross that had filtered through the room's closed curtains. She returned to the bed. "Better?"

"Yeah. Where are we?"

"The hospital. What happened to you last night? You had us all really worried." Allan wasn't paying much attention to Kendra's words; he was just staring at her with a wicked grin on his face. Kendra smiled in the dark. "What?" Allan pulled her close. "Allan, what are you doing?"

He brought her hand to his mouth and kissed it. Allan answered, "Tasting you," and began to work his way up Kendra's arm, kissing and nibbling. He said, "I'm hungry."

"I can't believe you. You should be resting." Allan slipped his hand up under her skirt. Kendra looked back to the doorway and said, "Someone could come in."

"Then we'd better hurry." Allan gave Kendra a lecherous smile and pulled her onto the bed.

———

Jenny was still grimacing from the last swallow of stale coffee when she crushed the Styrofoam cup and dropped it into a trash can. Someone had directed her to the doctor's lounge, and now she could see Chet, asleep in what appeared to be the only comfortable chair. Jenny crept into the room to peek at the chart in Chet's lap. She tried to free it from his grasp without waking him.

Chet awoke with a start. He checked his watch and stretched. "Allan's test results should be back in ten minutes."

"These aren't them?" Jenny sat and looked at Allan's chart.

"I'm having the data re-analyzed."

"Why?"

"I just wanted to be sure."

"Sure of what?" Chet didn't respond. Instead, he went to a vending machine and fished through his pockets for change. Jenny was too tired for patience. "Well?"

"The first results turned up something that I think—*I hope*—is wrong." Jenny prepared herself for the bad news. Chet sat facing her. "His pituitary and adrenal glands are enlarged. *Dangerously* enlarged, according to the data."

"And that means?"

"It could mean cancer, *if* the results are correct."

Jenny let the dreaded word rattled around in her head a moment before speaking. She asked, "So it couldn't be psychological?"

"No, it could. It *is*—I hope. It's just that his metabolism is running at four times normal. In fact, according to these numbers, all of his vitals are running at warp speed."

"Okay, so what's the worst case scenario?"

"The worst?" Chet took a deep breath, then exhaled slowly. "Progeria."

Jenny furrowed her brow. "That's that disease kids get. The one that makes them get old real fast, right?"

"And it's always terminal. Five-year-olds wither up like they were eighty. It's a horrible way to die. But adult onset is *extremely* rare."

"Could it be anything else?"

"The inflammation of the pituitary might be causing pressure on the brain. That could explain the mood swings. If it is cancer and it hasn't spread we can remove the pituitary and adrenal glands, and supply the missing hormones with synthetic substitutes through pills and injections. But it's a major and very risky procedure. Even if the surgery goes without a hitch, his life will never be the same."

"But the results might be wrong. Right?"

"Right." He tried for an encouraging smile. "So let's go see."

Jenny followed Chet into the hallway. She said, "Let's say it's psychological."

Chet nodded to a passing nurse and rounded the corner. "Whether it is or not—it wouldn't hurt to get him in to see Schultz."

"I hope Allan goes along."

"Just get him in here tomorrow. I don't care how you do it. Tell him it's to get the results of these tests. I'll work out the details with Schultz. In the meantime, don't say anything to him about his condition. I don't trust these results; if it *is* psychological a misdiagnosis of cancer could really set him off." Jenny stopped at the door to Allan's room. Chet kept walking. "Just make him rest, and keep an eye on him. With his system tweaked as high as it is he's gonna be bouncing off the walls." Chet hurried off down the hall and Jenny turned to the door.

Just as she was about to enter, Jenny saw shadows moving in the dark, through the one-foot squared portal in the door. Then she inched the door open and heard the sounds. At first she thought she was hallucinating. She closed the door, waited a moment, and then opened it again to be sure.

Yes, there was no doubt about it, those were the sounds of sex. It had been a while since she had heard them, and even longer since she had made them, but those were definitely the sounds. Suddenly, Jenny was caught by a painful spike of jealousy. She turned away from the door and headed for the exit.

83

After Kendra and Allan were spent, he kicked off the covers and leaned back against the headboard of the narrow hospital bed. Allan said, "Those Hindus really knew what they were talking about." Kendra groaned contentedly and laid her head in his lap, nuzzling the coarse hair. She could smell the sweet, musky scent of her body on his. There was a long silence as each did battle with their respective secrets. Finally, Kendra pulled away and sat on the edge of the bed.

Allan complained, "Hey—"

"You're too hot."

Allan studied Kendra for a moment before reaching out to touch her hair, and asked, "What do you think it'd be like to live forever?"

"Lonely."

Allan thought long and hard before he spoke again. Finally, he said, "I saw something last night."

"Yeah?" Kendra was staring off into space, trying hard to quell her guilt. "What?"

"Heaven. Or hell. I'm not sure, yet. It was whatever lies beyond death." Kendra didn't respond. Allan sat beside her and said, "Did you hear me?"

She averted her eyes and said, "I heard." Allan started to speak again, but Kendra interrupted: "But I don't want to know."

Now that Allan had made his decision he wanted the crushing weight of secrecy off his chest. He said, "I've done things to people, and seen things ...that have changed me. It has to stop. I have to stop it, but I don't know how or even if I can. My constant fever and appetite are all part of it. I think I'm living more than one lifetime simultaneously and it's aging me. I think ..." Kendra suddenly stood away from the bed and began to retrieve her clothes from the floor. Allan continued, "I know you think I'm crazy and I don't blame you, but you have to listen—"

"It's not that. I just don't want to know."

"But I need to tell you. I need to tell you everything." Allan climbed out of bed.

"What are you doing? You should be in bed."

"I feel fine. *Better than fine.*" He went to the closet to get his clothes. "We're going home. I have to get to my journal—to write it all down before I forget the details."

Kendra panicked, but tried not to show it. She returned to the bed, hoping to use more sex as a diversion. "How about another round before they bring in your breakfast?"

Allan returned to the bed. "Look, I just don't want any more secrets between us. And *this* is a big one."

She smiled and reached beneath Allan's paper hospital gown. "No, *this* is a big one."

"I'm serious. Don't make this a joke."

"C'mon ... Make love to me again."

"Is that all we're about? Fucking?" Allan reached for his clothes.

"C'mon baby, I was just—"

"I know exactly what you were doing." He tore off the robe, stepped into his pants and pulled them up fast.

"Fine. If you don't want sex—we don't have to have sex."

"Of course I want sex. I *always* want sex. You know that. But I also want *you.* It's like you hide behind this mask. You go into this seductive routine and a brick wall goes up behind your eyes. Your body's mine, but you—the *real* you—is hidden away."

Kendra avoided his probing eyes. "That's bullshit, Allan."

"There've been a few times when we've made love that you seemed to let the wall down a little, but for the most part all I get is the flesh."

"Maybe that's all there is to get." She felt touched and trapped and desperately lonely. "Maybe it's not a mask. Maybe I'm nothing but a cunt and tits and a mouth for sucking, and you don't get more because there is no more to get."

"No," he said, kissing her gently. "You're more than that." She tried to pull away, but he followed, whispering in her ear: "You're my salvation."

Kendra found his eyes in the dark and her own welled up with tears. "I'm *not*, Allan. I'd like to be, but I'm not."

"My mother said that my capacity to love would be my salvation and I love you, so you must be my salvation. She's never been wrong." Kendra bolted from the bed and Allan followed. He asked, "What's wrong?"

She fumbled with her clothes as spat out the words: "Fuck you."

"What did I say?"

Kendra glared at Allan, swatting the tears from her cheeks. Her words flew like an accusation: "You love me?" She raced across the room to retrieve her brassiere from the floor.

"What's wrong with that?"

Kendra laughed bitterly as she put on her bra and reached for her panties. "You love me. You *love* me?" She screamed, "Asshole!"

"What? Because I said I loved you?"

She yanked her lacy panties up so hard that they tore. "SHIT!"

Allan backed her into a corner, pleading: "Would you talk to me? Please."

"Just let me the hell outta here." She tried to push past him. He wouldn't yield. She was desperate. "Get the fuck out of my way, Allan! I have to go!"

"Look, if *you* don't love me, that's okay. I just needed to tell you. I wasn't trying to pressure you or anything."

She tried to push past again. Allan held his ground. Without warning she attacked him, pounding his bare chest with her fists as she screamed, "Leave me alone, goddamnit! Leave me alone! LEAVE ME ALONE!" Allan fought her fury with a containing embrace as Kendra continued to struggle and scream, "Let me go, Allan! I don't want to hurt you."

He held on, reassuring her: "Kendra, it's *okay* if you don't love me—"

Kendra blurted out, "But I do. *That's the problem!*" and gave up the fight. She went limp in Allan's arms and fought to catch her breath. "So let me go. Please."

Allan held her tight. Kendra resisted at first, then hugged him fiercely and whispered, "Please—let me go."

"No."

After a long time just standing there like that, Kendra pulled away and flopped down onto the bed. All of the fight had gone out of her. Kendra's voice was frail and small. "I hate you."

Allan lay beside her on the bed, panting. He stared up at the ceiling. "Don't take this the wrong way, but you're seriously fucked up."

Kendra laughed, emotionally and physically drained, and replied, "Kiss my ass."

"Give me five minutes. I'm a little tired right now."

Neither of them spoke again for a long time. They just lay side by side, holding hands, staring up at the ceiling and gasping for air. Gradually their breathing began to synchronize. They were still breathing as one when Kendra broke the silence. "What do we do now?"

"I don't know. Get married?"

Kendra stopped breathing completely … until she saw Allan's smile in the dark. She smacked him lightly on the leg and said, "You are an asshole." Allan groaned as he stood to finish dressing. Kendra asked, "Where do you think you're going?"

"Home. To get my journal. I need to show it to you."

Kendra's heart trilled. She said, "Haven't we shared enough revelations for one day?"

Allan took Kendra by the hand and pulled her up off of the bed. "You have to know everything—just like I'd expect you to share any dark secrets *you* might have."

Kendra tried to think. She couldn't let him go home and discover that she had taken the journal. Finally, she said, "Okay, I *do* have a secret."

"You do?"

"Yeah."

"What?" Allan stepped closer and took her hand.

Kendra thought for a long time before answering. "I have a son."

Allan looked into her eyes. The wall was gone. He asked, "Where?"

"Passaic." She let go of his hand and averted her eyes. "He lives with my parents."

"Wow. You have parents, too?"

She laughed bitterly. "Unfortunately, yes. My father's a bastard and my mother is a doormat." Kendra sighed. "Anyway, that's it ... my dark secret." She added, "But it's just one of many."

He stroked her hair and said, "What's so dark about that?"

"Other than the fact that I'm a shitty mother?"

"I'm sure you had a reason to leave him there."

"I did." It took Kendra a moment to find her voice again. The memory burned. "I do."

Allan kissed her and climbed from the bed. "I want to meet him."

"No."

"Take me to meet your son."

"I can't."

"Let's go—right now. We'll rent a car. It's Sunday. They should be around, right?"

"Allan, I haven't been there in almost a year."

"Then it's settled. We'll start with your secret—then I'll tell you mine. Okay?"

"*No.*" Kendra felt trapped. She insisted, "It's *not* okay."

"Okay, then let's go back to the apartment and we'll start with my secret."

"Allan, you don't understand ..." She tried to think of something to say that might change his mind, but it was clear by the defiant look on Allan's face that he wasn't going to budge. Finally, Kendra sighed and said, "Okay. I guess."

Allan kissed her and said, "Good. Let's go. We'll call Jenny from the road."

84

They made the drive in silence. Allan tried several times to start up a conversation, or just to make Kendra laugh, but it was no use. When they took the New Jersey Turnpike to Passaic, Allan noticed that Kendra's grip on the steering wheel tightened, the muscles of her forearms clenched beneath the skin. Allan asked, "Was this a mistake?"

Kendra said, "Yes," and pulled into her parents' driveway. She turned off the car's motor and stared at the humble two-bedroom tract home that sat before them. "God, this is an ugly house."

Allan fidgeted, unsure as to whether or not he should get out of the car. Kendra was just as likely to start the engine, back up and tear away from the house as she was to open the door and step out. Allan said, "It looks nice from the outside. Very *Leave It To Beaver*."

Kendra studied the fluted awning over the garage. The paint was peeling. She said, "I can't believe I brought you here. I must be outta my fucking mind."

Just then the front door opened and a frumpy white woman started down the cracked concrete walkway. She looked as if she'd been plucked from the heart of the bible belt. The woman stopped to pull a weed that had grown through a gap where a tree root had raised one of the concrete sections above the others. The woman groaned as she straightened up again, then called toward the car: "Well, you comin' in, or not?" Her breath was visible in the brisk afternoon air.

Kendra called back weakly, "Hi Mom," and chewed her fingernails for a moment longer before stepping out of the car. Allan got out to watch the reunion, a little surprised at himself for never having considered that one of Kendra's parents might be Caucasian. But then again, he had never really thought of her as any particular race or color, just as beautiful, funny, and bright. The women stood two paces apart in an awkward silence. The family resemblance was clear; Kendra had her mother's sharp features, and their eyes were the same, as was the slightly sway-backed stance that made both women's derrieres jut out at a decidedly sexy angle.

"'Hi Mom?'" Kendra's mother managed a smile. "Is that all you got to say to me?" That's when they hugged. Allan couldn't tell who had initiated the embrace. One minute they were staring at each other with arms crossed—and the next they were holding onto each other for dear life. When they finally separated, Kendra's mother was smiling in earnest. She wiped a tear from her daughter's cheek and said, "Now, none of that." Kendra's mother turned to Allan. "Don't be afraid. We don't bite much."

Allan stepped forward, offering his hand. "Hi. I'm Allan."

"Good to know you, Allan. I'm Leonor. Call me Lenny. Come on in. Supper's almost ready."

85

The interior of the house was as cold and Spartan as the man seated at the head of the table. The furnishings were dark wood covered with handmade doilies. After an hour with Kendra's parents, Allan had come to believe that the combination of dark wood and lace was symbolic of the relationship. Not just because Kendra's father was black and proud, though he was both, but because he was so unyielding, and she had tried so desperately to soften a marriage and a man whose rigidity made every moment an uncomfortable one.

Allan tried to get comfortable in the straight-backed dining room chair, helping himself to a third slab of pot roast. He said, "This is great, Lenny," and she seemed surprised by his praise. Allan thought she probably wasn't used to compliments. Allan turned to Kendra's father and said, "Your wife sure knows how to cook, sir."

The stoic man at the head of the table grunted an acknowledgment, but didn't look up from his food. He chewed exactly twenty-two times before swallowing, and then muttered, "Potatoes."

Lenny passed the mashed potatoes. She was used to her husband's moods. "I'm sorry Matthew wouldn't come out for dinner. He's like that sometimes."

Kendra said, "Only when I'm here, mother." These were her first words since taking her seat at her father's table.

Lenny searched for a new topic to fill the silence. "Allan, what is it that you do?"

Kendra answered for Allan: "He's a writer. He wrote a book about an African tribe called the Shantu." Kendra's father made a small, skeptical sound. To Allan it was nothing, but to Kendra it was a slap in the face. She threw down her napkin and pushed away from the table. "Okay, that's it—"

Kendra's father fixed her with a cold stare. His voice was calm and quiet. "Sit down, whore." He pushed his chair back from the table and added, "*I'm* leaving."

Kendra was stunned silent.

Lenny made a small, pained sound as her husband rose from the table and stormed off into the den. A moment later he had switched on the TV and turned up the volume. Lenny folded her napkin and said, "Well, I guess that's that."

Allan had to pick his jaw up off the floor. He asked, "What happened?"

Lenny began to clear the dishes as she spoke: "He's never been one to forgive and forget. I made him promise to behave himself, but ..." Lenny shrugged it off and disappeared into the kitchen. "You know how *that* goes."

Kendra was staring down into her plate, pushing her peas into her potatoes. She whispered, "Gee, thanks so much for suggesting this, Allan."

"What happened? I don't get it."

Kendra stood and started toward the bedrooms. "There's nothing to get, Allan. Absolutely nothing."

Allan called after her, "Are you okay?"

"I'm gonna give my son a kiss, if he'll let me, then I'm getting the hell out of here. If you wanna meet him—this is your chance."

Allan followed Kendra down a narrow hallway lined with fading photographs. Many showed an unhappy little girl who could have only been Kendra. The poses were uniformly rigid and the smiles were forced, beneath dead eyes. Allan recognized the sadness in Kendra's young face and wished that he could comfort the child that she once was. Kendra had stopped at the door near the end of the hall and was waiting for him. Allan sensed her apprehension as he approached. She wanted him there beside her, although she'd have never admitted it. Kendra listened at the door before knocking. The TV inside the room was tuned to an old Bruce Lee movie.

Allan could hear Lee's signature labored grunts and high-pitched battle cries.

Kendra knocked twice before speaking to the closed door: "Matthew? It's me."

A strained voice inside the room said, "Go away."

Kendra rested the flat of her palm against the door and spoke into the painted wood. "I'm leaving now, so if you want to see me you'd better open up." There was a long silence before the knob turned and the door opened—just a crack. Kendra pushed against the door. Matthew was lying on the bed with his face less than a foot away from the TV. He was nine years old and already very handsome. From the doorway, Kendra said, "You're not even going to look at me?"

"Why should I?" He didn't look back. "I got a picture."

Kendra suddenly seemed very tired. She turned back to Allan. "Okay, you've seen him—at least the back of his head. Can we go now?"

Matthew glanced back over his shoulder. "Who's he?"

"A friend of mine. He wanted to meet you."

"Why?"

Allan took a step closer. "I didn't know about you until this morning."

"That figures."

Kendra tried to lead Allan away, unable to take any more. "Please, can we go?"

Allan sat on the edge of the bed and spoke to Matthew with quiet sincerity. "I really like your mother and I think she likes me. So when she told me about you—I wanted to meet you. Anything wrong with that?"

Matthew gave Allan the once-over and, for a moment, it looked as though he might soften. But then, just as suddenly as it had come, the hopeful moment evaporated. Matthew returned his attention to Bruce. The boy said, "He looks like a dweeb."

Kendra left the room and stomped down the hallway. Allan started to follow, but then stopped at the door. He wanted to say something wise to this angry boy before he left, something that might make a difference. But before Allan could come up with anything, Matthew reached forward, turned up the sound, and said, "Goodbye, dweeb."

86

Allan ran from the house and tried to catch up with Kendra, but she was walking too fast. Her heels clicked on the sidewalk like a stuttered K as she sped down the block past little cloned tract houses. Allan called after her, "Where are you going? The car's back there."

"I forgot my keys." Kendra wasn't crying. Not anymore. "And I'm not going back in there."

"So we're gonna *walk* back to the city?" Allan was trying hard to keep up with her.

"Just give me a minute alone."

"Why alone? Maybe I can help."

"You've done a great job so far."

Allan said, "I didn't know it would be like this."

Kendra stepped into a large crack in the sidewalk and broke the heel of her shoe. She cried, "*Shit!*" and bent over to dislodge the heel while trying to balance on one foot. "Goddamn it!"

Allan finally caught up and offered his shoulder for Kendra to lean on. He said, "I had no idea it would be this bad. I'm sorry."

Kendra snapped back: "I'm not." She tossed away the broken shoe and sat on the grass. "It makes it easier to stay away."

Allan sat beside her on the grass and asked, "You gonna be all right?" Kendra remained silent. Allan said, "Maybe he'll get over it as he grows older—the anger."

"Who? My father, or my son? They both hate me, and they have every right." Kendra kicked off her remaining shoe. "My father worked so hard to make a good life for us. Sometimes the neighbors didn't even want us on the block. But he's just so ..." She stared off into space, remembering. "I can't live in a cage. His rules worked for him, but things are different now. *People* are different. I'm different. If I wanna be wild—I'm gonna be wild. And if I wanna be loud—" she called back to the house, "*I'll be loud!* I don't give a fuck if people stare, or if they have a problem with me. Tough shit. Get over it already."

"Why's your father so mad at you?"

"He's got his reasons."

"But to call you a ... In front of a total stranger."

Kendra studied Allan's hand, tracing her forefinger along the creases of his palm. She said, "You've got a long lifeline."

Allan thought, *If she only knew*, but he asked, "What could you have done to deserve that kind of treatment?"

"Apart from getting pregnant at sixteen? I was in jail. A long time ago."

"Why?"

"Drugs." She debated for a moment, then decided to edit. "Among other things. He bailed me out, then took me to court to get custody of Matthew. He was just a baby, then." She thought about it, then looked away, adding, "So was I."

Allan wanted to ask more, but didn't. Instead, he leaned forward and kissed her. "It doesn't matter. At least, not to me."

Kendra tried to smile, but only managed a cynical sneer. "Saint Allan, right?"

"What about your mother? Why does she stay?"

"She used to be so strong. So *defiant*. Over the years the world wore her down until his arms became the last safe place on earth." Kendra sighed. "According to her."

They shared an intimate moment of silence, sitting close, looking into each other's eyes. Finally, Allan said, "Maybe we've *both* made mistakes, Done horrible things." He was looking at her, although he was really speaking to himself. "*Unforgivable things.* But we're still here. We still have the chance to make it right. Or maybe not right, exactly, but a little better."

Kendra looked away, having had enough show-and-tell for one day. She said, "I'm cold. Can we go?"

Allan started back toward the house. "Wait here. I'll be right back."

Kendra lay back onto the grass and stared up at the sky, just as she had as a child. She used to find so many happy things in the clouds. Hopeful things. Today their mysteries had faded, and all they posed was a threat of rain. She closed her eyes and wished herself far away from this place, and from the person she had become. Suddenly Kendra sensed someone approaching and heard him sit on the grass beside her. Kendra's eyes were still closed when she asked, "Are you ready?"

"Oh yes. Very ready."

Kendra jumped as if she'd heard the rattle of a snake, and cried, "What are *you* doing here?"

Argus looked different. He seemed less stuffy than he had before. It may have been because she had always seen him in a suit, and now he was dressed in Dockers and a casual pullover shirt. But there was something else, too—a raw edge that must have been hidden beneath the slick facade. He said, "You two make a cute couple. A slut and a killer. But happily ever after?" He shook his head and whispered, "Don't think so."

Kendra looked toward the house. She said, "Allan will be back any minute."

Argus stretched out on the grass. He asked, "Heard the news?"

Kendra ignored the question and said instead, "You followed us?" She stood away from him and saw his car parked down the block.

Argus continued: "There was a murder last night." He picked a flower and smelled it. "At Saint Luke's. Pretty grisly stuff."

"If he sees you—"

"Whoever did it ripped the poor guy's eyes out." Argus offered her Allan's journal. "You should read this. It's a real page-turner."

Kendra thought about Matthew. Now Argus knew where he lived. She reached for the journal, trying to stay calm. Kendra said, "Okay. I'll read it."

Argus touched her hand with his forefinger as she took the journal. "I don't think you will. But you *should.* You'd be surprised what our boy is capable of."

Kendra tried to hide her fear beneath a casual tone of voice. She said, "You got what you wanted. You don't need me anymore."

"Oh no, I need you now more than ever—to keep an eye on him for me. And to let me know if any more nosy old men come around snooping."

"I've done what you wanted. I got you the journal. I can't do this anymore."

Argus delivered a sharp, unexpected backhand to the side of Kendra's face that sent her sprawling backwards onto the grass. He then reclined beside her, rested his hand on her throat. He hissed, "Why don't you ask Allan what he can do." Argus' breath on Kendra's cheek was hot and foul. "Better yet, ask him to show

you. I think you'll be surprised." Argus kissed her violently. She bit
his lip hard enough to draw blood and he released her. Kendra
made a run for it, but Argus caught her bare foot, jerking her back
to the ground with a frustrated cry. She clawed for her discarded
shoe, and drove its heel into Argus' face. He grabbed handfuls of
her clothes, dragging her back into his arms. She thrashed and
screamed as he began to choke her.

A young boy across the street called out, "Hey! I'm telling!"
and ran into his house to do just that.

Argus loosened his hold on Kendra's throat, and whispered in
her ear, "Shhh ... There will be time for this later."

Kendra gasped for breath and said, "Fuck you," then tried to
pull away.

Argus tightened his grip again. "You will do as I tell you until I
tell you to stop." He released Kendra and she rolled away, coughing. "And leave the fucking curtains open." Kendra held her
tongue and tried to catch her breath. Argus said, "You know, it
makes me feel good to know that my son is being initiated by such
a pro. After all this is over you might consider a career in the movies. You look great when you fuck."

Kendra suddenly drove her elbow into Argus' face and rolled
away as blood trickled from his nose. She grabbed the journal and
hobbled toward the house, promising, "Touch me again—or go
near my kid—and I'll kill you." Argus laughed, and she went bal-
listic—screaming loud enough to bring the neighbors to their windows: "I swear to God—I'll fucking kill you!"

87

Douglas mashed his armload of groceries between his body
and the wall in order to free one hand. He reached down to pat
his left pocket, then his right, cursing himself for not getting his
keys out sooner. Conservationists be damned, he liked plastic bags
better; the paper ones simply offered no decent handhold. Keys
in hand, Douglas leaned over to the door while struggling to keep
the bags from falling. He tried to insert his key in the lock, and
found the door ajar. Douglas called out, "Juana?"

There was no answer.

Douglas gathered his bags and nudged the door open with his foot. He said, "Juana, you left the door open." Douglas used his shoulder to flip on the kitchen light switch, and set his bags down on the counter while the fluorescent overheads flickered to life. The kitchen was a mess, and suddenly Douglas was annoyed. He said, "Juana?", then, for no rational reason, he was afraid. Douglas yelled, "Juana?" as he hurried toward the bedroom. It was only thirty steps away from the kitchen, but in that space of time Douglas' heart leapt into his throat, his pulse skyrocketed, and he broke into a cold sweat. He whispered, "Please God, Please God, Please God ..." as he ran through the living room.

The ventilator!

He didn't hear the ventilator.

It's been switched off! Oh my God, what have I ...

Then he heard it: the familiar mechanical whirring, interrupted by measured puffs of oxygen as they were pumped into Elizabeth's body. Douglas stopped a few feet from the bed, eyes welling up with tears. She was safe. He suddenly felt weak-kneed and limp. His own runaway heartbeat must have masked the sound of the machines. Then something registered in the periphery of his senses, but the forming thought was interrupted by the sound of the front door closing.

Juana mumbled, "Pendejo! You think you're funny, huh. Some big joke."

Douglas stepped out of the bedroom and asked, "Where the hell were you?"

Juana jumped and clutched her open hand to her chest. She said, "Dios mio, Mr. Geffner! You scared me."

"*I scared you?* You left my wife alone."

"It was only for a second. A man knocked on the door and said someone was breaking into my car, so I ran downstairs to—"

"You don't have a car."

"My brother loaned me his today. I was running late and—"

Douglas turned away. His limbs felt like they were made of lead. He said, "Go home, Juana. And don't come back."

"But Mr. Geffner—"

He spoke slowly and succinctly: "Goodbye, Juana."

Juana stood there for a moment, dumbfounded, and then gathered her things while Douglas stood in the middle of the bedroom scrubbing his face with his hands. Once Juana had gone, Douglas locked and bolted the door before returning to the bedroom. That was when he saw the rose in Elizabeth's hand.

Douglas blinked, but when he opened his eyes again, it was still there—like a rabbit pulled from a hat. And then his eyes found the business card he had left in Argus' office, propped against Elizabeth's blanketed leg.

Part V

౸ ◈ ౺

Like the spokes of a wheel ...

88

Jenny was flipping through all two hundred and ten cable channels. Again. She'd been restless and bored all night, nagged by a vague emotion she didn't care to identify.

Whatcha doin' home alone, Cinderella? Prince out havin' a ball? In New York for one week and here you sit, starin' at the tube like a brain-dead housewife—all alone and feelin' blue. You coulda done that back at home, babe. So Allan's fucked up. Let him work it out with Superslut. Faster than a speeding boner! More powerful than a multiple orgasm! It's a bird, IT'S A PLANE ...

Christ, take a pill already. So she's a bitch. So she's got secrets. Big fuckin' deal. Get over yourself.

Something on the eleven o'clock news caught Jenny's attention. The lead story was a fresh and particularly gruesome murder. Just as the over-coiffed anchorguy was about to say where the victim was found, Allan unlocked the front door. Jenny flipped the channel to an old movie and tried to appear engrossed. She wasn't about to be caught brooding. When Jenny spoke she didn't look away from the TV, just propped her feet up onto the coffee table and tried to sound casual. "Have a good time with the folks?"

Allan hung up his coat and said, "Depends on your definition of good."

Jenny muted the sound and turned toward the door with something very much on her mind. She said, "Hey, I want to apologize. I've been a real pain in the ass—"

Kendra, out of sight thus far, stepped through the front door, out of breath. "He said it was okay to park out front as long as I hurry." She looked to Allan and then to Jenny. Kendra said, "Sorry, did I interrupt again?"

Jenny considered completing her thought, but she didn't like the smirk on Kendra's face. Jenny switched off the TV and rose from the couch. "Nope. I was just going to bed. I'll get out of your way—"

Kendra said, "I'm not staying," and rushed back to Allan's bedroom, clutching her purse. "I just forgot something."

Jenny approached Allan and asked, "How you feeling?"

"Tired." He yawned.

"She wore you out, huh?" Jenny had spoken before thinking and immediately regretted it. Allan cocked his head and waited for elaboration. Jenny said, "Sorry. It's just that ...I saw you two ... In the hospital room."

"Oh." Allan blushed.

His embarrassment helped diffuse Jenny's bitterness. She shook her head and gave Allan a lecherous smile. "I said it before and I'll say it again—you do have a cute little ass." Allan chewed his lower lip and averted his eyes while Jenny reveled in his discomfort. When their eyes met again, there was a new tension between them, a pleasant, prickly heat. Jenny turned toward the guest bedroom and started to walk away, but her gaze kept wandering back to Allan. She said, "I'm gonna get ready for bed. See you in the morning."

"Ah … Okay. Good night." Allan was at a loss. This new *thing* between them had blindsided him.

As Jenny passed Allan's bedroom, she caught a glimpse of Kendra at the bureau. Jenny stopped, turned back, and peeked around the corner just in time to see Kendra return Allan's journal to its proper place.

Kendra locked eyes with Jenny and asked, "What?"

Jenny said, "Every time I see you—you've got your hands in Allan's drawers." Kendra closed the drawer casually and moved toward the door. Jenny asked, "Did you find what you were looking for?"

Kendra tried to pass, but Jenny blocked her path. Kendra asked, "What now? A catfight? I thought we were past this."

Jenny spoke slowly and plainly: "You'd better not hurt him."

Kendra tried to laugh off the cryptic comment, but only managed a guilty, strangled sound. She said, "Look, I don't need your shit. I don't like this any more than—" Kendra caught herself. "Get out of my way. Please."

Jenny let Kendra pass, but called after her, "You don't like *this?* What's *this*, Kendra?"

———————

By the time Allan had seen Kendra off, locked up, and turned out the lights, Jenny was brushing her teeth in the master bathroom. The cavernous room was done in black marble with gold fixtures, double sinks, and an Olympic-sized sunken tub. The room actually looked more like a mausoleum than a bathroom. Allan stopped in the doorway, watching Jenny's hips and breasts sway beneath her oversized T-shirt as she brushed.

Jenny saw him standing there as she swished and spat. She said, "Pretty sexy, huh?" Her voice echoed in the cold, stone room. Allan watched Jenny pull her hair back and then fasten it with a rubber band. She ran the hot water and said, "This bathroom's bigger than my whole apartment." Jenny tested the water, adjusted the cold-to-hot ratio, and began to wash her face. "Totally pretentious, though I must confess that while you were out with what's-her-name I took a bubble bath in that God-awful tub and it was pretty fucking amazing." She bent over the sink and splashed more warm water onto her face.

Allan said, "I'm sorry, Jen."

Jenny said, "Huh?" as she worked the soapy lather into her pores.

Allan spoke a little louder: "I haven't been a very good friend lately."

Jenny rinsed and turned off the water. She dried her face with a plush white guest towel. "Yeah, well neither have I."

"What do you mean?"

"I should be happy for you and Kendra. She's every guy's wet dream."

"You don't like her." Allan sat on the edge of the tub.

"I don't know her, but I don't trust her. She's hiding something."

"You know anyone who isn't hiding *something?*"

Jenny thought about it as she brushed her long auburn hair, finally answering, "Yeah. Me."

"No secrets? Not one?"

She set her brush on the vanity and took a step toward Allan. "Nope." She looked him straight in the eye. "Not from *you*."

Allan began to squirm. He asked, "What's that supposed to mean?"

"You ever gonna tell me what happened last night?"

Allan hesitated, and then said, "No." Jenny moved closer and Allan could smell her; sweet and soapy. He said, "Jen ..." Jenny was studying his mouth and wondering what it would be like to touch the tip of her tongue to his lips when Allan asked, "Do you believe in God?"

Jenny blinked and turned her attention from his lips to his eyes. They had gotten so light that it was almost freaky. She would have to ask Chet about that. But now, eerie eyes aside, she could tell that Allan was scared. Jenny asked, "You mean *literally*?"

"Yeah. God, heaven, hell ... the whole thing."

Jenny took a step back. "I don't know. I'd like to." She seemed at a loss. "But ...I don't know."

"I don't want to live forever, Jen."

"Live forever?" She wanted to laugh, but he seemed so deadly serious.

"But I don't want to die, either. Not *now*." He furrowed his brow, sat on the edge of the tub and said, "I don't even know if I can die."

"C'mon Allan, don't get weird on me again."

Allan didn't react for a long time, and then he shook his head abruptly as if to toss a troubling thought from his brain. Allan seemed wistful as he reached out to touch Jenny's face—but stopped short. He withdrew his hand, looked away, and moved toward the door. "Did the locksmith come today?"

"Yeah." Jenny's thoughts and emotions were muddled. "But I told you it wasn't necessary. I know it won't happen again."

Allan stopped in the doorway, but didn't turn back to face her. "You should go home, Jen. It's not safe here."

Jenny pretended to be offended. She said, "What, three days isn't soon enough for you? You wanna get rid of me even sooner?"

"It's not that," and rubbed his temples. Dread had attached itself to Allan's psyche like an ominous shadow. He said, "Just lock your door okay?"

"Go to bed. You look like shit."

"Promise me you'll lock your door."

The implied warning hung in the air and clung to the walls, transforming the marbled bathroom into a cavernous tomb and the moment into a scene from one of those old Christopher Lee movies where the wizened vampire hunter warns the maiden fair not to remove her oh-so-attractive garlic necklace. Jenny pushed the thought away, folded her arms across her breasts and said, "Yeah. Okay. I'll lock it." Allan started down the hall toward his room and Jenny remembered Chet. She called out: "Oh yeah, I forgot to tell you—Chet wants us back at the hospital tomorrow morning."

"What for?"

"The results of the tests."

Allan muttered, "It doesn't matter."

"He said it was important."

There was a long silence before he spoke again. "Fine. Goodnight."

"Night." Jenny watched Allan enter his darkened room and shut the door. She switched off the bathroom light and found herself whistling in the dark on her way back to the guest room. Once inside, Jenny used the shiny new deadbolt, just as she had promised.

89

The next morning an awkward silence stood between Allan and Jenny like a cold, gray wall. It had been a long night and neither one of them had slept well. Allan had paced the apartment, ranting and raving till four in the morning. He even tapped at Jenny's door at one point, but she didn't like the odd quality of his voice and pretended to be asleep. In that moment she was thankful for the lock on her door and Allan's earlier insistence upon her use of it.

In the light of day Allan had no memory of his actions and he questioned Jenny about the furnishings that had been toppled during his tirade. She told him what had happened. He grew quiet, and then asked if he had done anything ...bad. She reassured him and they went out to breakfast. It was a sullen meal, so different from the one they had shared on her first day in town, though nothing could suppress Allan's insatiable appetite.

Now, after a final round of coaxing, they had arrived at the hospital. There were police officers and press everywhere. It took ten minutes just to cross the lobby. Allan was about to stop a passing reporter to ask what had happened when it hit him.

The headache. The pounding in his ears like drums.

The old man's feeble screams.

Floating in mud.

Allan stopped so quickly that a policeman who had been two paces behind ran right into him. Allan turned back to the entrance, panicked, and found the cop's eyes upon him. Allan mumbled, "Sorry," looked away, and pushed back toward the front doors. He felt a hand on his arm and knew—this was it. Someone had recognized him.

"Allan?"

He turned and was almost disappointed to find it was only Jenny. Allan stammered, "Jen. I ...I've gotta get outta here."

"Allan, you *promised*."

"He scanned the crowd nervously, squirming beneath her determined grip. Allan said, "I know, but I—"

"I don't wanna say you owe me this, Allan." She waited for his full attention before continuing: "But you do." Allan hesitated a moment before lowering his eyes and allowing Jenny to lead him through the crowd and into the hospital's main hallway.

———

Chet was in the doctor's lounge pouring himself and another intern a cup of coffee when Jenny and Allan entered. Chet said, "I was beginning to think you two weren't going to show."

Allan noticed that the stranger beside his friend was staring at him rather intently. Allan replied, "She didn't give me much choice." The other intern sipped his coffee and watched Allan without blinking. Uneasy, Allan said, "We can talk later, if you're in the middle of something."

"No, no." Chet stepped forward, smiling a little too broadly. "In fact, I wanted you to meet a friend of mine."

The stranger stepped forward to offer his hand. "Calvin Shultz. Nice to meet you, Allan."

Allan warily accepted the intern's hand. The arrogant young doctor had chiseled, Nordic features, a cocky demeanor, and ice-blue eyes. Allan looked to Chet and asked, "What's going on?"

Chet's face flushed, and he replied, "Going on? Nothing. We just ..."

Allan turned to Jenny for the truth. "Jenny?"

She explained, "Chet and I thought it might be a good idea if you talked to someone."

Calvin took a seat, still studying Allan as if he was a specimen under a microscope. He said, "I'm a psychiatry intern, Allan. If you'd like to talk—I'm a good listener. If not ... that's okay, too."

Allan turned toward the door to leave just as a young police officer entered. Allan froze.

The officer said, "Excuse me. They said there was coffee in here?" The officer spotted the pot. "There we go. You don't mind, do you?"

Chet stepped aside. "Actually, we were in the middle of something—"

The cop reached for the coffee pot. "Be outta your hair in two shakes, Doc. Just needed something to take my mind off that mess you got in the ICU. The older guys say you get used to it, but—" He shuddered as he poured. "—Jesus, Mary, and Joseph. How could someone do somethin' like that to another person?"

Allan looked out into the hallway. There were still cops and press everywhere. He felt trapped and nauseous.

Calvin said, "What's it gonna be, Allan?" and checked his watch. "I've got a consultation in thirty minutes."

The cop glanced up at Allan as he filled a Styrofoam cup.

Jenny whispered, "Allan, *please* ..."

"Fine." Allan took the seat opposite Calvin and folded his arms. "But you're wasting your time."

Calvin gave Allan a confident smile. "No problem. I was born rich. I majored in time-wasting at Harvard."

Chet went to the door and whispered something to Jenny. She turned to Allan and said, "We'll be in the lobby," then followed the young cop out of the room before Allan had a chance to protest.

When they were alone, Allan turned to Calvin and said, "I'm not crazy."

Calvin laughed. "No one said you were, Allan. But you do hear voices. Right?"

"No." Allan was taken aback. "I mean ...yes ...but not like that. I just ...don't sleep a lot."

"Why don't you sleep, Allan?"

Allan began to fidget. "I've just got a lot on my mind, I guess." He looked back toward the door and saw dark blue uniforms passing the window. "I black out sometimes. Not often, but when I do—I can't remember what they've done. And that scares me. I'll admit that."

Something registered in Calvin's bright eyes. He asked, "Who are *they*?"

Allan's face flushed. "I didn't mean they. I meant I. I can't remember what I've done."

"You just said you couldn't remember what *they* had done."

Allan was getting angry now. He said, "That wasn't what I meant."

"If you do hear voices, Allan, and especially if you're suffering black-outs in conjunction with those voices—these can be symptoms of a rather serious condition."

Allan laughed. "I'm not delusional, if that's what you mean."

"Actually, I was guessing paranoid schizophrenia."

Allan glanced back at the door, expecting armed officers to burst into the room with guns drawn at any moment. He said, "I'm not paranoid. And I'm not schizophrenic, at least not in the traditional sense." Allan considered this for a moment. How he wished the professor would take over and put this arrogant snot in his place, but the cavalry was nowhere in sight. Allan said, "Forget it. I can't expect you to understand. I don't fully understand it myself."

Calvin leaned forward and challenged, "Try me."

Okay Cal, here's the scoop. I kill people and collect their souls. But the big joke is that the souls don't blend. They just bounce around inside my head—waiting for me to sleep or just let my guard down so they can take over. So you see, I'm really not a lunatic. Just a monster. Got a pill for that, mister GQ?

"Allan?"

Allan was imagining the glee with which Calvin would greet his confession. He'd make Allan the star of his own personal freak show. Articles would be written and papers presented. Calvin might even come up with a catchy label for Allan's "syndrome." A moment later, Allan rejoined the cocky intern in the here-and-now. Calvin's smug smile was still in place. Allan said, "Sorry. *We* were just discussing the matter."

Calvin caught the sarcasm and recognized a locked door when he saw one. He said, "Suit yourself, Allan," and checked his watch again. "If you change your mind and want to talk have Chet get in touch with me." He added casually, "You know, there are medications that can help quiet the voices."

This got Allan's attention. He asked, "Which medications?"

Calvin headed for the door as he listed: "Haldol, Clozapine, Fluphenacine. But they're only prescribed in conjunction with psychotherapy."

"They work?" Allan fought back hope. "These drugs ... They can really get rid of the voices?"

"In many cases, yes."

Allan stopped Calvin as he was turning to leave. There was more than a twinge of desperation in his voice as he smiled and said, "Let's try the medication *without* therapy. You could write a prescription right now, couldn't you?"

Now it was Calvin's turn to smile. If this kid was a true paranoid schizophrenia, which was very rare, this case had publication potential. And Calvin had played him just right. Calvin said, "Yes, I *could*. But I won't. I'll prescribe the medication only with a commitment of long-term therapy."

Allan insisted, "I couldn't do that."

Calvin shrugged, patted Allan on the shoulder, and then walked away. "It's your choice, Allan. Let me know if you change your mind."

90

"This guy came into my *home!* He touched my wife, for Christ's sake!"

Detective McCrae leaned back in his chair and clasped his hands behind his head. He said, "I understand your anger, Mr. Geffner—"

"No you don't." Douglas was trembling. "You have no idea."

"All right—I don't, but you've given us nothing we can use. Just a lot of speculation and a few questionable military records."

Douglas said, "He told my nurse that her car was being broken into—to lure her out of the house."

"*Maybe.* But she told you there was no one in the hallway when she opened the door. Right?"

"What about the card?" Douglas dropped the business card onto the detective's desk.

McCrae said, "*Your* card, with *your* handwriting on the back."

Lucci added, "And your fingerprints all over it."

McCrae stood and stretched. It had been a long day. He said, "The nurse left the door open, so it's not even breaking and entering—just entering. And all he did, even if it *was* Argus Steele, was put a flower in your wife's hand. By legal standards he did nothing threatening."

"But it was a threat. It was a warning."

Lucci and McCrae sighed in unison, almost as if they had rehearsed it. Lucci said, Let's not go down that road again, Mr. Geffner. We told you, the Steele file is closed. He had no motive to kill his wife."

McCrae said, "The insurance money didn't even go to him."

Lucci added, "–and he had no opportunity."

McCrae referred to his notes. "An eyewitness was with him from an hour before the accident to a half an hour after. And a twenty-story fall onto a crowded sidewalk doesn't leave much doubt as to the time of death."

Douglas asked, "So what am I supposed to do if he comes back?"

Lucci shrugged and suggested, "You could always buy a gun."

"Great. One more angry man running around the city with a gun. And what's that boy supposed to do? His son. He's living in Steele's apartment. Someone should warn him. I simply cannot accept—"

"Douglas Geffner?" An overweight officer at a corner desk was holding his phone's receiver and calling across the room: "Is there a Douglas Geffner here?"

"I'm Douglas Geffner." Douglas started across the room, dread closing in around him.

The officer handed the phone to Geffner. "Guy says he's your neighbor, and you left this number for him in case of emergency. What, you never heard of a cell phone?"

"Sorry. My phone's battery died the other day." The officer snorted in disgust and walked away. Douglas raised the receiver to his ear and his mouth went dry.

91

Allan and Jenny sat on opposite sides of the subway car despite the relative emptiness of the midday train. Jenny crossed the aisle and claimed the seat beside Allan. She said, brightly, "You've got your book signing party tonight, right?" Allan remained silent as he stared out the window. Jenny sighed and said, "Look, you're right. I should've been straight with you. It's just that you've been acting so fucking weird lately. I'm worried. And a little scared."

Allan spoke quietly as he watched the street names stenciled on the tiled walls of the stations whiz past: "Scared of me?"

"Of you." She took his hand. "And for you."

The tension between them was punctuated by the steady clunk of the passing tracks beneath them and the creaking groans of the shifting compartments. Allan said, "He thinks there are drugs that might help me—that friend of Chet's."

Jenny sensed the hesitation in Allan's voice and said, "But?"

"He won't give them to me unless I sign on for psychotherapy."

Jenny chose her words carefully. "That wouldn't be so bad. Would it?"

He looked at her for the first time since she'd sat down beside him. His eyes were narrowed and his jaw set. "That's the last thing I need right now. He'd lock me up in a padded room and throw away the key." Allan sensed Jenny's growing anxiety and tried to bite back his anger. "I'm sorry, Jen. I just can't." He turned back to the window and his voice softened: "Anyway, two more days and you'll be safe. Maybe if I can get that medicine ..."

"I thought I might stay until we figure out—"

"*No. You have to leave.*" Allan was gripping her hand more tightly than he had intended, speaking in a trembling whisper: "I don't know how much longer I can fight it, Jen. Please—I don't want you to see me this way." He stopped talking then, and looked into her eyes. And for a moment she saw a glimpse of the friend that she'd had so long ago. "Please Jen ... Go home. Before it's too late."

She hugged him and held him close. "Okay, I'll go. If that's what you want."

92

Douglas had fallen asleep in the chair beside his wife's hospital bed. The Geffners' neighbor, whom he had asked to sit with Elizabeth, had called the paramedics as soon as she began to seize. Had the neighbor called for help a moment later, it would have been too late. Douglas' grandson and his wife had been with him at the hospital for most of the day, trying to keep his spirits up. Douglas was relieved when they finally left him to his grief. It took too much effort to speak.

The doctor said it was a matter of weeks now, but Douglas knew better; Elizabeth was ready. It would be a day or two at the most, and Douglas would not leave her side. He would hold her withered hand, brush her thinning hair, and whisper in her ear as the machines churned and clicked ...and her precious life ebbed away.

But now he was dreaming. And in his dreams he and Elizabeth were young and healthy. She was breathtaking, he was brilliant, and they had their whole lives ahead of them.

93

The nightclub was packed, the music was loud and the people were beautiful. Allan happily autographed copies of his book while Jenny watched. His mood swings were so wild and frequent, now. He was sullen from the train trip home—right up until the moment they arrived at the party. Then something seemed to click. It was as if a channel had been changed; Allan became gregarious and confident, working the crowd like a pro. But still, the fact that Kendra hadn't shown had bothered him. Allan waved Jenny over and spoke softly as he signed another book: "Did you call?"

"Yes. *Again.* Still no answer. Just forget about her and enjoy yourself."

Allan returned to the task at hand, a little less enthusiastically. Jenny finished her drink and crossed the dance floor to get a refill, squeezing past bouncing businessmen and twitching intellectuals trying to keep time to the music. Jenny had just reached the bar when she spotted Kendra, standing in the doorway, trying to decide whether or not to come in. She wore a simple silk dress that would have seemed plain on anyone else, but somehow managed to look wicked on her.

Jenny watched the men rush Kendra like an army of ants descending on a picnic lunch, but the main course just ignored them and pushed past. Kendra approached and Jenny turned away to rejoin Allan. Kendra called after her, "Where is he, Jenny?"

"You're late. Have another date?" Jenny started back across the dance floor.

"Could you give me a break?" Kendra followed. "Just for tonight. Please."

Jenny raised her voice to be heard above the music: "Give me one good reason."

"Allan." Kendra put her hand on Jenny's shoulder. Jenny stopped and turned to face her. "Please. For Allan."

The urgency in Kendra's eyes seemed to blunt Jenny's anger. Jenny gestured toward the line of people waiting to speak to Allan and said, "Follow the yellow brick road."

Kendra looked Jenny right in the eye and read her thoughts aloud: "You're right. He *does* deserve better." Kendra disappeared into the crowd. Jenny considered going after her, but opted for a breath of fresh air instead and headed for the door.

Kendra weaved through the dancers as she made her way to Allan. She came up behind him and whispered in his ear—and his face lit up. He excused himself, allowing Kendra to lead him past

Ellen, Chet, and Laughton on the way to the dance floor. Allan asked, "What was so important?" as Kendra pulled him into the gyrating crowd. But she couldn't hear him. Allan raised his voice to be heard above the music: "I said, *what's so important?*"

The frenetic song came to an end. Kendra kissed Allan and answered, "Me. And you." A moment later a slow song began. Kendra spoke as they danced: "I'm sorry I'm late." She straightened his tie. "I had a lot of thinking to do."

"Anything you'd like to share with the class?"

"Later." Kendra seemed apprehensive. "We've got a lot of things to talk about, Allan." She kissed him again. "I'm glad I'm here to see this."

"See what?"

"The way everyone admires you."

"They admire the professor. It was his work. Everything I have is because of him." He touched her face, adding, "Even you."

"No, Allan. It's all *yours*, and I'm glad to be with you."

"This sounds like a 'no matter what happens' speech."

Kendra almost confessed right there and then, but lost her nerve, knowing full well that once she said what had to be said Allan might never look at her this way again. She rested her head on his shoulder and said, "I'm sorry. I'm not used to feeling this way. But I think I like it."

Allan kissed her as the song ended. He said, "Me, too." The next song was a fast one. Allan took Kendra's hand and tried to lead her from the dance floor. "Let's go."

She pulled him back and said, "Hey, where do you think you're going?"

"Huh uh. Not me. I don't dance. Don't ask me."

"Just follow me. You'll be fine."

He watched Kendra's body move seductively beneath her clingy silk dress. Allan said, "My God. That's unnatural. My body doesn't go that way. How about if I just stand here and twitch every now and then?"

"Fine. Just don't leave me." Allan launched into the White Boy Shuffle. Kendra suppressed a laugh before closing her eyes and giving herself over to the pulse of the music. Making the decision to tell Allan everything had lifted the weight of the world from her shoulders. In an hour he might hate her, and in a week she and her son would be a thousand miles away, but now, in this moment, they were together and happy and she felt free.

Allan kept shuffling as Kendra let loose during a particularly hypnotic percussion solo. He blushed when she rubbed her body against his and then, just when he wanted more, backed away. Allan's smile began to fade as vague recognition tugged at the back of his brain. There was something about the way she moved. Something familiar.

As Kendra danced, eyes closed, she had inadvertently incorporated parts of the Kali routine into her movements. When the song had finally ended and she opened her eyes, Kendra saw Allan standing dead still, staring. His face was pale and his eyes were open wide. She asked, "What's wrong?" and tried to catch her breath. "Allan? What is it?"

"It was *you?*" Allan continued to stare, horrified.

"What?"

"Your dance." Allan's wounded stare became an unspoken accusation. He backed away. "It was you."

It was only then that Kendra realized what she had done and gasped. "Allan—" He turned toward the door and pushed his way through the crowd. Kendra followed, her voice crackling with desperation: "Allan, please ..."

———

When Kendra emerged from the nightclub, Allan was already a half a block ahead of her. She ran after him, pleading, "Allan, let me explain."

He stopped suddenly and turned on her. "All right—explain. I wanna hear it."

The moment upon her, Kendra groped for the words that she had rehearsed so many times during the last few days. But she came up empty. After a moment, Allan turned and began to walk away. Finally, Kendra blurted out, "He hired me."

Allan stopped, but didn't look back. There was no question as to who *he* was. Allan asked, "To do what? Drive me crazy?"

"To figure out why you were so different when you came back from Zaire. I was supposed to get close to you. Find out what happened."

"Get close?" Allan's laugh was venomous. He turned to face her. "So, what were your findings?"

"I ...found the DVDs. And your journal."

"Did *he* read it?"

"Yes."

"So he paid you to fuck me?"

Kendra looked Allan square in the eye and began to cry for the first time in years. "I'm so sorry, Allan."

After a moment of painful eye contact, Allan began to pace. He looked up at the stars and asked, "Did you read it?"

"No. Not really. I couldn't." Allan studied her face, trying to glean the truth, and then turned back to the stars. Destiny, which he'd always envisioned as a distant beacon, now felt like quick-sand, choking and relentless—responding to his every attempt to escape with a decisive downward pull. Kendra took a cautious step closer, but she and Allan were still miles apart. She followed his gaze upward and said, "I guess we should've paid closer attention." Kendra stood quietly beside Allan for a long time before walking away, leaving him alone beneath the stars.

As Kendra's footsteps grew distant, another set approached. Jenny had been watching from a distance. She touched Allan's shoulder and said, "I'm sorry."

"No you're not, Jen."

She shuffled her feet a bit and answered, "No. I guess I'm not." She took a step closer, wanting so much to comfort him. She asked, "Can we go home?"

The pain in Allan's head was back with a vengeance. He winced and said, "I can't think. I need that fucking medicine." Allan rubbed his temples as he walked away, calling back, "Will you be okay?"

Jenny was hurt, but hiding it. She answered, "Yeah. I'll get Chet to give me a ride."

Allan said, "Go home, Jen. And lock the door," before staggering off into the night, clutching his throbbing head in his hands.

94

Allan's journal had a strange effect on his father. Argus knew that it must have taken something unusual to bring about the recent dramatic changes in his son, but *this?* Ever since the discovery of Allan's secret, Argus had been obsessed with the idea of performing the Shantu ritual. He found himself distracted at the office and in a perpetual state of restlessness. His thoughts kept drifting back to the floating platform and the violence that his son had committed there in the hopes of a better life.

But was a better life Allan's *true* motivation?

Argus had been neglecting his clients since Allan's return. Now things had gotten serious. Several big accounts had found other representation and Argus didn't care. His thoughts were all of Allan and Africa and blood, though not strangers' blood—as it had always been before. It wasn't until Argus stopped to pick up the pretty young hitchhiker that the truth revealed itself to him, and the voice in his head whispered, "Soon, he will come for you."

Argus had come to the conclusion that it wasn't really a better life that Allan was after. It was power. It was a weapon; the ability to possess another man's soul. To replace God. Surely, this was the ultimate weapon. And what better test of that weapon could there be than to kill your own father? Your creator? But now Argus knew the secret, too. He smiled to himself and thought, *The cat's out of the bag, son. Meow, meow ...*

"Hey, you okay?" The hitchhiker was nervous. The stranger behind the wheel had driven three miles without a single word.

"I am now," Argus said, relieved. "The cat's out of the bag."

The slender girl, still shivering beneath her oversized army jacket, reached for the car's heater. "Okay if I turn on the heat? It's colder than a witch's tit out there."

Argus was amused. "A what?"

"A witch's tit." The girl's crooked smiled sparked in the moonlight and she flipped her dirty blonde hair back from her face. "You never heard that one before? My momma used to say it all the time. We lived up in the hills, and it was cold as a witch's tit most of the damn time."

"Which hills?"

"Kentucky. That's where my people are from."

Argus looked over at the girl and wondered what it would be like to be inside the young stranger. Or even better—what it would be like to have her inside him. She must have sensed something then because, while still looking straight ahead at the road, she inched toward the door and rested her hand on the release. She said, "Hey, you know what—you can drop me at the next corner."

"Why?"

"I got some friends who live around here." She tried to sound casual. "Maybe they'll let me crash at their place tonight."

Argus said, "Sure," and pulled over to the road's shoulder. He slipped the Jag into neutral and added, "No problem."

The hitchhiker hesitated before opening the door. After all, he *had* pulled over when she asked. The girl looked him over, still unsure, and said, "Thanks."

He asked, "Something wrong?"

The hitchhiker pulled the release and opened the door. A howling wind swept the heated air from the car. She hesitated, dreading the thought of an hour or more on the side of the road before another car happened by—if one came at all. She said, "Oh, wait a minute. Is this ...?" She strained to read an imaginary street sign up ahead. "Yeah ... No, they don't live here. I mean, not *anymore*." She closed the door.

"So you *do* want a ride?"

She sighed, watching through the window as icy winds whipped leaves and trash around the car. "Look, the thing is ... I meet a lot of weirdos on the road."

"And you thought I was one of them."

"Yeah. I mean, I didn't know. But you were starin' at me like you might be."

"I'm sorry. I didn't mean to scare you."

"I mean, if it's just sex you're after—I'll do *that*."

Argus arched his eyebrows. "You will?"

"For a place to sleep and maybe dinner or somethin'—yeah. You're not bad lookin' for an older guy." She huddled in her over-sized coat again. "But if you're into some weird kinda trip ..."

A weird trip? Yes, indeedy, a real E-Ticket ride.

Argus said, "I hadn't really thought about sex, but your offer is tempting." He leaned over and moved her faded army jacket aside, revealing the pert swell of the girl's breasts beneath a threadbare sweater.

She asked, "What? Now?"

"Why not?" He slipped his hand beneath the sweater and felt the trapped heat of her taut young flesh. He said, "Everyone's tucked away in their warm little beds."

"Yeah, well, that's what I was hopin' for. A nice warm bed."

He promised, "Later," and felt her nipple harden beneath his fingertips. Was it sexual excitement ...the cold ...or was she afraid? The last possibility inspired an instant erection.

The weary young hitchhiker looked around and saw no pedestrians on the street. Decided, but not thrilled, she unbuttoned her jeans. "But you'll still give me a place to sleep—after?"

"You have my word as a gentleman. Tonight, you will have a bed."

She shimmied out of her jeans. "Can you at least turn the heater back on?" Argus turned on the heater and tugged at his belt. She said, "Oh yeah, I should warn you—I got my period."

He said, "That's okay," as he pressed the button to lock the doors, reached for the penknife in his pocket, and descended upon the half-naked girl with a reassuring smile. "I don't mind blood."

––––––––––

A few hours later Argus said, "Goodnight," and dumped the girl's body onto a bed of discarded newspapers in an alley behind a neighborhood candy store. He had worried about the lack of euphoria, which Allan had described so vividly in his journal, though Argus did feel exhilarated. He checked his reflection in the Jag's lighted vanity mirror and used a monogrammed hankie to dab the blood from the corners of his mouth. Other than a few blades of dead grass and some traces of mud, the interior of the car was pristine. Argus had done his business in an empty lot a few miles away and had carefully wrapped the sodden corpse in her oversized coat for transport.

It had been hard to keep the girl under control while he searched for a suitable location for the ritual. Argus had planned to strangle her, but after leaving the car, en route to the abandoned lot, she had bolted. When he tackled her to the ground, her head struck a concrete foundation, cracked wide open and robbed Argus of his favorite part of the hunt. Death was only moments away. He had studied her eyes as she twitched and mumbled in the moonlight about warm beds and lost loves. And then, as she drew her final breath, Argus thought he saw something. It could have just been the pooling of a tear or the reflection of the moon, but he wasn't about to miss the opportunity.

The little silver knife was well sized for the task, though Argus felt distanced by the steel. Later, he decided that the use of a weapon detracted from the primal intimacy of the ritual. Oh well, it was a learning process. There was always next time.

95

Calvin said goodbye to a fellow intern and hurried across the parking lot. By the time he reached his silver BMW, the young intern's nose had already gone Rudolph-red from the cold. He switched off the Beamer's alarm and fumbled for his keys.

"Excuse me—"

Calvin made a startled sound and turned to find Allan watching him from the shadows. He said, "Shit. You scared me."

On another day Allan might have been pleased by the trace of panic in the cocky intern's voice. But right now he could think of nothing but the pain. Allan said, "I really need that medicine."

Calvin noticed that Allan was without a coat, despite the sub-zero temperature. Steam was rising from his skin as if he'd just stepped out of a long hot shower. "It's Allan, right?" Calvin unlocked his car. "I told you, Allan—I can only prescribe those medications as an element of ongoing psychotherapy. Harassing me is not going to change my mind. So you've got a decision to make, Allan. Go home, think about it, and when you're ready to do something about your condition—give me a call." Calvin started to get into his car.

Allan's eyes were squeezed shut by the searing pain in his head; the voices, the drums, and the hunger that had already begun to build again. It was all too much. Allan grabbed Calvin by the arm and warned, "I *need* that medicine."

Calvin's pinched expression betrayed his fear. His mind was racing as he tried to remember the proper tack to take when dealing with a potentially violent patient. Calvin said, "Look Allan, why don't we go inside. You must be cold—"

"I'm not going anywhere without that medicine." Allan's stare was intense and his grip on Calvin's arm relentless.

"Okay, Allan. Come by tomorrow morning and I'll write you up a scrip." The intern looked across the parking lot for a guard or a nurse. He said, "I'm sorry. I hadn't realized just how serious your problem was."

Allan loosened his hold on the other man's arm—just for an instant—giving Calvin the opportunity to dive into the car and slam the door closed. Allan reached for the door handle, but Calvin had already engaged the lock. Calvin turned the ignition key, but the engine was cold and hesitant. Allan hammered on the roof as Calvin tried a second time and the BMW purred to life too late. Allan's fist smashed through the driver's side window and Calvin screamed. The intern floored the accelerator, but the BMW's emergency brake was still engaged and the car was going nowhere. Now Allan had a handful of Calvin's hair and he was pulling his head through the jagged hole in the glass. The intern stomped on the gas pedal, leaned on the horn and screamed for help, in vain, until Allan positioned his throat over the serrated edge of the broken glass and pulled down with all of his strength.

———

Allan ducked into the surgeons' locker room and shucked off his blood-soaked clothes as a gurney was being rushed out to the smashed BMW. He had released the emergency brake after finishing with Calvin, causing the car to speed across the parking lot and crash into the side wall of the maternity wing. Dazed and covered in blood and gore, Allan found it ironic that the hospital itself proved to be the ideal hiding place. He had staggered through the bustling hallways for a good ten minutes with barely a second glance from the overworked staff before locating the showers. Now, beneath the purifying heat of the water, he felt invigorated.

Allan watched Calvin's blood run down his naked torso, pool with the water on the shower's tiled floor, and trickle down the drain as if it were inconsequential. In fact, this time had been easier. Without The Sight and the desperate need that accompanied it, the act itself was far less traumatic—at least for *Allan*. The transference process had also been quicker and less spasmodic. And while the euphoria that Allan had come to crave had also diminished, he was still left with a pleasant buzz. As for guilt, he guessed there would be very little this time. The intern was a means to an end. Period. Allan said aloud, "He would have made a lousy doctor anyway."

He turned off the water and went to Calvin's locker. Allan dialed in the combination from memory and swung open the metal door, revealing a large mirror affixed to the inside. He muttered, "Vain little prick," as he glanced at himself in the mirror. He looked young and healthy again. Allan thought, *The more souls I take—the more my metabolism increases. And the quicker my metabolism runs—the faster I age. But with each new acquisition comes a rebirth. Interesting.* He reached for Calvin's surgical blues and mused aloud, "So, I'm damned if I do and damned if I don't."

96

Jenny had been pacing the apartment for hours. Allan was right. It was time to go home and lock the doors. The simplicity of her life back in New Mexico sounded good right about now. Besides, Allan didn't want her help. He wanted to suffer alone—to play the martyr. Fine, he could freak out with impunity and pine for Superslut all he wanted, just as long as she didn't have to stick around to see it. So Jenny had packed her bags and written the note. There was a flight home tonight and she'd be on it. If he wanted her help—he knew the number. The door wouldn't be locked, exactly, but for now she needed it closed.

Jenny didn't read the note after signing her name to it, she just tacked it up on the fridge where she knew Allan would find it. At first she felt relieved, but then she was overcome by a feeling of emptiness. Still, she wouldn't allow herself to buckle. Jenny planted herself on the couch and tuned the TV to an *I Love Lucy* marathon to pass the remaining hour before the cab was scheduled to pick her up for the airport. But the canned laughter and wacky antics on the screen didn't bring the comfort she'd hoped for.

Jenny tried to dismiss the restlessness she felt as guilt for leaving her friend to face his demons alone, but it was more than that. It was as if she felt his presence in the room, watching her. She must have looked over her shoulder twenty times in the space of one episode of the old TV show, but the feeling of being watched never dissipated. Finally, too nervous to sit still a moment longer, Jenny turned up the televised laughter, and returned to pacing. She paced the living room, then the dining room. She paced the hallway, and then checked the guest room a fourth time for forgotten articles of clothing that she knew wouldn't be there.

If it wasn't for her—I could have helped him. He would have let me. She really fucked him good, in more ways than one. What is she hiding? And what's the fascination with Allan's journal?

Dirty details of their bedroom acrobatics—or secrets?

His, or hers?

Jenny mulled it over while wandering down the hallway toward Allan's room. She stopped at his door and hesitated, then entered. Jenny moved to the dresser quickly, before she lost her nerve, and opened the drawer where she had seen Kendra digging. She didn't stop to think or reconsider—just attacked the drawer, determined to dig up the root of this mystery. The journal was easy to find, not even hidden really. But as she stood there with it in her hand, Jenny found herself unable to betray her friend's trust. Now the feeling of being watched was stronger than ever. She told herself it was her conscience, and returned the book to Allan's drawer.

She felt better after shutting the door to his room, but still not at ease. And then, on her way down the long, dark hallway, something caught Jenny's eye. A door that had always been closed was now ajar. Jenny approached the door, remembering that Allan had pointed this room out as his father's office. But he had said that it was always locked. Wherever they had lived, throughout Allan's childhood, there had always been one room that was off limits to everyone but Argus. Jenny smiled as she remembered Allan's sarcastic tone when he had referred to his father's sanctuary as the "Bat Cave".

So why was it open now? Had Allan's father been here? Wasn't he supposed to be on an extended business trip? Jenny tapped on the door and whispered, "Hello ...?" After receiving no response, she opened the door and found the most ordinary office imaginable: a big oak desk by the window, leather wing chairs, and an overloaded bookshelf. Boring.

But Jenny wasn't relieved by the normalcy of the room. In fact, she felt more tense than ever. There was something wrong here, though it was nothing visual. The room looked like any other lawyer's office. But there was *something* ... She ventured into the room to check out the books on the shelves. Reference stuff mainly, with a few Grisham novels here and there. But the something was stronger here.

Was it a sound?

No.

A feeling?

Definitely, but more than that.

"It's a smell." Jenny jumped at the sound of her own voice. She hadn't intended to say that aloud. The distant TV laugh track mocked her anxiety, and she suddenly felt very foolish. As she sniffed the air, trying to track down the mysterious odor, Jenny began to have fun with her own foolishness.

Sniff, sniff here ...

Sniff, sniff there ...

The smell seemed stronger near the closet door. She stepped away to be sure—and then returned, still sniffing like a determined hound. Yes, the smell was definitely more pronounced here. Probably a dead rat or something, caught in a trap. She supposed even the rich were troubled by the occasional curious rodent. Ready to prove her hypothesis, she turned the ornate, brass handle to the walk-in closet and opened the door.

Jenny stepped inside the pitch black space and covered her nose and mouth while waiting for her eyes to adjust. The smell of putrid flesh was strong indeed, but it was another smell that set off Jenny's internal alarm. An acrid, salty smell.

Sweat.

Gradually her eyes adjusted to the dark, and she realized that the huge closet was nearly empty. Then Jenny saw him crouched on the army cot a few feet to the left of her. She saw his narrowed eyes and the flat black stare, and she turned to run but it was too late. Argus pounced—leaping over half-filled cardboard boxes—and he had one arm wrapped around her neck and the other hand clamped over her mouth before she could scream. Jenny tried to fight, but Argus was in control. For every evasive move she attempted, he answered with the perfect counter. Argus didn't say a word as he choked Jenny. She heard his hot, labored breathing in her ear, and she felt something poking her where his pelvis pressed against her back. As her vision began to blur, Jenny used the last of her strength to stomp Argus' instep and slip away, a trick that she had learned in a college self-defense course. He let out an animalistic grunt and then pulled her back into his arms to finish the job.

The last things Jenny saw before the lights went out were the walls on either side of the cot. Polaroids of lifeless women in awkward positions floated before her, paired with bits of what looked, and smelled, like decayed flesh. Suddenly too tired to care, Jenny closed her eyes and sank down into the dark as distant TV Lucy whined, "Oh Rickeeeee!"

Allan returned to the apartment a little after 3 a.m., pills in hand. Everything at the hospital had gone without a hitch. He'd had no trouble passing for Calvin in the pharmacy. In fact, the pretty young student manning the counter had even flirted with him as she filled the prescriptions for Fluphenacine and Clozapine. She was sure she'd heard his name around the hospital, though she didn't think they had actually met before. Allan agreed, and assured her that if they *had* met—he would certainly remember. The girl got a little flustered after losing count of the pills, and glanced back to see if Allan had caught her blunder. He had smiled then, assuring her that he wasn't really the demanding and arrogant snot that the hospital gossips would have her believe.

And when she asked for a signature, Allan didn't give it a second thought; he knew his handwriting would match Calvin's perfectly.

The only surprise of the evening had come when Allan learned, during his fusion with the intern, that cocky Calvin's life hadn't been nearly as idyllic as he would have had the world believe. The intern had had a lonely childhood filled with abuse and neglect. And there was a vague, bittersweet memory that seemed central to Calvin's psyche: a radiant girl. No, a woman. Giselle was her name. But initially, Allan could glean little more than the name. This memory was buried deep and had been jealously guarded for a lifetime.

Allan went to the kitchen for water to wash down the pills. He had already taken 100mg of Clozapine, but it hadn't kicked in yet. Maybe a Fluphenacine chaser would do the trick. As it turned out, Calvin hadn't really known as much about these drugs as he'd pretended. The bits of Calvin's memory that Allan could tap into were unclear when it came to dosage and side-effects, and Calvin himself wasn't volunteering anything yet.

Allan thought, *Come on Cal, play nice with the other kids*, as he turned to the refrigerator for a snack and found Jenny's note. He read it twice and tacked it back up, feeling both relieved and disappointed.

She's safe. That's what matters. But now we're all alone with the nightmares and good old Dad.

Allan said, "Fuck him," to no one in particular. He liked the conviction in his voice but feared that his courage might be short-lived. After making two huge sandwiches, Allan moved through the silent apartment carrying his plate and glass. He stopped by the guest room, just to be sure that Jenny had gone, and was taken aback by the feeling of emptiness that washed over him.

Allan reached the threshold of his mother's room, but turned back when he heard a sound. He put his plate on the dresser and walked slowly back to the "Bat Cave". The door was ajar. He said, "Jenny?" and took a cautious step closer. "Is someone here?" Allan placed the palm of his hand on the door and collected his thoughts before proceeding. How many times as a child—and since—had he speculated on what might lie inside the forbidden room? He whispered, "I'm coming in, okay?" There was no protest from within, so he pushed the door open, but the room was empty.

97

The brief walk from the market to Kendra's apartment seemed endless. The whole thing was so stupid. She wasn't in love with Allan, regardless of what she had said. The words had just had just come out like the inky smokescreen of a frightened squid. She had to divert his attention, that's all.

Just let it go!

Mr. Delveccio, the old man from the fourth floor, was camped-out on the stoop, reading the paper, just as he did every morning. He saw Kendra coming and jumped for the door, tipping his hat. As he said, "Morning," his ill-fitting choppers clacked against his bony gums. "That's a real pretty dress you got there."

"Thanks, Mr. D." Kendra forced a smile, moved through the open doorway and started up the stairs. She knew that the old man was still staring. He always stared when she walked away.

Mr. D called after her, "Did that young man catch up with you?"

Kendra stopped halfway up the second flight of stairs. Her bags were getting heavy and she sometimes had a hard time understanding him. She called down, "What?"

Mr. D opened his mouth and pressed his thumb up against the roof of his dentures to set them properly, then said, "About an hour ago. I told him you usually do your marketing on Tuesdays. He said he'd try back later."

Allan.

She hadn't expected that, or the pleasant rush of adrenaline that came with the thought of seeing him again. Kendra asked, "Did he seem ...mad?"

The old man thought it over, enjoying the view from below, and answered, "Now that you mention it he *did* seem a bit peevish."

Great. He just came to give me shit. Just what I need.

Kendra said, "Thanks, Mr. D. If he shows up again—tell him I've moved."

"Okay, I'll do it." He watched Kendra continue her climb. Then the old man called out, "Argus," and Kendra nearly dropped her bags. Mr. Delveccio seemed quite proud of himself as he announced, "That was his name. *Argus.*"

Kendra boarded the subway still carrying her groceries, looking over her shoulder every three steps. She hadn't even stopped to think—just turned and ran—not even taking the time to pack a suitcase or feed the cat. She had no doubt that Argus would kill her if he found her. She didn't know how she knew, but she knew. Kendra had been out of breath and frantic when she called her mother while descending the urine-soaked steps that led down into the subway station. Matthew needed to stay with Aunt Liz—no questions and no discussion. She would explain later.

Kendra found a seat amid the noontime crowd, still feeling that *he* was nearby, watching. She could return the money—she didn't even want it now—but that wouldn't be enough for him. Not by a long shot. Argus was much more than dangerous, but Kendra had no intention of finding out how much more. She would lie low, long enough to liquidate her CDs, mutual funds, and stocks. And she would have a will drawn up, just in case. It would take a couple of weeks to get everything done, then she was gone. It didn't really matter where, just as long as there was a time zone or two between her and Argus.

But what about Allan? Could she leave him alone with his father? Kendra had been the only buffer between them, and now ... She couldn't think about that now. There was no time for thinking, or feeling. Especially feeling. It was strictly self-preservation time. Liquidate and evacuate.

Brooklyn. Kendra emerged from the station and caught a cab. Arlene's place was only ten blocks away, but the bags felt like concrete blocks in her arms and her head was throbbing. Maybe she was overreacting. Argus was an asshole. But a killer? Maybe if she returned his money—he might back off and she could return to her old life. It wasn't much, but it was familiar. Yeah, maybe if she just called him and said ...

Stop it. You're not calling, you're not going back, and your life will never be the same again. Not ever. Your instincts have kept you alive so far—now's not the time to go soft. What about that john you turned down in `91—the guy with the droopy eyelid. You had no real reason, just a feeling. So that other girl was beaten and raped instead of you.

The cabbie cleared his throat. The car was stopped at the curb. He said, "Hey lady, you smell real nice and all, but I got other fares waitin'."

Kendra handed him a twenty on her way out the door.

98

"K? Where the hell have you been?" Arlene, a porcelain-skinned, zaftig brunette with oversized breasts, opened the door and allowed Kendra to transfer the groceries into her arms.

Kendra said, "These are for you."

"Uh ...thanks." Arlene was confused. She brought the bags to the kitchen and started to unload. "Angela's been trying to reach you for weeks. She thinks you went out on your own. I told her no way. Have you?"

"Can I stay here with you?" Kendra went to the window and checked the street. No sign of Argus. Kendra added, "For a week? Maybe two?"

Arlene found melted ice cream all over everything in one bag. She grimaced and asked, "What's going on, Kendra?" as she rinsed butter brickle from a swordfish steak. "You in trouble?"

Kendra was scattered, unfocused. She said, "If it's a problem, I can go to a hotel. I just thought—"

"It's no problem. Stay as long as you want." Arlene's attention was drawn to Kendra's frantic expression and constant nail-biting, and she asked, "Are you okay?"

"No." Kendra looked out the window again. "But I *will* be."

"You wanna talk?" Arlene moved closer, wiping her hands on a dishtowel.

"Huh?" Kendra dragged her attention away from the window. She had never noticed just how kind her friend's eyes were. Kendra relaxed a little and replied, "No, not really. That okay?"

"No problem." Arlene reached out to give her friend a hug, and Kendra welcomed the contact. Arlene said, "If you wanna talk—I'm here."

99

The next morning Kendra and Arlene jockeyed for position in front of the bathroom mirror. Kendra accidentally nudged Arlene's elbow, causing her to apply lipstick to her cheek. She said, "Shit, Leenie. I'm sorry."

"Jesus, it's college all over again." Arlene wiped away the lipstick, trying to maintain her sense of humor. "You were a mirror hog back then, too."

"What about you? A different guy *every night.* It was like trying to sleep on the set of a porno flick."

Arlene laughed. "So I was majoring in sex and you were majoring in interior design. Can I help it if I found my true calling before you did? Besides, we both ended up with the same degree, girl."

Kendra sobered. "Yeah. I guess we did."

Arlene saw the pain in Kendra's eyes and cursed her own big mouth. She said, "Hey, it's not so bad. Nice things, free dinners, being the center of their world—even if it's only for a few hours. Shit, a few seconds in some cases. But hey, it could be a hell of a lot worse."

Kendra sat on the closed toilet seat lid and asked, "You ever think about gettin' out, Leenie?"

Arlene stepped on a scale and cringed at the numbers. "Me? No." She took off her sweater and checked again. "But if I don't lay off the Ben and Jerry's I may be forced into retirement." Arlene unbuttoned her jeans and began to squeeze out of them.

Kendra smiled and said, "I'm outta here," as she stepped out of the room. "There's no telling what's coming off next."

Arlene squeezed out of her pants and tip-toed back onto the scale. She called to Kendra, "Hey, how much do you think my implants weigh? Ten pounds? Fifteen?"

Kendra smiled and waved. "See ya' later. I'm going to the bank. Want me to pick up some Chinese on the way home?"

"Mmm, yeah. And call Angela." Arlene removed her bra and panties and balanced on one foot as she continued to stare down at the numbers on the scale. "Maybe I should start charging by the pound."

100

Kendra's cat was on the couch shredding a silk throw-pillow when someone came down the outer hallway and slipped a key in the lock. The cat darted into the bedroom, certain that there would be trouble when the mess was discovered. The door swung open on complaining hinges. The silhouette in the doorway hesitated before entering, and then moved forward in the dark.

She nearly tripped on something and shouted, "Shit!" Nothing seemed to be in its proper place. She tried the light switch, but nothing happened. She muttered, "Great," and began her labored journey across the room, groping and stumbling over toppled furniture and broken knickknacks. She banged her shin on an endtable and called out, "Fucking cat! It was only *two days*." She made her way to the window and threw open the curtains, but the moonlight didn't shed much light on the demolished room. There was one thing that the moonlight *did* make clear, however: this mess wasn't made by a cat.

Stay calm.

She started to feel her way back toward the door.

Just stay calm, keep quiet and walk out the door. Just walk out the fucking door and don't stop to think.

"Meow."

She stopped in the middle of the room and remembered the cat.

"M-e-e-o-w ..."

No, that *wasn't* the cat. She bolted across the room and stumbled over a toppled ottoman. She hit the floor scrambling for the door, but it was too late. Argus was upon her, hissing like a spurned lover: "Did you think you could just walk away from me?" She tried to answer, but his hands were around her throat. She struck out in the dark, but couldn't find his face. He squeezed harder, whispering, "I hate quitters. Are you a fucking quitter, Kendra?" Her lungs were burning now. Her eyes were open wide and tearing. She managed to grab a handful of his hair and pull as he straddled her for better leverage. He growled, "Say it! Say, 'I'm a fucking quitter! I'm a fucking quitter and I deserve to die!'"

She made a gasping sound, wanting desperately to explain. But he was squeezing so hard and her lungs were threatening to explode and the room was spinning. She found his eyes and clawed, but he jerked away before she did any serious damage, and chomped her forefinger between his teeth. She howled and bucked, trying to smash his testicles with her knee, but her strength was fading ...and her vision blurring ...and it suddenly didn't seem to matter so much anymore.

When she had stopped moving and her arms had fallen slack, Argus spat the severed tip of her finger onto the floor and stood away from the body. He plugged in a lamp and switched it on, savoring the coppery taste of the blood.

Arlene stared at him with vacant eyes. Her skirt had been hiked up in the struggle and her thigh-high stockings shredded. It took a moment for the truth of the situation to sink in, but when it did—Argus was infuriated. He kicked the lifeless body and screamed, *"You fucking whore! Where are you?"*

He glared at Arlene, trying to determine the appropriate punishment for her complicity, and she stared back with vague indifference. Then Argus noticed the provocative pose, the hiked skirt with a swatch of white cotton peeking out from beneath. And her eyes; they were quite beautiful in the moonlight. Soft and vacant. But there was something else. Something deeper. Perhaps it was a secret. Perhaps it was her soul calling to him.

There had been no 'soul transference', as it had been described in Allan's journal, when Argus had taken the young hitchhiker's eyes. At first Argus thought he had felt something akin to a psycho-spiritual rush. But later he realized that it was just the thrill of the hunt and the sweet release that had always followed it. Nice, but not enough. Not anymore. Argus needed the ultimate weapon if he was going to confront God's messenger.

Argus said aloud, "If at first, you don't succeed ..." as he returned from the bathroom, razor in hand. Argus stripped and laid down beside Arlene, whispering in her ear, "Can you forgive me?"

101

Argus was in a foul mood when he let himself into Arlene's apartment with the key from her purse. He had followed the procedure outlined in Allan's journal to the letter—again—and had felt nothing supernatural. Why didn't it work for him? What was so fucking special about Allan? After a brief check of the bedrooms and bathroom, Argus decided to wait. He went to the fridge and pulled out the half-eaten carton of take-out moo shoo duck. Argus plopped down on the couch and kicked off his shoes. He was flipping through the TV channels when he noticed the blinking light on the answering machine.

The first three messages were nothing, but the third... Argus skipped back to the beginning of the message and grabbed the pad and pen near the phone. A familiar voice said, "Hi, Leenie. It's Kendra. I called Angela and I guess she's got a job for me tonight. A tag-team in a penthouse at the Westin. Probably gave me a nerd—just to get me back. I don't know. I'm really not into it. Anyway ... Didn't want you to worry. See ya'."

102

There were only two penthouse suites at the Park Avenue Westin. The first was occupied by an older couple who were celebrating their fiftieth anniversary. Argus could tell that they didn't have real money by their luggage, which he had followed up from the lobby. Those powder-blue Samsonites with their dings and scuffs looked like they would have been more at home in a

Hawaiian bargain hotel than the thousand-dollar-a-night suite at the Westin.

Argus listened at the door of the second suite, the one with the "Do Not Disturb" sign out, but heard nothing. He thought about finding a maid and pretending to be locked out, but he didn't like leaving witnesses who might be able to identify him. So he decided to take a chance—and knocked. If she opened the door he could push his way in. The john Kendra mentioned didn't sound like he'd be any trouble. A nerd—that's what she'd called him. Regardless, he wasn't likely to go out of his way to protect a whore. And he was even *less* likely to call the cops. Argus heard a voice from inside, but couldn't decide if it was Kendra's or not. He knocked again and the doorknob turned. The voice said, "Yes?"

Argus threw his shoulder into the door and the girl draped in an oversized bath towel flew backwards onto the floor, screaming. He stepped into the room, kicked the door closed, and fell on top of her. It wasn't Kendra. Argus covered her mouth with his hand and whispered, "Where is she? Is she here?" The frightened girl's eyes moved to the bathroom door and then back to Argus. The shower was running, and Argus thought he could hear groans beneath the sounds of water. He looked around the room; clothes were scattered everywhere and there were lines of coke waiting on the coffee table. He looked to the bathroom door again and then back to the girl. He said, "She's in there? Kendra?" The girl hesitated, and then nodded yes. Argus promised, "If you're lying I'll kill you," then moved his hand away from her mouth to allow a response.

She sobbed, "I...I don't know her name. I never met her before tonight—I swear. They sent me to fill in at the last minute." The girl saw the look on Argus' face and spoke in a rush: "Please don't hurt me I won't tell anyone I promise if you just—" The water stopped, and Argus covered her mouth again and tried to think. The girl twisted away and knocked over a table. The vase that sat atop it crashed to the floor. Argus pulled her back to him by the hair, but she managed a feeble scream before he broke her neck with a sharp twist of her head.

Argus got to his feet but it was too late. The bathroom door was thrown open and sopping-wet Latino, armed with a handgun, emerged firing. The hooker in the bathroom screamed as Argus dove behind the couch and the Latino continued to shoot and shout, *"Come on motherfucker! Come and get me, you chickenshit bastard!"*

Argus kept low and counted the rounds; two more and the coked-out spic's gun would be empty. So much for the nerd Argus had hoped for. Argus had been hit in the shoulder and there was a lot of blood, but the pain was tolerable. He edged toward the door and another shot rang out. One left.

"Come on, motherfucker! Show your face!" Argus tried to slow the stream of blood from his shoulder while waiting for the final round. But the spic was holding onto it, moving closer. Argus could see his bare feet through the space under the couch, leaving wet footprints on the hardwood floor as he approached. The hooker in the bathroom continued to shriek.

The Latino screamed, "Shut the fuck up, bitch!" and took another cautious step forward.

He was close, now. Too close. But in another three steps he might just be close enough. Argus counted to five then took a deep breath and drove into the couch with his good shoulder— pushing it up into the naked gunman. The Latino discharged his last round into the couch. It ripped through fabric and wood and lodged in the thick muscle of Argus' thigh, but Argus kept driving forward. The Latino fell backward and Argus flipped the heavy antique couch on top of him, and then made a run for the door.

Argus' wounds screamed, but he didn't slow. He heard furniture toppling behind him, and was in the hallway and halfway to the elevator when the other man tackled him to the floor. The Latino said, "Not so fast, motherfucker! I wanna have a little talk with you." Argus was pinned to the floor, face down, as the other man delivered a flurry of mind-numbing blows to his kidneys. The Latino grabbed a handful of Argus' hair and pulled his head back. "Who sent you?"

Argus growled, "Fuck you."

The Latino slammed Argus' face into the floor, breaking his nose, then pulled his head back up again. He repeated, *"Who sent you?"* Argus began to mumble something and the Latino leaned down close to listen. Argus waited until the other man was within range then swung his elbow back, connecting to the side of his head with a loud crack. The startled Latino released Argus, just for an instant, but it was long enough. Argus pushed through the red wall of pain and bucked his attacker off of him.

As he flipped the Latino onto his back, Argus saw the scream-ing hooker inside the room—an Asian girl with long hair—run to the body of the other whore, then scramble for the phone. Argus straddled the Latino and pummeled his face with his fists, then brought his knee up to rest on the other man's throat. The Latino took a swing, but he was still disoriented by the blows to the face, and Argus blocked the punches easily. Then Argus brought his weight down onto the knee that was on the other man's throat and the Latino sputtered, "You're dead, man! You're fuckin' dead!"

The door to the other suite opened and the Samsonite couple poked their heads out—then quickly retreated to call downstairs. Argus was amazed at how fast a good plan could go to shit. The Latino made a move for Argus' crotch, but Argus caught his hand and twisted it hard enough to break the wrist. He whispered, "See something you like, faggot?"

The Latino's face was turning blue as he struggled against the pressure on his windpipe. Argus reached back between the other man's legs and said, "Is this what you had in mind, you greasy fuck?" Argus found the Latino's testicles and squeezed hard. The Latino convulsed and his purple lips moved wildly, though there was no air to carry his words. Argus released and then squeezed again, harder this time—until he felt something pop. The Latino's watering eyes opened comically wide, and then fluttered shut.

The elevator was coming. Argus rolled off of the other man and hobbled toward the stairs, barely reaching the safety of the stairwell before the elevator doors opened.

103

Kendra had spent the day shopping after blowing off the job at the Westin. She was ready for a new life, and that included a new line of work. She bought baggy slacks, sweaters, and anything else that looked good on her without looking sexy. And, despite her best efforts, she thought about Allan: his sweet, boyish charm and his insatiable appetite for all things, including sex. His haunting eyes.

His secrets.

The taxi turned left onto Park Avenue and was immediately grid-locked. Kendra looked up to find the Westin dead ahead and thought, *How's that for the fickle finger of fate? Right in your eye, Kendra.* She asked the cabbie, "What's going on?"

The cabbie lit up a cigar and settled in to watch the meter run. "Cops. Someone must've tried to skip out on their hotel bill." Kendra chewed her nails and studied the crowd gathered in front of the Westin. She felt a chill, even before she saw the shrouded corpses being wheeled from the lobby on a paramedic's gurney. Kendra jumped out of the cab and the driver said, "Hey, lady!"

"Sorry." She snatched some money from her bag and tossed it to the cabbie.

The cabbie called after her, "Hey, what about my tip?"

But Kendra didn't hear his complaints. She was wrapped up in a bad feeling, and every step closer to the hotel just made it worse.

Sylvia, a petite Korean girl with long black hair, had been told to wait for a detective in one of the lobby's plush guest chairs, though the hotel's manager was currently protesting that order. Sylvia had raccoon eyes from crying through her mascara and her attention kept skittering across the room, as if she was looking for someone.

Kendra said, "Sylvia?"

The girl flinched, and then saw that it was only Kendra. She said, "Shit, you scared me."

"What happened?" Kendra sat and took Sylvia's hand.

"F-f-f...Fuckin' psycho." Sylvia's teeth chattered as she shivered beneath the blanket that had been wrapped around her. She sipped coffee from a Styrofoam cup.

Kendra asked, "Who? The nerd?"

"Huh? No. The other guy."

"What other guy?" Kendra was distracted by the three-hundred-pound detective who was walking towards them.

Sylvia said, "The freak who killed the new girl and the john. I don't know how he got in, but he was fuckin' crazy."

This got Kendra's attention. "What did he look like? The freak."

"Older guy. Short hair, big shoulders... Scary." Sylvia fought another chill. "I don't know. He looked like a *psycho.*"

The detective addressed Kendra with a cynical eye. "Who are you?"

"A friend of Sylvia's." Kendra stood and turned to go. "I was just leaving."

"I'm Detective Koenig. Do you have a name, friend?"

"Kendra."

The detective looked troubled as he tried to catch his breath. The walk across the room had been an effort. He asked, "Kendra what?"

Kendra lied as she headed for the door: "Smith."

He referred to his notes and said, "You wouldn't happen to be the same Kendra *Smith* who lives at 2025 East Quint Street?" Kendra stopped and the detective added, "Apartment 3D? 'Cause the description of this perp matches the guy someone saw over there." Kendra turned back to face him. Her face had gone the color of ash, but she remained silent. The detective clucked his tongue and shook his head. "If so, you might consider checking into a hotel for the night—after we have a little talk."

Kendra's tongue felt numb and fat. She said, "I'm staying with a friend."

The detective looked down at his notebook again, and said, "Hope she's not five-six, brunette … about a hundred and forty-five pounds."

Kendra sat, fighting tears, and said, "One-forty-eight this morning."

"Her name wouldn't happen to be Smith, too?"

"No." She brushed away a lone tear with her forefinger and glared at the detective. "Her name was Arlene, and she was my friend."

The detective sighed and slipped the notepad into his coat pocket. "Then I think we'd better have that talk."

104

"Most days I've got a shitload of questions and no answers. Today I'm Wikipedia. All I'm missing is the right question. Kinda like that old game show—*Jeopardy!*. The common answer in these murders seems to be you. Now help me out with the question, Ms. *Smith*."

Detective McCrae passed by and noticed the attractive woman seated in the chair opposite Koenig's desk. As he returned to his paperwork McCrae thought, "Some guys have all the luck."

Kendra saw the handsome black cop checking her out from across the room, but didn't have anything to offer him except tears. She continued to fidget in the molded plastic chair, trying not to think of Arlene and those last horrible moments of her life that had been spent at Argus' mercy.

Oh Leenie, I never thought—

Koenig cleared his throat and said, "Excuse me? Are we havin' a conversation here, or not?"

Kendra sniped, "Aren't you guys supposed to have partners? Detectives always have partners on TV."

"My partner's out sick, but not much around here works like it does on TV. We don't get to have sex with pretty D.A.s, we seldom solve crimes in an hour, and our version of Good Cop, Bad Cop is Good Cop, Tired Cop." My partner usually plays the good cop, so please cut to the chase, Ms. Smith. Are you gonna help us out, or do we cut you loose and wait to read about your murder in the morning papers, after your boyfriend catches up with you?"

105

Despite the constant chatter of voices in his head, the last few weeks had been the loneliest of Allan's life. Calvin's anti-psychotics had helped, but not enough. Both the drums and The Sight were back again, indicating that the cycle was accelerating again. Allan's reflection confirmed his fears. His complexion had gone ashen and his hair and nail growth had reached an alarming rate. Allan's appetite had also increased, and his copious perspiration had taken on an odd odor, a dusty, sweet smell that reminded Allan of dead flowers. Had Tonga smelled that way? Allan couldn't remember.

Kendra's betrayal had really put Allan over the edge. Now even combining the new drugs with a massive dose of Valium couldn't silence the voices that each had an opinion on this, and every other matter. And, to his dismay, Allan was beginning to have difficulty distinguishing between their thoughts and his own.

You're better off without her, my boy.

But Jesus, Mary and Joseph—she sure was a nice little piece of ass. In my day, we had a word for a woman like that.

Fuck the bitch.

Allan tried to immerse himself in his work, but even his books couldn't hold his attention. So when Ellen asked him to attend another one of her little gatherings, Allan welcomed the distraction.

106

He circulated through the crowd, looking tense and frazzled. Many of the guests assumed that Allan's dark glasses were either an affectation brought about by his recent success, or an attempt to hide a new addiction. Laughton spotted him and tried to approach, but his path was blocked by a tall, dark man who could have been a sadistic eighteenth-century painter. The man was fawning over an exotic, melon-breasted creature of questionable gender. Laughton called out, "Allan!" and Allan dodged around a corner, hurried up the stairs, and started down a less populated hallway.

"Allan..."

He heard Laughton's voice approaching from the spiral staircase and tried to duck into an empty room, but a naked man was lying atop a huge pile of fur coats on the bed, masturbating. Allan quickly closed the door on the guest's climactic moans and scanned the hallway for another option. A bra-less older woman in a glittering mesh blouse exited a bathroom two doors down. Allan watched her bounce past, impressed with her plastic surgeon's handiwork, and then slipped into the room.

Allan locked the bathroom door, lowered the toilet's lid, and took a seat—enjoying the sudden silence. This bathroom was far smaller and funkier than the others in the house. The tile needed replacing and the walls had been scrubbed so many times that the old paint had begun to show through the current coat. Perhaps this was the kids' bathroom, or maybe a servant's. Allan heard a sound from behind the flowered shower curtain, and he pulled it aside.

"Oh, hi," said Ellen Chonce, who was lying in the tub. Her tone was oddly casual, considering the circumstances: she had broken her wine glass and was using the jagged shards to slash her arms and legs. Ellen hummed while drawing a razor-sharp piece of glass across her thigh as if it were a crayon.

Allan said, "Jesus Christ, Ellen! What are you doing?" and took the glass away from her. He then began to wrap her bleeding limbs in guest towels.

She extended her arms for a big hug and cried out, "Oh, Allan! It's you! I'm so glad!"

Allan grabbed a bottle of disinfectant from the medicine cabinet and began to clean Ellen's wounds. He said, "You really did a job on yourself."

"This? This is nothin'. I'm in training for the suicidal Olympics. The fifty-yard gash, don't ya' know." She laughed bitterly. "May I have a drink of your drink?" She reached for his gin and tonic while surveying the room. "Cute little shitter, don't you think? You know, you'd be surprised at the things you hear when you hide in a busy bathroom for an evening." She grimaced as she guzzled Allan's drink. "Surprised and horrified."

Allan took his glass from Ellen and said, "I think it's time you called it a night. Did you come with someone?"

"I came with him, but he'll be *cumming* with someone else."

"Ellen, please, help me out here."

"My husband has found himself an object of desire." She snickered as her head lolled back onto the cool ceramic slope of the tub. "The big titted drag queen."

"Oh, that's your husband?" Allan remembered the dark man and his curious companion.

Ellen said, "Hope he gets the bitch home, tears off its dress, and gets a big fistful of dick." Ellen broke into a fit of hysterical laughter.

Allan picked up the broken bits of glass that covered and surrounded Ellen, laughing along with her, despite the seriousness
of her predicament. He said, "I'm sure if your husband knew the
situation—"

"Her ..." She corrected herself: "*Its* ... situation?"

"*Yours.*"

Ellen dismissed the comment with a wave. She said, "Oh, he
knows. I tell him all the time. But he'll take her home—*it* home—
and fuck her—him—in our bed." Her amusement began to wane.
"Hey, what the hell. At least I won't have to watch this time."

Allan said, "Ellen, this is none of my business."

"He's sterile, so he doesn't care who he fucks. He says it doesn't
count. It's not *real.* Not unless there could be a baby." Her tone
turned singsong: "But there can *never* be babies, so it can never be
real. So sad. Soooo saaaad."

"Ellen... I'm sorry."

"He shoots blanks but believe me—it still hurts."

Allan helped Ellen stand and said, "C'mon. Let's get you
home."

———

Ellen slept as Allan drove her car. She mumbled, "Johnny. Billy.
Charley. Harvey. No, not Harvey ... that's ugly. Bob junior—that's
it! Bob junior. Robert." She smiled in her sleep and crooned,
"Bobby."

Allan said, "Ellen, you need to tell me exactly where on Fifth
you live." She continued to smile in her sleep, but didn't respond.
"Ellen, I need an address." She continued to mumble and giggle
but offered no address. Finally, Allan sighed and turned the car
around.

107

He entered the penthouse carrying Ellen over one shoulder.
The closing door startled her awake, and she mumbled, "Sir, are
you trying to take advantage of me?"

"*Now* you decide to talk." Allan hurried to the guest bedroom, puffing beneath the dead weight of the drunken woman. He deposited Ellen into the bed, fully clothed, but she looked uncomfortable. Allan asked, "Can you take off your clothes by yourself?" There was no response from Ellen, so Allan removed her shoes and rolled her onto one side to unzip her dress. As Allan struggled to remove the garment, Ellen mumbled something about babies.

After stripping Ellen down to her slip, Allan sat to catch his breath, studying his guest's troubled face as she slept. He took a plastic vial from his coat pocket and popped five Valium and two Clozapine into his mouth, while Ellen argued with someone in her dreams. Allan whispered, "What are you thinking?" and moved to the bed. He let his fingertips linger at her closed eyelids. He asked Ellen, "How did this happen to you?"

The hunger was back with a vengeance, but Allan restrained himself. He removed his hands from Ellen's face and stared at them, suddenly amazed by the things of which they had been capable. Could this *really* be his destiny: to feed on the souls of the dying and the wretched? Disgusted, Allan stood abruptly, switched off the light and left the room.

He paced the darkened hallways of the apartment, trying to distract himself from the hunger and the drums. If only Jenny were still here. No, it was good that she was gone, that she was *safe*. Hers would be one life that he would not destroy in the name of intellectual curiosity, though Allan's growing addiction seemed to be quickly becoming his primary motivation. And yet the *need to know* still drew him like a drunk to his drink. But Jenny had no secrets from Allan and, therefore, nothing to reveal.

She had no secrets and that was good. It was less tempting that way—as long as Allan kept stewardship of his body, which he now thought of as *The Body*, rather than purely his own. No secrets. Perhaps that's what they would put on his tombstone. That was, if he could die at all.

108

Argus' rented room was a pig sty. Cartons of take-out food and paperwork were scattered everywhere. Argus sat by the window, dividing his attention between spying on Allan, via telescope, and the evening news. A special report was airing on TV that detailed the recent wave of bizarre and brutal murders that had plagued the city. The killer, who had left the bulk of his victims raped and mutilated, had been dubbed the Uptown Ripper by the tabloid journalists. When pressed for details, officials revealed that the killer had taken a certain part, or parts, of the victims' bodies with him, they assumed as a trophy. They would not reveal which part.

A muffled cry came from the bedroom and Argus turned up the TV's volume. The Samsonite couple from the Westin appeared on camera, describing Argus in detail. Then another eyewitness, the old man from Kendra's apartment, came on to confirm that the police composite from the Samsonite couple fit the stranger he had seen exiting Kendra's apartment to a tee.

Argus limped into the bathroom. He flipped on the lights and unbuttoned his shirt to change the dressing on his shoulder. The jagged hole was starting to scab where the bullet had passed through the upper biceps. Argus' left eye was blackened and his broken nose was still swollen. He noticed that blood had begun to seep through his pant leg again, so he slipped the pants off, and sat on the edge of the tub to take a look. The sanitary napkin that he had taped there to absorb the blood was soaked. Argus had dug the bullet out of his quadriceps with a sterilized steak knife and a long pair of tweezers purchased from a nearby pharmacy. He also bought a sewing kit and a box of birthday candles.

The searing pain Argus felt during the extraction had doubled his vision and caused him to chip a tooth when he bit through the leather belt that he held between his teeth. But he saw the pain as an opportunity to test his mettle. Argus managed to remain conscious until he had sewn the hole in his leg closed with a needle and thread, and had melted wax over the stitches to slow the bleeding.

But that was four days ago and blood was still trickling from the stitches. He would have to reopen the wound and then cauterize it in order to seal it closed. Argus moved to the kitchenette and turned on one of the tiny stove's gas burners. He found a spatula and held the metal blade over the flame until it glowed red.

109

Allan tried to work, but his mind kept returning to the vulnerable woman in the next room.

Ellen, Goddamn it! She has a name. Ellen. She has a name and a life and she doesn't want to die. SHE DOESN'T REALLY WANT TO DIE.

Allan paced back and forth from the window to the door. He almost stepped out into the hallway several times, but managed to stop himself. Allan flopped onto the bed and buried his nose in a book. He cut a hunk of cheese from a plate that he'd brought to his room and popped it into his mouth. It tasted foul and he spat it out onto the floor. Hot, worn-out, and still unable to concentrate—Allan pulled off his clothes and climbed into bed, creating space for himself by pushing the scattered papers and books onto the floor.

A few minutes later Allan's bedroom door opened and Ellen staggered in. She crept to the bed, slipped beneath the covers, and covered Allan's mouth with her own. Allan's mind had drifted to thoughts of Kendra and he began to respond, but didn't recognize the taste of these lips. He opened his eyes and pulled away. "Ellen?"

"Please don't send me away." She covered his face with kisses.

Allan tried not to look into Ellen's eyes, which radiated a seductive purple glow. Allan pleaded, "Ellen, don't do this," and was horrified to realize that he was actually salivating. Allan pushed Ellen away and said, "You have to get out of here."

"You think I'm ugly, too. That's it isn't it?"

"No."

"You're lying." After a sullen moment, she turned to face him, wanting desperately to believe. She asked, "Really? You think I'm pretty?"

"Yes, but—"

"You think I'm pretty." She kissed him again. "You *said it*—and you can't take it back!"

Allan fought his hunger and pushed Ellen gently away. He said, "Ellen, please..."

Ellen reached for Allan's crotch and purred, "Have you ever fantasized about a menage?"

"A what?" Allan tried to deflect her roving hand.

"You know—two women and you. Or you and another guy, sharing a woman. I'd do that with you if you want."

"What?" Allan was shocked enough to let down his guard and Ellen took full advantage of the opportunity. She slipped her hand beneath the covers and found him ready.

"Mmm... Feels like *someone* likes the idea."

Allan didn't resist her touch. He said, "You've really done that?"

Ellen pulled back the covers and kissed his chest. "My husband will only screw me if another person's there with us."

Allan's lust was tempered by sympathy. He said, "I'm sorry."

Ellen complained as she continued to play with him; "No, no, no... Don't go soft on me." She bit his nipple and increased the tempo of her movements. She murmured, "That's better." Allan's hungers were overshadowing his judgment. Ellen tongued his ear and whispered, "Sometimes it's with another woman, but he usually brings a guy. If it's a woman, he'll let me just watch. But if it's a guy—I have to participate."

"Why?"

"He likes to watch me fuck other men because he shoots blanks. He says that if I make it with another guy—"

"It's real?"

"Yeah." She straddled Allan's fevered body and ground herself against his erection. "So if you and I made it—it would be real." Ellen suddenly stopped and asked, "You don't shoot blanks do you?"

"I don't think so."

Ellen said, "Good," and continued to rub against him. "Then it could be *real.* And it would be just you and me ..." She reached down to guide him. "... and I could pretend you love me." Allan made a frustrated sound, rolled out from beneath her, and headed for the kitchen. She said, "What's wrong? Did I do something wrong?"

Allan said, "I'm gonna make some coffee. I don't think you need sex. I think you need someone to talk to."

Ellen threw herself face down on the bed and screamed into the mattress, *"Coffee?"* She sat up and yelled, "Are you fucking nuts?"

Allan called from the other room, "I can't hear you. Just a second."

"No. *Now.* Come here!" Allan didn't answer. Ellen pleaded, "Pleeeease."

Allan said, "What?" and returned to the doorway carrying a bag of imported coffee beans. His erection waggled at half-mast before him. He asked, "Do you take cream and sugar?"

"Come on... Come here."

Allan took a cautious step closer and said, "Ellen, I don't want to take advantage of you." He looked into her luminescent purple eyes and whispered, "And I don't want to hurt you."

Ellen struck a suggestive pose, her eyelids drooping from too much alcohol, and answered, "But what if I wanna be hurt?"

"That makes it harder." Allan took another step, fighting the sounds of drums in his head.

Ellen stood and said, "I can see that," and then gently led him back to the bed by his penis.

Ellen kissed Allan and he meant to say, "Stop," but all that emerged was a groan. "Ellen," Allan spoke through clenched teeth as he fought to control himself: "I really don't want to hurt you."

She stroked him and said, "Well, well ... We have a pretty high opinion of ourselves, don't we?" and then she removed her bra and panties.

They embraced and Allan fought both hungers: for the body and the soul. Between kisses he said, "I just wanted to help."

Ellen bit his lip and answered, "If you really wanted to help you should have left me to bleed to death in that bathtub. I didn't ask you to rescue me. But you did, so now you're responsible for my happiness." She chewed his neck and whispered, "So make me happy already."

"The House of Drums."

"Hmm?"

Allan murmured, "I am the House of Drums now."

Ellen chewed on his earlobe and whispered, "I just wanna eat you up." Allan's response was a hungry moan as he finally gave in. He lifted Ellen up and she wrapped her legs around his waist.

Argus saw the change in his son through the eye of his telescope. Suddenly Allan's touch appeared more clinical than it had been before and his expression was devoid of its former tenderness. The heat was building between Allan and Ellen, but Argus knew his son's true objective.

Ellen tightened her legs around Allan's waist, wrapped her arm around his neck and reached down between their bodies with her free hand. She panted, "Gimme, gimme, gimme," and made an adjustment—then lowered her weight onto him. Ellen gasped, "Jesus, you're on fire," and Allan began to move to the sounds of drums in his head. She moaned, "Mmm... Oh, yeah—like *that*." Ellen saw the intensity in his eyes and asked, "Did my little secret turn you on?"

"Yes."

"I've got more you know." Allan carried Ellen over to the window, where he allowed the ledge to help support her weight. Between excited gasps she said, "I've got lots of secrets. Do you want me to tell them to you?"

Allan answered, "Yes," and lowered his mouth to her breasts as he thrust his hips forward, "Tell me your secrets."

Ellen said, "You first," then licked the sweet-smelling sweat that had gathered in the fleshy hollow beneath Allan's Adam's apple.

Allan admitted, "I only have one, but you don't want to know it."

"Mmm..." She scratched her nails across his back as he pressed forward. Ellen insisted, "Now you *have* to tell me."

Allan pulled away to the point of withdrawal, teasing, and warned, "Be sure it's what you want."

Ellen reached for him and whined, "No! I mean—yes. I want it, I want it."

He moved forward and then withdrew again. "You want my secret? Or just—" He jabbed his hips forward.

"Oh...I want it all." Ellen was teetering on the verge of orgasm. She panted, "I want your body *and* your fucking secret!" and she dug her nails into his ass. Allan began to thrust faster and she lost control, screaming, "Oh, fuck! Tell me! *Tell me—so I can cum!*" Her body suddenly tensed and Allan continued to thrust. Ellen cried out and began to shudder.

Allan brought his razor-sharp fingernails up to her throat, but she didn't notice; she was thrashing wildly, eyes closed in exquisite agony. Then, when Ellen was at her peak, Allan grabbed her by the hair and slashed his talons across her throat. Ellen's cries of pleasure turned shrill as he severed her jugular—then crunched through her windpipe. Ellen opened her eyes and stared at Allan— horrified beyond reason.

He whispered, "Don't be afraid. I will give you a home."

Ellen's response was unintelligible—just a sputtering gurgle that spattered Allan's torso with blood. Her eyes were wide and wild and her body still shaking with the echoes of her orgasm, inexplicably heightened by a rush of adrenaline born of pain and terror. It was a gruesome feat of physiology that sent her into violent convulsions. Allan watched, stone-faced, as Ellen's body finally went limp and the smoke gathered in her eyes.

He lowered her to the floor and waited until the fruit was ripe, and then Allan used his bloody fingernails to harvest Ellen's tortured soul. After it was done, he sat with her head in his lap until the fusion began.

Standing alone at the entrance to an ancient cavern. A distant spark becomes a beacon, and then expands into a ball of flame that swells from the cave's depths to engulf him.

Suddenly, he finds himself among an endless parade of naked strangers. He is conjoined with men and women in every conceivable combination. Ellen's husband, sometimes involved and sometimes merely a spectator, looks on with a mixture of disgust and desire.

Allan stumbled blindly into the living room, his hands and face covered with Ellen's blood. He fell to the floor screaming in pain and pleasure as he relived Ellen's miserable life.

110

Kendra had passed through JFK's security checkpoint and hurried on to her gate. Detective Koenig had warned her not to leave town, but right now the threat of arrest was the least of her worries. The detective had accepted Kendra's pretended ignorance of the Westin situation with surprisingly little resistance. In fact, too little resistance. But there wasn't time to think of that now. She would board the plane and be far away from both Argus and Koenig by morning. Once she had found a place, Kendra would have her mother take Matthew out of hiding and put him on a plane. The drama would give Kendra's father more emotional ammunition to use against her, but he would ultimately do whatever was necessary to keep his grandson safe.

Kendra arrived at the gate and found that her flight had been delayed. The information desk offered little real information, apart from an estimated departure time that was two hours away, at a minimum. That would make it 6 a.m., just in time to watch the sun rise. Kendra wandered around the airport for a while, oblivious to the fact that two of Koenig's men had been tailing her from the moment she'd left the police station. Finally, Kendra stopped at a payphone, thinking, "You should at least warn him. You owe him that much." After picking up and replacing the receiver several times, Kendra plunked in some change and dialed the number.

111

The phone rang for a long time before the sound finally found its way to Allan's senses. As he pulled himself toward the phone, Allan was still trapped in the agonizing sexual kaleidoscope that had been Ellen's life. Allan flailed out, knocking the handset from its cradle during a convulsion, then clawed for the phone blindly, screaming, "Help me!"

When Allan's face began to change into Ellen's, he shrieked like someone set aflame, while a faint voice came from the phone's receiver: "Allan? ALLAN?" But Allan had lost the ability to form words and he was suddenly—

Looking up from an operating table, just coming out of the anesthesia. Two nearby nurses gossip, unaware that patient is conscious and terrified.

"She didn't even know who the father was. Got hysterical in Doctor Hoffman's office."

"I feel sorry for her. Did you see the cigarette burns on her thighs?"

Allan sits up on the operating table and wails as blood soaks through his surgical gown.

The room turns liquid and, when it solidifies again, becomes a desert highway. Allan stands apart from Ellen, facing her on the road. Beside her are the ICU patient, the boxer, Calvin and the professor. Allan watches as all five souls merge into an explosion of white light.

The light gradually fades, and Allan finds himself back in the penthouse living room, cross-legged on a meditation cushion. Floating. The room is filled with blood. Beneath the surface swim the ghostly images of all of the world's lost souls. They reach out to him, begging for a home. Allan topples from the cushion and fights his way across the sea of souls—toward the sunlight ...

112

"Allan?"

It took a moment for Allan to realize that the voice was in the room, not in his head. He blinked, trying hard to focus. Allan was covered in blood.

"You look like shit." Argus stood above his son.

Allan tried to coordinate his limbs and mind enough to untangle himself from the phone cord and offer a plausible explanation for his current condition. He asked, "What...what are you doing here?"

Argus watched his son struggle into a seated position and then kicked him in the face—sending him sprawling back to the floor. He said, "It's time."

113

Kendra checked her watch again as the taxi squealed around the corner. She said, "Can't you make this pile of shit go any faster?"

The cabbie growled, "Watch it lady. She's temperamental."

Kendra reached into her purse, extracted a hundred-dollar bill, and showed it to the cabbie. "Maybe you can have a talk with her. We're gonna need to lose that car behind us." The driver took one look at the bill—and the temperamental cab suddenly perked up.

Back in the trailing unmarked police car, the officers had called in to notify Koenig as they sped through the city. Koenig barked over the radio, "What's going on, Johnson?"

"She's in a helluva hurry, sir."

"Any idea where she's headed?"

"Hold on. She's pulling over at a pawn shop."

———————

Kendra ran into the store and up to the counter where an old woman was seated behind bulletproof safety glass. Kendra said, "I think I need a gun."

The scraggy storekeep seemed skeptical. She said, "What kind?"

"I don't know. A big one. Something easy to shoot."

The old woman was amused. She asked, "Got a cheatin' beau or somethin'?"

"Are you gonna sell me a gun or not?"

"You know about the seven-day waitin' period, right?"

Kendra removed her gold Rolex and slid it under the safety glass. "Check the date on that. I think it's set a week ahead."

114

Allan was still reeling when Argus returned from the bedroom and limped to the kitchen. Allan got shakily to his feet as his father poured himself a cup of coffee. Argus said, "I've gotta hand it to you—you do nice work." Allan staggered toward the front door while Argus added sugar to his coffee. "Locked and bolted. Why don't you go wash up? You'll feel better."

Allan went to his mother's bedroom, still in a daze, and locked the door. As he walked through the room, on the way to the bathroom, Allan saw Ellen's feet sticking out from behind the bed. He approached the body. Faced for the first time with the proof of his crime, Allan was suddenly nauseous. He covered his mouth and ran to the bathroom.

Allan pushed up the toilet seat and dove to his knees as the grisly contents of his stomach spewed into the bowl. He kept his eyes closed as he convulsed—over and over again—afraid to see what had been inside of him. Afterward, he rested his head against the cool porcelain and vowed in a small, frail voice: "No more."

Allan struggled to his feet, washed the blood from his face and hands, and then returned to Ellen. He paused at the foot of the bed, gathering his strength, and then went to the body. Allan covered Ellen with a blanket and then sat down beside her to weep—for her and for the boy who had dreamed of becoming a man, but became a monster instead.

Argus was on the other side of the locked door. He said, "I've got a surprise for you, son."

Allan wiped away his tears, slipped into a pair of pants and searched in vain for a way out. Then he heard Jenny's weak and trembling voice call out his name. Allan froze—then turned his attention to the door. Argus must have done something to her then, because Jenny screamed in pain before calling out, "Allan don't open the door!"

Allan ran to the door and threw it open, crying, "Jenny!"

"Not so fast, son." Argus backed away from the door. He had a butcher knife at Jenny's throat and her blackened eyes were wild with fear. Jenny's hair was matted with sweat and blood. Her clothes were torn and smelled of urine.

Allan pushed away the thoughts of what Argus had done to her as he fought to stay level and focused. He took a step forward and said, "Let her go and you can have me. I won't fight you. I don't even care anymore. Just let her go. Please."

Argus said, "I want you to do something for me, son," and took another step backward, toward the livingroom.

Jenny pleaded, "Allan, don't listen to him."

Allan said, "I'll do *anything* you want. Just let her go."

"All right." Argus backed up into the living room with the knife pressed to Jenny's throat. "I want you to show me."

———

The cab screeched to a halt outside of the building. Kendra jumped out and ran past the doorman. She barely caught the elevator and punched the button marked "Penthouse". The elderly insomniacs beside Kendra huddled together as she extracted the revolver from her purse and checked it to make sure it was loaded.

The police detectives who had been following Kendra entered the building a moment later and tried to catch the elevator.

Johnny the doorman blocked their path and said, "Can I help you?"

Allan pleaded, "Don't kill her! Please!"

"What did you say in your journal? 'I have an appetite for knowledge that is all-consuming.'" As Argus spoke, the edge of the knife nicked Jenny's throat and drew a bead of blood. "Pretentious horse shit. You like to kill. So do I. Like father—like son. The only difference is that I don't make excuses." He applied pressure to the blade and Jenny whimpered. "There's only one thing that I need to learn. And you're going to teach me." Allan was about to make his move when Kendra hurried her key into the lock. Argus swung around to face the door using Jenny as a shield as Kendra entered—gun upraised. Argus said, "Oh, good. More company."

Kendra aimed the gun at Argus with trembling hands, commanding, "Put the knife down."

Allan said, "Kendra—"

Kendra screamed at Argus, "Put the fucking knife down!" Argus kept the knife in place and took a step forward. Kendra saw the look of desperation in Jenny's eyes and cocked the trigger. She said, "I'll do it. I swear I will."

Argus took another step closer. He whispered, "No, you won't."

They were only two paces apart, now. Kendra suddenly felt light-headed and the gun seemed very heavy. She said, "Why won't I?"

Argus tossed Jenny aside and hissed, "You're too fucking weak. You're too—"

BANG.

Argus looked confused. There was a hole in his chest and blood was pumping out, but he felt nothing. He took another step toward Kendra and she closed her eyes before squeezing the trigger a second time.

BANG.

This time, she missed. Argus leapt for Kendra and sent the gun spinning across the floor. Argus brought the knife to Kendra's throat and slit it unceremoniously.

Allan screamed, *"No!"* and scrambled from Jenny to Kendra, but there was nothing he could do. The blood just kept pouring through his fingers as he tried to staunch its flow and Kendra gurgled and sputtered toward death.

Argus, slumped against the wall, commanded, "Show me!"

Allan sobbed, "Kendra! Don't die on me. Please."

Kendra looked up at Allan and tried to tell him how sorry she was, but her mouth was filled with blood. Allan cradled her head in his lap and kissed her forehead. Then he saw the smoke glistening in her eyes like diamonds as Kendra's soul prepared to exit her body.

Argus screamed, "Do it now! Before it's too late!"

Allan hesitated before raising his fingers to Kendra's eyes—to gently close them for the last time. He said, "No," and held her tight as she drew her final breath before her soul took flight.

Argus staggered back from the kitchen, tossed a handful of knives onto the floor and grabbed Allan by the hair to drag him away from Kendra's lifeless body. He hissed, "You make me sick!" Allan leapt to his feet and tackled his father to the floor, knocking the butcher knife from his hand. Argus taunted Allan as they grappled in an awkward embrace: "You're too much like your mother. Even after all this, you're too much like *her* to hurt me. She didn't even put up a fight." Allan reached for one of the knives, but Argus caught his hand in time. He said, "I *had* to let her go. I didn't deserve her. But you always knew that, didn't you?" Argus broke free and clambered for the butcher knife while Allan went for one of the others. Father and son gasped for breath as they circled each other—looking for an opening.

Allan said, "It was you? You killed her."

"No, I set her free. And after it was done I could breathe again."

Jenny called out, "Allan!" from the corner where she had retrieved the gun.

Argus turned toward the sound and Allan took the opportunity to lunge at his father—driving the knife into his stomach. Allan said, "You're right. We *are* alike. I *will* enjoy killing you."

Despite his wounds, Argus answered with a crushing blow to Allan's jaw that sent him to the ground. The knife still protruding from his body, Argus pinned his son to the hardwood floor and said, "It's time for us to finally get together, son."

Jenny called out, "Get away from him. *Now!*" and leveled the gun. Argus looked at her with a secret hidden beneath his smile and said, "Do it, bitch!"

The first shot shattered a lamp on the other side of the room. Jenny took another step closer, held her breath, and fired again. This time the bullet hit its mark, entering Argus' back and ripping another hole in his chest as it exited.

Allan tried to reach the knives, but they were out of range. Argus extended his son's right arm to the side and drove an ice pick through the palm of his hand—nailing it to the hardwood floor, then reached for the carving fork and did the same with Allan's left hand.

Another shot rang out, this time from behind Jenny. The detectives were in the doorway with their guns trained on Argus. The first detective's bullet had torn through Argus' throat.

Argus began to choke on his own blood, but he still managed to remain on top of Allan. The second detective fired—shattering Argus' cheekbone and tearing away the right side of his face. Argus touched the gory hole, fascinated by the damage one bullet could do. He looked out at the faint amber glow of the sun on the horizon through drooping eyelids. At last … it was *his* turn to die. Father and son looked at each other and Allan saw the smoke in Argus' eyes burning white-hot. Argus' speech was slurred and sleepy: "You can see it, can't you?"

Allan was blinded by the evil intensity of his father's soul, now pooled in his eyes. And then there was a horrible moment of unspoken communication between them. Allan knew exactly what his father was thinking, even before the dying man raised his murderous hands to his own eyes and clawed them out. Allan screamed, "N-o-o-o-o!" as he tried to free himself, but Argus was determined. Allan choked on the bloody tissue as his father forced it blindly down his son's throat, jamming his fingers into Allan's mouth while Allan fought back with his teeth—biting those fingers to the bones.

Jenny and the detectives rushed forward, but it was too late.

It was done.

His dying act complete, Argus' lifeless body slumped to the floor. Jenny pushed the dead weight of Argus' corpse off of Allan while the detectives released him from his crucifixion. The hollow sounds of the carving fork and ice pick being pulled from the hardwood floor were muted by Allan's wails.

There was blood everywhere. Allan struggled to his feet, making a low, guttural sound like a dying animal. Jenny watched helplessly as Allan staggered through the house, screaming as he saw through his father's eyes:

Whistling in a crosstown cab, long-stemmed roses on the seat beside him. He watches the city pass in a blue-gray blur.

Looking up at the penthouse from the street below. French doors stand open. Sheer white curtains dance on a gentle breeze.

The doorman is asleep at his post. Allan moves calmly past and boards the elevator, leaving the scent of roses lingering in the lobby.

His key in the lock...quiet. The mechanism has been recently oiled. Trapped within his own body, Allan calls out, "STOP THIS! YOU CAN'T MAKE ME DO THIS!" as his hand-tooled shoes move silently across gray marbled floors.

He approaches his mother's bedroom, shadow bowing in the graceful curves of crystal sculptures that line the hallway. Diti wheels herself out onto the balcony to share the sunset with her Persian cat, Sasha. A cool breeze whispers, inspiring the wind chimes, and Diti turns to meet it. Her sightless irises are clouded white.

She rests her hand on the railing, feeling its scarce warmth—an echo of the setting sun. The guardrail responds to her touch, moving slightly, sending concrete crumbles trickling to the deck's textured surface. The bolts that hold the wrought iron in place have come loose from the bricked outcropping, but Diti seems unaware.

Allan pleads, "Stop this! PLEASE!"

But she hears only the laughter of children in the wind, and smiles. Sasha jumps up onto Diti's lap and glares at Allan, baring her teeth and hissing.

Allan begs as he creeps closer, "Mother, please turn around. Please turn around!"

Sasha nuzzles Diti, while keeping an eye on Allan.

Diti strokes the cat's silky coat.

Allan moves closer...

The cat purrs.

Closer...

Diti feels the last rays of sunshine on her face.

Closer...

Allan howls, "N-O-O-O-O!" as his shadow steals the sunlight from his mother's smile.

But still—Diti does not hear him.

The cat jumps to the ground and Allan caresses the wheelchair's hand-grips. He whispers, "Can you forgive me?"

Diti reaches back over her shoulder to lay her hand lovingly atop her son's and answers, "It was your Destiny."

Allan has no choice. He sends the chair forward, her knees meet the railing—it gives way—and she's gone.

"N-O-O-O-O-O-O!" Allan continued to wail as he pressed himself flat against the bathroom door, and then crumpled to the floor, blind to all but the horrors in his mind. He wept as he waited for the sound. And then the horrific memory began to repeat itself for the first of a thousand times.

Allan ran blindly though the house and slammed into the sliding glass door, then fumbled for the latch as Jenny followed, screaming, "What are you doing? Allan, what's going on?"

He threw open the door and rushed toward the railing. The small surviving voice that was still his own wanted to go over the side, as his mother had—wanted to join her outline on the pavement below and put and end to this inhuman suffering bequeathed to him by his father. But Jenny managed to grab Allan before he reached the railing, and she pulled him to the ground. She struggled to hold him in a futile gesture of protection, whispering, "It'll be okay. It'll be okay..."

Allan writhed, arms outstretched toward the heavens, lips moving in silently litany as he pleaded with God. But there would be no reprieve. Jenny embraced him as he bucked and drew a sharp breath inward, and then made a sound like no other she had ever heard. It was the sound of Good and Evil fusing together in one body—one mind. One soul. Allan's pain was immeasurable and his screams were the sounds of the damned. And as he stared into the dawn of a new day, Allan's anguished howls built and merged with the sounds of sirens.

And now for something completely different from
Brad Marlowe:

Sleepwalker: The Last Sandman
(Reviews, Synopsis, and Sample Chapters)

Praise for Sleepwalker: The Last Sandman

(*The following comments were excerpted from* <u>*Amazon.com*</u>
reader reviews)

"I absolutely LOVED "Sleepwalker: The Last Sandman. The story was imaginative, fresh, and extremely enjoyable to read." – flipoid (South Georgia)

"Many authors can make fantasy exciting and others can make reality realistic, but to be able to do both is something you don't often see in YA novels." –Alexmarie (Syracuse, New York)

"While "Sleepwalker: The Last Sandman" sits comfortably in the same niche as the works of Neil Gaiman and Terry Pratchett, Marlowe holds true to his own unique creative vision." – Old Granny

"I don't say this very often about books but this was simply brilliant." – SerenityFL (Miami)

"This is a wonderful book suitable for many age groups. It's part fairy tale, part fantasy, part action adventure. (...) It would make a GREAT movie, with the characters rivaling those of the Harry Potter series." – FantasyReader (Indiana USA)

"This book touched on many subjects and emotions that I, as a mother of a teenager who is rapidly preparing to go out on her own, was deeply touched by. The love of children for their parents, the love of parents for their children, the strength of children, the weaknesses in even the best parent figures - all of these themes come into play in Sleepwalker: The Last Sandman..." – Alexmarie (Syracuse, New York)

"It's one of those fun, engrossing reads, that anyone from 9 to 90 will like." – OhEmGee!

"I would recommend this book to ALL ages!!! While it could be considered a children's book, as they would enjoy it, it is also very much an adult book!!!" – A. Fox (Chicago)

"I REALLY didn't want it to end! (...) Something happened when I finished this book that I can't remember happening to me before. I went back and re-read the first few chapters and enjoyed them almost as much as the exciting final ones. They were so much more meaningful the second time around after becoming friends with this family." – SueS

"I loved this book! It brought back memories of my favorite childhood stories, Peter Pan and Narnia, and the fantastic worlds in which they were set." – Wendy D. (Williamsport, PA)

Story Synopsis

ON A WARM SUMMER NIGHT, atop a second-hand bed with Spiderman sheets, in a modest farmhouse in Iowa, two young brothers committed their deepest fears to the leathery lavender pages of a strange, blank journal. Sean and Cole Golden's shared terror was a malevolent shadow that they believed would come for them, in their dreams. But the shadow's threat had been nothing more than that – until the boys named him Mr. Brink, and etched his likeness onto those enchanted pages.

Thirty years later, Cole Golden – now grown into a man – is pressed by his own children to reveal the incredible adventure that began with that simple act, so long ago. An act which not only resulted in the abduction of Cole and his brother Sean, but also caused the Sandman to be ripped from his throne—and robbed the citizens of the world of their ability to dream.

A dark force was born from the uncommon imaginations of Sean and Cole Golden on that long-ago night, casting a cold shadow over Nod, the ever-changing land of dreams. Jake (the boys' cynical father) was forced to resurrect the imaginative child within in order to cross the adult-proof barrier separating the real from the surreal. In Nod, a world literally made of our dreams, the younger Jake set out to rescue Sean, Cole, and the Sandman before the sleep-deprived citizens of the world burned everything to the ground.

Aided by a trio of Dreamers (children with nothing except their dreams in our world, who have been adopted by the Sandman), Jake encountered bizarre characters and wondrous locales as he discovered the transformative qualities of belief, the enduring power of love, and his own Destiny. He faced physical manifestations of all manner of dreams, including a treacherous money forest, Lost Lake (where mankind's collected regrets churn beneath black waters), They and Them (monochromatic Siamese twins who are the architects of The Rules for accountants and elementary school teachers), The Tree of Hope, and Death himself—who turned out to be a pretty nice guy.

But despite the wondrous locales and characters contained in the story, there is a current of authentic emotion tethering the whimsical fantasy elements to a credible reality like the string of a bright red balloon tied around a child's wrist.

SLEEPWALKER: THE LAST SANDMAN is a modern fantasy without wizards, faeries, dragons, or vampires. It is an exploration of the origin of dreams and the tale of a world-weary, broken-hearted father's love for the sons he has neglected far too long. It is a fantastical journey through lost love and rediscovered hope that led to redemption—for one family, and the world entire.

A thematic cousin to PETER PAN and ALICE'S ADVENTURES IN WONDERLAND, this unique adventure offers emotional complexity to mature readers while delivering a thrilling ride for the young and the young at heart.

Prologue

There were no shadows in the place some call Nod until the night he was created. He emerged from nothing, glistening ink-black beneath flickering pinholes in the sky that hinted at a world on the other side. There is no moon in Nod so, until his arrival, there had never been nighttime shadows, or anything to fear.

He threw back his head and howled in pain, his amorphous form warping and twisting as it grasped for stability, but in his infancy the dark man was unable to hold any shape for more than a moment. The awful sounds of his agony, as he tried to solidify, gradually hardened and grew into a thundering battle cry. In time, he began to look vaguely human, but his sharp black outline continued to ripple. To anyone witnessing this beginning of the end, the man made of shadows would have been little more than a sinister silhouette, cut from dirty black paper, which blotted out the wondrous landscape of Nod even as it moved through it.

The shadow man glided down a grassy slope that was wet with dew. His dark form fell across the lush foliage and a deadly frost immediately descended upon it. The man approached the Stream of Consciousness, which teemed with Random Ideas, as well as more cohesive schools of Thought. Together, these sparks of creativity swam beneath the surface of the sacred water, as they had from The Beginning. One of the Great Ideas (a large Iridescent) leapt excitedly into the air, hovered for a moment, and then splashed back into the burbling emerald water. It wasn't quite ready to fly.

The shadow man had mass now. He stepped into the Stream of Consciousness, causing the water's temperature to plummet and the ideas within to grow stagnant. A miserable, high-pitched keening emerged from the stream in frantic bubbles and the shadow man, who had been stepping up onto the opposite bank when he heard the sounds, realized the suffering of the stream's inhabitants, due to the chilling effect of his presence. His curiosity piqued, the dark man stepped back down into the stream and watched chunks of ice begin to form on its surface. Within seconds the water had turned to slush. A moment later the stream was frozen solid, and the ideas within were lost forever.

The shadow man looked down at his legs, which had been encased in ice, and he allowed them to dissolve into sooty smoke. He stepped up onto the other side of the stream, made his body solid once again, and then set out to make a home for himself in this strange new world.

Chapter 1

No Place like Home

The churning tires of an aging BMW spat back a serpentine cloud of dust, shrouding the rural Iowan landscape in an eerie yellow haze and trailing the vehicle like a lit fuse. The narrow dirt road ended abruptly at a ramshackle clapboard farmhouse that was to be the Golden family's new home. It was their Aunt Sissy's house, which she had left to Cole Golden and his older brother, Sean, in her will. Just as a dog's owner can come to resemble its canine companion over time, the farmhouse mirrored Sissy's no frills facade and unimaginative, sensible construction.

Cole's wife, Elizabeth, had lost her job at an A-list advertising agency back in New York City, and had been unable to find another position that paid even *half* of her former salary. Cole was a stay-at-home dad who had been educating Charlene and Zane (the couple's precocious 11-year-old twins) from home for the last five years. So the cash-strapped family had reluctantly accepted Cole's aunt's posthumous gift, and had moved to Iowa to start a new life amid the towering pecan trees and bittersweet memories of Cole's childhood.

The mud-splattered vehicle stopped in front of the old farmhouse that had been a cheerful shade of blue many years ago, but now stood ghostly gray in the twilight. One of the car's rear windows was lowered, and Charly peered out at the run-down structure in disgust. Her iPod's earbuds were still lodged firmly in place and she spoke too loudly. "Was it always this ugly?"

Zane said, "It looks like the creepy house in that lame old movie you like, Dad." The boy's eager face appeared beside his sister's in the open window. "You think Aunt Sissy's ghost still haunts the halls at night, carrying her severed head?"

"She died of old age, Z, she *wasn't* beheaded," Cole climbed out of the passenger's side of the car, groaning and stretching his aching legs, adding: "And that's not a very nice thing to say."

Zane and Charly got out of the car to stand beside their father. Cole nudged his square eyeglasses up the bridge of his nose with a forefinger, and looked at the farmhouse warily. Zane said, "Sorry, Dad. Aunt Sissy was cool. Cranky, but cool." Cole didn't respond. He was staring at the house with a look of trepidation and child-like wonder that Zane had never seen on his father's face. The gangly preteen said, "Dad? You okay?"

"Huh?" Cole shook himself from his secret thoughts and slung an arm around his son's narrow shoulders. "Yeah. You know, Sissy raised me in this house."

"When Grandpa Jake was gone, right?"

"Right." Cole smiled and kissed the top of his son's head, inhaling the familiar scent of his hair, thinking that Zane would be too tall for that familiar gesture of affection in another six months and was, perhaps, too old already. It was just one more vestigial connection between a father and his kids, assigned to the memory drawer along with all the kissed boo-boos and sweet Santa lies of early childhood.

Charly removed her earbuds and carefully wound their cords around her iPod. "Dad, next time you write Grandpa Jake tell him I want to come explore the world with him. I mean—we probably can't even get DSL out here. Not to mention a decent slice. And look at the house..."

"That's *enough*, Charly." Cole added, with a note of finality: "It is what it is, and we're *all* going to make the best of it."

Zane said, "You think Grandpa Jake would come visit us here?"

Cole was touched by the hopeful expression on his son's face. He rumpled Zane's hair and answered, "He would if he could."

Charly said, "Yeah, right. I know he's supposedly out exploring the world and all, but he can't show up in person every now and then? Or even call?"

Zane said, "I've never heard you ask to return one of his presents."

Charly answered, "How could I—even if I wanted to? They just show up on our doorstep."

"So?"

"So no return address, doofus. How weird is *that?*"

"A little, I guess."

"You guess? You *know*, Z. And it's a lot more than a *little* weird. I mean, how many kids do you know that've never even met their own grandfather? Unless he already croaked before they were born."

Zane looked down at the dirt, offering an unhappy shrug in response. The abrupt change in the boy's mood was not lost on his father, but before Cole could offer consolation Elizabeth Avila-Golden emerged from the car with her jacket in-hand, talking loudly into her sleek, black cell phone. She was a short, feisty Latina whose dusky skin tones were mirrored in her daughter's exotic beauty, though Zane was as white and Anglo-looking as his father. In fact, Zane's natural coloring was so pallid that his sister had started calling him Casper several years earlier. The nickname had stuck, much to Zane's chagrin.

Elizabeth's expensive, canary-yellow business suit stood in stark contrast to the jeans and short-sleeved T-shirts worn by the rest of the family. She tossed her long, curly black hair and laughed. "Well, you tell him if he wants the best it's gonna cost him. My campaign for Happy Dog netted a 25 percent sales increase in the first quarter alone. Jason Boggs can't even come close to those numbers. He's a nice guy, but..." Elizabeth stopped to listen for a moment. When she spoke again her voice had lost some of its sparkle. She said, "No problem. Call me back when they've made a decision, but don't let them wait too long. Make sure they know that I have other offers. Thanks, Vicky." Elizabeth snapped the phone closed and looked at the house. She let out a sigh of disgust and turned to Cole. "Did I tell you that the movers left a voice mail? They unloaded our things yesterday."

Charly asked, "Do you really have other offers, Mom?"

Elizabeth brushed a lock of auburn hair away from her daughter's probing brown eyes and said, "I *will*. Don't worry. We won't be here long." Elizabeth shivered and put on her jacket. "We'd better go in. It's freezing out here." She huddled down into her coat and made a run for the house, as if rushing for shelter from an arctic snowstorm. The rest of the family was amused by her theatrics as a warm breeze rustled the branches of the pecan trees overhead. Elizabeth considered anything below eighty degrees to be sweater weather and anything below seventy downright intolerable.

Chapter 2

The Promise

Later that night, Cole stood in the middle of a dark, empty room on the second floor. Two large windows looked out onto the endless rows of neglected pecan trees that surrounded the house. This was the bedroom that Cole and his brother Sean had shared as boys. A patch of stars sparkled in the sky like diamonds on deep blue velvet. But the night's beauty was wasted on Cole, who was transfixed by an incongruous patch of crumbling brickwork that jutted from the interior wall, directly between the two windows. The structure looked like an oversized fireplace mantel, without the fireplace, and was six feet wide, rising from floor to ceiling.

Cole approached the odd addition, transferred the old book that he was carrying to one hand, and reached out with the other to touch the bricks. His movements were so tentative that you'd think the rust-colored bricks might spring to life at any moment and take a bite out of him. He spoke to himself in a hoarse whisper. "How about it, Cole? Do you still believe?"

"Believe what, Dad?" Zane stood in the doorway, carrying a moving carton that had been labeled 'Z's Room - Top Secret' with a fat black marker.

"Probably can't believe we have to live in this dump. I know *I* can't." Charly joined her brother in the doorway. She'd been coming down the hallway from the other direction, lugging a bulging fuchsia suitcase. Charly peered into the darkened room with distaste, and spoke in a sarcastic tone. "Nice."

Cole took a quick step back from the bricked section of the wall and held the book behind his back. He said, "C'mon, it's not all bad. Your rooms are a lot bigger than the ones back in our old apartment in the city."

Charly narrowed her eyes and dropped the suitcase to the dusty hardwood floor with a thud. "What's up, Dad? You've got the same look Zane gets when Mom busts him."

Zane said, "Like you're such an angel."

"Shut up, Casper."

"You shut up."

Cole said, "Hey. That's enough."

Charly gave her brother a hard look before returning her attention to Cole. She asked, "What's with the book?"

Cole's cheeks reddened. "Shouldn't you two be in bed by now?"

Zane and Charly stepped into the room, curiosity piqued by their father's odd behavior. Zane said, "Yeah, Dad, what *is* with the book?"

Cole feigned innocence and said, "Book?" Charly switched on the overhead light, causing her father to squint against its sudden intensity, his eyes having become accustomed to the darkness. But the light reminded Cole of something, and he seemed relieved. Cole brought the book around to show his children. Its scuffed green suede cover had seen better days. "Oh, *this* book?"

Charly took the worn volume from her father's hands and thumbed through it. The cover and pages appeared to be blank. "What is it? Some kind of journal?"

Zane said, "It's just a blank book. Why are you hiding a blank book, Dad?"

Cole averted his eyes and shrugged. Charly and Zane exchanged a puzzled look. Something was definitely afoot. Charly said, "Dad, when we were little you told us that you had never lied to us and that you never would. Not about *anything*. Big or small."

Zane said, "Yeah, you *promised*, Dad."

Cole remained silent.

Charly said, "So, why were you in a dark room, staring at a brick wall, hiding a blank book?"

Cole's shoulders slumped beneath the weight of the sacred promise that he had made to his children. A promise that he had, so far, never broken. He said, "Okay," and reached for the book. "But it's not a short answer, and I'm not sure you really want to know. I guess what I mean is... I've never been able to decide whether or not you *should* know, and I doubt that you'll believe me if I tell you. And even if I tell you and you believe me, you might regret ever asking."

Zane was intrigued. He asked, "Why?"

"Because if I tell you, *and if you believe*, your lives will never be the same again."

Charly narrowed her eyes and waggled her fingers in front of her face while making spooky ghost sounds. "Ooooh, creepy." She laughed. "Our lives will never be the same again? As if an old blank book is gonna rip a hole in the fabric of the universe, like some retarded episode of Star Tre."

Cole had to smile, but he met his daughter's eyes and answered seriously. "It can, Charly. And if you believe what I tell you, it *will*. "

Zane was incredulous. He asked, "And that's a *promise*?"

"Yes, Z. That's a *promise*."

Chapter 3

One Last Story

Cole knocked twice, entered Charly's new room, and closed the door behind him without a word. Zane and his sister stopped talking abruptly and turned their attention to the book in their father's hand. The twins sat Indian-style, facing each other on Charly's frilly canopy bed, which looked out of place amid the Rock N' Roll band posters taped to the bedroom walls. Cole paused by the door. He looked over at his kids with and expression of dopey parental nostalgia.

Zane said, "What?"

"You two, sitting together on the bed like that. When you were little, you'd huddle together every night to hear me read bedtime stories." Cole used his foot to nudge an unopened moving carton close to the window and he sat down upon it.

Charly said, "That was a long time ago."

Zane said, "Yeah, back before we couldn't stand each other," and both he and Charly laughed in good-natured agreement.

Cole smiled, knowing how much his kids loved each other, despite the requisite sibling antagonism that they dished out on a daily basis. "I guess this'll probably be the last story I ever read aloud to you guys." Cole looked down at the book in his lap and ran his fingertips across the cover, which was still blank beneath the warm yellow lamplight. "I guess that's appropriate. But I wonder..." Cole fell silent, lost in thought.

A look of concern passed between the twins. Charly said, "Dad?"

Zane added, "You wonder what?"

Cole looked up from the book and met his kids' probing eyes. "I wonder if it's too late for you to believe."

Zane said seriously, "I don't know about Charly, Dad, but if you tell me something and you say it's true, I'm gonna believe you." Zane looked over at his sister and she nodded in agreement.

Cole made his decision. "All right, then, let's get started." He reached for the lamp and switched it off, leaving the room in darkness. "We'll have to wait a moment for our eyes to adjust."

Gradually, the room seemed to brighten as the light from the star-filled sky shone through the bedroom window and fell across the book in Cole's lap. The twins were about to ask what their father was up to when Zane noticed that the cover of the book now showed a luminous illustration of a teenage boy fighting off a shadowy creature while two smaller boys cowered behind their protector. The youngest was depicted with square eyeglasses.

Zane said, "What the..." and reached for the book. Cole allowed his son to take it from him.

Cole explained, "It can only be read by starlight." Zane looked up with a question in his eyes, and his father held up his hand in a stalling gesture. "We'll get to that."

Charly moved closer to her brother in order to read the book's title aloud. "The Book of Dreams." Zane and his sister flipped through the pages, which were now filled with handwritten text and painted illustrations that glowed beneath the starlight. Charly switched on the bedside lamp and the text disappeared, but now the kids could see that the book's lavender pages were thick and leathery with what looked like fine golden filaments woven into the paper. Charly switched the light off again, and the handwritten words shimmered back into view.

Zane looked up at the stars and back down to the book, trying to make sense of the strange phenomenon. He said, "It's like those secret codes in cereal boxes you can only read through red plastic."

Charly handed the book back to Cole. "Okay, very weird, Dad. But why all the drama? Why not just leave the book, and let us read it ourselves?"

"You could never make sense of my father's handwriting. I can barely read it myself."

Zane's eyes lit up. He asked, "Grandpa Jake wrote that?"

Cole nodded. "It's his story, and mine. And your Uncle Sean's." The kids hung on their father's every word. Cole continued, "It explains everything you've ever asked me about your grandfather that I couldn't answer, and a lot about me and my brother that I've never told you. And it has something to do with this house, too. I guess that's partly why I decided to tell you now, on our first night here. That, and my promise."

Charly said, "Not to ever lie to us."

"Yes. It was *that* more than anything. Besides, you're both old enough to hear the story and mature enough to decide for yourselves whether or not to believe it. So..." Cole cleared his throat and took a deep breath before turning to the first page. The kids got comfortable and waited wide-eyed in the starlight for the story that would change their lives forever. Cole exhaled, adjusted his square eyeglasses, and opened the book to the first page.

Sleepwalker: The Last Sandman
is available now for the kindle and in paperback at www.amazon.com

Coming in June 2014

Pop Shot
A Dex Wexler Production

Dex Wexler is a struggling director of independent films, a newly-divorced father of two preteen boys, and a nice guy with limited prospects. Apart from his close relationship with his sons and his friendship with his eccentric repertory of fellow filmmakers, Dex's life has never looked bleaker. But when he's coerced into posing as the director of a big-budget X-rated production in order to assist an investigation into the suspicious suicides of a string of young girls who had recently auditioned for porn films, Dex's unremarkable life takes a dark and unexpected turn.

www.ingramcontent.com/pod-product-compliance
Lightning Source LLC
Chambersburg PA
CBHW030643260626
47157CB00007B/2465